THE MARK OF CHAOS AND CREATION

ARABELLA K. FEDERICO

THE MARK OF CHAOS AND CREATION

Pisces Moon
PUBLISHING
L.L.C.

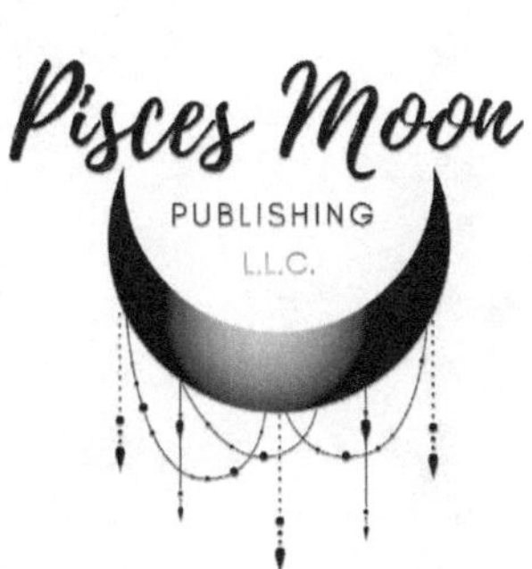

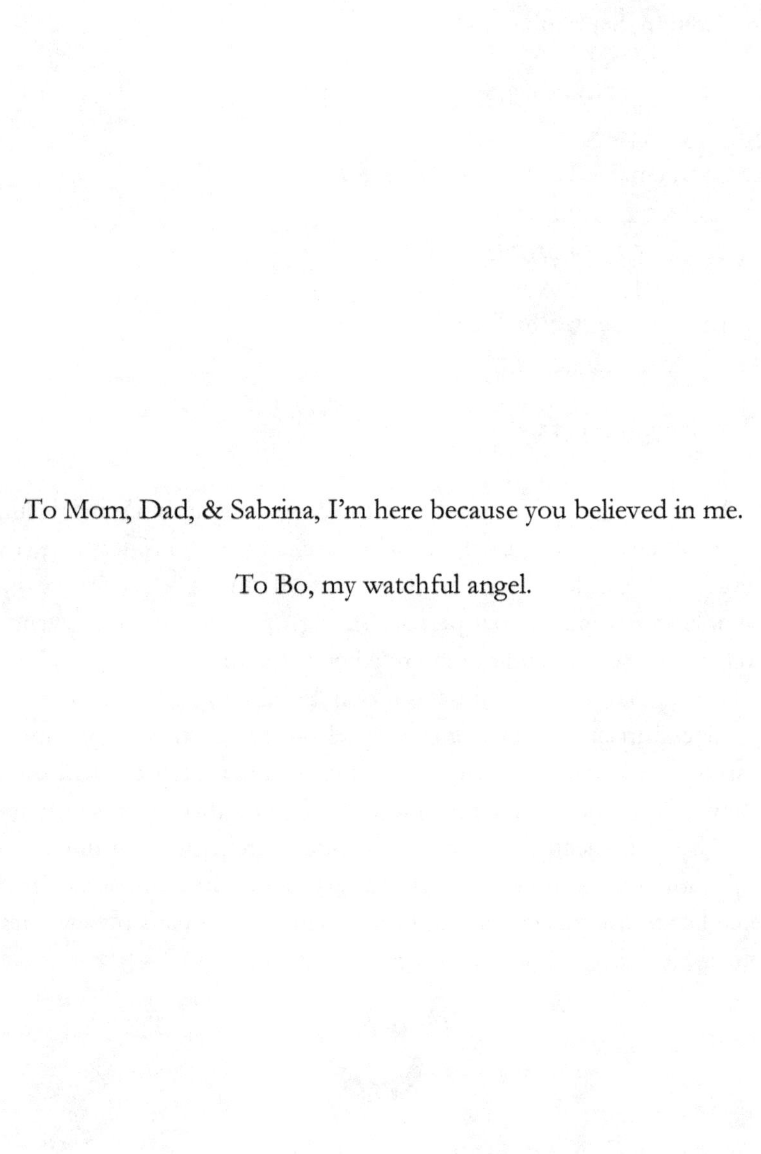

To Mom, Dad, & Sabrina, I'm here because you believed in me.

To Bo, my watchful angel.

Pisces Moon
PUBLISHING
LLC

THE ELENDRIL CRYSTALS

	MAGIC		RINGER MAGIC
	ANTIMATTER		MENTAL MANIPULATION
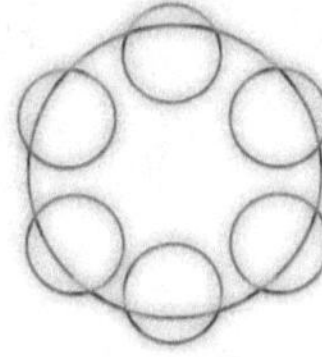	GRAVITY MANIPULATION		HEALING
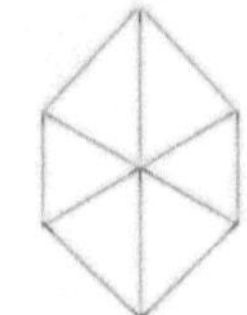	REANIMATE THE DEAD		DREAM WALKER
	RENGENERATION		MEMORY MANIPULATION
	BODY MANIPULATION		VISUAL MANIPULATION
	ELEMENTAL CONTROL		SENSORY MANIPULATION

PROLOGUE

Year 2104
Five years after the Devouring

Monsters are nothing but bullies who like to hide in the dark, but I find that what they fear the most is the very darkness they run to—and themselves.

Even though in this situation it may appear as if I'm in the wrong, I'm not.

The dining room is alight with the sounds of children slurping and chewing and running around when I grab the collar of the boy's shirt and drag him off the table. But then I'm caught before I can do anything else.

"Karalevine Ruzz, you let that boy go right this moment, young lady," Amera scolds. She's one of the six mothers who care for the kids dumped off at Naresteé Orphanage.

"Yeah *Karalevine*," my best friend says tauntingly, his pointed canines on full display. Food sits half-chewed inside his mouth. "Let the bully go, or else the Arianyte Empire will come snatch you out of your bed tonight for being such a badass."

Arianyte owns this orphanage. This is where they unload all the kids they orphaned. But that isn't my story. My parents abandoned me without a war with aliens as an excuse.

"Language, Gavrielle!" Amera's voice is a sharp hiss, and as her delicate footsteps approach us, the wall of children that circled around our dinner table quickly scatter away like rats. The boy I've grabbed is crying, snot crusted along his nose. Why is it that when I confront this mean boy, he doesn't seem so scary anymore? All it takes is a strict look from Amera and I drop him with a loud thunk.

"He—" I try to defend myself, but she hushes me with a sharp "Shh!"

"Don't you dare tell me he started it," she says. She picks the boy up and instructs him to sit beside me, with Gavrielle on the other side, food still on his plate.

"He shoved that girl's hair into her food. He wouldn't stop, then he spit in her bowl and told her it was worthless just like her."

Hands on her hips, Amera looks down her nose at me. She's pretending to be mad, I realize, because her eyes glint in the way I recognize. She's known to play favorites. I'm the favorite. She's my favorite, too, the closest thing to a mother I've ever had in this overcrowded place. She would braid my hair, taught me how to read, and she recently gave me 'the talk'; claiming every twelve year old was required to listen to it.

"That's when you come get one of us. No physical contact with other children, Karalevine, you know this. We've told you many times."

I shrug. I don't know what she's talking about.

"She only dragged him off the table and he started wailing," Gavrielle says.

Amera's brows lift higher than the ceiling, skeptical.

"Lovely, then the both of you can skip dessert and go upstairs. Separate rooms." The tone in her voice sharpens with her last words.

Crossing my arms, I say, "I hope Arianyte comes and takes me away from this stupid place." But of course, I don't mean that.

Her eyes go wide, as if I've struck her, fear flashing a dark shadow there.

"The aliens won't actually come take us, will they?" the bully asks. He's such a baby.

"Of course not, Tommy," she says, but her voice sounds wrong, and her face is stiff and weird. Why is she acting so strange all of a sudden? "Remember what we taught you all about the Devouring Accords? The treaty says they're not allowed to take any children away."

"Yet they still took control of the planet. That's why they call it the Devouring. They basically devoured us all," Gavrielle says in a deep, maniacal voice. He would know because he isn't even from Earth. The war is why him and his parents came here in the first place.

"Oh, stop it, you're scaring him," Amera says. She swoops her arms and points to the stairs.

Enough said.

Both Gav and I walk across the large room, along the rows of long dinner tables full of kids with dirty hair and ratty clothes. When we both notice Amera's attention has already been drawn elsewhere, the two of us dart up the stairs together.

We don't really follow the rules around here.

The sound of the dinner rush fades behind us as the two of us reach the third floor. Gav leads me to the large room where the boys sleep, which is a replica of the girls' room on the floor below, right down to how the sun's rays cut through the persistent dust in the air at twilight. It even has the same musky odor as the room I sleep in.

The entire space is lined with rows and rows of small, lumpy beds with squeaky metal frames. The boys made the beds this morning with not a single brown blanket or flat pillow out of place.

As he reaches beneath his tiny bed, his wild, violet eyes twinkle like the night sky. "I'm actually glad she sent us away. There's been something I've wanted to show you."

Smiling, I sit on his bed next to him, excited. I rarely get surprises.

When Gavrielle carefully hands me a bundle of fluff, my eyes widen and my heart shoots up to my throat, not having expected this.

"They're . . ." I take a deep breath, and I tenderly hold the perfect bouquet of wish-ready dandelions tied together with a shoestring.

Nobody's ever given me flowers before.

This is something Gavrielle has always done, even here, in this awful place: he somehow knows the perfect way to make me feel seen. It's why he's my best friend.

My only friend.

Gavrielle is shunned by everyone in this orphanage because he's from another star system, another planet—literally, he's as alien as you can get. And alien means Arianyte. The fact his parents came to Earth to assist humans in winning the war doesn't seem to matter to the people here. It makes no difference to me that he's an alien, that we look so opposite to each other. His long, braided hair is as white as snow, whereas mine is blacker than a raven's. He is tall and I am the runt of the litter. Ying and

3

yang, black and white, yet we each have a little of the other within us. He has some of my strength, and I have some of his playfulness. He's my best friend, practically human-looking, human enough for me.

Maybe one day he could be more than that?

"Actually," he says, nervously looking down at his feet, one shoe missing its laces. "Well, let me show you."

Before my eyes, the dandelions transform from overlooked weeds into a bouquet of voluptuous, stunning flowers. The stems are thick black licorice, the buds are full and teeming, and the leaves as black as night. Each petal gradually tapers to a brilliant turquoise and bright teal at the tips. I did not know such a color existed. Their forms are wide, layered, and full. They're the most beautiful illusion he's ever made.

Both of our gazes are drawn to his right hand, where an enchanting symbol sits between his pointer finger and thumb, where it's been his entire life like a birthmark. It's no bigger than a quarter and looks more like a circular, geometric flower than any birthmark I've ever seen, but that's what we call it. We assume the magic is made from the mark because he says it feels tingly whenever he makes his illusions.

"Your abilities are incredible, Gav." I exhale in awe. These flowers make me feel like he isn't a giant pile of cooties.

"I wanted to see them again before I forgot what they looked like. They were my mother's favorite." His cheeks flush and eyes flash with memories he so desperately grips to. At least with his magic, he can remember them.

We sit side by side together on his tiny bed, laughing as we reminisce about all the jokes and pranks he's been playing on the kids and the mothers here.

"You're going to get caught," I tell him, shaking my head and sniffing his flowers. They don't smell like much, which I find a bit disappointing. They look so real it's hard to imagine they're an illusion.

"They'll never figure out it's me," he claims, his violet eyes confident. "Plus, if they do, I'll just blame it on you."

I shove him playfully, the two of us laughing. "Not like that'll be anything new."

My bare toes curl. I need to try and be better, but it's like trouble seems to find me.

I'm a little perplexed when Gav doesn't reply, and when I look over at him, his face is taut, and his body unnaturally still—like a predator's.

"Gav, what is it?" I stare at his profile. He suddenly looks so much older than twelve.

"Do you hear that?" he asks, his pointed ears razor sharp. I pause, hearing nothing.

Seconds later, the screaming begins.

Cries from the first floor drive a lump in my throat, and it grows larger with each shattering dinner plate. The entire first floor transforms into a cacophony of screams, wails, and clashing booms.

That's when I hear their boots pounding against the wooden steps.

The two of us immediately rush to the windows and peek out. We look at each other in horror when we see the aliens' spaceships parked on the front lawn.

But why . . .?

Gavrielle snatches the flowers from my grasp and points to the opposite corner of the dusty room. "We have to hide. Go to your spot. Now!"

"Come with me. I can't open it by myself."

The two of us zigzag between the rows of beds, the pitter-patter of our feet barely audible above the awful sounds of chaos below. My pounding heartrate beats in time with boots getting closer and closer.

We reach the farthest pillar from the doorway. Gavrielle grips both sides of the wooden pillar and heaves the panel off. A plume of dust catches in the sunset's rays.

My heart's thrashing and heat rushes into my chest like a tsunami. "Come in with me." The two of us stare into the hollow pillar. It's barely wide enough to fit one of us, let alone both.

Our gazes lock, and I'm sure the panic in his violet gaze is reflected in my teal eyes.

"I know somewhere else I can hide." He hands the panel to me and sprints for the cubbies faster than a cheetah.

They're coming, and we've both run out of time to hide.

As I slip inside the tight musky space, fear grips me. I can't line the panel back up, fingernails straining as I clumsily try to fit the panel back in place with trembling hands. *No, no, no!* Beyond my breath's ragged echoes, I can hear the roaring thunder of voices. They're right outside the room.

The panel slips from my clammy hands and falls forward. Terror spikes through me. My gasp is so loud that I'm sure I've revealed my hiding place, but thanks to my quick reflexes, I lunge out and snatch the panel.

Gavrielle hisses, and I realize I only have milliseconds to hide.

Then they appear.

The Arianyte Empire has arrived . . .

I place the panel along the pillar as softly as I can, but it doesn't line up perfectly, and I'm left with a sliver of light cutting through the stuffy darkness.

I don't know where Gavrielle is.

A soft, almost dainty female voice rings onto the third floor as black-metal soldiers spread out in the room, yet this voice is dripping with brutal authority. I can't see where it's coming from.

"Spread out, I want a thorough search of every single room. We must examine every child. There are no exceptions. Remember, we're looking for a geometric symbol made up of two triangles pointed up and down to form a star shape, but any unusual markings must be flagged and separated from the other children. According to the informant, the Star is at this orphanage, as well as another marked child. Search every single one. These symbols are likely to be located on the chest or hands. You will recognize them."

My blood turns to ice. As unique as Gavrielle's birthmark is, he's not the only one that has one. It's why we're so close. I, too, have a special mark. Mine is twice the size of Gav's, maybe a little smaller than a baseball, and sits directly over my heart on my chest. A mark shaped like a star made of triangles, one a lot like the voice described.

As reality sinks in, that mark tingles and burns . . . the Arianyte Empire is here *for me*.

For us both.

Peeking out from the space inside the pillar, I see the soldiers fanning out into the room. There's no telling what race of alien lurks beneath their sleek black uniforms made of movable metal. Arianyte hides their faces behind fully encompassing helmets that shine with no face, mouth, or eyes—only a stripe of cyan where the eyes should be. Their sleek bodies resemble humans, but that's where the similarities end. The weapons in their hands are long and foreign looking. Why do they need weapons to come search for children?

Gavrielle's abilities appeared a year ago, but no powers have ever manifested for me. Although, the more I hyperventilate inside this darkness, the more the mark burns like fire. It's never so much as itched before this night, and Gav always mentions how much his tingles when he creates magic.

Beds are thrown around the room, shoved and broken in search of us. The metal against metal fries my nerves. They rip cupboards off their hinges, and tapestries along windows are carelessly strewn about.

That's when I see her, the one giving orders.

She's as alien as I've ever seen; the picture they hang of her isn't the same as seeing her up close. The dark freckles across her nose are a striking contrast to the blood red eyes and intimidating gaze that even her photograph couldn't erase. She's so much scarier than her picture ever could imply. This is Naresteé. The alien they named the orphanage after.

Her striking horns grow out of the top part of her head and sweep back along her black hair in a slight curve. Her dark-blue-and-green skin is wrapped in a tight black outfit that accentuates her strong body.

Everyone talks about her like she is some kind of savior or something, but she looks more like a bully to me, and I know bullies well. The burning over my mark swells to an unbearable level.

Then they find Gavrielle.

"Look how simple this is," a soldier mocks as three of them hold Gavrielle down. They restrain Gavrielle on one of the beds and hold his hand up to Naresteé as she walks across the room. "There's one right here on his hand. Looks like that informant of yours was right after all."

Naresteé walks up to him, snatching his wrist with her clawed fingernails, examining Gav with icy, disinterested eyes. Like this is just another chore for her to tick off her list of duties. "I'll inform him we discovered a direct match to a symbol within our database. He's definitely who we're searching for. Continue looking for the Star amongst the other children: it's our top priority."

Inform who?

No, this can't be happening, I think, panic taking root in my bones. They can't take him. He can't leave me. I need him, I need him so I'm not alone.

But if they take me too . . .

Another female voice enters the room, and I peek through the slit.

"You said the Star is here; we searched this entire orphanage. Where is she?" Naresteé asks, and I'm stunned to see whose face walks into frame.

Amera.

"She's likely inside that pillar over there," her soft voice betrays. She peers down at her feet in shame.

She's the informant . . .

"Kara, come out peacefully now. They won't hurt you or Gavrielle. They promised me you'll both be well taken care of. You both know that you're very special and need very special attention we can't give you here. Now come out, please."

She betrayed me . . . she betrayed *us.*

How could she do this?

"I want the cato credits you promised in exchange," I hear Amera whisper to Naresteé, not knowing my pointed ears can hear her. I wish I hadn't.

A single set of heavy boots approach my hiding place. I press my back against the pillar as if I could vanish within it. The dark figure blocks out the sliver of light and the *bam bam bam bam bam* of my heart shoots up like a rocket in my ears and I think I'm going to pass out from the pain in my chest.

My pounding heart nearly drowns out Gavrielle's screams of protest.

The mark on my chest suddenly flickers on like a light switch, and a purple-pink glow illuminates the surrounding darkness. The star mark is *glowing.* I feel like I'm going to turn into a ball of fire.

The soldier's gun is raised at me, but I didn't do anything wrong . . .

Then everything explodes.

I'm enveloped in darkness.

A darkness so deep, so boundless, that I know the moment I come out of it, I'm never going to be the same girl ever again. Some part of me knows this.

My wet lashes open to blue stunners whizzing past my slick cheeks, ears ringing like bells. There's a lingering sizzle on my chest that brings me back to reality. A dreadful reality.

Then I'm running. Stunners fly by me. Wet grass meets my bare feet. I run and run and run, not even remembering how I got outside, let alone down from the third floor. The smell of smoke and burning things is nauseating. The violent orange flame burns against the dark night of the surrounding forest. Once I hit the tree line, I see the lines of other children being taken into the ship Arianyte arrived on. More voices follow close behind as they hunt for me.

What happened?

Where's Gav?

What have I done?

What have I done?

I'm so confused, so turned around and lost that I trip on a rock and plummet face first into the slick forest ground.

I need to go back for him. I need to . . .

"*Survive*," some voice inside answers. I need to survive.

Go into the city maybe . . . I need to make it to the city. Lose them there.

Rage at Arianyte burns like the stars above me. Each one represents a boundless amount of hatred, which expands with each moment. All that remains is darkness and burning fire.

Unable to bear it a second longer, I get up from the dirt and flee; but the fury remains.

I'll never be able to outrun it completely.

I'll tire of running eventually. And someday, I'll be strong enough to become the one hunting them.

Hunting the person who ordered this. The one who did this to me Hunting *her*.

And I'll go after them all. They'll know what it's like to be *devoured*.

CHAPTER I

THE ARIANYTE EMPIRE DECREE #5

FOR THE SAFETY OF EARTH'S PEOPLE AND
EXTRATERRESTRIAL TRAVELERS, THE SOLAR SYSTEM
POLICING OF ARIANYTE RETRIEVALS, REWARDS,
OPERATIONS, AND WARRANTS—A.K.A. SSPARROW—WILL
BE GIVEN FULL AUTHORITY TO POLICE AND REGULATE
THE PEOPLE OF EARTH AND THE SOLAR SYSTEM IN WHICH
IT RESIDES (THE AURORA SYSTEM) UNDER ARIANYTE LAW
AND THE DEVOURING ACCORDS.

Six years later

They still consider grand theft auto a crime under Arianyte law, and it's much more enforced within the major metropolises like Zarmenia City, but does that stop me?

Never.

Because the last thing I care about are the laws of this corrupt empire.

"Don't forget to pull the registration out so the owner doesn't get their head chopped off if this van somehow gets into the occupation's hands. I don't want an innocent person going down for what we're doing tonight." I rummage through the back of this handyman's hover-van, stolen only moments ago by the three of us. I tiptoe around loose tools and worker's supplies as the hover zooms around another street block into the heart of the city. "Maybe take it easy on the corners, will you?"

All I can see of Dimitri is his bald head poking over the driver's seat headrest. "You can think of every little detail you want, but your little revenge plot is still going to be doomed."

I flip an old paint bucket upside down to sit on and lock eyes with Dimitri in the rearview mirror. His best friend, Connar, is sitting idly in the passenger seat, prone to his own skepticism about what's going to happen tonight. Lights from the city make their way into the back of the van like peeping eyes, likely judging me too.

"One, the boss wants you here—so you're here," I say, trying my best to sound like I know what I'm doing. "Two, we know what these sky-rats are up to during this meeting. We know Arianyte wants to negotiate terms of the Devouring Accords, which can only be bad news for all of us. Yes, it's a risky plan, but the rewards for succeeding can be substantial."

The reward for me will be substantial.

The two guys are silent, and that awful gut feeling I get when I know nobody believes in me bubbles up. I question everything about my plan for tonight, but I can't let that deter me now. Not when I'm on the verge of getting everything I want—of getting everything I *need*.

Both men are several years older than me, somewhere in their midtwenties, and they've always looked at me like being seventeen is far too young to be pioneering this type of mission. All the humans—or Terrans—in the Terran Resistance see me differently, and it's for the same reason the aliens of Arianyte continue to hunt me down.

Arianyte came for Gavrielle; sooner or later they'll come for me too. Everything hinges on this moment for me because it could mean the end. The end of running in fear. To looking over my shoulder every single day, wondering if Arianyte will capture me. The day they took Gav taught me anyone can betray me. Arianyte can take anyone from me. It defined me, and now, finding Gav is critical to my peace. The two intertwine and are irrevocably linked, all culminating in the ultimate revenge.

Destroying the Arianyte Empire.

What they did—what they continue to do—they deserve to pay. And I'll do whatever it takes, even if it means sacrificing my humanity in the process. If it means ending whatever suffering Gavrielle has endured these last six years, then I'll sacrifice whatever I must. I deserve no less after what I've done. It's the only redemption I have.

"Kidnapping their commander is more dangerous than anything we've done in a long, long time," Connar says. His strawberry-blond head and eyebrows glow in the dark cabin as he peers over the seat at me. "It's only riskier if we were making an attempt on the head honcho himself. People get vaporized for getting too close to these alien freakshows. We've run many sophisticated hits on Arianyte, and every single one of them has failed to bring in a substantial target. We'll be lucky if we can stop this event at all. The capturing and bringing in of this second-in-command—is virtually insane. If the boss didn't order us to be here, we'd be as far away from you as possible. But the boss wants the meeting stopped, so it's your lucky day."

"Well," Dimitri begins, his voice skeptical. "Step one is complete. We got the hover-van. Now it's up to Kara to complete step two. We're passing onto Crannan Street now. You're sure Trinity will be waiting for us with the stolen badge?"

"She'll be there. Trinity may be a daddy's girl, but that's not the only reason the boss trusts her: she always comes through," I say, feeling a twinge of jealousy bloom inside me at the closeness of their relationship, something that I could only dream of. Being an orphan leaves you with daddy issues. "No doubt she's gobbling up that Annanaka dinner from that Lyran restaurant near the tattoo shop where I work. She swears by this other star system's food, says it's the best in the city. Personally, I think they just fry up cats and call it space-food."

"Disgusting squids." Connar groans the slur for extraterrestrials, or "extras" for short.

Once we stop, I hop out of the hover-van and slam the back door. I approach Dimitri along the driver's side. "Stay here, and if you even think about leaving, I'll come for both your heads."

His laugh chases me as I make my way across the wet street and into the heart of the city. Lights reflect off the slick roads like fairy lights. They bounce off the thick mist still lingering in the air. The sounds of hovers humming a foot above the pavement almost drown out the rail lines buzzing above my head. I shiver in my leather jacket as I walk down Crannan Street towards where I'm due to meet Trinity, whipping out my electronic smoke pen to manage my anxiety. The nicotine flavored like watermelon and peaches and a twinge of mint helps me relax.

My knee-high boots step over soggy flyers painted with faces of missing children as I make my way through the heavy fog that blankets the city in an eerie glow of neon signs. Silver skyscrapers reach towards the stars, their long shiny fingers pointing upwards and disappearing into the mist overhead. Flying vehicles putter between the spotless windows. Like a snake slithering through grass, the rail lines glide above businesses, their support beams popping out of the concrete ground like weeds. We're living in a practical snow globe, encasing us all in alien steel and rainbow lights.

The city used to be in a place called Ontario, Canada, but that city had an unfortunate 'accident' and Arianyte built Zarmenia on top of Ontario's ashes with its own sustainable grid and everything. It's controlled one hundred percent by their foreign tech. They like to remind the public of that any chance they can get, with their propaganda signs and SSPARROW recruitment videos playing on the hologram projections that pop up randomly on the sidewalks. Giant screens with choreographed images make it look like joining the SSPARROW enforcement is something akin to being a patriot; the epic advertisements appear very convincing for some people.

As I approach the street corner I pass through nearly every day, I dig into my bag and I pull out a few pieces of jerky I saved for my friend, Sadie. The husky-mix street dog approaches me with a wag of her black tail, those blue and brown eyes and that sweet graying muzzle always smiling despite her circumstances. I don't have much time to pet her, but I bend down and make sure she gets something to eat. I wish I could take her home; I've tried sneaking her into my loft on several occasions, but my landlord caught me and has threatened to kick me out. Her bark follows me, and I promise more food to come tomorrow before work as I continue down the crowded streets.

If all goes well tonight, that is. I can't think of what'll happen to the stray dog if I don't make it.

My eyes are fixed on my Dezlar device when I feel a clammy hand clench around my upper arm like a vise.

Stopping in my tracks, I look over to see an old woman with long gray hair standing beside me, looking woefully out of place in the crowd with her raggedy black robes and feral-looking eyes. I scan beyond her wild hair; she's positioned outside a shop where the Cherry Red neon sign reads: 'Free 5-minute psychic reading.' Claiming palmistry, off-world tarot cards, past-life-regression sessions, and more. The entire shop looks ridiculous and is one more cheesy sign away from being a full-out scam.

"How about a look at your past lives, deary? Your aura is showing me you've lived many lives before this one. Crazy lives! Would you like to know which star systems you originate from? Yes, very interesting," she clangs. Her glowing irises are a mix of the Mustard Yellow and Pumpkin Orange tattoo ink I use, and those eyes pierce directly into my soul as if they were a set of spears. She has a twitchy mouth framed by thin, translucent lips that bounce even when she's not speaking. She's not Terran, and whatever species she is shoots a terrifying chill through my bones. Before the Devouring, this woman would have freaked out the entire planet. Aliens used to be viewed as entertainment, like the little green men of science fiction lore. Things like aliens or magic were purely fantasy and wishful thinking back then. Now, things like extraterrestrial food trucks and subways that fly above our heads are as common as a person walking their dog. It may be a three-headed beast that somewhat resembles a German Shepard, but still.

"No thank you." I don't have time for this hokey stuff. Any true psychic would have been snatched up by Arianyte years ago, and I've got to get to Trinity.

"You'll be back." She smiles confidently, her rotted teeth glinting at me. "The green-eyed devil will be your undoing tonight." And with a wink, she turns and disappears into her shop. I blink dumbly in the middle of the sidewalk, the crowd moving awkwardly around me.

The green-eyed devil?

Rubbing my eyebrows with my pointed acrylic nails, I force my feet to keep moving towards Trinity. She hates it when I'm late. That woman is a scam artist and is simply trying to get my mind reeling in order for me to come back and pay her cato credits so she can make up more ridiculous stories. I'm gullible, but I'm not that desperate. Maybe I should have asked her if this alien heist mission is going to succeed tonight? From the sounds of it, a *green devil* is coming to ruin it all.

So scary.

The only devil in this scenario is Arianyte.

And maybe me.

After about five more minutes, I finally make it to the tattoo shop. Outside, the vertical neon sign that reads 'Tattoos' sputters its bright Grass Green color into the night, glowing alongside the Tomato Red sign that advertises our rare old-school method of ink-and-needle tattooing. People nowadays use Arianyte tattooing tech, but it's not the same. Only preselected images can be used: they create no actual artwork.

The boss, Geonni—Trinity's father and the leader of the Terran Resistance himself—he's the person who saved me from the streets after I fled the orphanage. He brought me to the rebels, gave me a home, a purpose, and a channel for my anger at what happened. Geonni then taught me how to tattoo in the midst of all this chaos, how to see the differences in every color's multiple shades, and how they can be finessed and molded into something that'll never leave you. It took me years to trust after Amera's betrayal, and many nights I wonder if I trust anyone at all. Geonni, Trinity, and the entire Resistance are the closest thing I have to a family, and even though it's not a perfect pairing and we have our issues, I owe them everything.

The screen directly implanted into the glass door is switched to closed. The anxiety grows in my belly as I proceed down the busy street. My nose is buried in my Dezlar device; its thin glass is diamond-shaped as I scroll through its transparent screen in one hand and puff on my smoke pen in my other. By the time I reach the Lyran restaurant I release a grateful breath that Trinity is standing there waiting for me, munching on some mystery creature fired and skewered onto a stick. *Gross.*

"You're late," she says by way of greeting, shoving herself off the side of the building with so much force that her Ebony Raven box braids swing across her Apple Red bomber jacket.

We begin walking in the direction I came from, the only sound between us her incessant chewing.

"Did you manage to steal the badge?" I whisper close to her ear, fearing a SSPARROW walking by could hear, or worse, an Arianyte spy who's likely ratted out people for less. A twinge of anxiety spikes through me as Trinity crinkles her freckled nose in concern. Was there a problem? Was she unable to steal the badge? If we don't have that badge, we're completely screwed. It's our only way inside the meeting.

She takes another bite, and I cringe as her teeth sink into the flesh of the poor creature, shredding it off like a ravenous Reptilian. The lip gloss on her luscious lips doesn't move an inch, and I stare at her, my impatience evident on my face as the pressure in my chest grows to that of a nuclear bomb.

"Oh, my stars, calm down girl. I got the badge. I'm only messing with you." She laughs, tension seeping out of my body in an instant. I should know her well enough by now to have spotted her ruse. "Those SSPARROW sky-rats won't even know it's gone until tomorrow at the earliest. When they wake up from the large bumps I put on their skulls, that is."

Relaxing my shoulders, I look away from her and take another swig from my smoke pen.

"Pops does want me to reiterate some things first before we go through with this insane proposal of yours," she starts, and I immediately feel my defenses fly up.

"I don't need you to tell me what he's told me a million times already," I protest, annoyed that they don't trust me to handle this. "Geonni always does this. Just let me do this mission the way I planned, please. It'll work out if we all stick to the plan."

Chucking her alien meat into the nearest trash bin, Trinity sighs heavily. "You should have let me tell him it was my idea; it would've saved us both a lot of grief."

It also wouldn't have given me any credit for when it goes right, either.

I grab her arm and stop us both. "We're going to get the second-in-command," I promise, more to myself than to Trinity. But she knows how much this means to me, what it'll mean to the entire Resistance if we catch her.

"Maybe, but do you know what you're up against?" she asks. "The meeting between Arianyte and Terrans is going to be fully equipped with advanced facial-recognition cameras, heat-seeking drones, three-dozen SSPARROW soldiers, and that doesn't even consider the Terran's security protocols that each official brings with them. You know what'll happen if you get caught?"

Rolling my eyes, I exhale a large puff of sweet-smelling smoke into the street as we walk back to the hover. "Yes, they'll do their alien voodoo on me and brainwash my mind into eternal servitude. *I know.*"

Trinity makes a disgusted noise, shakes her head, and swats my smoke away from her face, the red lights of the virtual reality booths bouncing off her dark-brown skin. "Reconditioning is no joke, Kara. They use torture techniques that strip down your identity and implant new memories into your head. You'll no less know your own name, and that star symbol on your chest will be a weapon the occupation will gladly take advantage of. You of all people should be wary of what they'd do if they finally got their claws on you. Stars only know what they did to your little friend. Or have you forgotten that?"

"I've never forgotten about him," I snap back, the edge in my voice harsher than I intended. Trinity knows what a touchy subject Gavrielle is. She's been there on the nights I've cried and driven myself mad over his loss. The scabbed-over fissure within me gets sliced open again, and the emotion that escapes is enough to render me speechless. It hurts so much I have to close it back up again like a poorly sutured wound on a battlefield. I'll deal with it later, heal it properly—later. "It's why I'm doing this. To find him. You know I'm not going to be able to live like this much longer. Without knowing what happened to him, I just—"

"Completely lose your mind and do crazy shit?" Trinity finishes for me. I go to deny it, but we both know that I can't. This mission is proof of how crazy losing Gav has made me.

Trinity side-glances me. "Any other reason?"

"Perhaps I'm secretly vying for your position at the top of the Resistance next to your father?" I joke, but deep down, it's not a joke at all. And we both know it.

"You're so lucky I like you, girl. You better nail this mission tonight if you want Pops to elevate you. A lot is a stake; I know you won't be happy in your current position as lookout if you fail. Not to mention it's been almost six years, and this is our only lead on finding Gavrielle. Keep that power of yours under control. It'll likely be your blessing tonight, or your curse."

My one weapon to get my revenge.

To get Gav.

To finally get my place in the Resistance.

Smiling, I link her arm with mine as the hover comes into view. "Let's bring down these ass-licking squids, shall we?"

CHAPTER 2

THE ARIANYTE EMPIRE DECREE #4

THE TERRAN GOVERNMENT SHALL RETAIN MINIMAL
RIGHTS AND AUTHORITY TO GOVERN TERRAN
INHABITANTS ONLY WITHIN THEIR PERSPECTIVE ZONES,
PER THE DEVOURING ACCORDS.

"Okay, let's run the plan through one last time." The four of us drive towards the meeting between the Terran government and Arianyte. "The meeting is going to be taking place at the Capitol building—you know, the one with the long steps and the big white pillars? The rebel sources say there's going to be a one-block perimeter three-hundred-and-sixty degrees around the building. The only entrance in and out is through Dankova Way."

"Not to mention completely guarded by SSPARROWs, cameras, drones . . . and stars-knows-what else," Dimitri interrupts, and from the back of the messy van, I glare over at Trinity, silently expressing my annoyance at the patronizing tone for the second time tonight.

Smiling with no amount of sweetness whatsoever, I continue, "Trinity, Connar, and I will hide back here while Dimitri drives up to the checkpoint, flashes the badge, and gets us past the SSPARROW guards. Once inside, you'll drive me up to the building directly across from the Capitol building's face. I'll scale the building and wait for our major players to arrive. The three of you will park the hover-van close by, change into your stolen SSPARROW uniforms, and blend in with the rest of the soldiers guarding the event. Now, once the Arianyte official arrives, I'll use my powers to cause a disruption. That's when you'll snatch them up and get the hell outta dodge, swing back to pick me up, and we'll exit the same way we entered. I've got an additional sedative that's safe for extras. I'll leave it inside the center console in case you need it."

"How will we know you've given the signal?" Connar asks as he makes his way past the clutter of maintenance supplies and into the back of the van alongside me.

I chuckle to myself as Trinity says, "Oh, trust us, you'll know."

Peeking out the dirt-frosted windshield, I see the line of hovers spanning out from the perimeter checkpoint.

"Okay, it's go-time. Whatever you do, don't let them open the back doors. If they find us, they'll kill us."

Sighing heavily, Dimitri turns the van to get in line. "We're totally getting caught. We're going to get vaporized like the others who've tried this crazy shit. They're going to probe us."

"Oh my stars, shut up," I hiss as the hover approaches the checkpoint.

It's going to be fine, we got this.

I can't see much, but there are at least ten SSPARROW soldiers guarding the entrance, likely more. Those metal-clad black forms are perched on every street corner in the city, along with their patrol units known as nests. One thing that's different from the soldiers that raided the orphanage is the Arianyte logo that's now plastered on the arms, backs, and helmets of every uniform. Somewhat resembling the letter *A*, but with more pointed, sloping edges, the logo is bright crimson red that fades into a deep night black. They literally slap that oppressive symbol on everything, like the rail line tubes, any production they develop and distribute, the products they produce, posters, anything within their government. Its sinister shape always gave me the feeling of an eerie night.

Dimitri rolls down the window with an impressive squeaking sound.

"Credentials," the SSPARROW demands. He displays a long rifle, black as night and complex with a glowing stripe of blue down the side. I try not to let my hands shake. It happens every time I got close to one of them. Every single time. Trinity grabs me and we hold onto each other nervously, the way we used to when the rebels would come home blazed in the middle of the night when we were kids.

I'm okay, I'm okay . . . I tell myself, heat rising inside me. *I'm in control. These assholes cannot hurt me. They won't be taking anyone.*

Fumbling his words like a total imbecile, Dimitri searches the cluttered van for the badge. Why is it taking him so long to find something I'd given him two seconds ago?

"It's here somewhere . . . I just had it." His voice trembles.

Idiot, idiot, idiot.

"Your credentials," the SSPARROW repeats, and even behind the voice-altering software of the helmet, I can hear the impatience.

The three of us hiding in the back eye each other nervously, my heart rate ticking up in a flash of anxiety. The star-shaped mark on my chest tingles in response to my emotions, the two irrevocably linked.

"Check the back," the nest leader instructs, and panic seizes me.

"No!" Dimitri's voice is too shaky and desperate to not be suspicious. "Sorry, here. My badge is here."

The idiot in the driver's seat hands the soldier the badge, and the SSPARROW leader scans it with a flat, silver device. It beeps softly, glowing red. My stomach drops.

"This says you're not supposed to be here tonight," the soldier tells Dimitri, and I hold back a curse. I glare at Trinity with a mix of anger and fear. She assured me the badge she stole was of a SSPARROW who was assigned to this mission. As a backup we even had our tech guy double check this specific badge would work. Unless, she never did any of those things.

Nervously, Dimitri says, "Can you try it one more time? It's always glitchy."

Fat chance. We're doomed.

Looking at another guard, the SSPARROW reluctantly scans the badge again, and to my shock, the scanner glows bright green.

Oh, thank the stars themselves.

We each let out heavy sighs of relief as Dimitri rolls the window up and slowly drives through.

"Holy stars, that was too close," I say, gliding my hands through my long hair. "We all need to relax and play it cool." Giving Trinity an apologetic glance for not believing in her, I include myself in this.

It only takes us a few minutes to arrive at my drop off point. We pass several nests along the way, including Terran security as well, all dressed in black with communication devices visible.

"Just slow to a crawl and I'll hop out," I instruct as I finish tying my hair back into a low ponytail. I'm dressed all in tight black clothing to hopefully blend into the shadows. "Remember, grab the alien leader and get back to the van as quickly as possible. It's going to be chaotic, but as long as you keep your uniforms on, nobody should suspect you're actually kidnapping them. They'll assume you're doing your protective duties and getting the alien outta there. I'll be waiting down by the building's side for you when you're done. Again, if you leave me here, I'll have your heads."

Slapping me on the back, Trinity winks confidently at me. "Don't worry, I won't let them abandon you, girl."

I smile at that.

"Go, before a sky-rat spots us." Connar ushers me out the back door of the hover-van.

Hitting the asphalt is a little more jarring than I had expected, and the hover zooms off within seconds.

I'm alone.

The time is now.

But let's not count the cookies before they're baked, or the eggs before they're hatched, or count the Grays before they've . . . Well, that's merely a dirty stereotype I'm perpetuating. The point is, I've arrived, but anything can happen.

I tiptoe towards the building's side face. All signs, screens, and lights are shut off, and it looks like a ghost town compared to the rest of the city. A persistent buzzing sound gains strength, and I break into a sprint and hide behind a smelly dumpster. An Arianyte drone flies by. It's sleek, black, and shaped like a stingray, but much less wide. A blood-red light illuminates its belly. The cameras are located on the entirety of its bulbous head at the front of it, giving it a three-sixty view. Some anti-gravity tech I don't understand holds it up, and it barely makes any noise since there are no blades propelling it. I'm only able to hear it coming because of my slightly pointed ears and higher-than-average hearing. After seeing nothing amiss, it pitters off, and I release another tension-filled breath. Another one of these close calls and I'm going to see them as bad omens.

The alleyway isn't much to look at. Pretty empty, aside from a rusty old lamp illuminating the stinking trash bucket I stand next to. A door sits below the lamp, and out of curiosity, I grip its handle to see if it's unlocked, but it isn't. Looks like it's time to scale the building.

Pulling my backpack over one shoulder, I pluck out one of my favorite devices Geonni made for the Resistance. The leader's tinkering mind is more brilliant than he realizes. It's shaped almost like a gun but has a two-inch diameter barrel. Smiling and giddy with anticipation, I close one eye and take aim for the top of the building. It's hard to see through all the fog, but the device screen replacing the rear sights locks onto the ledge of the building between two crosshairs, beeping red once it's officially locked. I pull the trigger, and with a slight recoil, it shoots a claw straight up into the sky. I lose sight of it as it disappears into the foggy night. The whining of the attached rope as it flies straight up is my only indication it's still zooming upwards. Seconds later, I feel the rope pull taut, and a green light appears on the screen, indicating the claw is locked onto the building's ledge.

"This is going to be so awesome," I whisper, my chest filling with butterflies. "And per usual, there's nobody here to witness how badass I am."

Just you, Kara, just you.

I unhook the rope from the device, clip the hooks on the loops of my pants, and take a deep, anticipating breath. Shaking my head at how crazy this is about to be, I gently pull on the rope three quick times.

A squeal escapes my lips as cold wind whips at my face and ponytail and I'm sucked up the side of the building. The light around me zooms from the yellow glow of the lamp to the darkness of the fog, to the bright lights of Zarmenia City in mere seconds.

I may as well be flying.

The ledge arrives far too quickly for my liking, and I climb over it with ease.

Zarmenia is all lights and colors and skyscrapers in front of me, a kaleidoscope prison of oppression masked in technological advancements. The air up here doesn't reek of the overcrowded bodies and the garbage where I live, and I take a breath of clean air. In the black sky above, there are more ships than stars. Arianyte's Azurite mothership shines brighter than the moon as it floats in orbit. I've never known the skyline without the gigantic ship floating up there.

The farthest corner of the roof looks out over the large white Capitol building, a place where a democracy used to conduct business, but those days are long gone. There are dozens of low-ground-hovers down there, bringing in the local and out-of-Zone Terran government officials as they come to 'negotiate terms' between Arianyte and us. But it's more likely to sell out humanity for money, power, and greed.

Eight stories below me, the chess masters of this game laugh and mingle, completely unaware of all the people out there suffering from their decisions.

I get the planet was dying before Arianyte came. They haven't erased that history, at least. I can even stretch my empathy far enough to understand the deal our Terran leaders made through the Devouring Accords: to give away human beings to these monsters in exchange for saving the planet that would not have survived otherwise. The second deal was a much better one than the first, where Arianyte demanded thirty percent of the population, including children, given to them over fifty years. *Children.* The new deal amended the child Tributes, but I and many others know that's a fallacy and only a matter of timing for Arianyte. I've seen with my own eyes how they pluck children from orphanages or streets and corral them into spaceships, never to be seen again. The Hijacked exist, Arianyte is taking them, and the Terrans are allowing it.

But why they're allowing it . . . one of the many things I'm going to find out. If I do anything tonight that's worth this risk, it'll be worth it for them. Gav isn't the only child who has suffered because of Arianyte.

Amongst the SSPARROW soldiers, I see our first out-of-Zoners. This Terran's name is unknown to me, but his face is way too beautiful to be trusted. He's a dark-haired, sky-blue eyed talker whose clothes cost more than most people's homes, yet he's constantly preaching how he's 'one of the people.' Next are a few local government officials that live within

Zone 77, the home of Zarmenia City. First is Jamie Chen, a fancy lady who brings her two purebred huskies with her everywhere, including this meeting. She's as much of a brown-noser as our next couple: Mr. and Mrs. Devil Incarnate. The Dawsons love and live the high life, spewing their riches and proper manners all over high society. Not a blond hair is out of place on their immaculately styled heads. If I could snatch up these Terrans tonight in addition to my target, I would.

Next time.

My chest leans over the edge, wind blowing softly, and I take a deep breath. Pushing down all my feelings from today, I call forth something much more substantial and way more volatile than a teenage girl's emotions.

I call forth a force of nature.

The monster within me awakens, eye popping open after a long sleep, famished and gluttonous, ready to devour and destroy.

That's what I do . . . it's what I am. I never said I was proud of it, only that I'm learning how to use this curse for the greater good. Whatever cruel god cast such a horrific hex upon me is surely regretting it now. I'm powerful, strong, undeniable.

I can do this.

It begins with a rush to my brain, a high that's so pleasurable I doubt even heroin could compare. My cheeks flush. I flourish in the wave of heat that blooms inside me, letting it shower me from my head to my chest, to my belly, then to my legs and toes. It fills me with an energy of raw power, and it feels so good my toes curl in delight. Nothing else matters but this pure state of euphoric bliss. If someone took this feeling from me, I know I'd do terrible things in order to get it back. To feel *this*. The mark stings, then burns, spiking before it lights up the surrounding darkness in a glorious purple-pink glow that reflects off my skin, hair, and clothing.

It's almost ready . . . and it only gets better from here.

I know my target has arrived by the incredibly sophisticated hover coasting up beside the white marble steps. Its rounded edges and oval shape allow it to glide in on bulbous wheels with spokes that light up blue and pink. Its back end has scales that glow neon blue and flap like a dragon's. The Terran bodies surrounding the hover are tense with anticipation, and my anxiety spikes as the driver, a gray alien in a small tuxedo, releases the door that opens skyward.

The woman that elegantly exits the hover is tall and exceptionally beautiful in a tight-fitted black gown that sparkles like the night sky. Her skin is a gradient combination of dark Forest Green and Navy Blue, the high slit in her dress revealing the blue subtly stippling in a patterned texture around her thighs and shoulders. Her hair is a black-and-red ombre, cut to her shoulders in big curls. Given all that makes her stand out, none of those things is her most identifying feature. On top of her head are two thick horns curved at the tips, growing towards the back side of her head. The alien's face is a striking mask of privilege, and she looks exactly the same as she did when I watched her from that hiding spot six years ago. Back then, I was a different girl. When I hid inside that pillar, I was terrified and weak and helpless. This is Arianyte's second-in-command, Naresteé, and I'm finally going to pay her back for what she took from me six years ago. It's all been about this very moment, my revenge and my salvation all at once. She's the key to everything. To impressing the Resistance by stopping this meeting and bringing her in, and then once she's in our custody, to finding Gavrielle by getting the information out of her by any means necessary.

Gav is out there somewhere—alive. He must be, and this is the night I make good on the promise I made as I ran away, leaving him alone like the coward I was.

Not anymore.

It's time. Finally, after years of running and hiding and preparing, it's time.

Time to come for the ones who came for me.

CHAPTER 3

IN GOOD FAITH, BOTH ARIANYTE AND THE NATIVE SPECIES OF EARTH, TERRANS, AGREE TO END ALL FORMS OF VIOLENCE AND UNREST. WITH THE SIGNING OF THE "DEVOURING ACCORDS," A PROPOSITIONAL AGREEMENT BETWEEN BOTH PARTIES, EACH SIDE SUBMITS IN GOOD FAITH THAT PEACE CAN BE SUSTAINED FROM THIS POINT FORWARD AS OUTLINED IN THE DEVOURING ACCORDS.

Narestéé speaks with some Terrans, smiling a white and wicked smile full of manipulative teeth.

I grip the building's edge hard, the mark fueling itself up, the feeling I soar for coming in fast like a bullet down a barrel of a gun. Yet something catches my eye, and I stare curiously.

I almost fall to my feet.

No.

Connar's dumbass is walking around down there, dressed in his SSPARROW uniform, without his helmet on. Rule number one for any sky-rat soldier: never remove the helmet. You'd be surprised what people can do to each other when the occupation secures their anonymity. Why in Jupiter's rings has this redheaded stepchild taken off his helmet? Why aren't Trinity and Dimitri stopping him? Perhaps they know it'll draw too much attention? And it looks like he's zoned out in a daze, but when I squint and look closer, I see his eyes are glowing *green* like he's possessed by some demon.

My eyes dart around, searching each of the bodies and the hovers and the corrupt politicians for the source of whatever's controlling him. Thankfully, nobody down there has seemed to notice Connar as he slowly stalks across the white steps, but that's only going to last so long. Seeing a SSPARROW with their helmet off is as rare as Arianyte admitting they lie to the public. It never happens. He's a normal Terran, the guy has no abilities to speak of, and although he isn't particularly on board with this mission, he doesn't have a death wish.

Then I see someone, someone I can only describe as a green-eyed devil.

Wearing a long tan trench coat that goes to the ground, a man hides deep in the shadows behind the white marbled steps. From my high vantage point, I can see those intense glowing-green eyes illuminating out of the shadowed alcove. He's covered mostly in darkness, and all I can make out is a head of stark white hair combed back from a steep, pointed hairline. And a face framed by two enormous, pointed ears that—from this distance and angle—look a lot like devil horns. His skin tone is dark green and practically blends into the night. He appears to be some unknown type of extraterrestrial. The dread that overcomes me is palpable. Who is this guy?

Those glowing-green eyes are transfixed directly on Connar. Both sets of eyes match.

I can only surmise one is controlling the other—and it's easy to guess which is which.

What the hell?

Then Connar's gun rises up, pointing right at Narestee's head.

What kind of freaky puppet-master is this guy? And wait—if she gets killed, that means everything I've planned for will die with her.

A feeling of dread blankets me as the air becomes almost static with an energy that I've never felt before. My breath becomes heavier and heavier, and I feel the buildings closing in on me. A pressure builds and grows like a magic bean stock inside my belly. Nausea rolls over me in waves. The building I stand on appears to grow higher and higher, taking me on a wild ride I know is all inside my head. The star mark on my body, the thing that burns like hellfire, almost comes undone right here and now. This person hiding behind the steps, he is something *evil*. I don't know how, but I can *feel* him.

I can't lose my bearings, not here, not now.

Keep it together, you don't want another incident. This will not be a repeat of the orphanage.

A soft twinning sounds to my left, and I turn sharply, feeling like a deer caught in a hunter's crosshairs.

Standing five feet away is a man aiming a bow and arrow directly at me. I stiffen.

He couldn't be over eighteen, and his hair is a pale dishwater-blond, instantly reminding me of Gavrielle. My heart skips and I gasp. Could it really be him?

"Now, now, Thumbelina, let's take it easy. Whatever you're about to do, don't," the guy says, but I barely hear him over the pounding in my head.

"Gav?" I breathe, my heart beating in hopeful anxiety, all thoughts of the green-eyed devil disappearing like smoke in my hands.

"What's a gav?" he asks in a confused tone, brows knitting together. He inches closer, bow taut. I instantly deflate as he comes into better view.

This person is not Gavrielle, and I'm stupid to believe he could have been, even for a split second. The first thing that tells me it's not Gav is his eyes. They're an ink blend of Midnight Navy and Royal Cobalt, creating a rich, depthless sapphire color, nowhere near the violet of my old friend's eyes. His shoulder-length hair is a mousier blond than the icy white of Gavrielle's, which isn't cascading down his back or braided in my old friend's home-world style. His facial structure is much more angular and sharper than Gav's face shape, and this person's ears are rounded, not pointed. A clear Terran, and Gav is from an entirely different star system. Disappointment from even that small pinprick of hope shatters me.

It even sucks more than the fact that an arrow is being pointed directly at my face.

His timing is impeccably awful.

I look back down to the building, searching for Connar with wild eyes. How has anyone not noticed him yet? He's closer to her, maybe a quarter way across the steps.

"Stop your power now," Blondie says, and my eyes shoot back to him, wondering how he knows I'm even calling forth any type of magical power in the first place. Could Arianyte have known I was planning on being here somehow? He's dressed casually, nothing like a SSPARROW, and despite the chill in the air tonight, he's only wearing a slim black tank that accentuates his muscled chest. The cargo pants he's sporting seem to have plenty of room for additional weapons. He clearly has the body of a warrior; that's apparent off the bat.

"Who the hell are you?" I ask breathlessly, my power growing more and more with every second—burning hot. I also seriously question if this guy just called me *Thumbelina*. I'm short, but holy stars, come up with something a little more creative.

"I'm someone who can help you," he claims, inching ever closer. "All you need to do is stop increasing your power. Shut it off. You don't have to do this."

Scoffing, I look him up and down with disgust, nails digging into the building's edge. This boy's skin has little color to it, and the dozens upon dozens of tattoos help him not appear so washed out. Yet, the tattoos are well done, and I immediately notice they're inked in the traditional ink-and-needle style. Costly. They trail all the way up and down his muscled arms. He even has one or two across his ringed fingers and partially exposed chest.

Turning towards him full-on, I look this dangerously beautiful boy in the eyes. I'd hate him even if he wasn't pointing an arrow at me, purely for all the stupid shit he'd cause me to do in the name of getting those eyes to look at me with more than the testiness that's reflected there now. Plus, you can't trust a guy who looks as good as he does. He's too beautiful, and he knows it. I can already tell by that cocky smirk.

"Easy now . . ." He actually backs up this time, like he's afraid of me. "I don't want to shoot you. Stop your power. Now."

"I don't have any power," I claim, but he laughs softly in response.

How does he know?

Our sharp breaths are the only sound. This opportunity is too rare, too important for me to miss. It looks as if I'm going to have to take this guy out. Why he's appeared here, at this very moment, is highly suspect.

Wondering at which angle I should dodge his arrow, I'm about to pounce when a tattoo on his chest catches my eye. Over his heart is a circle, and riding along its rim are six other miniature circles, all spaced perfectly apart. I know this mark somehow . . . It triggers something long ago forgotten in me that I never realized I had lost, and it sticks out like a sore thumb next to the other tattoos there. It isn't shaded with ink. The geometric shape is unmistakable. It's a clear marking almost identical to mine, but a different shape.

How can this be? My body goes hot, and so does the sister mark on my own chest. I see the magenta light from my mark before my vision goes completely black.

The wind whips the long white hair against my face. I vaguely have a sense of myself, but all my memories and sense of Kara bleed into the vision before me, erasing anything but the current moment. I am somewhere else . . . someone else. My feet stand in a rocky, dirt-covered, and barren place. I am not on Earth. The overwhelming sense of déjà vu and dread overtakes me, and Kara disappears . . .

The dust-covered scene is a reddish haze, nothing but dirt and rock for miles. I'm terrified and trembling in my tall, powerful body. I wear high boots and leathers made for fighting. I can't stop shaking, and panic has overwhelmed me in a way I can't describe. Only that it's primal and all-consuming.

I'm clenching the arms of my comrade. The two of us stand face-to-face. His skin is a pale turquoise, smooth and overlaying large muscles, paired with sturdy legs. The wind blows so hard our long white manes of hair intertwine together, becoming indistinguishable. Long pointed ears and eyes so vivid blue stare back at me with anguish saturating them. In the center of his chest is a birthmark near the dip in his collarbone. I know this shape . . . that circle with smaller rings spaced directly over it peeks out at me. Our blessing and our curse. He's talking to me, dark lips moving, handsome face worried and body tense, yet his words remain distant sounding, like they're underwater. The feeling of his hand gently caressing my arm brings me into my body more by the second. My connection to him is everything.

A spaceship sits to my right. Other figures are running around rapidly and with tactical purpose. We've crash-landed on this small moon, thanking whatever gods exist that it has an atmosphere we can breathe. Although, the wild wind blows the orange dust and dirt around us like a glowing orange hellscape. No life, let alone intelligent life, survived here. The sense of doom looming over us all is nauseating.

"We can't separate," he begs, and my attention returns to the man before me. "I need to stay with you. I'm not leaving you."

"We don't have a choice," I say, and I believe my words with all my heart, despite them breaking it. "It's more dangerous if we stay together. He's after me foremost, but you're a strong second. You don't understand, Erodis—after what I've done, he's never going to stop coming after me. I've already put you and the others in so much danger, so you need to go. We'll meet back here once Father fixes the ship. Father only needs an hour, he said. We can stall until then and finally escape this insanity forever. Then we'll be free. We'll be safe."

I press my hand over the mark on his chest. His eyes want to fight my every word.

Others around us give quick goodbyes, people I deeply love and care for. They're nothing but shapes and shadows in my peripheral; my focus is only on the man before me. I wave them goodbye as they disperse into the orange. Hopefully, they'll be able to avoid our pursuer until we can escape for good.

It's hard not to feel responsible for all this.

I'm supposed to have led them—protected them. What I've done instead is damn them.

The promise of the person pursuing us rings in my memory. His clear threat a very real reminder of how outnumbered we are and how stupid I am to think we'd ever get away. He's never going to let me go. Believing so has been a fantasy.

By releasing the information to the galaxy at large, I signed all our death warrants.

And now the bone collector is coming to reap his bounty.

In blood.

"You both need to go," a voice tells us from somewhere close, but I don't look over to see that person's face. I can only see one face: his face. The face I love more than any other.

His hands cup my cheeks, and I lean into his scent, spicy and earthy and strong—so familiar it hurts. I don't want to leave it. I want it to keep me warm and safe so that I never have to be this afraid again. Lips kiss my forehead as he brushes my white hair from my eyes. He lingers there, and I feel his massive body shaking. My warrior love, he never shakes. I look into the painful pools of his eyes, rimming and glossy with tears, the weight of a galaxy reflecting back at me. So blue, so intense, so anguished.

What have I done?

I push myself away from him, force myself to go.

32

Leaving him like this, knowing it could be the last time we ever see each other, I want to scream. This is all because of me, because of my stupid choices.

How could I ever forgive myself?

How could they?

If I were them, I wouldn't be able to.

"Zariya!" he yells as I dash from him. I continue to run. It's what's safest for him, but it hurts the most. "I love you!" he shouts, but I can't turn back to him. If I look back, I'll never be able to leave him. Yet, his words echo in my mind, and I love him too.

I should have told him I love him too.

CHAPTER 4

I gasp as if I've almost drowned, unaware of my surroundings or even my sense of self.

What the hell?

My neck whips around wildly, and I stumble around in literal circles. My equilibrium throws me completely off-kilter. I'm unsure of where I am in time and space.

Forcing a deep breath, body trembling, I look around and do my best to stabilize myself.

I'm on the rooftop, standing in the exact same spot I was in before . . . before this dream or vision or whatever the hell I just experienced.

It doesn't appear that much time has passed, and I was standing upright the entire time.

What the hell?

Blondie stands in the same place as well, probably wondering what the hell is going on with me, but when I look closer, his eyes appear unfocused. I wave a hand in front of his face, and nothing. He's in a trance. Then as if he snaps out of it, he tumbles on his feet like he's dizzy or something.

But Blondie isn't my biggest problem, because while I've been off in dreamland or wherever the hell I've been, my mark's power has only been growing and growing unchecked.

And I'm mere moments away from losing complete control.

Shouting from below grabs my attention, and I'm reminded of Connar.

Turning back and looking down, I see a dozen SSPARROWs all pointing their weapons at him. His eyes are back to normal. He looks absolutely terrified, hands up in the air, rifle on the ground.

This is bad.

"Hey!" Blondie yells at me, but I ignore him as I lean over the edge.

What's happening? Everything is crumbling. My one shot at stopping the one and only Arianyte Empire is dissolving before my eyes. I can't let this happen.

When I look back to where the alien man was hiding in the shadows, I find his green, glowing stare pinning its haunting gaze directly up at me.

And my stomach drops to the asphalt eight stories down, the control of my power tumbling along with it.

Hyperventilating, I feel claustrophobic and trapped. Like I'm inside that pillar in the orphanage, out of control, with no escape, watching as everything I care for is about to be taken away.

Everything has fallen apart so quickly, my entire plan shattering before my eyes.

"Step away from the ledge of the building now."

Oh my stars, will this guy ever *shut up*?

A blast from a SSPARROW disruptor sounds right before my power surges up through my body and out into the unexpecting people below.

A Raspberry Fuchsia light glows from within my arms and hands, and the burn is white hot as pure energy erupts in a misty lightning that bombards the Capitol building below. I barely register what's happening because the high is so intense my knees buckle, and the only thing keeping me upright is the ledge itself. Not even my most pleasurable, exhilarating moments could ever compare to the way this power makes me feel. I'm no longer that scared girl from inside that pillar—I'm a god. The utter collapse of my plan and all the consequences sure to come all vanish. It breathes strength into me I do not possess on my own. The light alone erupting from it is blinding, the mark on my chest glowing just as brightly. The brilliant massive colored light, ghosts of sunset orange and violet purple, pure ungovernable energy makes its way across the street as it destroys and demolishes hovers, marble, and pillars. Pillars and marble crumble in a white avalanche of rocky chunks. That valve to my power is now wide open, and I cannot stop it, not even a little.

A part of me tries to aim my power towards the man with the creepy glowing eyes, and it clobbers a hover-car instead. It goes flying up into the air in a ball of fire and smoke. Concrete goes flying in all directions. People cover their heads and frantically run for safety. Screams burst out like bulleted rain, pelleting into me: *guilt, guilt, guilt.*

I am out of control.

But I don't care.

I should—but it's hard to when it feels this good. When all the pain disappears and is replaced with the strength of a thousand stars.

I don't know or care what happened to Blondie; for his sake I hope he was smart enough to take cover.

As the power keeps rushing in like a toxic lover, it goes to work numbing the bad feelings away. To make me feel good for the first time in so long . . . My guilt melts and disappears, and I'm satisfyingly numb. To not have the rage and hate for myself bubbling, simmering at every moment is the pinnacle of cool, safe waters. Is it so wrong to want to feel good? Why does everyone harp on me for wanting to find my friend and a place to belong?

My hair and jacket whip and thrash from the heat wave that comes from within me until finally, I'm able to rein it in enough to stop the manifestation of energy. I fall backwards and land flat on my back. Breaths accost the silence around me. The mark sizzles on my chest like a freshly pressed brand. The euphoria is already fading away, seeping out of me as if I had a leak in my soul.

Then all the regret and self-hatred hits me harder than a baseball bat to the head. How could I have allowed myself to actually enjoy that? How disgusting am I? Every pain, hurt, and regret hits me with no buffer to block the feelings.

People are screaming down below. Those sounds will haunt my dreams for years to come. At least the SSPARROW sirens aren't blaring yet. The air smells of burning things, and I pray to the stars that I hadn't hurt Trinity, Dimitri, or Connar. Or blown our target to bits. Geonni is totally going to find out about this. Would he kick me out of the Resistance for making a scene this big? For potentially hurting his daughter, possibly killing her? If the latter were true, I'd be completely shunned at best. Not to mention, my only friend would be dead at my own hand. Stars, what's wrong with me? Maybe they're all okay? Maybe they'd still be able to grab Naresteé and bring her back to the hover-van if they weren't injured?

Yeah, right . . . I need to stop being so delusional.

I utterly failed.

I should never have gone through with this.

Now, my one lead on Gav, my one chance to impress Geonni and be taken seriously by the Resistance is gone. The mere thought of running from Arianyte for the rest of my life absolutely wrecks me. Everything has completely blown up.

Literally.

"Don't move," an angry voice commands me. Blondie has survived. Lucky me.

Rolling to my side, my body drained, I know I can't fight back. Fortunately for Blondie.

As I look up, I see his arrow is inches from my face. The look of utter disgust tells me he has no issues firing that arrow if I so much as sneeze.

"There are innocent people down there," Blondie sneers. He lifts me up like I weigh nothing and plants me beside him, his hands a firm clasp around my wrists.

I'm too full of self-loathing to fight back, and as the SSPARROW soldiers arrive, barking orders and demanding surrender, I don't fight them.

"I'm with Arianyte." Blondie finally lets go of me, and one of the soldiers manhandles me to my feet. "Scan my Dez."

Holding up his Dezlar, the SSPARROW scans the handheld device with the same scanner used at the barrier, and it lights up green. This little shit does work for Arianyte.

"Traitorous rat," I hiss, spitting at Blondie's dark boots.

The red-colored SSPARROW cuffs my wrists behind my back roughly, ordering another cyan soldier to wrap a cold metal collar around my neck like a damn dog. A red SSPARROW is a high-ranking soldier; they sent the big guns over to me—a compliment at least.

"Oh, don't worry, honey. You'll be seeing a lot of us traitors after what you've done tonight," the metal soldier coos, the altered voice as disturbing as he intends.

Blondie steps directly in front of me, standing clear over me at six five or taller. I crane my neck to kiss the sky in order to meet his incredulous stare. The light from the fires below reflects off those eyes. His head is shaking subtly, like I'm the most disgusting thing he's ever seen. The hatred coming off him is as palpable as the smell of burning flesh and hair.

And the feeling is mutual.

He ruined *everything*.

We stare each other down, neither one giving up first. I won't, I refuse.

Snatching me roughly from the SSPARROW leader, Blondie forcefully walks me towards a sky-hover that landed on the roof a few minutes ago, and I loathe that his smell of sage and cinnamon is as pleasing to me as it is.

This is all his fault, and he's leading me to my demise.

However, I can't help but grin a tiny bit at the fact that I accomplished one thing at a minimum. This meeting sure isn't happening now, but the cost for that has been raised tenfold.

As hard as I try, I can't keep Blondie from feeling my bones quake as he sits next to me and the hover takes off into the air. Destination–Hell.

CHAPTER 5

ANY PERSONS, TERRESTRIAL OR EXTRATERRESTRIAL, FOUND TO HAVE UNNATURAL ABILITIES LEVEL ONE THROUGH FIVE SHALL BE DETAINED AND SUBSEQUENTLY EVALUATED FOR ANY THREATS TO THE EMPIRE OR THE AURORA SYSTEM AND ITS FUNCTIONING. THOSE WHO DO NOT WILLINGLY ASSIST IN ARIANYTE'S INTERESTS AND PURSUITS SHALL BE SUBJECT TO "RECONDITIONING."

I can take a punch pretty dang well; I've been taking hits even before my training with the Resistance, but a punch to the face by a metal SSPARROW fist . . . now that hurts like a *bitch*.

"You know"—I spit blood onto the closest sky-rat's boot—"I prefer it when you tase me, if I'm being perfectly honest. You hit like a bunch of little girls."

The small interrogation room is extremely claustrophobic, with all five metal bodies crammed in among the dark imposing walls. Being forced into the confinement facility, where criminals are processed, is a complete mess. I made sure of that. The hover landed in front of the tall black building with glowing red lights etched into the steel in patterns of lines and cryptic shapes. The word 'confinement' glows red at its center. Squirming, buckling my knees, using my colorful language skills—I even tried fake tears, but that clearly wasn't convincing enough for anybody.

There was a brief moment when I managed to wrangle out of Blondie's grasp, but that bastard managed to get his hands around me again pretty quickly. If I accomplished anything, I hurt his pride, because such a big guy really shouldn't have needed two additional SSPARROWs to help get a tiny girl like me into this building. Ultimately, they strapped me down to this confinement chair once deep inside, after I got lucky and kneed Blondie directly in the balls.

That's when they opted to bring in the heavy artillery—the interrogation SSPARROWs.

The single, dim red light sways slightly because one of the taller soldiers keeps bonking it with his fat head. The long wand taser bites me in the ribs again, burning directly through my shirt and skin.

They try again, distorted voices bouncing off the dark walls that feel endless and suffocating all at once. "Why were you at the meeting, and how did you get inside the perimeter?"

I want to go home.

"You're all so tough, beating up a girl tied down to a chair. You tell your wives you do this type of thing?" I taunt, doing anything to avoid their questions. I'm not showing it, but I'm scared out of my mind.

Absolutely terrified.

I screwed myself so hard, hurt so many people . . . My powers, they got so out of control, but it was only because of Blondie and that bizarre vision. Whatever that vision was, it set me off. I didn't intend to hurt anyone but the one person who deserved to be hurt, that squid Naresteé. For all I know, she could be dead, and my hopes of finding Gav along with her. Forget the rebels welcoming me back with a hero's welcome. Who am I kidding? All my hopes for tonight are as far off as me and Blondie having a romantic dinner together.

Everyone tried to warn me and I didn't listen. And now, because I was solely focused on my ambition and revenge, I've hurt people and I've hurt myself. It's not what I meant to do, I—

The door to my cell opens and my thoughts snap back to my horrendous predicament. Trinity's warning about Reconditioning rings out in my memory, and my body trembles more from fear than from pain.

What is Arianyte going to do to me? Will they figure out that I'm the person they've been hunting for? Will they notice my mark?

Then the last person I expect to enter walks in, and I'm startled into stillness.

I'm taken aback by his entire appearance. His whole demeanor is a low-key, pick-me shit type of vibe, a Demon Prince from the Seven Circles of Hell edition, like he totally fits into the dungeons of his own making. Dressed all in black, his perfectly ironed slacks and pull-over jacket are as expensive as clothing can get. He drips of affluent prestige and influence—of power. All that's missing is a crown of darkness.

My inferiority blooms fully as I sit here before him—blood trickling from my nose, bruises forming under my eyes, and sweat dripping down my body in buckets. This person is light-years and leagues above me in every single way. He's an extraterrestrial. One that I've seen nearly every day of my life, yet never met before. His race is unknown, which means he's from a planet very far away. But I know his face from all the photos he's hung up of himself across the world. Someone within Arianyte gave the order to come after me. Was it him? Was he the one who's hunted me down since I was a child? Did his mouth form the words that ordered Naresteé to the orphanage that night? His aura a seductive and mysterious shadow I can't help but be drawn into instantly—that darkness dances around me. We're not strangers to the other's madness.

The SSPARROWs part for him, and he approaches me slowly, his celestial-black eyes making my skin tingle as they methodically hover over every inch of my body. They pause on my chest, and I know exactly what's caught his eye, and it's not what typical men see. The other tattoos are there to hide the star-shaped mark, its intricacies detailed enough to pass for a tattoo at first glance. Hide it in plain sight—that was Geonni's idea. It worked. At least, until it didn't. Until now.

Arianyte has finally found me after all these years.

"You're the leader of Arianyte," I breathe, not knowing what else to say.

It makes sense for it to be him, why he'd be here.

Blondie shuffles in behind him, quietly watching.

This powerful alien bends down directly before me, eye to eye, our faces mere inches apart. Damn, he's hot. His face is all sharp edges, high cheek bones, and pointed ears. His nose is slightly too big for his face, and he's definitely as attractive as the leader of Arianyte would be.

However, despite him being even more beautiful than Blondie, it's the power he wields and his attitude that gives him his edge.

"You are exquisite." He speaks each word with so much intent and flavor that it causes me to recoil. Why would *he* say that to *me*?

A smile reveals two sets of pointed canines on his top row. "You don't agree?"

"Uhh . . ." is all my jostled mind can manage.

"Uncuff her," he orders, never taking his gaze away from mine.

I hate myself for flinching when the soldiers' stiff fingers touch my skin.

"And remove this collar as well."

"But sir—"

"Do as I say," he orders, voice calm and far more reassuring than I'd expect it to be.

I don't realize how heavy the metal shackle around my throat is until they remove it.

"Allow me to introduce myself, I'm Malakyte Ardeen." He finally averts his gaze. He pulls a jet-black satin handkerchief from his pocket, slowly brings it to my lip, and dabs the blood there. "And technically, I'm not the leader of Arianyte. My parents control the empire. I merely own Earth."

As he continues to wipe the blood from my face, I chuckle cynically, wondering who in the galaxy gave him the audacity. "You *own* Earth? Wow, the taxes on this place must be through the roof."

He laughs and shoos off the soldiers. We're alone, aside from Blondie's brooding form hiding in the corner like some annoyed wraith. "You have no idea."

His thumb touches the cut on my bottom lip, and I shudder at the frigid touch. He's cold-blooded. Adorning his wicked smile like a crown, those dual sets of pointed canines frame dark-blue lips. I hadn't noticed the cold pouring off him, but I feel it now as if it's a billowing gust, and I shiver from it.

I'm grateful when he stands, free from his chill and his gaze, but my heart drops when he asks, "Who is Trinity Monterey?"

CHAPTER 6

IN EXCHANGE FOR TECHNOLOGICAL ADVANCEMENTS, MEDICAL BREAKTHROUGHS, ALL THE MANY FEATS AND ENDEAVORS THE ARIANYTE EMPIRE HAS BESTOWED ONTO EARTH, A TOTAL SUM OF FIFTEEN PERCENT OF THE TERRAN POPULATION WILL BE RANDOMLY SELECTED ANNUALLY TO SERVE THE EMPIRE AS IT SEES FIT. THESE PEOPLE WILL FOREVER BE KNOWN AS TRIBUTES, AND THEY SHALL ASSIST THE EMPIRE IN BUILDING AND SUSTAINING LIFE WITHIN THE AURORA SYSTEM.

Oh, stars . . .

"See, Miss Ruzz," the cold-blooded alien begins while I curse myself for the fact he already found out my identity. If he knows who I am, and if he knows who Trinity is, then what else does he know about us? "You've created an unfortunate situation. Thirty people are hospitalized, including a valuable member of my council. An attempted kidnap on her was nearly successful: something I find wholly disturbing. Thank the stars she was able to get away from her kidnappers at the last minute. Why, by all observations, does it appear like you're at the heart of all of this?"

"I didn't—"

He holds a long, boney finger up to stop me. The eerie red light of the room bounces off his pale skin, making him look like some sort of vampire overlord minutes away from sucking me dry.

His words make my stomach curdle. Attempted kidnapping? That means the boys and Trinity were unsuccessful in kidnapping Naresteé.

Dammit.

But are they okay?

"I want to remind you that as a Junior Citizen, you're a ward of Arianyte until your eighteenth birthday, meaning legally, you belong to me. Not that I need that pretext to hold you after tonight. But understand, you are now in my custody. Now, a young woman was found at the scene, Miss Trinity Monterey, who has been rumored to have strong ties to the Resistance for years and is the daughter of the infamous Geonni Monterey. Pardon my assumptions, Miss Ruzz, but it appears that you attacked my event on behalf of the Resistance as an act of terrorism and made an attempt at kidnapping my second-in-command."

I hear his words, but all I can think is *They have Trinity* . . .

There is no way I can let Arianyte take another person from me. Not again . . . I won't survive if this happens again.

"No." My mind fumbles to come up with some explanation, some excuse. He knows everything. How did he piece it all together so fast? "No. I don't even know who that is."

Malakyte's eyes narrow. "You're telling me that the daughter of a supposed rebel leader simply happened to be inside a highly restricted zone tonight of all nights? If that's the story you want to stick with, Miss Ruzz, it isn't a very advantageous one. That doesn't explain why you were up on that roof, and why my partner was almost kidnapped and nearly killed. We have the owner of the hover as well, and they claim to know nothing of these events either. Only your face was detected on my cameras."

Those idiots didn't remove the identification papers from the hover-van . . .

I'm so dead. At least it doesn't sound like they found Dimitri or Connar, which is incredible considering Connar was being controlled by—

"I didn't know I was even there," I blurt out, playing as innocent and vulnerable as I can. I don't care what I have to do to get out of this, what types of lies or doe eyes I need to make in order to play this off as believable. People don't take me seriously. I'm a measly five foot one with an innocent face; nobody sees me for what I truly am. I use that to my advantage. If I play this off right, I can get out of this.

If.

A dark brow raises as the alien looks down at me. Blondie half laughs, half coughs awkwardly.

Think, you idiot. Think! Before he Reconditions you and you're his slave for the rest of your life.

Coming up with the story on the spot, I weave my lie as best I can, praying to whatever stars that my intuition is right. This major leap is a dangerous line to tow, but it's sink or swim at this point. "The last thing I remember is walking through the city tonight, and this creepy man approached me. He was wearing a long trench coat and had big ears. He was an extra—an extraterrestrial, like you. But not like you—you. He was green, I think. Not a common race. And he had these scary, awful glowing-green eyes, and then it all went blank."

My voice comes out so shaky I make little sense, but that's all by design. If I confuse the hell out of him, maybe he'll buy this bullshit story.

I'm not hopeful.

Malakyte's skepticism shifts to intense interest. I don't know if what I saw happening to Connar matches up with the story I'm telling now, yet it appeared as though Connar was being controlled by the green-devil guy, however implausible that fact may be—I know what I saw.

"He made me . . ." I pretend to confess, looking away as if in shame. "He made me do all that stuff. I don't know about your commander or whoever you said was almost kidnapped. Maybe he used me to create a distraction and have someone take her? I don't know, I only remember he was right there in the street with me one minute, then the next I'm on top of some rooftop, SSPARROWs and this douchebag with a bow and arrow in my face. I swear, I didn't do this."

The alien before me searches my eyes intently and suspiciously. He smells expensive and educated, likely smart enough to smell all my bullshit.

Malakyte then looks into the corner of the tiny cell, motioning to Blondie.

Oh, shit. My heart begins to pound in my ears. He'll be able to confirm that I'm lying about being controlled.

"Was Deimos there?" Malakyte asks Blondie. *They know this guy's name?* "Was he controlling her? Were her eyes glowing green?"

Blondie and I look at each other, and I have no assumption he's going to say anything other than the truth.

"Your parents were down at that meeting," Malakyte coaxes. "I'm sure emotions were running high, but something as specific as this would certainly be observed."

Folding his arms, Blondie looks passively disinterested.

"I definitely felt Deimos there," he claims. "However, I didn't get on to the rooftop in time to see any evidence she was being controlled by him, but it's entirely possible. There was a report of a SSPARROW soldier acting erratically without his mask on, eyes vacant and emitting a green light. Could have been our guy. We know he likes to cause major disruptions: it's what he's been doing for months."

He's lying.

Why? If I almost killed his parents, why would he ever cover for me? What game is he playing?

The alien leader looks back at me, uncertainty playing out on his beautiful face.

"Are you saying he's the terrorist who's been all over the news? The one blowing up nests and stuff? He's the one that kidnapped me?" I play as dumb as I can.

The two men look at me, and I'm not sure if I've convinced them these events are the truth or not, but what I have created is doubt.

"The devil made me do it, huh, Thumbelina?" Blondie mocks, and I roll my eyes in annoyance. *Jerk.*

"Please, you've got to believe me. I didn't do it. This psychopath made me use—" I pause, not knowing how to approach talking about this radical power Arianyte is likely highly interested in controlling.

"We know all about that thing, so don't try to hide it," Blondie says.

My stomach does another flip-flop as I realize there's no point in hiding it when they already seem to know more about it than I do.

"I don't even know how to use it," I confess, and it's the truth for once. All good lies have some version of the truth embedded within them. "Or what it even is."

"What you have is an extremely powerful weapon known as an Elendril crystal. It's one of six." Malakyte's head points towards Blondie, where his mark sits above his heart, the same place as mine, but I refuse to look at it again for fear of it triggering another one of those wacky visions. Didn't the alien man in that vision have the exact same mark as Blondie?

"Ardelle has one, as do two others who are a part of an exclusive squadron I've assembled of Starseed warriors."

"Starseed?"

"Those who have Elendril crystals. Those like you."

Ardelle clarifies further. "The extraterrestrial you claim took control of you is Deimos, and he's a deadly, slippery squid. He has a crystal that allows him to control the bodies of others, their voices, whole body autonomy—everything."

"That's why his eyes were glowing," I say, putting the pieces together. Mine glow the same way when I use my power, only a different color. According to the rebels, it looks quite creepy. Why hadn't I connected the dots sooner?

"And the sixth crystal? Who are they?" I ask, continuing to draw the attention away from me.

"It's heavily fortified within Arianyte and is none of your concern," Malakyte answers quickly, coming to stand directly beside me. Although I'm no longer strapped down, I continue to sit in the chair with my knees pulled in close to my chest, and when Malakyte faces me once more, I wiggle, highly uncomfortable. "I've been searching a long time for you, Miss Ruzz," he says, and it makes me shiver. What will happen now that he finally has me? What awful punishment will his power bestow upon me? And what about Trinity? The owner of the van? I put them here.

This entire thing, all that I've done . . . It's all starting to feel like a wake-up call where I've been plunged into ice water.

"What do you want from me?" I ask defeatedly.

Malakyte's eyes remain focused on me like I'm a puzzle he can't quite solve. "I genuinely can't stomach my city being terrorized by Deimos.

The only ones strong enough to stop him are those like him. A special breed. Someone very rare. As rare as you, perhaps?" The backs of his fingers slide down my cheek, causing my skin to go all goosey and the hairs on my arms to stand straight up from the coldness of him. He makes me extremely nervous.

"Become one of my Starseeds. Help them find and bring Deimos in alive. Work for me personally, alongside the other Starseeds, then you and Miss Monterey will both be pardoned for tonight's incident. It seems Deimos was the culprit, and since you have no record, I can take you on your word this has all been a ruinous misunderstanding. But I will say that I don't take the attempted kidnapping of my partner lightly. I will dig into this further, and I hope I do not discover you are involved. My grace for you will extend no further, and I guarantee your experiences will be far more unpleasant than what you've experienced here this night. Do you understand, Miss Ruzz?"

I wasn't exactly sure what I expected to happen once Arianyte finally got their hands on me. Whether it be Reconditioning or forcing me into something terrible, this isn't what I had in mind.

And that the leader of Arianyte believed my story is even more shocking.

By all accounts, I lost tonight, but did I? The meeting was interrupted, and everyone in the Resistance will know that I did that. Sure, getting caught by the enemy has me ten seconds away from shitting bricks, but maybe it's not as big of a loss as I initially thought. Maybe I can work through this awful circumstance. I surely didn't intend to become a martyr tonight, but I've always been willing to sacrifice myself for what I believe in. Perhaps I can work this, and I can still find Gav—bring him home? I didn't get what I wanted out of this mission, but neither did Arianyte. There are still winners, it just isn't either of us. Likely, many children have been saved by the impeding of this meeting, and I feel good about that, at least.

Although, I can't discount the predicament I've found myself in. Arianyte—the damn Arianyte Empire—is about to have full control of me if I agree to this.

"And if I say no?" My voice is weak, and I look down, away from those piercing onyx eyes.

He sighs heavily, as if he's contemplating all the terrible ways he can ruin a young woman's life. "Miss Monterey will be sent up to the Azurite Fleet to work as one of the human Tributes—her family, as well. We always need more assets to work up on the mothership. As for you . . ." He clicks his tongue, his large Adam's apple bobbing along his pale neck. "It would pain me greatly, nevertheless, Reconditioning would aggressively be imposed in order to ensure cooperation with an Unnatural Ability that powerful. You're at the top of my power scale, Miss Ruzz. That makes you incredibly dangerous. Take my offer so you can keep your memories."

Well, shit . . .

"You can't go home, of course. You'll go live with Ardelle and the other Starseeds so I can ensure your cooperation," Malakyte clarifies, and a bit of me cringes at the mere thought of having to live with Blondie.

Malakyte bends over me, both hands on the chair's arms. I hunch down like a frightened dog, pushing myself against the metal chair as if I could somehow escape the frost radiating off him.

"So, what will it be?"

My mouth hangs slightly open as I painfully and uncomfortably search this monster's eyes for any hint that he's bluffing. He's not. Malakyte Ardeen, Prince of Arianyte, will make good on his threats. Of this I have zero doubt.

He clearly doesn't believe I don't know Trinity, otherwise he wouldn't be using her as a bargaining chip to get me to agree to this. The prince must really want me on his little team, because he's willing to let the daughter of the Terran Resistance's leader walk out of here in exchange for my cooperation. I messed up tonight, big time, but not even Geonni can discount the set of cojones I've got for the decision I'm going to make.

Am I seriously about to do this? To agree to work with *Arianyte*? With the enemy? Wouldn't this make me a traitor to the Resistance? A sellout? A coward?

A dark horse . . .

Could I manage to pull something like that off? Go full trojan horse on their ass and bring down Arianyte from within?

A dangerous thought . . . one even more foolish than my attempt on Naresteé. As tempting of an idea as that is, I've gotten myself into enough trouble by being selfish and reckless.

"Alright," I begin, knowing I'm backed up against a wall with incredibly crappy options. "I'll be one of your Starseeds if, and only if, you let Trinity go. The owner of the hover-van, too. They're both innocent victims, like me."

Malakyte seems to ponder my counteroffer for longer than I'd like him to. "Miss Monterey is my collateral that you don't skip town or do anything foolish. If another incident occurs—any other suspicious occurrences—I will track her down and she's going to be the one responsible for it. Do you understand?"

There's the Arianyte I know so well. The power Malakyte wields flexes before my eyes, reminding me that I may have pulled a fast one on him tonight, but that he's the one in control, and I'm merely a pawn in his game.

"I've searched so long for you. I'd be laden with grief to have something unfortunate happen to my Star. Don't disappoint me."

Maybe it's the bad girl in me that's drawn to the bad boy in him, I don't know, but something about all that dark power is enticing when it should be repulsive. He's everything I've been fighting against; he's the reason Gav was taken away from me. However, he's offering me a lifeline where I'd otherwise drown, and despite all my hatred for him, I reluctantly take it.

CHAPTER 7

ANY PERSONS LIVING WITHIN THE AURORA SYSTEM FOR FIVE YEARS OR MORE MAY TAKE PART IN THE COMPETITION ARENA GAME KNOWN AS "THE TITAN GAMES." THE WINNER OF THE TITAN GAMES SHALL RECEIVE GENEROUS FINANCIAL COMPENSATION ALONG WITH AN INVITATION TO THE EXCLUSIVE AZURITE FLEET, WHERE THEY'D BE GIVEN ACCESS TO INTERSTELLAR TRAVEL BROUGHT TO THEM BY THE GENEROUS LEADERS OF ARIANYTE.

"You don't need to hold onto me so tightly." I pull on Blondie's—Ardelle's—grip on my arm as he aggressively walks me out of the confinement building, something I didn't think was going to happen once I was dragged inside.

I'm lucky. Too lucky.

It doesn't sit right.

I should be Reconditioned. I should be his puppet and his pawn and his weapon. That's what I've been told ever since my powers manifested. By Trinity, by Geonni, and by the rest of the rebels who know about my powers. Something is going on here, and I'm going to find out what it is.

Blondie doesn't loosen his grip. We walk past SSPARROWs and non-SSPARROW Arianyte workers alike. Most of them extras, at least twenty different alien species, and they all work for the enemy.

I guess I do too now.

"Did you piss off your hair stylist or something?" he asks dully, commenting on the teal ends of my hair, the same color as Gav's flowers.

I take my free hand and shove my middle finger directly into his face before he swats it away.

"Jance is waiting," Ardelle says.

"Who's Jance?"

Blondie doesn't answer.

We exit the foreboding building, the red lights that glow on the outside casting the foggy night into a haunting, bloody mist. I never want to see this building again. I gulp down the chilly air like I haven't breathed in a thousand years.

A black ground-hover idles outside the building. A handsome, rugged man in his midthirties leans against the hover with his arms crossed and one foot up against the running board. He wears black pants covered in buckles and straps, a berry maroon-and-black adorned with buckles, clips, and heavy detailing around the shoulders.

The moment the man sees me, he pushes himself off the hover and eyes me with surprise, almost like he's seen a ghost. He covers up his startled slip quickly, however, and closes the last few feet between us, coming up to tower over me like a giant. His tan skin peeks through his close-cropped beard, the same raven-black color as his intentionally messy hairstyle that dances along the top of his head.

"You must be Jance." I force my arm out of Ardelle's grip. He lets me go finally and steps away from me like I'm contagious or something.

"He's your Ringer," Ardelle informs me.

I inch back. "What the hell is a Ringer?"

Jance holds out his hand to me, and I awkwardly shake it. But when I see why he truly held his hand out to me, I'm shocked.

"What?" I shout out, bringing the man's hand in close. "How is my mark on this dude's hand?" Nestled right between his pointer finger and thumb is a smaller, darker version of the star mark on my chest. The *exact* same star mark. Even down to the three small lines that meet in the center of the small triangle.

"Looks like you may belong here a little more than you realized, Thumbelina." Ardelle smirks, eyebrows raised.

I scoff rudely but hold back the snarky comment already forming on my tongue.

"I'm driving; she's all yours," Blondie says, disappearing to the driver's side of the hover.

"Why is my mark on your hand?" I ask this Jance dude one more time, my voice impatient. This is bizarre because Gavrielle's symbol is in the exact same spot as this guy's mark. But Gav's mark is not my star mark; it's a completely different shape. It has to be connected to these Elendril crystals somehow.

"It's Karalevine, right?" An old-world New Zealand accent comes on thick with his deeply textured voice. That entire continent is currently underwater, and guessing by the color of his skin tone, he's one of the natives from that area.

"Just call me Kara," I tell him.

His nearly black eyes look at me with curious inquisitiveness, returning to the same expression he wore upon first seeing me. Noticing me notice him, he assures me they'll explain all the details to me soon, and I reluctantly climb into the back seat simply to end this awkward introduction.

I run the events of the night repeatedly in my tired mind. My emotions are too numb to feel the full magnitude of what's happened, of what I've done. The emotions I do feel are a jumbled mess of guilt, embarrassment, and frustration.

How many people did I hurt? Not only physically, but in multiple other ways? Not to mention Blondie's parents were down there, and this guy is going to loathe me for all of eternity most likely.

What's wrong with me? Why do I do this? Why am I like this? I ruin everything and I hate myself for it more and more each time I do. It wasn't intentional, but I suppose that doesn't matter to the people who are impacted by my actions, does it?

The awkward silence and perpetual glances from them both in the rearview mirror get to be too much, so I finally ask a question in hopes of gaining some information.

"So, since you're a Starseed like me, you have a mark on your chest too. I noticed at rest it's the color of a bruise or birthmark, and like mine, it's directly over your heart."

Blondie nods, and we make eye contact in the rearview mirror.

"Yes," he deadpans like that information is super obvious. "That's where the symbol is located for all the Starseeds."

"And when you use your power, does the mark begin to glow and turn a color? Mine lights up like a sun, practically. What is your power, by the way?"

We take a sharp turn leading onto groundway Z-11, which leads out of the city and into the surrounding mountainside that cups the city of Zarmenia in its hands. I wonder where they're taking me.

"I control gravity," he informs me, and my brows raise in surprise. "And Jance can imprint anything into a person's mind because he's your Ringer, but the whole Ringer thing is a story for another day."

So, the Ringers, whatever they are, have magic too, apparently. Not to mention this Jance guy and his abilities are terrifying.

I suddenly feel an odd pull in the center of my stomach, and when I glance away from the dwindling lights of the city fading behind us and back to the rearview mirror, Ardelle's eyes are glowing red within the pupils. My long strands of hair begin floating around me in soft, long tendrils. The necklace around my neck begins to float, as if I were suddenly floating on the moon. Then, as quickly as it began, my hair softly falls back against my shoulders. I briefly see the red glow of Ardelle's mark reflecting on the steering wheel before it fades out completely. I try not to think of the vision the mark triggered.

"Different colors for different marks, then?" I clarify, knowing that my mark glows purple when I use my magic, and he answers in the affirmative with a grumble.

Crazy. If only Gavrielle was here with me to see this.

About ten minutes pass before we're slithering up the mountainside, the rainbow lights of the city still visible on certain turns. Only the rich live up here, away from the bodies squished on top of each other but still close enough to the city where the commute is rather short. I'm unsure what to expect, but after we begin to slow on one last turn, we slowly travel up a steep driveway where lights peek out from a house at the top.

This is a song and dance I am used to, walking into a new home where I don't know a soul and certainly don't belong. Those are the hardest nights.

Awkward situation number two for the orphan moving into a new home: the Inspection, the very first look at where I would get into trouble for breaking rules I never knew existed.

Grumbling, I hop out of the hover and am shocked by what I see. The hover sits in a long, wide driveway. Most of the property is shrouded in complete darkness, which makes me wonder where I am, at first. By my guess, we're in the sprawling tree-filled mountainside that encircles the city, which twinkles down below a massive, steep cliff face like a rainbow metropolis. The ledge overlooks all of Zarmenia City.

It is one hell of a view. The skyscrapers, all the bright neon lights, even the Titan Games arena, are lit up like the sun. Its vast bowl shape looks like a shining crater from this distance and altitude. The sky-hovers appear like little bugs buzzing around the city. Arianyte's mothership in the sky above looks even bigger and brighter all the way up here. It plays footsie with the moon as it hovers in Earth's orbit. The stars seem to twinkle ten times brighter than I'm used to seeing. I haven't seen so much of the night sky since the orphanage, and I know Gav would have loved this view. There are so many stars, so many more than what I could ever see from the city. It's breathtaking. Is Gav looking at these stars at this very moment? Does he ever wonder about his home-world? Does he ever wonder about me?

A high-pitched squeal snaps my attention towards a girl with legs for days. I don't know which is more beautiful, this girl who runs into Ardelle's arms or the house she emerges from.

"Thank the stars you're back!" She wraps her arms around Ardelle, meeting his height without shoes on.

"Not what you were imagining?" Jance says from behind me as I gape at the mansion, its many windows and elegant design. "I built this place after I left my post as general for the Terrans in the war. My late wife left me a considerable amount of cato credits and always wanted a place in the wilderness. I like to think I built this place for her. I equipped the house with a full training area where we can help you refine your skills: archery and firearm accessible, a surgical suite, an indoor pool, anything you could want or need."

He fought with the rebels . . . but is now working for Arianyte? Could he do both? Could I?

"Wow, was your wife some sort of long-lost queen or something?"

His face remains blank, and I instantly feel terrible. *Great one, Kara . . .*

"You'll have your own room with an attached bath. I can imagine this is a very abrupt change for you, but know you'll be safe here."

Safe from who?

Jance walks towards the front door. The house from the outside looks enormous. Elaborate pillars frame an entryway where plants and windows all group together in a statement of pleasant greetings. It has multiple levels, and a few rooms on the upper levels have their lights on. A three-hover garage veers off to the right of the house near the tree line. The rest of the house is invisible beyond the darkness of the forest.

"Oh, please tell me that's our Star?" The tall girl gawks at me with an absolute grin on her face as I approach the twelve-foot-high entry door. She wears pajama shorts paired with a matching blue shirt, a cartoon unicorn head on the center. Her hair is a shoulder-length choppy haircut that's longer in the front and colored pastel blue. The dye job is perfection, completely even and smooth like butter. She's thin, but all lean muscle. Looking at her, I feel inadequate.

"Unfortunately," Ardelle says with a snarky twang, and the girl looks over at him with a scrunched freckled nose and her tongue sticking out.

"Be nice, big brother. She doesn't look like the type of girl to take much of your crap."

I already like her.

She gives me a giant hug and I repress a moan from the beating I've taken. I awkwardly pat her back a few times, hoping she'll let me go.

"I'm so glad we finally found you. I'm Pacey. We're going to have so much fun together, I already feel it. Love your hair, by the way."

I try to see if she has a mark, too, but her shirt is covering her chest. Her hand is free of any mark or symbol. "What did you guys do to her?

She looks dreadful. Come inside, I'll show you around. Do you want some hot chocolate?"

I decline the offer, and Ardelle makes another shrewd comment about how I thoroughly got the crap beat out of myself.

Maybe since Arianyte took Gavrielle, he was brought together with these people? It's more than possible, and my heart swells at the possibility, pushing my wearied, aching soul forward.

They styled the house in a modern-vintage aesthetic, with décor and art that screamed sophistication and taste. Bold, chunky pops of color draw the eye in every direction. It's clean, with lots of white-and-black walls, accents and simplistic furnishings giving pops of color here and there. Beyond the entryway, the winding staircase of floating wooden steps and an intricate black-metal railing is a definite showpiece. A giant, floating, three-dimensional arrangement that resembles a flower hangs next to the stairs. It bathes the space in a tender, relaxing glow of warm yellow.

Awkward situation number three for the orphan moving into a new home: the Vibe. I'm a big feeler. How things feel to me is an immediate indication of how a new home will be. Here, this place—it's warm. Not warm in temperature but warm in energy. I'm thrown off by it, by how comfortable it feels.

A gilded cage is still that—a cage.

"Is there anyone else here who has a marking on their hand like you?" I ask Jance. "Around my age, maybe?"

Jance's brows crease. "There are other Ringers, yes, but they're all my age, late thirties."

My heart plummets to the marble flooring. Even the smell of pumpkin-pie candles can't stop nausea from rolling into my gut, and I want to hurl up every ounce of hope I stupidly allowed myself to feel.

Gavrielle isn't here.

But why not, if Arianyte took him? Why wouldn't he be here? He's clearly connected to all this. It simply doesn't make sense, and anger fills up the space hope left behind.

"Listen." I turn to the three of them. "This is a nice place you got here and all, but I don't want to be here. So, I'm going to make things perfectly clear. You may force me to find Deimos, pretend that I'm a part of your little club or whatever, but this is nothing more than punishment for something I didn't even do. I don't trust you, and I'm not interested in joining your little *squad*."

Silence is my response.

Good.

"I'll take you to your room," Jance says, the deep texture in his voice doing its best to cover the awkward tension between them and me. He turns and heads down a hall with mounted light fixtures resembling tree branches. Smooth hardwood floors pave the way.

"Well, that went well," Pacey says when I'm halfway down the hallway. Normally I would be out of hearing range, but not with these pointy ears—I can hear everything.

It isn't her words that sting and remind me of how much of a piece of crap I am, it's Ardelle's. "Yeah, she's a total psycho, trust me."

Nothing I don't already know.

Ignoring them, I map the way Jance takes me up the stairs to the third floor. My room is the second door on the right, its black wood carved with fancy flowing patterns. The rose-gold handle is cold to the touch.

The size of the room hits me foremost because it's bigger than the entire loft I'm currently renting. Latte-colored walls with Marshmallow White trim gives the room a warm vibe off the bat. The ceiling light is a concave cutout, casting a soft, comforting glow onto the dusty-rose-colored curtains, rugs, and accent furniture. The vanity is identical to the dresser: rustic, linen-cream colored, and vintage-looking, but with a dainty pink cushioned seat sitting beside the vanity.

"This room is very nice," I say softly, trying to make up for my outburst moments ago. The king-sized bed has a puffy comforter and pillows of all sizes. I find the remote and turn on the curved television atop the vintage dresser, if only to drown out the tense silence between us.

Feeling his eyes on me again, I look at Jance and wait for him to lock me in or go over the long list of rules I'm supposed to follow, but he stares at me instead. It's awkward enough that I almost tell him to get out. Thankfully, he softly tells me goodnight and shuts the door behind him. I walk up to the door, see the lock is on the inside, and lock myself in. A small measure of safety, but at least the lock is on this side of the door for once.

CHAPTER 8

They woke me up at the butt crack of dawn so they could 'assess my skill level in combat in order to train me properly for Deimos.' I learned what that meant after the massive breakfast. I gluttonously ate way too much. I regretted eating all that bacon—a food only the rich can afford—because I got my ass whopped, and that bacon is still doing somersaults in my stomach.

And this has all been made worse by the fact it was Blondie himself facilitating my second beatdown in less than twenty-four-hours.

The sly smirk on his lips told me he enjoyed it. Just like he probably enjoyed ripping me away from my entire life and throwing me into a job where I work for my biggest enemy.

I didn't say anything about my injuries, but after about ten minutes of my sore body not able to fight back in any substantial way, it's clear I'm useless like this. Jance puts an end to my day-one assessment down in the basement when Ardelle lays me flat on my ass.

Reaching his hand down, Ardelle offers to help me to my feet.

I slap it out of my face and stand on my own, scowling. I don't typically get beat so easily, but I'm sore and I also don't want them to know how good of a fighter I actually am, not until I can evaluate them further. They're not the only ones doing an assessment.

"I didn't realize Arianyte did such a number on you," Jance says. "Next time, tell us."

After I wipe myself off, the tour of the downstairs continues with Jance and Ardelle. They walk me through the large space.

The windows and sliding door light up the entire basement with the glow of fresh morning light. A multitude of weights and free-standing workout equipment stand against the wall made of mirrors, a punching bag sits idly by the bigger machines, and beyond that are the mats and a free area with a multitude of weapons hanging on the wall. This place is great, although, the pressure to perform right now is giving me anxiety. Do I show them what my powers can do, or will that make things even worse? Typically, people are frightened by my powers. Will they report back to Malakyte how strong I actually am? Will it change things?

"You've really got a nice place here," I tell the two of them, my ribs still throbbing.

Before either of them can reply, a petite Japanese woman confidently walks into the basement, her sleek shoulder-length hair swaying. She and Jance lock eyes before her gaze shifts to me.

"Kara, this is Saris. Sylo's Ringer," Jance tells me as she approaches, reaching her hand out for me to shake. I take it, surprised by her strong grip, and see the diamond mark on her hand in the same spot as Jance's and Gavrielle's.

"And Sylo is . . . ?" I ask, still confused about what a Ringer even is and what it means. Nobody has really gotten to that yet.

"Oh, he's a royal thorn in my side, I'll tell you that right now," the woman says with a semi-joking tone, her Asian accent hardly noticeable. The vibe I get from Saris is badass, take-no-shit, not-even-from-the-devil kind of lady. "He's one of the other Starseeds, like you and Ardelle. We're excited to have you here, Kara, and as the weapon's expert in the house, I'm curious to see what experience you have."

My brows raise. I wasn't expecting that.

How do I explain that I'm trained in all of those weapons? *Oh, by the way, I've been bunking with the Resistance the last six years—you know, your enemy—and although I don't appear like it now, I'm actually a lethal machine trained to take Arianyte down someday.*

"Wow, that's exciting. Show me what you got," I say with an excited smile. The woman and I walk towards the side of the basement gym where we find an armory stocked with as many weapons as the Resistance has.

The entire wall is lined with every type of disruptor pistol, from handguns to full automatic rifles similar to the ones the SSPARROWs use. I see Blondie's bow and arrows up there, along with axes, a pair of sai, throwing stars, brass and spiked knuckles, and even grenades. My eyes light up at my favorite section of this massive wall of goodies, where I spot several different types of swords and blades. Katana, tachi and wakizashi—the katana and wakizashi I prefer due to my small size— and then there's the basic broadsword and two-handed sword, both considerably too long for me. A rapier hangs vertically on the edge of the wall, completing the blades with a few daggers ranging in size on the right.

I whistle in impressed fashion, genuinely giddy. The guys in the Resistance would freak if they saw all this.

"Not so grumpy to be here, now, are we?" Ardelle chimes in, busting up my good buzz. I shoot him a dirty look. He continues, "What do you say? Do we give the new girl a crash course in all these weapons, show her that you pull the trigger on the guns—not push it? There shouldn't be any special treatment because she's new."

Placing my hands on my hips, I glare at Blondie and hope he spontaneously catches fire.

"Here's an idea. Can you show me how to use my powers instead?" *So i can blast Blondie halfway to Hell.*

Ardelle laughs as if I told a halfway decent joke.

Jance shoots him a dirty look. "We're going to wait on that for now. Your crystal's power is pure antimatter. We want to assess you before we go off the deep end."

"Antimatter? What's that?"

"It's only the deadliest force in all of existence," Ardelle comments artfully.

"Antimatter is highly destructive," Jance echoes. "Everything on Earth is regular, boring old matter with their subatomic particles charged to the positive. What comes from you is matter's complete opposite on a subatomic level. You emit pure antimatter that alone does nothing until it hits regular matter. When the two matters combine, it creates annihilation."

Annihilation?

"Well, that makes sense."

Jance steals my attention back. "Let's take a break. Ahren wants to meet you, anyway."

"I have to see someone else?" I ask, not wanting to leave the beautiful wall of weapons, especially for awkward situation number five for the orphan moving into a new home: the Introductions. *The worst.*

Saris places a firm hand on my shoulder. "Don't worry, they'll be here when you return. After you visit with Ahren and meet the rest of the team, we can go over each of these in detail."

Jance leads me out of the gym and down the hallway to where the other side of the huge basement comes into view.

We pass the elevator that brought us down here, the stairs beside it.

Jance points to another door some twenty feet down. "That door leads to the surgical suite, but it's a sterile room so stay out of there."

I whistle loudly. Fancy.

"Ahren is our resident doctor. He keeps us out of the hospital. Trust me, it's better that way."

We pass a few doors that are marked specifically for their purposes: exams, x-rays, and other fancy imaging. Then we enter a room that resembles a medical lab. The room is lit with a soft-blue light glowing from underneath cabinets and small table lamps here and there, sitting next to machines of all sizes. Tubes, syringes, gauze, gloves, and other medical supplies are semi-organized and thrown about. It's an organized mess, if I'm being generous. Sitting hunched over a microscope is a man in his late thirties, wearing a white lab coat with his blond hair combed back in a simple, sophisticated hairstyle. He turns to us and smiles warmly, genuinely.

"Ah, you must be our new recruit." He stands and walks towards us. "I'm Dr. Johnson, but you can call me Ahren. No need for the doctor formalities. I hear you may have a few injuries from last night, is that right? Take a seat there." He points to a swivel chair. I sit and find Jance already gone, leaving me alone with the doctor.

"Yeah . . . but it's nothing serious. I'll live."

His smile is genuinely sad. "That's what I feared you'd say. How they treat captives over there is beyond my comprehension. I am sorry that happened to you. I never feel as if violence should be the answer if other means can be reached first. How do you feel about me running a few tests? Nothing invasive, but I'd like to see how your body is functioning in general. Especially with what I know of your history of an unstable childhood, which could have led to deficiencies and disease. You should also be aware that you will inevitably have physical effects from your crystal, so it's important you're monitored closely. Are you afraid of needles?"

The man performs a myriad of tests: x-rays, blood and urine, weight, muscle indexing, and some other crap I don't know what it's for. It's been a long time since I've seen a doctor. He works with gentle hands, not rushing, but methodically going through his tasks as if he's done them a million times. He's very different from Jance in the sense he has a quiet confidence, a soft soul. His face is calm and clean shaven, with eyes a common shade of blue that lends to the appeal of his handsome face.

"Can I ask you something?" I press, the silence driving me nuts, and his soft smile is all the answer I need. "They explained to me about the crystals, but what's the marks on the hands all about? And what in star's name is a Ringer?"

Rolling on his chair to where we took my x-rays, he takes a remote and points to some panel on the wall that lights up, revealing a digital version of my x-ray. I jump out of my chair and dash over to the screen.

"What in the world?" I gasp as I look at the image there. Of me. "Is that the—"

"Elendril crystal? Yes," Ahren interrupts, but I get the sense he feels bad about doing so.

Right in the dead center of my heart, surrounded by black and sticking out in stark white, is the Elendril crystal.

"Why is it all jagged?" I cock my head to the side and pop an eyebrow. "It looks like a spikey ball with pokey things."

"Well, if you think about it, it looks like naturally formed crystal we would find here on Earth. Typically found in the quartz or amethyst family. That's why we gave it that name—crystal."

"And this whole time I never knew it was there. Can it come out? I don't understand how it got there. From what I can remember, I was born with this crazy thing."

The doctor shakes his head, zipping back towards me in his chair. "Unfortunately, if the crystal comes out, it causes death. It's so integrated into the muscle of the heart that when removed, it'll completely destroy the interventricular septum. That's the wall of cardiac tissue that separates the right and left ventricles. I'm aware that's all doctor speak. Essentially, it destroys the heart muscle. Brutally. And to answer your other question, you were born with it. We all were."

"And a Ringer is . . . ?" I ask again. "How come Jance has my star mark on his hand? Whose do you have?"

Ahren removes his black gloves and shows me the mark there, identical to Ardelle's. I suddenly feel extreme amounts of pity for the doctor. What incredibly bad luck.

"Think of the marks on our hands as somewhat of a sidekick to the superhero that is the Elendril. It gives us—the sidekicks—abilities as well. They differ from the chief hero, but they're connected to each other. Malakyte told us the nickname 'Starseed' is to categorize you from us."

"That's why the marks are the same," I conclude, finally able to connect the dots. "They're a pair."

"Precisely." Ahren smiles and grabs up all the discarded garbage he created from his tests. "You'll find over time that there's a special connection between Starseeds and Ringers; it's difficult to quantify."

My mind spins. If Gavrielle's mark is on the same spot as the others, that must mean he's a Ringer. But whose Ringer is he? Whenever Gav was using his abilities, often playing jokes or pranks on the kids at the orphanage, his eyes would glow green inside the pupils. Strikingly similar to someone else I've seen recently. If they're a pair, and assuming the colors match up, then that means . . . oh stars. He's a Ringer for *Deimos*.

"So the only Ringers we know of are you, Jance, and Saris?" I ask again, hoping against hope he may know something the others do not.

As he snatches up a ridiculous number of blood vials, Ahren shrugs, his doctor façade already coming undone. "Correct."

Where are you, Gav?

"How do the Ringers get their powers if they themselves don't have a crystal?" These crystal things are beginning to make my brain hurt.

Ahren contemplates my question for a moment before saying, "I think it's due to the enormity of the raw power of these magical artifacts. Perhaps without the split in power, all this magic alone would be too much for any one being to handle. How it works precisely is beyond my scope of knowledge; these are ancient celestial artifacts, after all. However they work, how they appeared in each of us and why, is a big mystery. Ardelle and Pacey are siblings, which can lead us to some data that familial relationships can play a role in the connections between Starseed and Ringer. As we see with Ardelle and me, that's not always the case. Plus, with your mysterious past, you may have a deeper connection to one of us than you know of. You never know."

Woah, yeah. Definite brain ache with this stuff.

"What abilities do you have?" I ask, needing to come back down to Earth with a simpler question this time.

"I have the wonderful ability to heal the body," he explains. "It's why I became a doctor. I want to help people. It gives me purpose. If you'll let me, I can heal the burns and bruises from last night. I'm sure they're painful. I can imagine Saris already wants to begin training. The others too. We're all curious to see what you can do."

His chuckle is light and I can see his affection towards each of them. Like they're all one big happy family.

This is not the image of Arianyte I've been imagining the last six years, and it's beginning to mess with my mind.

CHAPTER 9

etting out of that house was a nightmare. The concept that I have a job didn't seem to resonate with these people, and after an argument with Ardelle, he suggested they put an actual tracker on me. The look on Ardelle's face when he put it on made me want to punch him in that beautiful, stupid face of his. He thinks he's better than me. It's clear by how he acts.

Jerk.

But Ardelle can suck it because all I care about is making sure Trinity is safely out of Arianyte's clutches.

I finish up my last client early and walk to the back room, the old-world rock music from the twenty-first century blasting in the otherwise awkward silence. I struggle back here for almost ten minutes trying to get this damn tracker off my wrist.

Finally slipping it off, I pocket it, grab my bag, and leave Brim—the shop's main manager since Geonni no longer inks anymore—and the shop without another word. Brim is likely watching me as I hide the tracker behind the 'Tattoos' neon sign, but he won't move it. He knows what it's for. He knows Arianyte owns me now.

Everyone's going to know.

I wouldn't be walking free otherwise.

Because I don't want my new Starseed friends to know where I live, I creep in the building's shadows towards my loft as soon as I ditch the tracker. There are valuable items to me there, some of them being drawings of Gavrielle I made years ago when I realized I was forgetting his face. Not only that, I was forgetting the symbol on his hand. I knew even back then our two marks were linked somehow, so I drew his, trying to remember the exact way its round, petal shape looked as each piece curved and wrapped around itself to make a perfect, mandala shape. I need that drawing; I need to compare it to my theory that he's Deimos's Ringer. It's likely, simply by doing the math and knowing the two are pairs, but I need that confirmation.

Slipping through the main entrance to my building unnoticed as I usually do, I take the stairs two at a time. This place is a crap hole. Rats scurry away at the sounds of my footsteps, driving them into darker places. It definitely is nothing like Jance's house, but it is my own space. The years of living under other people's expectations in foster homes, orphanages, and even with Geonni, was suffocating. To have my own place is freeing. I'm only accountable to myself, and it was great for a while, although it was also extremely lonely. I didn't realize how deafening the silence of solitude would become. Trinity was right when she told me I'd regret moving here, but at the time I thought she was just pissed that I was leaving her.

Once I get to the floor where my loft is, I make the immediate right turn towards the door at the end of the hallway, then I stop in my tracks.

The door to my loft is ajar.

This can't be possible. My security measures are top notch. The door itself has three locks, one of them a fingerprint scanner. I'm immediately puzzled by how the camera embedded within the lock didn't alert me, and I frantically check my Dezlar to see what happened. When I watch the last recorded footage, it only reveals a shadow crossing by, and the entire thing goes black. Inching closer to the lock, I see that it's been blasted by a disruptor pistol, the entire thing blown to hell.

Warning bells immediately go off, my hackles raising like a wolf's.

Is this person still inside? What'll happen if I confront them? Does this have anything to do with Malakyte or Deimos or even the rebels? It could be anyone inside there. Anyone with a motive to kill, to kidnap, or to keep me quiet.

My star mark begins tingling. The roaring of blood pounds in my ears and my knees begin to shake. I'm such a baby, holy stars. I've got nothing to protect myself with, and if this crystal goes off, so does half of this building. Thank the stars Ahren healed me this morning, because

I can at least fight. Although, it doesn't make me feel very safe as I stand frozen outside the door.

Sliding it open slowly, its hinges screaming like a blaring alarm, I open my loft door to a disaster.

It's completely and utterly trashed.

It's small enough for me to see almost the entire space, and I see no one. Squatting, I pick up the small lamp that flickers on the floor and set it upright, my hairs standing on end. Shit is everywhere. My mouth is dry as I try to breathe, looking around in horror at the sight of my few belongings being cascaded around as if they mean nothing. And though this place never truly felt safe, or warm, or like a real home, I still feel a deep sense of violation. The coffee table has been flipped over, the raggedy couch that came with the place cut up, its cushions brutally murdered, fluff all over the place. The few printed copies of used books I had on my shelves about tattooing and art lay shredded, my heart aching at the sight of them. Cabinets lay open or dangling off their hinges, and my clothes are strewn over the bed and floor.

What in star's name . . .

My creep of a landlord, the asshole he is, is going to freak when he sees the place. As the thoughts of my immediate safety calm down a little bit, my next panic is how much it's going to cost to repair all of this. Apprenticeship does not pay well, and I've barely been making it as is.

I scurry towards the drawer where I keep all my older drawings, and I gasp when I see the entire drawer is empty. Standing in my kitchen, stunned, I blink and look in the drawer again, somehow expecting the drawings to magically be there.

No. No, no, no.

Out of pure panic, I open other drawers, knowing the drawings aren't in there. I then go to a more logical step and rummage through all the crap strewn about. The broken dishes in and out of the cupboards, the tipped over cereal boxes on the counter, I even look in the fridge—the drawings are gone. Gone–gone. Gavrielle's face and mark along with them.

Anger roils in me, half at whoever did this and half at myself. How long has it been since I looked at the drawings? Months? A year? I . . . I don't know if I remember his face anymore.

Is this what they came for, or is it simply what they found? Either way, I know now that they're interested in Gav and the Elendril crystals, and therefore it could be anyone who broke in here. The rebels, Deimos, or even Malakyte. What would have happened if they found me here instead of an empty loft?

I stuff some clothes in a backpack, snatch up the only plant I have, and ditch the place before anyone can return. I leave with the feeling of my loft stuck on me like a parasite, its darkness following me around like a demon looking for a way inside. I can't shake it, but I know I have to switch gears. A clouded and distracted mind will not serve me well as I head to the leader of the Resistance.

The more I think of Geonni on my walk down the busy street, the more I wonder if he's the one who ordered the break-in. It would make sense. His daughter had been caught by Arianyte. I'm sure Dimitri and Connar told him about last night, that Arianyte snatched me up as well. It'd be prudent of him to destroy any evidence of their involvement or locations.

The anxiety that blooms inside at Geonni's potential reaction makes me question why I'm going there in the first place, and I shudder against the crisp afternoon air. If Trinity isn't there . . . stars only know what'll happen to me.

Passing the psychic's door from last night, I pause. Her sign, identical to the one at the tattoo shop, is switched to closed. A part of me wishes the woman was there, especially after the experiences of last night. I should have listened to her. I should bust in there and demand she tell me who broke into my loft, but I continue walking instead and try not to think of everything I've lost in such a short period of time. It's starting to pile up, and it's starting to hurt.

After juggling my plant as I dig into my pocket for the spare smoke pen I've snagged from the tattoo shop, I gingerly puff on the device. I'm so rattled at the stolen drawings that not even the multiple hits of nicotine help me relax. And I desperately need to relax.

What's this growing anxiety? It seems the farther I get away from my loft, the worse I feel. Perhaps reality is setting in? An ice-cold tickle spindles its way up my spine as I weave in and out of people on the street. A man bumps my shoulder, his face hidden beneath a ratty black hoodie, and I pause when I see his eyes are glowing green. At least, I think. The glance was only a fraction of a second; perhaps I'm seeing things. It's only PTSD from last night; there's no way this Deimos guy is around here, in broad daylight.

My Dezlar rings, and I grunt in annoyance as I juggle my plant and smoke pen while reaching into my back pocket for it. The number is blocked. Maybe it's someone from Jance's house? I flick the translucent-glass interface and bring it up to my ear, slinking into an alleyway to ensure they don't hear any street sounds.

"What do you guys want?" I say as a way of greeting. "I'm coming back to the house. How many times do I have to tell you that?"

"You shouldn't be out walking the streets of the city alone. It's dangerous. There are predators out here."

The voice on the other end chills me to the bone. It's a mocking tone, if not a little breathy, but confident.

Freezing, my mouth hangs ajar as I stand with my back against the alley wall, peeking out from the shadows. How does this person know I'm out walking about? Are they watching me? Do they see me right now?

Scanning the surrounding street, buildings, and parked hovers, I don't see anyone suspicious.

"You won't be able to see me," the caller clarifies, and I zip back into the darkness of the alley, holding my potted plant close to my chest as if it'll protect me somehow.

"Who is this? What do you want?" I ask, but I think I already know the answer to the first question.

A soft chuckle is his initial response. "You have something that doesn't belong to you."

My mark tingles as my fear spikes from the threat in his tone. The clear correlation between this call and my trashed loft makes me now suspect him over the others: *Deimos.*

But what was he searching for? Does he possibly know Gav is his Ringer, and that's why the drawings were stolen? That would make a lot of sense.

Being so done with this conversation, I take the shaking Dezlar from my ear and hang up. I bolt out of the alleyway and dash towards my destination, hoping to the stars Deimos won't pop out of a shadow.

After speed walking down block after block with no incident, I finally arrive at the tall brick building nestled up against a grocery store. I finally feel safe enough to let myself breathe normally again. Completely unassuming, the building looks like any old brownstone and is one of the old-world buildings not destroyed in the war, yet the entire Terran Resistance lies within. Before my loft, I lived here for years while they trained me in combat, weapons, and spying. What they couldn't train me in was how to use the stupid crystal or whatever I'm supposed to call it now. My mark has been a mystery to all of them, but maybe now that I'm around others who also have experience with this insane type of power that could change; I could change?

I open the heavy entranceway door. It opens to a small foyer that smells a bit mildewy, where three men armed to the teeth are lounging. They tense as I walk in, as do I at their reactions.

"Nice plant," one of them says. I silently walk past them to the stairs, the tension thicker than sludge.

The giant set of stairs is a deep blood-red velvet carpet that's worn down and dulled in the center. They line the cream-colored walls that are garnished with Renaissance art from the old world, which somehow survived the Great Purge. All the artwork reminds me of are the missing sketches that are now in someone else's hands.

After climbing eight stories, I arrive at the top level, where Emma and Bradley stand guard. Each holds a carbine-aluminum AR-15 with digital firepower, meaning they never run out of bullets because the bullets are created within the magazines themselves. They're energized bullet rounds. Someone tried to explain the science to me once, but it went over my head.

Once the pair sees me, they each grip one Sunset Gold handle, opening the Apple Red door in one smooth motion. I scowl as Emma and Bradley close the door behind me, but only after they scan me for a recording transmitter and demand I leave my backpack and plant outside the room.

It hurts they don't trust me.

Sitting at a large mahogany desk in a leather-bound chair is an eccentric man who can easily be described as rough around the edges. He's older than Jance, somewhere in his fifties. His tightly wound, close-cropped hair is graying along the edges of his cool-toned brunette skin, and his thick black beard had gray hairs that waved back at me. He wore sunglasses despite being inside, and a faded suede suit in the ink shade Cherry Bomb.

"Kara"—Geonni, the leader of the Resistance, opens his arms wide—"I'm surprised to see you out and about, considering your royal screw up last night."

My eyes dart to the young female standing to his right, and I sigh in heavy relief. Trinity perches in her usual spot beside him. Her skin isn't as dark as her father's but had the same cool tone, and her Honeycomb Brown eyes shine bright as she looks at me. The wall-length window behind them casts their faces in shadow. Her hunter-green cargo pants make her lower body look slightly bigger than her tightly toned upper body, both abs and muscled arms on display in her black cropped tank. At least she doesn't look as beat up as I was, but the two of them are eyeing me more than suspiciously.

Smiling awkwardly, I try to ignore what's being implied—that I'm a spy. It seems as if their minds are practically made up, so was it them who broke into my loft? Can I no longer trust the Resistance?

"Well, first off, you're welcome for freeing you. That was me, by the way. Second, it turns out they would rather work with me than submit me to Reconditioning. I was able to make up some lie that got me out of most of the trouble, but they're still making me work for them. I came here to assure you they have no clue about my connection to the Resistance. My cover is safe. We're all safe," I say, taking a seat across from Geonni at the desk while Trinity stays standing. "They sort of suspect you guys of being rebels, although that's nothing we didn't already know."

Those sunglasses, ones he never takes off, dip as he looks down his nose at me. "Arianyte doesn't simply let people go, do they, Trinity?"

"They sure don't, Pops."

"They let *you* go," I protest, "in exchange for my . . . *cooperation*."

"We really appreciate you getting me outta there, Kara, we do," Trinity begins, and I can already see where this is going. "But that's the thing—the Prince of Arianyte lets the rebel leader's daughter go? For you?"

I groan with frustration, tipping my head back to the ceiling. "They want me to help find some terrorist or something. His name is Deimos."

My stomach twists. I shudder at the mere mention of his name. What does he want from me?

Geonni cackles, and I don't miss the condescending tone. He asks, "So your identity is still a secret within Arianyte? They have no idea you belong to the Resistance? And you lied your way out of culpability for the attack on their meeting and second-in-command last night how, exactly?"

"Well, I want to say that I stopped the meeting, number one. Number two, I did my part perfectly. It's Trinity, Connar, and Dimitri who couldn't bring it home. Blame them. Three, I told you, I was convincing."

Father and daughter eye each other skeptically—Trinity clearly not happy about me throwing her under the bus, but I continue answering Geonni's question, explaining to him what occurred last night and how I was able to slip out of any culpability for the attack.

His dark brows rise slightly. Geonni's smile reveals the gap in his front two teeth. "So, what you're saying is that instead of punishment, you're working for Arianyte now? That doesn't sound like you."

This interrogation doesn't sound like you.

Shrugging, I wrap the teal ends of my hair around my fingers nervously. "It was either help them or be Reconditioned. What would you have chosen?"

Trinity walks around the desk and over to my chair. The tension in the room is becoming palpable, and I feel stupid for not assuming they would suspect me of being a spy given the circumstances. They know all about how spying works, they do it all the time, they've trained me in how to pull it off. If the Resistance thinks I'm spying on them for Arianyte in exchange for my freedom . . . I don't know if I'm going to walk out of this building.

"I'd never put this Resistance in jeopardy. You saved me from the streets, Geonni. Taught me how to tattoo, gave me purpose. After Arianyte tried to take me from the orphanage—after they took Gavrielle—it was you who took me in. You trained me from that point on so I could get my revenge on them. We know how many kids go missing every week. The Hijacked are real. I'd never betray them, or you, or my friend who's counting on me to find him," I say passionately, looking straight into his sunglasses. It's the truth, but as Trinity sits on the armrest of the chair, I can feel something off in her energy.

"Maybe she's telling the truth, Pops?" Trinity suggests. I did save her, after all.

Geonni's hands come together, a few oversized rings touching his chin. "I want to believe you, I really do, but the circumstances are fishy. We know how ruthless Arianyte is, and they simply let you go after an attack like that? Freeing such a high-level target such as Trinity? I've never seen it. Even if you're not complicit, they could've followed you here."

"It's because of this," I say, unzipping my coat and pulling down my shirt to reveal the mark. "It's useful to them, the same way it's useful to you. There are others in this group they've assigned me to. They've got similar marks with abilities. They think they can train me to control it."

Trinity laughs. "Tell them good luck with that."

I can feel her warm breath on my cheek and smell her spicy perfume.

"What can I do to prove to you I'm not in league with them? You already raided my loft, so you know—"

"Your loft was raided?" Geonni interrupts, his voice concerned. Head tilting sightly, I can tell Geonni is glancing at his daughter as she sits over my shoulder like my personal little devil. "That wasn't us."

I'm relieved to see the genuine surprise and concern on both their faces, but I'm also chilled to know that means there's only two suspects left, and neither are good.

"It's likely Arianyte is looking into you."

His guess is likely correct, but he didn't see the way those glowing-green eyes of Deimos looked at me last night . . . His vibe wasn't merely creepy, it was predatory.

"Which makes my story all the more believable," I say, hopeful they'll believe me now.

The small uptick of his lips, the shine of his one gold tooth that only shows when he smiles a certain way, fills me in on what's actually going on here way too late in the game. I suddenly feel even stupider, wondering if they've just boxed me into a corner that I can't get out of—intentionally. My hackles rise.

I know who I'm talking with, how they think and what they're all about. It's not hard to guess what they're insinuating. They knew it was true the whole time.

"If you're about to ask me to spy on Arian—"

"I thought she said she wanted to prove to us she's not in league with Arianyte to save her own ass, right, Pops?" Trinity purrs, her voice as sweet as a crisp apple on a fall afternoon hover-ride.

Now it's my turn to laugh. "Jupiter's rings, yeah, but not in a way that'll get me killed. You know who I'm involved with. Their head guy is literally a cold-blooded squid, and he made it quite clear that if I even sneeze wrong, I'm dead. I'd love to shoot them down, but I'm not going anywhere near that." It's suicide.

"You will if you want to finally find Gavrielle," Trinity suggests, and I open my mouth to deny it, but then I stop, mind turning. His drawings are gone—someone took them. If I can only find him, then I can assure whoever took them doesn't get to him first. Finding him is essential to my peace; I cannot continue living without knowing what happened to him. Can I say no to these people and risk losing them too?

Moving his hands around, Geonni continues his daughter's train of thought, almost like it was planned out from the beginning. "Let's say, hypothetically, you get inside their computer systems. We could access that information and search for him. Find out if he survived your unfortunate . . . fit back at the orphanage."

A fit. That's a great word for what I did that day—*not*.

Leaning back in my chair, I cross my arms, defiant. "You've never cared to help me find him before now."

"I've always helped you with the Hijacked," Trinity argues, and she's partially correct. She and I grew up here together. However, the older we grew, the more I wanted to be involved in leadership with her father, which she found threatening. It caused the first rift. Then, I moved out. I thought it would make her happy. I thought she'd see it as me stepping off her toes, but she and Geonni took it personally.

My Dezlar catches my eye. Ardelle is scheduled to pick me up in less than twenty minutes, and I need to get back to the shop where the tracker is before then.

"You and I have an opportunity here, Kara, a big one," Geonni begins. "To end the occupation of Earth and the entire Aurora System. End the Hijacked, because as we know, you saw Arianyte taking those children from the orphanage like they were cattle. And you've seen the missing posters, but those are simply the ones with families that care to report them missing. What about all the homeless youth that go unreported? Kids like you. Arianyte has them, and we can stop them with your help. We can stop the trafficking of all Terrans. Get a leg up on them for the first time. No one but you has this type of access to them and their operations. You can be the one who makes all the difference."

The last time I tried to get a leg up on Arianyte, I ended up in the terrible position I'm in now. This experience changed my perspective a bit. It showed me where I was going wrong. I still want all the same things, but I'm not sure how to get them anymore.

"I'm not sure if violence is the answer anymore," I say weakly, my head low. Trinity makes a sympathetic yet disbelieving sound in her throat. I know it sounds ridiculous coming from me; however, the screams of all those people dying and in pain didn't sound ridiculous in my nightmares last night.

"We don't need you to commit violence, do we, Pops?"

Geonni leans in even closer and I hold my stare in the black reflective pools of his sunglasses. Surprising me, he takes them off. His left eye is milky white while the other eye is a rich, dark brown with hues of mahogany and ridged with passion and resolve. "The Arianyte prince did this to me." He points to his blind eye, ghostly and unfocused. "Years ago, when I was the closest anyone had ever gotten to taking his head. It was long ago, but us Terrans remember the scars they put upon us. Visible and invisible."

"And you know what they did to my mother, Kara." Trinity's voice is sad as she sits behind me, and I lean my head against her arm in solidarity. I know all too well what they did to her mother, Geonni's wife, Martha. "She's up there on their mothership as a slave! With hundreds of thousands of other people they claim rights to under the Devouring Accords. Tributes my ass. They're slaves. Modern day slaves. We've got to stop them."

I frown, the anger that's always simmering right under my skin flaring to life. "I'm sorry." I mean it. I know how deep those scars go.

I'm riddled with them.

Visible and invisible.

Geonni puts his glasses back on, and to be honest, I'm glad he does.

He pulls something out of a drawer and throws it across the desk. It's an insignificant item, no bigger than a quarter, its flat and half-circle shaded in Blueberry Blue.

"Take this. It's a UVB drive. Plug it into any Arianyte computer system, and we'll take care of the rest. No violence. We'll make finding Gav a priority as a good-faith gesture to you, for all you're risking by doing this."

The clock is ticking down. I either need to agree to this madness, or I need to leave, likely abandoning all goodwill with the Geonni and Trinity while I'm at it.

And all hopes of finding my friend, of discovering if I . . . if he is even still alive.

Yet, Gav is all that matters, and I'll do anything to get him back. Even if it means putting myself and others at great risk. I just need to make sure that I don't fail. This is what I've trained all these years for, after all. If anyone can do this, it's me.

Snatching up the UVB drive, I curse my foolish self.

CHAPTER 10

Awkward situation number seven when coming into a new home: the First Supper. Better phrased, 'Eat your peas or get your ass beat,' as my old foster mother Margrethe used to say. The entire house sits down for dinner together on the first night after my arrival, but I've yet to meet the last member of the team, his seat empty beside Pacey as we wait. My mind is still reeling from the events of today, both at my loft and with Geonni and Trinity. The more I think about who could have broken in and stolen my drawings, the more confused I become as to who it could've been. Deimos would have a good motivation to find his Ringer, surely. Then what about Arianyte?

When I got back to the house, I immediately locked myself into my bedroom and attempted to draw Gavrielle's face again, but it didn't look right, and neither did his mark. He feels even more lost to me now, and I just can't stand not knowing what's going on here.

As I sit on Pacey's other side, she attempts to pull me out of my thoughts by asking me questions about myself that I begrudgingly answer. I glance down and see what looks to be many small scars on her left forearm. I blink in realization—those scars are self-inflicted. Seeing this pains me. She seems like such a happy girl; what happened in her life to cause these scars? I can't help but be extremely curious as to what drove her to such drastic actions of self-harm. Pacey and I continue to converse when the empty seat beside her finally fills with a body.

"Oh hey, new girl," the boy's smooth voice drawls as he slides into his chair, eyeing the dinner with eagerness. The young man about my age is of average height, lean, and dressed in washed-out black jeans with high-top sneakers and a studded leather jacket with the collar popped.

"Hey," I say as I twist in my chair to face him, forcing myself to smile—although it isn't all that hard. His hair is like a shiny raven's wing, and he has gorgeous eyes that are a bright mossy green that's almost unseen in people with his brown, Latino skin tone. I typically used the color of his eyes for detailed background and lighting work in my tattoos. This teen boy doesn't seem to understand how beautiful he is, even though he is the leanest of all the guys here. Talk about teenage heartthrob.

"I'm Sylo. I meant to say hey earlier, but Pace and I were busy trying to dig up some weird interference. My girl here is the best with computers: she's practically a weapon of mass destruction."

Pacey smiles up at him as he stabs his fork into a green bean. They couldn't be talking about some signals regarding the UVB drive, could they?

His chest is exposed and so is his crystal, looking identical to the diamond-shaped one I saw earlier on Saris. The final Starseed—aside from the one Arianyte has hidden somewhere.

My fork greedily scoops up a large mouthful of mashed potatoes and gravy, and I melt the instant it touches my tongue. Food. Actual food. The chicken breast is juicy and flavorful, the green beans crisp and fresh, the fruit juice tangy and sweet. I've died and went to heaven, my body levitating above this luscious spread of food. My apprentice credits don't allow me to eat food this good.

"The food is delicious, thank you," I say to no one as I take another bite, appreciating each one.

"You're welcome, Kara. Jance and Saris cooked tonight." Ahren smiles suspiciously between the two adults. Saris freezes at Ahren's silent implication of something more happening there. Looks like my eyes did catch a connection between them this morning.

"It isn't poisoned, is it?" I say jokingly, but I realize the moment the words leave my mouth it was highly distasteful, and the table awkwardly looks at each other. "I mean, it's Arianyte, so . . ." I stuff as much food into my mouth as possible so I don't continue digging my own grave. I know Geonni would've laughed at it.

Taking a sip of wine, Saris looks over at Sylo, who looks like he really needs to say something. And he does. "I get Terrans who work for Arianyte have a bad rap, but my father isn't like that. He's one of the highest-ranking SSPARROWs and he does good work for this city. Arianyte simply wants peace and order and to help the people here. Look at all we've learned from the aliens. Ask Ahren what advances in medicine they've given. Saris has been to every single colony in Aurora, including a trip to another star system. Those two things alone are miracles, but let's not forget how they've basically reversed global warming."

The snort I make is a reflex, and better than the gag forming in the back of my throat. His dad is a fricking sky-rat? Jupiter's rings . . . first Blondie and now him.

Sylo squints at me. "What about all the jobs and careers they've given people like my family?"

I've had this argument before—and nobody can win it.

"They added those jobs against all the millions of government and local police jobs that were lost when Arianyte overran the government at the end of the Terran Rebellion."

"Those people were corrupt," Sylo responds.

My eyes roll to the back of my skull. "Right. More corrupt than the literal occupation holding Earth hostage? Never mind they're a propaganda machine that controls the Network and most television stations. They took away our right to vote, for star's sake." The tension is building around me, but I don't care. They need to hear it. "Most nations had sovereign elections and democracies before they came, and little by little, they eroded our processes and rights. Nobody holds Arianyte accountable, and power begets power. For example, the human slaves they take each year; I'm sure the families of the Tributes and Hijacked don't agree with your flowery interpretation of a literal nightmare. They take and take, and nobody is there to stop them. You don't see the danger in that? Not to mention, you all genuinely think they're simply going to let us go after all this is over? Seriously? We're already slaves."

A few of them look down at their plates, picking at their food with wavering hope that Arianyte will grant them their freedom. This only ends one of two ways: we're either free and an enemy of the occupation, or they control and use us. People with Unnatural Abilities like us never go free, exactly like Geonni said earlier. His words echo in my ears, and the UVB drive in my pocket vibrates with the truth of it all. The only way out of this is to blast through it. To destroy them from within. I'm more determined than ever.

An awkward cough stops the conversation before it can go further. Saris draws my attention to her as she looks intently at her Starseed, but I know I need to stop.

People skills, people skills . . .

"So, what's everyone's superpowers?" I ask sheepishly, needing to discuss a new topic. I'm a bit shocked to say it out loud, actually. Geonni and the rebels always knew of my power, but they constantly made me feel more like a freak for having it, and I never felt safe embracing it. In all actuality, I hid it. Because I always knew Arianyte was searching for me, it seemed safest to hide it away like it didn't exist.

Pacey is the first to share. "Mine is hands down the best and most pragmatic," she claims. "I can control the natural elements. I basically have multiple powers. Fire, water, earth, air. Tell me who could beat that?"

"Babe," Sylo interrupts, smirking coolly. "I bring back the dead. It's way better."

"No, dude," Ardelle chimes in, breaking to swallow his food like a proper rich boy. "You reanimate the dead; there's a difference."

Oh, creepy.

I already know Ardelle can control gravity, Jance goes into people's minds (disturbing), and Ahren can heal.

"And you, Saris?" I ask.

Cutting her food into small bites with her knife, her smile is subtle but confident as she eyes Jance almost as if there's some inside joke there.

"Dreams," she tells me softly, still looking at Jance. "I can enter dreams."

"And Deimos?" I ask before the question has time to form within my mind as a stupid one. "All he can do is control people's bodies?"

Jance takes the mantle of answering. "He can also control the voice and any other bodily function. For magic like his and mine to work, eye contact is necessary. Keep that in mind."

Useful information to know, yet it's all the more chilling.

"Pacey," Saris says inquisitively. "Did you ever figure out what that strange signal you said popped up this afternoon was?"

Wait . . .

Taking a bite of her food, Pacey nods. Once she swallows, she turns and looks me dead in the eye. My food curdles. "I did," she says in a cheery tone, taking a sip of her drink through a bright-pink metal straw. "I'm pretty sure I took care of it."

She knows.

Her gaze tells me everything. How she could have picked up the UVB drive already is beyond me.

I need to get it out of this house—and fast.

But what's even more interesting is: why did this girl who I've only met a day ago lie for me? Shouldn't she have called me out in front of the entire table?

Things are getting interesting in this house.

CHAPTER II

The dead of night doesn't hold on tightly; it's a caress that quietly lasts until dawn shows its face. I have hours left until the sun kisses the sky again, and the nighttime shadows call my name sweetly as if we belonged together. And as that night draws deeper into itself, I have no choice but to act on the promise I made to find Gavrielle and do what must be done.

The UVB drive Geonni gave me is burning a black hole in my jean pocket as I tiptoe around the hardwood floors with bated breath.

A few days ago, Geonni gave me a choice. One, to use my unfortunate position within Arianyte to help the Resistance bring them down and in turn use that data to find my lost friend, Gavrielle. He's got to be the out there somewhere, even after what I did . . . I feel he's alive, he's out there somewhere. Or, I can do nothing and serve this corrupt tyrant Malakyte and hope to the stars I can be free afterward.

I've chosen option one.

This is happening now, or it isn't happening ever.

With the lights out in the house and only the glow of candle warmers and moonlight lighting my path, I feel tense as I make my way towards the kitchen.

Entering the wide-open space of the kitchen makes me feel exposed, like swimming over the deepest part of the ocean. The light above the oven shines down on me like a spotlight. I look around, paranoid someone will be up sneaking a midnight snack, but there's no one here but my own shadow.

The adults keep the hover keys in a very inconspicuous place: hanging up next to the coat rack by the door that leads to the garage. I snatch the keys to one of the hovers, and I'm slipping into my ankle-high boots when a sound of rustling causes my stomach to plummet.

"Going somewhere?"

My mouth is dry as I turn, hover keys jingling in my hand like bells. Pacey's long legs sport black leggings, and she wears a baggy black T-shirt that has a green T-rex head printed on the front.

This is the moment I've been fearing. It's barely been a few days and I'm already caught.

What do I do? What do I say?

"Where are you going?" she asks again when my frozen mouth doesn't answer.

Blinking rapidly, mind going blank, and face on absolute fire, something like the sound of an "um" comes out of my mouth.

Laughing far too loudly for my comfort level, she approaches me. "Wow, I really hope you're better at fighting the bad guys than you are at covering up your tracks. You're clearly sneaking out. Why?"

I breathe in my nose loudly, releasing it with a frustrated sigh.

Shit.

"I just need to get some air. Jance is a bit suffocating." It isn't technically a lie. The dude is intense, and he hovers way too much.

Pacey's smile is one of pity and skepticism, and it's abundantly clear that excuse doesn't pass the smell test. "I've spent my entire life dodging my brother's overprotective gaze, Kara. You can't bullshit me. Does it have anything to do with the fact that you lied to the others about that UVB drive?"

Super shit.

"I . . ." I stutter, taken aback at her fearless bluntness. So my suspicions were correct; she knew about the UVB drive the moment I brought it into the house. It must be emitting some sort of signal her defenses can pick up.

Which is even more strange. This is the Pacey who colored and cut my hair for me yesterday, who got her nails done, went shopping, and formed somewhat of a friendship with me these last few days as I've acclimated to my new life.

"Why didn't you tell anyone?" I ask, knowing the game is over.

"My brother thinks Arianyte can protect us. It's a long story, but we fled our home and our parents. It's complicated, but essentially, we're not safe there. We're only here because Arianyte claims they will keep our parents from our tail, which is harder than you'd think. They've got a lot of resources to burn. I really resonated with what you said about Arianyte not letting us go once we're done with Deimos. I think you're right about that, unfortunately. And I don't know, I guess I sort of see you as this rebel girl that could help us get out of all this eventually. You're the Star. Arianyte values you. I suppose I wanted to see what you were really about and what you were going to do with the drive before I detonated this trigger and mention it to everyone."

She looks down, something like shame flashing across her cheeks. "I know you despise Arianyte, and even though they may be useful to us now, that courtesy will only last as long as they need us for something. Our usefulness is dangling by a thread, contingent on how well we perform. They have the ability to turn people like us into mindless corpses. The Reconditioning they almost did on you . . . Well, let's say I won't be anyone's lab rat ever again. The only person who gets to define my life and my choices is *me*. It's okay not to like who we're working for, but you've got to start being honest with us. Otherwise, this isn't going to work."

She is right. I do have to be honest.

"How did you know about the drive?"

She shrugs casually. "My security systems flagged that thing the second you walked into the house with it. At first, I thought you were going to plant it in here. When you didn't, I realized it wasn't a bug meant for us. Which made me wonder where you were planning on planting it?"

I am impressed. "People really do underestimate you, Pacey Dawson."

She smiles at me, as if she knows all too well the truth of the fact. Sighing heavily, I let my body relax, knowing I have to do this very carefully. She may claim not to trust Arianyte; however, I have too much to lose to believe that completely. So I decide to tell her about Gavrielle. I recall the night Arianyte took him and feel the anxiety bloom in my chest so vividly that my mark tingles slightly. A good lie always has a little bit of truth in it.

"I managed to get away, but they took him. Arianyte took my friend. So, I went and picked up this drive because I want to try and find him. That's why I have it and that's where I was going tonight. To get into the Arianyte systems and try to find him. It's my fault he was taken, and I can't live with myself knowing he's out there somewhere, and I have this rare opportunity to find him."

I can tell by the look of sympathy and sadness on her face that the lie had successfully convinced her. Maybe I even convinced myself that I didn't do what I actually did, because the part I've conveniently left out of that story is the worst piece of all.

The girl approaches me and slides her feet into her shoes. Snatching up her coat, she holds out her hand. "I'll drive. I know the perfect place to plant this bad boy. We'll find your friend, I promise."

The drive down the mountain and into the city is quiet. Upbeat music plays softly in the background as we fly down the empty mountain roads, the rainbow cacophony of colors still dazzling brightly ahead of us as though the city never slept at all.

My suspicious mind debates whether I could genuinely trust her, even though I'm the lying one. She genuinely seems to want to help and would likely get in as much trouble as I would if we get caught, so hopefully this doesn't blow up in my face.

To calm my nerves, I ask Pacey a question that's been on my mind since we left the house. "You said you and Ardelle were running from your parents? What's all that about?"

I wonder if it has something to do with the scars on her arms.

Matter-of-factly she answers: "Our parents initially hired Ahren to work with several other physicians at our personal home, where we had an entire medical suite similar to the one back at the house. Ardelle and I really don't like going down there, but anyway, our parents used their wealth and influence to attempt the removal of our crystals."

"Wait, what?" I recoil from the notion altogether. "They tried to take the crystals out? Like, out—out?"

The hover is a smooth hum as Pacey answers. "Despite doctor after doctor explaining to our parents that our crystals are embedded in our hearts and any removal would kill us, they didn't want to hear it. They're Terran government officials; image is *everything* to them. When Arianyte announced the Unnatural Abilities scale, and both their children were at the top of that scale, it completely freaked them out. You know how people were after the Devouring: anything even minutely resembling an extraterrestrial got labeled a squid—got seen as *other* and *bad*. They spent years forcing Ardelle and me to undergo unnecessary tests, surgeries, procedures—mostly experimental—to satisfy their obsession over 'fixing us.' They never succeeded."

"How was Ahren involved?" I ask, not seeing him going along with something so horrible. I remember the x-ray he showed me, his explanation of the crystal's true integration with the heart and how removing it really is impossible. Guilt hits me hard. I had judged them, judged Ardelle based on my preconceived notions of him; and I was wrong. Living through that, especially at the hands of their parents, would have been awful. I know what abuse feels like, the types of scars it leaves on you.

They never go away.

For Pacey, they'll likely be with her forever, too.

Sighing, her lips purse at the mention of Ardelle's Ringer as she continues to stare straight ahead, her nose a steep slope. "Our parents hired him to work for them privately. Once he signed the Nondisclosure Agreement, they filled him in on our predicament. We didn't know about his marking, or even what the Elendril crystals were back then. We used to call them our magic badges."

Her laugh is sad, full of painful memories, but not all of them might have been so horrible. "Once Ahren realized what our parents were doing to us, he quit immediately. He tried to bring us with him, but we weren't ready then. It wasn't until it got so bad that we had no other choice but to leave. They're our parents, and we love them. They gave us a perfect life aside from this. They bribed and gave us anything we wanted in exchange for submitting to what the doctors wanted to do, but ultimately, they would've forced us regardless. So might as well get the new fresh item on the market to distract or numb the pain we had to endure. It was the only thing that got us through it. Well, and having each other, of course.”

“I'm really sorry you had to go through that,” I tell her, and I mean it. “Is that what the scars on your arm are from?”

Even though I'm only viewing the side of her face, I can tell her eyes are becoming glossy. The vibe shifts instantly.

Feeling terrible for asking, I try to take it back. “You don't need to—”

“No, it's okay,” she assures, sniffing loudly. “Ardelle saved me. He saved my life by getting me out of that house. I know what people think when they see my scars: they think I'm crazy. But I just had so much pain and I didn't know what to do with it. Sometimes, it was the only time I felt anything at all. Messed up, right?”

I shake my head vigorously. “I don't think it is. And I don't think you're crazy, Pacey. I've been through real shit too. And I may not have scars like yours to show for it, but I've hurt myself in other ways.”

Taking out my smoke pen, I crack the window, needing the calming effect of it right now.

We look at each other, and for a moment, it feels like we connect on a deeper level. Not because our experiences were similar in any sense of the word, but because we've both suffered and we both understand that the pain lingers in ways we may never fully understand. In ways that make us different from the people we were before. I want to be honest with her, share more of my truth, but I can't.

By the time the lights of Zarmenia hit us and we roll up to a large building on the outskirts of the city, my heart bounces in anticipation.

“Where are we? I don't recognize this building.”

Pacey puts the hover in park and shuts off the engine with a press of a button on the dash. “This is basically the heart of the city, the infrastructure hub of all operations like electricity, sewage, and water. Also hosting more modern amenities such as the Network, space flight schedules, all that stuff. From what I've gathered by hacking in, it's connected to the primary computer core up there.”

She points to the sky, where the command hub of Arianyte *truly* exists. An entire planet on space-wheels where Arianyte could jump from solar system to solar system. Hundreds of thousands of people of every alien race live on that highly guarded Azurite Fleet. The fact Pacey hacked herself this far into the Arianyte system is a feat on its own. Perhaps I could genuinely trust her if she's admitting this to me willingly. If this is a trap, it's one hell of a plan to get me.

"If we're able to get this into their system here . . ." I begin, my mind racing at the possibilities.

"Then we might get into the entire Arianyte systems and the Azurite Fleet too. Sort of a lot to find a long-lost friend." She eyes me a bit suspiciously, but I smile innocently, knowing I've never had a better opportunity to find Gav than this.

Geonni and Trinity are going to crap their pants once they realize what I've plugged their device into. This has to convince them that I'm on their side—one hundred percent.

We park a block away and walk in silence, our footsteps barely audible as I plan a way inside.

"Your brother is going to kill me if he finds out about this," I finally say, imagining how much more Ardelle would hate me if he knew what we were doing. We walk past eight-foot-high fences topped with barbed wire as well as a high brick wall framing the entire property. Security is tight here.

Pacey doesn't seem concerned. "My brother's heart is in the right place, and I agree he would freak if he knew what we were doing. That's why we're going to make sure he never finds out."

Savage.

"Plus, he's been up to his own sneaking around lately."

My brows raise at that admission. Where would he be going off to?

Both of us flinch and hide beside a concrete barricade as we see a SSPARROW walking casually alongside the building's entrance. The building itself is quite flat, looks to have a main entrance, and seems rather normal. This could have been any random utility building in the world; there was nothing alien about it. The only odd thing is the clear presence of high security. That, and Arianyte's stupid logo slapped over every surface.

Peeking over the barrier to see the soldier pacing back and forth in clear boredom, I say, "We can't just walk up to the front door. We need a plan."

Nodding in agreement, she looks around. I had grabbed a basic black mask from a costume shop the other day to cover my face, and Pacey snagged a pair of her stockings from the washroom before we left the house in order to cover hers.

"Do you feel that?" she asks, looking up as if she's sniffing the air. I look around, not seeing or sensing anything. "There's an electric charge in the air. It's weak, and rare for this time of year. Perhaps its residual from the power plant down the road. Either way, that SSPARROW suit looks awfully conductive to lightning, don't you think?"

Before I can even talk through it with her, I feel Pacey's crystal and see her eyes begin to glow, her pupils becoming aquamarine-colored pearls as her crystal mark starts glowing sky-blue under her shirt and coat. I didn't realize we could feel each other's powers like this, but squatting down next to her as she begins to manifest her crystal's magic, it becomes clear I feel something coming from her. It's similar to what I felt with Deimos at the Capitol building, but different. I wonder what her powers even are when a single strike of genuine lightning shoots down from the night sky right onto the soldier. It's a perfect hit, barely making a sound as it electrocutes him. His body slumps and flops to the ground in a smoking huff.

Holy stars . . .

"Problem solved." She stands and begins dashing towards the entryway. Looking around left and right, I see no one else as I follow her.

This girl is crazier than I am.

"You control lightning?" I ask in a hushed whisper, but Pacey shakes her head.

"Not technically. I control nature, and lightning is a by-product of the natural world."

Together, we drag the dead weight of the soldier back to where we were hiding. We snatch his small key card to get into the building.

Not wanting to walk right in the front door, we find a side entrance to sneak into.

"There are cameras up here," Pacey reminds me as we approach the entrance and slip on our extremely cheesy disguises. Pacey especially looks ridiculous with her black-and-white star tights cut up hastily and smooshed over her face. I flash the ID badge at the black pad next to the door's handle, and it unlocks with a soft beep and a green light.

Here we go.

Once inside, we look around but find nothing but a long, dimly lit hallway. On quiet toes, we make our way down an unassuming path that looks nothing like any alien-run outpost.

"You hacked this place before, so lead us to the computers," I instruct, wanting to get in and out as quickly as possible.

"I think it's this way," Pacey says as we take a left hesitantly. The halls are grungy beige, with awful florescent lights overhead and worn tile; nothing special catches my eye. I peek around, ready for a SSPARROW to pop out at any moment.

We don't see anyone.

Taking another turn, we peek around the corners, walking on spider's feet, barely breathing, anticipating a SSPARROW to pop out from behind every corner and shadow.

We continue through the hushed halls.

No soldiers appear.

"Where do you think all the SSPARROWs are?" Pacey whispers. "It's very unusual we haven't run into any yet."

"I was thinking the same thing," I answer, my voice full of suspicion. I assumed this place would be crawling with them, but there doesn't seem to be anybody home.

"Maybe we just got lucky tonight and they're at the company picnic?"

"Girl, nobody is that lucky."

Stalking through the halls, we come up to a set of double doors at the end of one.

Pacey nods her head forward, indicating that's where she believes the computer hub to be—I hope she's right.

The trembling in my legs hasn't stopped from the moment we stepped out of the hover, and I swear it feels like the earth below my feet is quaking by the time we slowly open the double doors.

I brace for whatever is behind them.

CHAPTER 12

We both hold our breath as the door opens with an eerie creak. We're greeted by the beeping of dozens of supercomputers. Swiveling my head left and right, I whisper, "Let's do a room check and do what we came here to do."

We split up, each of us hesitantly peeking down row after row of computer towers that reach all the way to the ceiling. Their sleek black shapes intuitively control the entire city of Zarmenia. The damage the Resistance could do by hacking into this place would be enormous. Pacey has no idea what she's willingly contributing to by being here, and I doubt her hesitancy about Arianyte would cause her to knowingly do *this*. We cannot get caught: if we do, I could get her captured or killed.

And I don't want to be responsible for another person's demise.

"Hey," I hear her whisper in a rushed tone, "I found one with a monitor."

Hustling towards the sound of her voice, I clear the remaining portion of the room for any signs of life. When I find her, she's standing before a monitor sitting on a desk next to some type of computer equipment that's taller than me. The monitor is turned off, while the larger mainframe breathes with life, beeping and bopping, with many flickering lights and fans keeping it cool.

"Give me the drive, I know where to insert it." She holds out her hand without looking away from the monitor as she slides into the chair and begins striking at the keyboard. Knowing I'm useless in this regard, I let her take the wheel on this one. Digging into my pocket, I find the drive, and I hand her what could potentially be both my salvation and the final nail in both our coffins.

Don't be stupid, don't get caught.

"It looks like it needs a password or something," I observe as the monitor boots on. A small box with a key icon pops up. "How are you going to—"

"Shhh!" she hisses. A black box appears above the password-protected login, and she's striking the keyboard as quickly as a warrior would with the sword and shield. She's already deep inside her hacker's zone; this is where she excels most. I can see it in the way her face lights up for the first time the whole night. Clearly, she's so passionate about what she's doing and how she wants to live her life. Given what her parents did to her and Ardelle, I would be too. Pacey doesn't want her parents or Arianyte to dictate her life. The last place she deserves to end up was locked away in some facility as a science experiment. My only hope is this entire thing doesn't lead to exactly that.

"I'm in," Pacey squeals, her bubbly bravado coming back to life like pink-bubblegum warmth flooding cheeks after a long day out in the cold. "Now, let's get to the good stuff."

After a few moments, she has several windows open, all of which show many security codes, protocols, and footage of the property. Fingers flying like a stealth jet, I watch as the footage of us skulking through the halls is promptly deleted. Smart, even though we are wearing masks, it's good to delete all evidence that we were ever in this place.

Then the moment of truth: she takes the UVB drive and inserts it into the mainframe.

The amount of relief that flows through me is stronger than I had expected. The Terran Resistance as a whole never took me seriously—always leaving me with this awful feeling of inadequacy. With that feeling that I never belonged. I can't say with confidence if I do or not, or where I fit in now, especially with Geonni and Trinity, but I want to make them proud and trust me again. With this one action, I'm setting in motion a series of events that will hopefully bring down Arianyte. That will ultimately land me back in their good graces.

Hopefully.

"Can you check something for me before we look for Gav? I want to know what they have on this Deimos guy."

Pacey mumbles some incoherent display of disgust, and it tells me exactly how she feels about him. A video opens after a few short keystrokes, revealing a dark scene from one of the Arianyte monitoring cameras. My stomach drops to the ground as I watch Deimos walking towards a large hover-van with an unconscious girl in his arms. The video changes angle to him loading her up into the van, then to him driving through half a dozen different cameras until he stops in an empty parking lot. Shortly after, another hover pulls up next to Deimos's van and my heart plummets. Getting out, Deimos and this man with a baseball cap converse for a few moments before they go to the back of the van and open it. They pile in at least half a dozen children into the other man's hover. The kids, ranging all the way from toddlers to teens, don't struggle. They don't fight, or cry, or beg to go back to wherever they came from. And when the hover finally drives away and Deimos is alone, I'm sick to my stomach.

"Kara . . ." Pacey says, already knowing what I'm about to say. "Ardelle and the others are totally on board with this new theory Arianyte proposed to us a few weeks ago that he's the one who's stealing children all over the city. We've already talked about this. Personally, I do think it seems a little too convenient, but this video looks really bad. The whole thing with this guy is hella suspicious."

So Arianyte is claiming Deimos is responsible for the Hijacked? Watching this video, it sure looks like he is. But if it's all Deimos . . . then that means what I saw at the orphanage would be, what then? None of this makes sense.

"No. No, there's got to be some other explanation for this."

The squeaking of the chair's wheels as she turns towards me is all I hear for a long moment before she says, "Maybe it is him? It could explain the Hijacked. Arianyte completely denies it. They're bound by the Accords; they can't just snatch kids off the streets."

But they do.

"I've seen Arianyte taking them . . ."

"That was years ago, right? When they took your friend? Malakyte doesn't seem like the type to do something like that. I know you've only met him that one time, but he's not this bad person you think he is. Maybe things have changed over time?"

I want to believe it's all Arianyte, because if it's not Arianyte . . .

Then what the hell am I doing?

I'd have to find another way to prove it.

To prove what I saw—that Arianyte is the one taking the Hijacked.

"We need to try and find Gavrielle." I abruptly change the subject, unwilling to let what I saw change anything about my opinion of Arianyte.

Before she can look for Gav, we both jump at the sound of someone coming through the doors. Looking at each other in horror, we freeze in panic. I fling my arms around trying to communicate, but she looks instantly confused under her makeshift mask. The sounds of heavy footsteps grow closer. The SSPARROW is two aisles from us and coming in hot when Pacey whispers, "Take off your mask."

"Are you insane?"

Ripping off her tights, hair static and sprawling in every direction, she points to my face with dramatic irritation. There's no time to question her, so reluctantly, I remove the plastic costume mask, and she instantly grabs the front of my coat and pulls me into her lap. Falling over on top of her, the chair squeaks with both our weights. She takes the back of my neck, brings me in close.

"Kiss me?" she whispers.

My eyes go wide. I'm so shocked by her request that I freeze. Then I hear the gears squeak from the guard's armor mere feet behind me and realize the ruse she's come up with. I begin kissing her full-on the mouth, and she kisses me back, both knowing this show has to look realistic. I'm surprised by how soft her lips are and how sweet she tastes.

"What the—" the SSPARROW says, clearly taken aback at seeing two females making out on his work chair.

Breaking the kiss, Pacey swivels us both towards the guard. "Oh! Wow, we didn't realize anybody would be coming in here. I know we're not supposed to take our uniforms off, but they're a little clunky and hard to maneuver around in, if you know what I'm saying."

If the stunned look on my face isn't obvious, then my body language surely is. It's a good ploy, clever even, but I'm straight and this is my first time kissing a girl.

I'm not prepared.

"Who the hell are you two?" the guard interrogates, his body language defensive. But we are two cute, unassuming girls. We don't particularly look like a threat. "We haven't assigned you to this outpost. I've never seen either of you girls before."

My mark is on fire, and my power bubbles right underneath my skin. I need to take care of this before it gets out of hand.

"This is Bird 337. I've got a level one breach in the computer room. This is not a drill. Send all units immediately."

Shit!

Before I can engage him hand-to-hand, the antimatter energy flies out of me in a flash. Hitting the SSPARROW right in the chest, the blast of purple light knocks him into one of the computer towers. The tower bobbles back and forth but doesn't fall over, unlike the soldier who is sprawled on the ground.

"What the hell?" Pacey gasps as I crawl off her.

"I'm sorry," I say, knowing what a royal mess up this is. "It just slipped out. I couldn't stop it."

Turning back to the computer and typing faster than I've ever seen anyone type before, she closes out all the windows while I go over to the fallen soldier. Thankfully, I find a pulse.

I turn back to her, and it looks like she's shutting everything down.

"No!" I rush towards her. "I need to look for Gav. Please, Pacey, it's why we came here."

She shakes her head and continues closing things out. "We can't. We've got to go or we're going to get caught. I've got to trigger my tape worm program to gummy up the security footage so we can get out of here without Arianyte showing up at the house with collars. That guy is going to wake up and give a description of our faces and your power, and we can't give them any more ammunition. These are crappy disguises. And I'm sure you don't want another one of those collars around your neck again."

My mouth opens to object, but she's right. We don't have time. I can practically hear the stampede of SSPARROWs barreling towards us as we speak, the thought triggering the memories of the night at the orphanage.

I got the drive inserted, that was priority number one. I was hoping I could try and find Gav tonight as a bonus; however, I've got to let that go. It doesn't mean my heart doesn't break from disappointment. It's like I continue to get close to him only to be shoved back even further.

I'll have to rely on the Resistance to find out what I could not tonight.

"Okay, I'm done," she says.

"Masks back on." My vision is half covered as my plastic mask covers my face again, and my breaths are loud inside the mask as we bolt for the door. Zigzagging through rows and rows of computers, we finally reach the doors and fly through them, Pacey's long legs several paces ahead of me.

Yet the moment we burst from the dark room and the florescent lights from the hall hit our senses, an imposing chunk of black and icy cyan thirty feet down the hallway sticks out against the light-colored walls. There's got to be at least a dozen of them down there.

"Hey!" an unnatural voice booms off the sterile walls. All of us freeze like animals in the wild.

"Well, we found our birdies," Pacey says as our eyes meet, wild with trepidation.

"Run!" I tell her, and we do.

My legs burn as we fly down hallways, sliding into each other as we zoom around corners, dodging stunner bullets flying down on us like rain.

A shriek echoes into the hall as Pacey gets hit in her low back with a stunner. She staggers, and I fly right past her.

"Go!" she cries as she sees me slow and hesitate. The nest of SSPARROWs is right on her ass. For a moment, I consider actually leaving her here as she hobbles forward. My heart is beating so loud I can barely hear her screaming at me. Her arms are swinging in front of her, pointing behind me.

Go. Go. *Go!*

Gavrielle's face, what's left of it from my memory anyway, flashes into my mind. Coming to a full stop, my legs a bowl of limp noodles, I realize there's no way I'm going to let them take her, not after tonight. If she's going, I'm going—there's no leaving anyone behind this time. Scared shitless or not, I have to force myself to move.

Now, get your ass over there and help her. You are not that little girl inside that pillar who was useless and afraid. You are a trained machine.

"Thumbelina, go!" she yells again as the first SSPARROW reaches her. At first, I wonder why she calls me by her brother's annoying nickname, but then I realize it's because she doesn't want to compromise my identity. How could she think of anyone but herself right now? She fights like a badass, agile, and strong as hell. Her kicks and punches land and the first guards are down in less than ten seconds, but the next three are already on her.

I rush back towards her, adrenaline pumping wildly and my crystal clawing ravenously under my skin, wanting out.

Knowing my fists would be of little use against this many of them, I snatch up a cyan weapon from a fallen SSPARROW and take aim at the mob attacking Pacey. My crystal will most likely strike her along with them because my aim and control are terrible, and I can't risk it. The gun is heavy and long in my hands, and I struggle to hold it upright, but I manage to aim decently enough. The stunner bullets do nothing but clang off their metal uniforms. The stunners' hooks have nothing to grab onto, no flesh to sink their long teeth into. Then I remember these guns have live ammunition capabilities.

Looking down at the weapon in my trembling hands, I try to find the switch to live ammo on the digital interface on top, but I can't hold it with one hand—it's too heavy. With a curse, I take a knee, but as I do, a SSPARROW comes charging right at me. I shriek, then drop the gun and blast him with my crystal's energy. He flies into the group, knocking a few others down with him in a trail of smoke.

After I lug the gun back onto my lap, I swipe at its interface. My finger shakes so wildly I can barely tap the correct settings on the screen, but I finally set the rifle to live ammo.

Some people call them birds, some call them sky-rats, but I'm calling them *dinner.*

"Get down!" My voice cracks as I shout into the fray. She does. Her death drop to the floor is almost immediate as I pull the trigger. Their uniforms are tough, but not durable enough to stop a bullet from this range. The firing mechanism is automatic and fast, much like the machine guns I practiced with inside the Resistance. My eyes meet Pacey's, and she nods.

Taking my aim to the right side, she plunges out of the mess of metal bodies and smoke, diving towards me.

"I'm right behind you, go," I yell out, knowing she's hurting like hell and needs the head start.

She doesn't argue.

"Bird 789 on mobile, we've got live fire situation at Main Outpost. I repeat, live fire assault on Main Outpost. Send nests immediately."

Pacey runs past me as I continue to shoot. Dropping the gun, I fly after her, barely catching her whizzing around a corner. My adrenaline pumps so fast I can barely tell which way is up, let alone the way out of this place. Hopefully Pacey has better composure than I do and remembers the specs so we can get out.

It doesn't take me long to catch up to her. When I do, I pull the stunner bullet teeth from her skin and chuck it to the floor.

"We're almost there," she says, panting through every hobbling step, pain evident in her face. The sky-rats are on our heels, but only a handful.

"You're not getting out of here! Surrender before you get yourselves killed," one guard yells at us, live ammo flying past our heads. But the distorted voice is correct. We probably aren't getting out of here alive.

"Keep running," I say between huffing breaths, too scared to look back.

Finally, we see the exit. We barrel through it.

The icy darkness feels like plunging into an arctic bath, the switch from bright fluorescent lights to the sudden blackness a jarring contrast.

"Go get the hover going. I'll hold them off," I tell Pacey, and she's already gone by the time the four SSPARROWs come through the metal door to meet me.

My eyes are wild things as they glow with the color of my crystal, and I laugh in pure exhilaration at how good it feels to allow my power loose.

Typically it's months apart that I get to use it, not days.

"*You know you want to end them,*" a voice whispers in my head. Although I've never heard it before, I know exactly who it is. *What* it is: my crystal. It's speaking to me, and with all this chaos and close calls, I'm itching to release it.

What I truly want is to stop running, to end my living nightmare of constantly looking over my shoulder for Arianyte or some monster to hurt me. They have hurt me, monsters and men alike, and I am so done with being a victim. Of not claiming who I truly am. I have power, and I am ready to use it if it comes down to myself or someone else. I'd hate myself even more if I let yet another person hurt me. Violate me, trap me, destroy me.

Never again.

"*Do it,*" the voice purrs as I feel high off the crystal's power flooding in. I can dust them in two seconds if I want to.

The SSPARROW soldiers must have sensed the danger because they back up defensively. Sparks dance around me, turning the concrete below my feet to powder. I stand my ground; I do not run or hide, and as I hold my chin high, I almost feel powerful.

They all turn and run back into the building. It's a smart move for them. The screeching of the hover's brakes follows shortly after. A twinge of disappointment fills me as my power quickly fades, seeping back into its hollow lair, and by the time we shoot out of the lot, I'm feeling more empty than full.

"Holy shit," Pacey squeals. Her eyes are on fire. "I can't believe we made it out of there. Nobody's following us, right?"

Looking in the side mirror, I see nothing but a dark road as we blast away. "We're good. Are you hurt?"

"I think I'm okay."

Nodding, I release the rest of my crystal's energy with a long sigh, hating my disappointment for not being able to use it.

Then I remember.

"Okay, so what was with that kiss?" I ask, already assuming the answer but wanting to know from her.

Pacey laughs out loud in that bubbly fashion I'm coming to enjoy. "It just came to my mind, and I acted. Who wouldn't believe two hot girls making out on the job, am I right?"

"But the guy didn't believe us," I counter, unable to keep a smile off my lips. "Besides, if I was going to kiss either of the siblings in the house, I figured it would have been your brother rather than you."

Her head snaps over to me so fast it almost flies right off her shoulders. My regret is instant.

"No, I didn't mean it like that. Don't you even—"

"Oh, my stars, you like him, don't you?" she gawks, her smile wider than the Azurite Fleet itself.

"No, he's a dick," I protest, arms crossing over my chest. "No offense. I just assumed, given the option, I'd pick the one of you that's more my type. So, does that mean you're . . ."

Taking her eyes off the road, she looks dead into mine. "Do I like girls? Sure. And boys . . . depends on the person. Maybe I'd even date an extraterrestrial if he was cute enough."

"You'd date an extra?"

Eyes curious and musing, she considers it. "Well, you know . . . if all the parts fit together."

My howling laughter is my response.

"So ,wait. If you're into both sexes, do you parents know? They don't seem like they'd be very accepting of that given who they are and what you've told me about them."

Pacey's sigh is heavy, and I can tell my question dampers the mood. "They don't know, and neither does Ardelle. I think, I mean, I don't know. It really just depends on the person. Sylo, for example, he's funny and goofy and beautiful . . . I just want to enjoy him. But also, I find girls so attractive, ya know? I guess I'm still figuring it out."

"No, it makes sense," I confirm. "Your secret is safe with me."

"Just so you know, I think my brother would be pretty satisfied if you kiss him the way you kissed me tonight."

"Yeah, no. That's never going to happen, girl. I'm just glad I can bring you back to him in one piece." For once, I did something right. There is no guilt or pain or regret. It's exhilarating. If only I was this brave six years ago.

When she finally looks over at me again, the light from the navigation screen is pronounced in her glossy eyes. "You came back for me." Her chin quivers a bit, and a ping of emotion swells in my chest. Something I haven't felt in a really long time.

What it's like to have a friend.

What it's like to do right by them.

"I wouldn't leave you behind." And for once, it feels good to tell the truth.

"I won't forget it," she promises, and after the experience we shared back there, I believe her.

There's nothing like almost getting captured and killed to bring two people together.

CHAPTER 13

THE ARIANYTE EMPIRE DECREE #2

IN ACCORDANCE WITH THE DEVOURING ACCORDS,
ARIANYTE WILL ASSIST IN THE RECOVERY OF EARTH'S
DAMAGED ECOSYSTEMS, AIR AND WATER QUALITY, AND
LOWER THE PLANET'S CORE TEMPERATURE IN AN ATTEMPT
TO REGAIN CLIMATE STABILITY.

I'm in the basement training room again, the air pungent with the smell of sweat and heaving breaths. Saris's fighting technique is as tight as I've ever seen.

"Your footwork is sloppy," she informs me as we go toe to toe on the mats, my breaths labored and ragged while hers remain as still as the Zarmenia River.

As Jance watches from the side with his arms crossed, he adds, "And you keep letting your arms drop." He is always watching—always looking at me with those eyes.

When it's time for a break, I ditch the gym and meet everyone upstairs. We eat lunch in the kitchen together. Like being put at the kid's table during the holidays, all the Starseeds sit at a separate table from the adults.

More details of the house have come into focus now that the shock has worn off. Like the stark white trim along the floors, ceilings, and doorframes popping out against black-and-white walls, with accent-colored walls here and there in select rooms. Each door is ornately carved, yet their clean lines seem to go well with the sense of nature that's depicted throughout, like along the fireplace and above doorways. The kitchen is massive. The state-of-the-art meteor-steel appliances are top notch and require a tenth of the energy to run and keep food cool. The marbled countertops are like a galaxy of grays, golds, and whites, giving the room a touch of old-world charm. And a delicious spread of food lies on every surface. It's the nicest kitchen I've ever set foot in, and I can't imagine ever feeling hungry again. It was nothing like my loft, but each time I think of it, my stomach roils with nausea.

"Are you a picky eater or something?" Ardelle asks. Sitting to my left, he watches me fiddle with the food on my plate, and I'm certain he feels like this is not the punishment I deserve for all the people I hurt at the Capitol building. The truth is, my nerves have spoiled any appetite I previously had. I used my powers last night. What if that's enough to connect Pacey and me?

To my right, Pacey multitasks by eating and messing with her Dez, seemingly not worried, and Sylo stares aimlessly at the television next to Pacey.

I consider what to say to Ardelle, not wanting to start yet another argument between us. We simply don't get along, we're too different. "No, although I remember the food at the Naresteé Orphanage was much less nutritious, and the money I make from apprenticing at the tattoo shop could never allow me to eat this way. It's good, I just feel a little weird about it. You wouldn't understand."

Although Ardelle and Pacey suffered at the hands of their parents, they never wanted for anything. They'd never know what it's like to go hungry, to be that desperate. Not with rich parents like theirs.

"No, but I'd think having that experience would make you appreciate this even more," Ardelle says, and he's not wrong. It should.

"Maybe it's more complicated than you realize." My voice is condescending at best. "Other people struggle out there, Ardelle. They don't all have lavish lives with rich families taking care of them, and when you grow up having to find food for yourself and being so hungry it literally drives you mad, it leaves you with scars that don't always make the most sense to others."

His eyes automatically go to his sister's wrists, the cuts there—the ones she gave to herself. And I understand because I have scars too. My scars are beneath my clothes, beneath my skin—and I've slashed myself time and time again. I understand her. But I doubt her brother does. And if he can't understand his own sister, how can he understand me?

Likely not wanting the conversation to switch to her, Pacey asks more questions about my past. "Did your friend Gav grow up at the orphanage with you?"

She already knows the answer to this question. Perhaps she's playing dumb for some reason or is trying to get me to tell the others about him.

Guzzling his glass of milk, Sylo chimes in. "Who is Gav? And wait, did we just jump over the fact they named an orphanage after that horned alien chick? The one you blasted?"

The way he says it makes me laugh a little. "They actually hung up a portrait of that scary chick at the orphanage. None of the kids wanted to go near it. We all believed she could hear and see us." We collectively giggle at that.

"Gavrielle was a boy that I met at the orphanage. He's actually an extra. I don't remember the name of the planet that he's from, but it was from far away. His parents came and fought for the Terrans, but they died in the war, and that's how we ended up at the orphanage together. We clicked instantly. I always had a problem fitting in."

"Couldn't imagine why," Ardelle mumbles, and Pacey shoots him a death glare from behind her Dez. Trying to backtrack, he asks, "I mean, where's this friend of yours now?"

Pacey and I lock eyes, and I see the sadness there. I look down at the dandelion tattoo on my forearm, the ache in my heart etched permanently on my skin in shade Dynamic Black. I've looked at it and made a thousand wishes, hoping a thousand times they'd come true. "Arianyte took him."

The table sits in silence, and if my instincts are right—which they usually are—the adults are listening in as well.

"The night he was taken, he gave me a bouquet of dandelions from the field behind the building. It was the very last interaction we had." And like clockwork, the guilt floods into me as sharply as any knife would, reminding me how much work I have to do in order to make things right. Do I tell them? That I wasn't the only one Naresteé came for that day? That my old lost friend is a more integral player in this larger game than any of us can know? Given the drawings of his face and mark had been stolen, I can't trust anyone with that information.

"So that's why you hate Arianyte so much," Sylo realizes, leaning back in his chair and putting together the truth of my hatred. With his dad being a SSPARROW, it should make us enemies.

None of them can fully understand what that night did to me, the pieces of me that were left behind, how it changed me forever. How I can't move on with my life without getting retribution for the only person who made me feel like I was worth loving. He took a broken little girl and made her smile after all she suffered at the last home she lived in. He was an alien boy, but I was the true outcast.

Pacey leans over the table towards Sylo. "You've never gotten me any flowers."

Feigning regret, Sylo smiles at her playful pouting. "You never asked, doll."

"I shouldn't have to ask, you big idiot, that's the point."

As I scroll through my Dez to distance myself from having to talk further about Gav, a weird glitch blacks out the screen for a split second, leaving it completely see-through as if it is off. This has happened several times in the last few days.

"Hey Pacey," I say, shaking the device in one hand and pulling her away from the guy she's totally crushing on. "My phone has been doing this weird glitch thing recently."

"That's odd. The alien tech in these devices is exceptionally precise. They don't glitch for no reason. You should have me look at it," she says as she takes a sip of her Pop Rocket, a drink so carbonated it literally pops inside the can.

Ardelle leans over to me and looks at it, and I smell the cinnamon and sage on him and reluctantly allow myself to enjoy it. "Maybe when you lost your Dezlar the other day, you dropped it, and that's how it ended up sitting on the ground where we found it. It's probably nothing. Plus, it's an older model."

I glare at him incredulously for the subtle dig at not having the newest, greatest device. When my Dezlar mysteriously disappeared for hours the other day, I could've accidentally dropped it, but I think I would have noticed that. It's attached to my hip, like it is with everyone else.

"Sure, I'll take your word over the expert," I say, trying to keep my voice light. Our spats happen over the dumbest things because we're clearly still pissed at each other for the way things went down that first night. At least, I am. He ruined all my plans, is the cause for why I'm in Arianyte's clutches. And although I get that he's probably irate that I almost blasted his parents—despite their contentious relationship—it doesn't make sense why he dislikes me so much.

Smiling wide, Pacey shines brighter than the Titan Games arena on finale night. "Did you hear that, big brother? She says I'm the *expert*."

It's nice to see a genuine smile on Ardelle's face for once; he always seems sad. "This time, I won't argue with you, Thumbelina."

Gasping dramatically, I punch him playfully on the shoulder. "Miracles actually do happen."

He shoulder bumps me back, attempting—I suppose—to match my level of tolerance for him; and I don't hate it.

"Don't push it," I grumble.

The four of us laugh, and in this small moment, things feel normal. All the awkward tension and irritation with Ardelle and the clear differences of opinion with Sylo seem to melt away and we can be normal teenagers. No pressure, no lies or arguments about which side is right or wrong—we're merely hanging out.

The adults even seem to have stopped eavesdropping.

And I don't hate it.

Then it all shatters.

A loud banging on the front door makes me jump, my heart rate skyrocketing and my crystal tingling in an automatic trigger response. The noise of slamming doors from my childhood still haunts me to this day.

Ardelle places a hand on my shoulder to steady me, and I'm surprised to see it helps ease that spike of anxiety shooting through me. More pounding and loud voices come from the front door demanding entry, and I immediately look over at Pacey, panicked. This cannot be what I fear it is, but the genuine concern in Pacey's big blue eyes tells me she's thinking the same thing.

Did Arianyte figure out it was Pacey and me who broke into their building last night?

"Jance, what's going on?" Ardelle stands up, his chair's legs skidding against the hardwood floor.

"I'm sure it's nothing." Jance's deep voice doesn't sound sure in the slightest, and he moves swiftly towards the front door as the bangs and demands for entry grow louder and more forceful.

All of us get up and follow, obviously curious about what's happening. The knock on the door says a lot, and it's more than urgency—it's a demand.

And I can only think of one person who has that type of audacity.

As Jance opens the heavy wooden door, sunlight shines into the foyer. A dark shadow greets us, and it is far from welcoming.

The icy air isn't what chills the mood instantly or causes the vibe of the house to plunge drastically.

It's who's standing in the doorway.

With a halo of SSPARROWs around him, Malakyte stands tall in the center of the doorway, staring down his sharp nose at the lot of us. He wears all black yet again, jet-black hair pulled back in a low ponytail as it cascades down his eloquent coat. It has a suede, almost filigree, pattern melded into the entire thing, with silver metal slabs on the top of the shoulder blades. And silver accent buttons halfway down the front to match. I can only speak for myself, but I feel rather underdressed. My leggings and tight crop top, dried sweat and dirty hair once again leave me with a less-than-desirable impression. Yet, his dark eyes seem to find me first.

Malakyte looks as furious as a raging bull.

"Malakyte," Jance says by way of greeting. "Naresteé, you're looking well," he adds awkwardly, but I can see the burns going up the left side of her neck as she stands beside the Arianyte prince. *Whoops.*

The look on his face makes me shiver. The storm clouds roaring in his eyes along with the tight setting of his jaw causes my crystal mark to tingle with fear.

"We all need to talk."

CHAPTER 14

"You want us to take a test to prove we're not lying?" Ardelle demands. All of us stand in the formal living room beside the front door.

The SSPARROWs are hauling multiple boxes full of alien tech into Jance's office, which sits on the other side of the foyer. We can't stop them.

Malakyte sits in a Cherry Red leather chair, one leg crossed over the other and a cocky smile on his face, but he is far from pleased. Naresteé stands beside him like a statue with resting bitch face. Her floor-length Forest Green coat has silver angel wings embroidered all the way down the back.

"There was a break-in at Main Outpost last night. Two young females seemed to easily overthrow two dozen of my SSPARROWs, plant a UVB drive, and successfully erase the footage of their ransacking. Reports said the girls had quote, 'magical powers.'"

It's Jance that automatically comes to our defense. "Well, that's terrible to hear, but that has nothing to do with us. Everyone was in the house last night. You can check the cameras. Nobody left."

There are cameras in this house? How did Pacey not tell me this? What if they look? They're going to see that we left and came back. I risk a glance at Pacey, but she doesn't seem to be nervous. I can only hope I look as composed because anxiety and fear are beginning to bubble up in my blood.

Malakyte's eyes, deathless pools that I can see tinkering away, remind me of the threat he promised me back in the confinement center. That if he finds out I'm involved with the Resistance, not only am I screwed, but Trinity will be too. The entire Resistance could be in jeopardy.

But I don't know how I'm getting out of this, and I'm sweating.

"There are only two young women in this house, so I want to begin my test on them," Malakyte says, nodding his head towards the equipment being hauled inside, and before I can ask questions, Ardelle speaks.

"You're not testing my sister, forget it."

Malakyte raises a thin black brow. "I wasn't asking, Mr. Dawson. She, and you, and everyone else in this house will take my test. Analysis is quick, painless, and highly accurate at detecting falsehoods. If you have nothing to conceal, you have no rationale for noncompliance."

"If this is because you suspect *her*—" Ardelle points at me and I shake my head like it's the rudest accusation ever. "—of working with the Resistance, then test her but don't force the rest of us in this crazy mess."

Rude.

Stepping into the fray, I say, "I'm not working with the rebels, asshole."

"Then let's take the test so I can return to much more important duties than having to babysit these adolescents." Malakyte claps his hands together and stands, and I can feel his cool chill as he walks past me and into Jance's office where the alien lie detector test is up and working. "Miss Dawson first, please."

I know PTSD personally—we're close friends—and something about this is triggering Pacey badly. Now whether it's because she knows we're about to be caught or if she's having some type of triggering moment from all the weird tests their parents put them through, I'm not sure. She's holding onto her brother for dear life. He places his arm around her shoulders and whispers something in her ear. She nods her head, his thumb softly caressing her shoulders. Gently, he forces her towards the room and walks her in. All the while, I'm wondering how bad it's going to be when everyone finds out about last night.

"Want to confess anything?" a sweet voice asks from directly behind me. I jump, stumbling into Jance, and he steadies me with his large hands. Naresteé smiles wickedly down at me; she's tall and imposing. Her black-to-blood-red ombre hair is curled at the ends, matching the blood red of her eyes. She's even scarier up close. I've thought about her every single day since the night she came for me and left with all those other children at the orphanage, including Gav. If she only knew what her fate would have been if those idiots Dimitri and Connar hadn't screwed it up. She got lucky, but I'm going to ensure her luck runs out. Because she knows what happened to my friend, and I'm going to do whatever I have to in order to find him again.

First, however, I need to find a way out of this for me and Pacey—and fast.

Ardelle looks absolutely livid when he leaves the room. Naresteé walks past us all and enters, closing the doors behind her. Two soldiers keep watch at the door, and the rest of their personal guards wait outside the house.

I nervously tap my acrylic nails together, their long black shapes making a click, click, click.

"Can you stop it?" Ardelle barks, his eyes blazing fire at me. "This is all your fault."

I open my mouth to argue, but Jance beats me to it.

"Ardelle, that's not fair, and you know it."

Ahren steps up and places a hand on Ardelle's shoulder, eyes soft and demeanor calm. Ahren is always the one to simmer down Ardelle. "Son, there's nothing invasive about this test. Several electrode pads, that's it. She'll be just fine." Ahren seems to have that chill, grandfatherly vibe despite his young age. I think it's called good bedside manner.

Although his Ringer's voice is assuring and clearheaded, Ardelle is far from either.

"It's not about that. It's what this brings up for her. She can't handle it. She's too fragile. I've barely gotten her nightmares to stop; now they're going to be triggered all over again."

She's probably more freaked out because she knows we're both screwed. Me more so, because I'm the one that's going to take the brunt of the punishment for this, not her. I have way more strikes against me than she does. However, she's in this position because of me. This whole ordeal has made me realize I was hurting the people surrounding me by my actions. Although I stand by doing whatever I can to save Gav and other Hijacked, I don't want to hurt anybody. I want to be a good person, but my life hasn't given me the luxury of being that girl. I have to do bad things to get results because nobody else is going to do it for me. To get justice or help save kids that are completely forgotten—kids like Gav and me.

A few minutes go by when Pacey shoots out from the room, visibly upset. Ardelle calls her name several times, but she ignores him and rushes up the stairs. Her bedroom door slams moments later, and then Naresteé stands in the doorway. She beckons me with the pointed-nail finger like some type of monster from a horror movie.

Lovely.

My body doesn't even feel like my own as I walk into the room. It's average-size, the bay window to my right letting in sunlight. The warm light bounces off the dark mahogany desk at the center. Malakyte sits in the main chair, both his legs kicked up on the desk, one crossed over the other. Several monitors are placed all around the desk, some facing him and a few facing me, but I feel his eyes once again prodding into me as I sit down in the chair across from him.

Naresteé aggressively presses the sticky pads onto both my wrists and the side of my neck before she stalks to the corner of the room. Knowing this is the bitch who took my friend—it takes everything in me not to blast her to high heaven.

The screen facing me looks like a live recording of me, and I watch as it zooms into my eyes, capturing every minute movement they make.

Malakyte looks over at one of his screens and then looks up at me. "This should be rather painless, as long as you tell the truth. I'm sure you remember our last conversation about any incidents that you may be involved in, Miss Ruzz."

"Please, call me Kara. And I assure you I haven't been involved in any *incidents*," I say, doing my best to hold eye contact.

I'm a dead girl. What is going to happen to Trinity? Would he place Trinity in the Tribute camps just like her mother, Geonni's wife? If anything happens to Trinity, both of them will blame me for it.

And what would Malakyte do to me?

"You expect me to believe you had zero involvement with what happened last night?" he asks. "Which would disappoint me immeasurably, by the way."

"I don't see why it would," I say as a way of not answering his question directly.

Malakyte looks almost hurt by my words. "You think I don't care about you?"

"You don't even know me."

He smiles, flashing one set of his pointed canines. "I think you'll be surprised to see I know you better than you think."

"You'd like to think that, wouldn't you?"

"Your heart rate sure is high," he says, pulling the same question-avoiding tactic.

Thinking on my feet, I make a bold claim. "Of course, it is. You won't stop flirting with me."

Naresteé snorts, and I can tell my words surprised the dark prince because he smiles devilishly.

"If I were flirting with you, Miss Ruzz, I'd tell you how beautiful you look today and how it pains me to do this."

Before I can even think about answering, Naresteé walks out of the room and slams the door shut. Apparently, that struck a nerve.

"Don't mind her, she's still recovering from what took place the other day at the Capitol building."

And I was a little raw over her kidnapping my best friend. She should get over it.

"Why do you care so much, Malakyte? You just met me. There are other powerful Starseeds here and you don't look at them the way you look at me. There's no reason you should be so focused on me."

I can see his gears turning behind his eyes again, his blue lips darker than navy, tilting upwards. In normal daylight, I can see his pale skin has a blueish undertone, like he just popped out of an ice-crusted river. "You truly don't realize how special you are, do you?"

"I'm not," I answer quickly, voice weak.

He watches me for many heartbeats until he finally says, "Your potential is unlimited. Trust me, you should know how rare you are. I do, and I don't squander such inimitable treasures."

"I'm not special."

Malakyte glances back at his screen and nods at the honest answer.

"Are the results live?" I ask.

"Not quite. I can see your vitals, but the computer generates the report after the algorithm analyzes all the data. I'll know if you're lying to me shortly."

Tension spikes through me. Between him and me. Stars only knows why I'm pulled towards him, but I despise it. I'd rather be drawn to Blondie than Malakyte.

"And then what?"

Then you're a dead girl whose mind is going to be Reconditioned into an Arianyte slave.

I wipe my wet palms on my leggings, trying to keep my composure. My nerves cause my mark to burn. This interaction with Malakyte makes me highly uncomfortable. He creates this heaviness within my chest, one that's exhilarating yet wildly terrifying all at once. Yet the darkness within him stirs the darkness in me, and the two of those wicked things recognize the other despite all the reasons they shouldn't. It's a dangerous dance, a horrible performance that's predicated on my ability to keep him both enticed and at bay all at once.

"Then I see what side you're truly on."

CHAPTER 15

After Malakyte questions me further, I leave the room in a heart-pounding haze. I'm pretty sure Naresteé hisses at me as I pass her, but I'm so mentally fried and freaked out I can't care about that witch.

I need to find Pacey and talk with her about what sort of excuse we could come up with to make this seem like it's something other than what it really is.

Pure treason.

Ardelle approaches me, his demeanor a lot calmer than earlier. I look at him, see his beautiful face, my fear making it so I don't instantly want to punch it. All the gorgeous artwork on his body is so pretty it hurts, and I can't keep my façade up. I'm so scared I'm latching onto anyone at this point. Even this jerk.

I grab onto his arms, and he seems a bit taken aback but doesn't shove me off. Honestly, I'm surprised he doesn't think my poverty will rub onto him. Instead, he brushes a strand of my hair behind my ear, hand hovering over the pointed tip.

"Thumbelina?" he whispers so only he and I can hear.

My eyes are telling him everything right now.

We did it. We did it and we're about to get caught, and I know you don't care about me, but I know you care about your sister and you have to do something or else we're going to be taken away, and I'm so scared—

"Thumbelina?" he repeats, that stupid nickname coated in something akin to . . . tenderness? Compassion? Empathy? Ardelle—caring about me?

"I need to go," I blurt out, the emotions roiling up inside me—confusing emotions—are too much for me to handle right now.

I don't stop when he calls me by that stupid nickname one last time. I dash up the stairs. Pacey's room is a few doors down from mine, and by the time I reach it, I'm close to vomiting on the pristine white carpet.

She jumps as I open her door. Her eyes are wide and wild, and her freshly dyed Bubblegum Pink hair is thrown up in two short ponytails. Her computer chair slides backwards on its wheels as she looks behind me to see if anyone else is with me. Our rooms are roughly the same size, but she designed hers with bright pops of pinks and bold black-and-white stripes. Fairy-light curtains and fake flowers and vines cover her window, as well as a chair that looks to be held up by vines hanging in the corner. Beside her perfectly made bed with a lush white comforter and fuzzy, striped pillows sits a modern makeup vanity surrounded by bright round bulbs.

"It's only me," I say, and she wildly beckons me inside with her hand.

"What are you doing?" I hiss. She turns back to strike her computer keyboard like a knight assails a dragon. Her computer desk is white but matches the style of the rest of her room with striped pen holders and hot-pink paper organizers. She wears a pair of old-school Lime Green headphones with cat ears on top of the band. "We should pack up our stuff and get the hell out of here before they take us out in cuffs and collars. Trust me, they suck. And why didn't you tell me the house has cameras? We're totally on camera last night."

"They didn't see us going anywhere," she says, and she stares intensely at her three computer monitors, each twenty inches wide and curved, taking up the entire length of her desk. "I took care of that last night. It's not what I'm worried about right now."

I walk over the fuzzy pink rug, sit on the gray quilted bench at the foot of her bed, and try not to worry myself sick.

"What are you doing over there?" I ask skeptically, internally questioning if I should ditch her and run into the woods while I still have a chance. Although, that's not who I am anymore—I proved that last night. I'll never be that person again. If we are going down, we're going down together, but it doesn't relieve the ass-clenching stress I'm feeling right now.

"Hopefully saving our hides." The clicking of her keyboard is as swift and precise as it was last night, but now that her own freedom is on the line, she's even more focused. I can only see her profile, but I swear she isn't even blinking.

"Oh, my stars, I'm actually in!" She cackles in disbelief, leaning over her desk, eyes glued to her monitors. "I genuinely didn't think I'd be able to find a way in, but it doesn't look like they've patched up the hole I made last night. Idiots."

"I think they've got bigger holes to plug," I say, knowing that they do. "What are you hacking into? What are you trying to do?"

Grinning wickedly, her mouth slightly too big for her face, she stares ahead intensely, cracking her neck with an aggressive snap.

"I'm going to change our results to say we were telling the truth."

I shoot up from the bench, meet her at her desk, and put my hands on both her shoulders. "You can do that? They won't see that we both totally failed the test?"

"Nails," she warns, and I retract my acrylic claws from her. "But yes, I'm changing our results now before Mr. Dracula down there goes through them. We both bombed it, by the way. See, it says so here." She points towards our results and each question that registered as a lie in the system. Ardelle's are popping into view as we speak, all clear, of course.

"How do we know someone hasn't already viewed them?" I ask, thinking of every contingency.

She takes a long time to answer. "We don't. We can only hope they haven't."

I pace the bedroom over and over for the next hour as each one of them downstairs gets meticulously tested.

"So, was that whole bit about you being upset about the test an act to get up here and change our results?" I ask when my mind wouldn't stop spinning out worst-case scenarios.

Pacey looks a bit insulted, but her face softens almost as quickly. "Not quite. Tests . . . they scare me. It doesn't matter how invasive they are or aren't, it's the—"

"Lack of control," I finish for her, and she nods. "I get it. I know what it's like to feel powerless. I've had a lot of that in my life too. Are you okay now?"

She looks sad for a minute, her enormous eyes as expressive as my own tend to be. Neither of us is able to keep our genuine emotions off our faces. "I'll be good once I know the leader of Arianyte isn't going to drag us out of this house and into his war chest."

Stars . . .

Someone knocks softly on the door and we both freeze, eyes wide and bodies tense. The door opens, hinges not making a sound, and I exhale loudly in relief to see Ardelle and Sylo poking their heads in.

Tension bursts through me for those few seconds as the boys stand there, not opening the door wide enough for us to see if there are soldiers accompanying them or not. My heart pounds in my ears.

"They're gone," Ardelle says, and the both of us let go of our shackled breaths in unison.

Ardelle crosses the bedroom as he forces his sister to look at him. "Are you okay?" The intensity at which he asks leads me to believe he's putting more emphasis on words he isn't directly saying. The worry is evident all over his face; he doesn't want his sister to be affected because that could trigger her into a spiral of unhealthy choices. He wants to protect her, I realize.

Pacey's scrunched nose makes it seem like she's somewhat annoyed by his overprotective nature, but also grateful. After assuring her brother she's alright, Ardelle leans in closely and kisses her forehead. A myriad of wordless communication passes between them in this moment, and as I watch, it's clear that Ardelle deeply loves his sister. By the looks of it, he'd do anything to keep her safe and happy and healthy. I get that. I'd do it for Gavrielle.

I only wish I had someone that devoted to me. Although, whatever lucky star has watched over me these last few days, I need to ensure I thank it.

CHAPTER 16

TRADITIONAL FRACKING AND OIL DRILLING ARE OUTLAWED, AS WELL AS ANY DETRIMENTAL ACT THAT NEGATIVELY AFFECTS THE PLANET, NATURAL WILDLIFE, ECOSYSTEMS, BODIES OF WATER, AND THE TERRESTRIAL-EXTRATERRESTRIAL POPULATIONS.

I still haven't gotten used to the quiet that surrounds this house. After living in noisy environments most of my life, the quiet is a little *too* quiet for me. Truly, it's the sound of the city that I miss most so far, the honking of hovers, the whizzing of drones as they spy on me through my tiny balcony back at my loft. I always used to hope one would saunter inside so I could capture it and take it apart. I wonder if the person who broke in has been back, if they were ever looking for me at all? It didn't take long for my landlord to find the mess, and he's been hounding me with messages I've strictly ignored.

Autumn has fully taken over, so there are no buzzing insects or nighttime crickets chirping to interrupt the never-ending silence of the trees and their secrets. They have their own language, however, one I hadn't heard for so long. Although I lived mostly within the city's steel boundaries, the Narestée Orphanage had a miniature forest next to it by an open field. They built it on the edge of the city, like the outcasts needed to be put in the backyard and away where nobody could see them.

It's an honest metaphor for me and my life.

The silence is broken up by the crunching of twigs and fallen leaves as I walk a tiny way into the tree line from the bottom back deck, enough so that I'm not seen but still close enough to have a good view of the house. Finding the familiar rock that's become my designated spot the last week or so, I plop down on it and remove my smoke pen with greedy fingers. The anxiety of today, of Malakyte barging in here with his soldiers and that horned-wench Naresteé, was too much. The pen vibrates slightly as I turn it on, the center of it glowing green, and as soon as I inhale a large hit, all of that tension seeps out of my body like a flip of a switch. For these precious minutes, I am safe. I don't have to worry or think about anything—I can just *be*.

Yet, my peace doesn't last long.

It was too close today, I think as I deeply inhale and release a giant puff of smoke, the icy air swirling together in a fruity cloud. *You could've gotten Pacey killed. And yourself.*

Straight up, Pacey saved both our hides today. I had no plan, no strategy, no excuse for why we could've been there. This all happened because I couldn't keep my powers inside and used them; that had to be what tipped Malakyte off to suspecting me. He's a lot sharper than I gave him credit for. It's also likely he doesn't believe my lies about Deimos controlling me at the Capitol building as much as I thought he did. Everyone in the house is probably thinking it—the Prince of Arianyte is the one saying it. Well, and Blondie, too.

I twirl the pen aimlessly between puffs. Something has to give. It has to be worth it in the end if I'm making such dramatic sacrifices for this cause because it's not only about me and my revenge or my need to please the rebels. There's Gav, my top priority. Then it's about saving the children Arianyte is taking in secret. I don't believe it could be Deimos taking them, regardless of what the video showed. Arianyte is up to something, something terrible and dark, and it's up to me to find out what it is and stop it. Every day I wait, another kid with no one else to look out for them will end up like Gavrielle. My next shot at Arianyte has to be much more carefully thought out. No more going balls to the wall. I need to strategize better. The Titan Games parade is coming up in two weeks and we're expected to be there. From this point till then, I need to come up with a smarter plan to strike Arianyte without putting others in danger.

Crunching footsteps snap me out of my thoughts. They're clearly coming from the direction of the house. A dark silhouette approaches me as they pass through the lights.

"Shit," I hiss slowly, standing up in a panic. My arms wave around sporadically in front of me, and I try in vain to disperse the fruity smelling air. It doesn't matter, because two seconds later Ardelle meets my gaze with an incredulous, judgmental leer.

Of course it would be him.

"You know Jance will kill you if he catches you smoking that death stick again. You should go farther out into the trees if you want to get away with it. I could smell that thing from the moment I stepped out of the hover." He approaches, stopping two feet away from me and my rock seat. Since I'm caught, I see no point in hiding the thing now, so I sit back down and take a long puff.

"Good thing he's not my dad then, isn't it?" My snarky tone is garnished with a smile that is far from sweet. "You took off shortly after the sky-rats left. Did you go somewhere you shouldn't have?"

He walks over to a large tree and leans against it, arms crossed. His black pants are baggy until they reach the knees, where they tighten up and disappear under his Shanghai Black leather boots. The pants have dramatic buckles and hooks and attachments that allow for weapons to be stored and easily accessed. His sweater is in shade Wedgwood Blue and Nightshade, the zipper coming up his left side rather than the center, while the collar flares around his chest, and the hood snaps on from the front and down his back. He wore a moderately thick silver chain around his neck, a few ridiculously expensive rings on his fingers, and a leather bracelet on his right wrist. His mark is covered up, and due to that wacky vision it triggered, I'm glad I can't see it. I never want that to happen again.

Ardelle squares his chin and almost looks a little defensive. "I have a life other than being here, Thumbelina."

"I have a real name, you know." I blow smoke in his face with the sole goal of irritating him.

Swatting the smoke away aggressively, he switches the subject. "That was intense today. It looked like you were a few seconds away from completely losing it. Why was that?"

Squinting at him, I take a long drag. "Well, the test spoke the truth. Maybe I have a little residual PTSD from the night you manhandled me into the confinement center? Did that ever cross your pampered little mind?"

"I'll make sure to be gentler the next time you get yourself into trouble, then."

Heat rises from my belly, flooding into my chest, and spills out into my cheeks and ears at the mere thought of him grabbing my body again. What happened between us today? What changed?

I still hate him.

I clear my throat, then say, "Well you won't have to worry about me getting into trouble. I'm a good girl now, don't you know that?"

We watch each other, the eye contact getting more intense by the millisecond. His eyes speak to me, they say a million things at once, yet I can't figure out what. The silence becomes its own sound, dancing in line with the rhythm of my increasing heart. Ardelle's presence alone, the memories of his powerful body as he trains and spars are flooding my mind as aggressively as I try to shoo them away. Just because I'm physically attracted to him doesn't mean anything. We're not compatible, we have absolutely zero in common.

He's an absolute pass.

"No," he says as he kicks himself off the tree and clears the space between us in two strides. "I think you are the trouble."

Sapphire Sky eyes dance in the darkness, the stars and moon reflecting inside those water lagoons.

"Maybe trouble isn't such a bad thing?" I test the waters, seeing how far he'll go down this road with me. How far I can draw him to the dark side, because why not? He messes with me often enough; it wouldn't hurt to get a little innocent payback. "Perhaps you've been a little too good your whole life and trouble is exactly what you need?"

The smoke pen must've been laced with drugs because I can't believe I actually said that.

His mocking chuckle confirms how ridiculous I'm being. He's not flirting with me—he's messing with me.

"If there wasn't so much at stake, then maybe I'd agree. But I can't afford trouble. I can't let my sister get hurt because of your wild choices."

My walls instantly fly up, made of hard steel and garnished with barbed wire. "What part of 'we passed the lie detector test' didn't you hear?"

He shrugs. Before I can do anything, I feel his crystal's power surge from out of nowhere. It's like someone took a rope tied to the center of my stomach and pulled. The stronger the crystal's energy output, the more intense the pull. He plucks my pen from my mouth, but not by his hand—by his magic. It bobs in the air between us as I watch, amazed. The pupils of his eyes glow ruby red behind the floating e-cigarette.

"To most people my gravity magic looks a lot like telekinesis," Ardelle begins, "but even though things may appear one way, they're truly something different entirely."

He lets my pen drop to the forest floor, then steps on it, its snapping plastic sounding like a breaking bone.

My mouth gapes open in shock. Point duly noted.

"Dude, what the hell?" I yell as I shove him off it, the pen now in two pieces, connected only by wires. The liquid nicotine seeps into the forest floor. "Those are super expensive."

Ardelle looks down at me with a proud smile. "These pens are horrendous for your health. There's a reason Jance pounced when he caught you with it: because there's no way you can keep up endurance-wise if you're puffing on that thing all day. I'm doing you a favor. You're a part of our team now. We need to count on you, not worry if your smoker's cough is going to slow you down when our lives are at stake."

I hadn't thought of it like that. Even so, he didn't have to break it.

"I get you're too posh and don't like me because I don't have money or grew up in a fancy mansion like you probably did, but that doesn't give you the right to be a jerk to me. I don't get you: your sister is a total sweetheart and so down to Earth, and yet you must've come out of the womb acting like a pompous dick from day one."

"You know nothing about me, or what I've been through."

"Same can be said to you. I don't like how you treat me."

We stare each other down again, our eyes in a miniature battle of wills. Sighing, he rustles his hand through his hair.

"I'm sorry," he says, his voice somewhat genuine as he takes a seat on my rock. "Pacey and I grew up in a totally different world from this one. It's so relaxed here, slow in the sense we don't have a million expectations being placed upon us. That's not how we grew up. Every minute was choreographed and monitored. Our parents are Terran government officials. The politics of their job bled into the fabric of our family. Strict was an understatement."

"Oh, sounds like a horrific life," I mock. Fire erupts behind that beautiful face of his.

"You wouldn't understand what it's like to have every expectation of you held up to the highest, most meticulous standards. At home, at school, at sports, in public. I doubt you had any standards growing up at all."

I whirl at him. "Yeah? Because my parents dumped me, is that what you're trying to say?"

Hurt flashes on his face and he shakes his head. "No, that's not what I meant at all."

I don't buy it. "And for your information, not like I have to justify anything to you, but I've been in several foster homes that all had different rules I was supposed to follow. How I was supposed to behave, be, act, and feel. And if I didn't, I—" Hesitating, I think about what I'm saying for once, and stop.

"Was punished for it?" he finishes for me, and I look up at him with the sad eyes of a sad girl.

"Something like that."

I cross my arms, closing myself off.

Ardelle shifts away, giving me space, and I can tell he feels bad for whatever reason. "We were never punished, per se, except for what we were born with. Our crystals were the ultimate sin against our parents' perfect image. It was the one thing they couldn't change, or manipulate, or make *perfect.*"

"Pacey told me what they did to you guys," I say, my demeanor softening for the genuine pity I feel for them both. Not even I would wish for parents like that.

Ardelle huffs softly, the fake smile he portrays coming and going quickly. Is this what he's doing? Wearing this façade he's had to build up over years to fit into a box he never fit into? "It's all the crystals' fault. If there was only a way to get rid of them, then everything would be perfect. We could go home."

My brows knit together in confusion. "But Ahren showed me the x-rays. He said they are impossible to remove without us dying."

"He's right," he snaps, but I can see actual regret there the moment it leaves his lips. "I'm only saying, if there was somehow a way to change that, then I'd do whatever I had to in order to make that happen. So that we could go home. Be a family again. Everything would be normal. We could be a normal family for once."

I've been in enough abusive and toxic situations to recognize one from a mile away, and Ardelle and Pacey's parents are one hundred percent abusers—they're simply rich abusers, so it at least makes it go down a hell of a lot easier.

"And you genuinely believe the crystals are the only problem? That if they magically went 'poof' all your family problems would go away? That's not typically how it works."

Ardelle shrugs. "I wouldn't say all, but most—yes. The crystals are the curse. If they were gone, our parents would have nothing to want to fix about us. Well, maybe aside from Pacey's constant hair color changes. If our mother saw her with that hair, she'd lose her mind."

Wait till mommy dearest figures out her picture-perfect daughter likes girls and is actually a badass hacker genius.

I wonder what she'd think if she saw her son talking to me right now? Would I not be good enough for her?

"I'm just saying, I don't think that's going to be the solution to your problems. It sounds like there are deeper, underlying issues there," I try telling him, although I doubt he'll be very receptive to what I have to say—what does an orphan girl like me know about families, anyway?

Ardelle's face appears sad, like he's completely helpless. "Have you ever failed someone so badly that it eats at you every single day? Pacey is my sister, my baby sister, despite us only being barely a year a part. She's everything to me—and I failed her. I let them hurt her and I . . ." His voice catches, and he can't go on.

"You'd be surprised by how much I understand."

He nods and leans forward, his elbows on his knees. The way he's sitting, with his hair all tangled up in his hood, he could've been Gav. He's not, I know, but maybe that's why I feel this attraction to him that's absolutely maddening. It's that he reminds me of my old friend. It's got to be the hair because that's where the similarities end. There's no mistaking the boys, they're different lives, different species, different everything.

Looking at Ardelle, I honestly feel bad for him. He doesn't see he's being abused by his own parents. And worse, he longs to go back to them despite their toxic effects on him and his sister. He doesn't see that crystal or no crystal, the two of them will never be perfect enough for the two monsters who raised them.

"Well, Blondie, I hope you find what you're looking for," I tell him, getting a nice whiff of his scent as I walk past him towards the house.

I can hear his loud steps cracking twigs as he follows behind me. "You are *the Star*," he says enigmatically. "Who knows, you may be the key to everything."

CHAPTER 17

The breeze tickles my cheeks and gently sways the baby hairs around my ears as I stand with Jance out in the freezing fall day. Pacey tied my hair up into a Dutch-braided mohawk and dressed me in a tight-fitting blue bodysuit. It does little to hold off the cold, and we can't afford any loose clothing today.

Not with what we're here for.

Jance and I stand in a large clearing in the woods close to the house. It's the size of a football field. Trees glow like fire in the sunlight, almost like a real-life painting. If I were going to tattoo these trees on someone, I'd use the colors Blood Orange, Starburst Red, Desert Sand Dark, Hard Orange, and Yellow Orchid. People don't realize how many colors actually go into creating art of any medium, and I think that's a lot like how people are. There's more depth to all of us than meets the eye.

But we aren't out here in the cold to enjoy the glorious transitions of the maples and oaks. We are here to finally awaken the beast.

"As your Ringer, I'm less susceptible to your powers than anyone else," Jance begins. "Although I'm not completely impervious to it. Don't kill me, kid."

I affectionately smile at the pet name, coming to like it—and Jance, despite myself.

"Can you tell me about your powers?" I dare ask, having been curious.

Shrugging, Jance explains, "I get inside people's heads. Technically I have the ability to affect brain chemistry, but it's a lot more complex than that. I can make a person see, feel, hear, taste, smell, whatever I want them to experience. Either within their minds or externally."

I shudder as I blink rapidly, the terrifying reality of my Ringer's powers scaring me a little. That's a lot of power for a person to have over others, and it scares me to think what someone with bad intentions could do to someone.

"Is it true that Starseeds and Ringers are supposed to feel a special connection?" I ask, having not felt that connection thus far. I tried telling myself it's because it's only been two weeks and that I'm being clingy and weird and doing that thing I do when I attach to people too quickly . . .

Jance peeks over the collar of his black coat at me, his stubble growing a little thick and his hair blowing in the wind.

"It's true," his gravelly voice confirms. "Yet, like anything else, it's a process."

That's code for: 'I don't feel it either.'

Why does that hurt so much? I shouldn't even care. *They're the enemy, remember?*

"You need to be extremely cautious when using this weapon." There's no segue; he dives right into why we're here. "The crystal uses your energy to produce the desired output of energy. It's something deeply intertwined with your emotions, so once the crystal depletes the physical and emotional energy, it will draw on your life force. If pushed too far, too quickly, without the opportunity to replenish the wells of energy, the crystal can and will take too much. It could put you into shock, organ failure, a coma, and it can even kill you. There are limits to these weapons. Do you understand what I'm telling you?"

"I do."

"First, let's get your mind into a relaxed state so we don't have another repeat of the Capitol building."

The wind is freezing as we sit across from each other in the center of the clearing. Jance's eyes that border on black peer into me like lasers. I want to forget that night entirely, how I failed so epically and ended up making this entire mess for myself. Not like I could tell him that.

"Calm your mind, don't think of anything else," he says, his voice calming and deep.

Annoying thoughts bounce into my mind like ping-pong balls. Like how I'd love to tattoo these trees on someone, or the way Ardelle's cologne of juniper berries, cinnamon, and sage hit me as he sparred with me this morning. I mentally scold myself for thinking of him like that.

Focus, Dammit!

"Now, focus on bringing up the start of the crystal's activation process. Turn it on," he says smoothly, his voice calm and sturdy.

Focusing, I bait my crystal with what I know it desires most of all— escape. It always wants to break free, it always wants me to use it.

Yet, like a ballet performer suddenly freezing on stage, nothing happens.

After zero movement, I open my eyes to see Jance staring at me inquisitively. He must feel that nothing is happening; the Ringers are also able to feel and sense the powers of the Elendril crystals.

"Take a deep breath in . . ." he says, a calming anchor for me as I listen to the deep grit and texture there, "and out. Do it again. Let your thoughts simply pass by, don't judge them or let them linger. Everything is irrelevant at this moment. There's nothing pressing, nothing urgent, nothing to do."

I do as Jance instructs, allowing my fears and hatred towards this power to float in and out of my mind, open to a new relationship with it.

"You know what it feels like when it begins . . . remember it. Feel the buzzing on your skin build. Let it."

But I've never simply *let it* do anything. It's always done what it wants, when it wants.

Doing as Jance suggests, bringing the feeling up to the front of my mind, I focus on it, but I don't feel much more than a pinprick. I sigh in frustration, and he urges me to relax and breathe. So I do, trying to bring out the power that I know is there. It's raw and vicious and practically has a mind of its own. But why is it so hard to control? To even bring forward?

After forty minutes of absolutely nothing happening, I open my eyes, annoyed with myself.

"Tell me what happens when you use it."

"You know what happens," I say allusively.

"Not from you."

I bite my lip in annoyance and reluctance. "Typically, it comes on when I'm in an intense situation. When my emotions are high, it's ready to go."

Jance crosses his meaty arms. "So, you're telling me when you're upset or angry, you find your power at its most optimal?"

I scoff. "Yeah, sure, you can say that."

"And, is it safe to surmise that if you're distraught, overwhelmed, and feeling chaotic, that the crystal feels uncontrollable?"

"It always feels uncontrollable," I say, "that's obvious."

"What's obvious is that Arianyte is going to throw you into Reconditioning if you don't figure this out. I don't want that for you."

I flinch back as if he's slapped me. My stomach drops to the cold ground I sit upon. His tone switched from patience and understanding to almost cruel. I really didn't expect him to be like this. My walls instantly fly up.

"Do you want to be sent back to confinement?" he asks, voice and expression as cold as the wind chill.

Sent back . . .

The tingling comes in fast after that. My chest blooms with hot shame under my dark one-piece outfit. It's abundantly clear that this arrangement is transactional, that I was forced to be here and they were forced to take me in. But after finding out about the Elendril crystals and the Ringer thing, I thought there could be some sort of connection—or at least the potential for one. I didn't care at first, but it's almost been like I could fit in here. All the potential with these people is what got me hopeful, despite knowing I should be cautious, and all that hope feels like it's shattering in this moment. A familiar feeling creeps up my spine like the icy hand of the Grim Reaper.

Unable to stand his eyes anymore, I spring to my feet and walk away, going nowhere in particular.

"Arianyte doesn't mess around, kid," he continues, coming around to circle me with his arms still crossed. "Now I can't imagine the things they do to people like us, and we're lucky Arianyte has let us remain autonomous with little intervention, but that comes with a cost. That cost is performance and deliverance of our duties. Do the job you agreed to."

"I'm trying," I sneer.

"Then prove it."

I close my eyes against the image of his betraying face and feel the wind and smell the surrounding pine and wet leaves in the air. The tingle over the mark is now a steady burn, and the purring of the beast licks its lips at the glorious temptation. It feels way better than it probably should.

"What's upsetting you so much about this conversation? How many times were you sent back from foster homes?"

"Shut up."

My emotions make me feel like I'm drowning; they're the hand that holds me underwater no matter how hard I thrash to grasp the air.

I open my eyes. Jance looks surprised by my words as his dark brows raise. "Well, that's not very nice, kid." His smell is like rum and coffee, with a touch of bergamot and strong masculinity.

"Leave me alone," I demand, feeling like I'm treading water here. There are feelings bubbling up that I don't want to feel, a crushing weight that feels like a serrated knife twisting and turning within my chest. It's a pain like nothing else—not being wanted. I'd rather someone stab me with an actual knife instead.

"I'm not going anywhere until you use that crystal."

"Screw the stupid crystal!" My voice raises, the mark flaring on my chest.

Dry leaves crunch as he follows behind me, not letting up on me or on his assault. The more I try to get away, the more he follows.

"Leave me alone," I repeat, continuing to stalk away from him. Jance grabs my wrist and pulls on it, and before I can stop myself, the crystal zaps him.

He gasps as he gets thrown on his ass fifteen feet away, and the smell of burning flesh fills the air. "Oh, stars!" I am definitely being kicked out now. They'll all hate me for sure if I hurt him. "I didn't mean to, I—"

Jance sits up with a smile on his face, his white teeth gleaming. He holds his palm out to me. It's smoking and charred. I wince. "Do it again," Jance demands, standing back up to his feet. "Come on. Arianyte won't be happy with that little spark. It's pathetic."

All the pity he got from me goes right out the window.

"Why? Why does it matter when you guys will just send me back when I ultimately don't do what you want?" That wound is raw, open, and actively bleeding. Truthfully, it's been bleeding for years. No tourniquet has stanched it, no aid to mend it; it's been nothing but a roaring river of self-pity and shame for as long as I can remember. I wasn't enough to be kept—to be chosen. I'm like a pretty doll. Normal and desirable on the outside, but once I'm no longer fun to play with, I get taken back to the store. Maybe I should tattoo a return policy on myself. That way, I'll never be blindsided again.

"What does that feel like?" he asks. I blink, the only sign of hurt I'll show.

Shaking my head angrily, I ask, "What are you doing?"

The biggest part of me wants this to be a way to egg me on, to push me towards an edge that would trigger my powers. I'm there, upon that edge—all it's going to take is one more shove.

The man shrugs. "I'm merely trying to assess you."

I roll my eyes.

"Use your magic."

"No." I don't want to. "I'll hurt you." *I'll kill you, and it'll give more people more reasons to hate me.*

"You won't," he says, taking a step closer.

"The first time my crystal manifested in its entirety, it blew an entire roof off a building. Several people were killed." *Gavrielle was . . .*

The pain pulls me deeper underwater, deeper and colder and darker downward.

I laugh cynically, remembering all the screams that day. How I didn't feel an ounce of pity or regret for blasting those sky-rats, all those emotions were saved for Gav.

Jance rubs his stubbled chin with his fingers, those emotional eyes of his betraying his cold façade. There's pain there, pain for me.

Or just plain pity. It's way worse.

The power swells up into my chest at the memories of that time, how broken I was after. Truthfully, I was broken way before, and it was Gav who continuously kept me together.

I immediately turn away from Jance, feeling my control slipping from my grasp. "Stay back."

It's hot and searing and raging—and it demands its freedom.

Jance tries stepping close to me yet again, and I put my hand between us.

"Let it go," Jance eases me, his voice serious. All taunting gone.

Stars, I want to. The pressure has built to such a level it's painful. Not only that, it's like all my worst impulses and desires are screaming—

no—*begging* me to release it. Though all I can think of are all the people I've hurt with this power—it's monstrous. It makes *me* a monster . . . a terroristic nightmare dressed up in pretty packaging.

"Please stay away." My voice shakes. The crystal is lit up, the pink-and-purple light on full display.

The mark screams.

"*Let me out! Let me out! Let me out!*"

If I hurt Jance by accident, they'd all hate me for it. Just like the Resistance.

Stupidly stepping closer, his face softens. "You can release it, Kara. It's okay."

"I . . ." I breathe, barely able to speak from the pressure.

"You must let it out once it reaches these levels. If you don't, the crystal will melt your body from the inside. You have control of this, not the other way around. Don't let it rule you."

There's still this resistant part of me that doesn't want this thing to ruin what I have here . . . like it's ruined so much in the past. Although Jance is correct—I can't hold this in.

In my peripheral, I see what looks like a shadowy figure standing on the edge of the tree line. It's behind Jance so he doesn't see it, and it looks like a man in a long coat with giant ears . . .

Deimos.

The crystal explodes.

Purple light envelops us both, and for a moment I wonder if I just obliterated Jance into dust or if he had disappeared into the light. The figure completely disappears from my mind. He becomes a distant memory as the head rush of the crystal's power blinds me. It turns the tears that fall from my eyes to steam before they reach the fullest part of my cheeks, but I don't cry because I'm sad or because it hurts. My tears fall because it feels so good to surrender to the power for the first time instead of doing everything possible to cage it. The pain of Jance's words vanishes and is replaced by a numbing release. It doesn't matter anymore. They can be like everyone else and leave if they want. As long as I have *this*, I'll be okay.

Falling to my knees, hair coming undone in a mess of teal curls, the initial high comes down. In its place comes a tsunami of emotions.

The glow around me fades until only my mark is glowing. The well of emotions that erupts out of me is stronger than any antimatter, and the wind carries my screams across the scorched landscape.

Relief floods me when I feel Jance's arms come around me then, and I grab onto him to keep from completely toppling over onto the charred ground. He's not dead. Scattered all over, like chaotic lightning barreled through here, are jagged scars on the earth. The entire field around us is smoking, dozens of tiny fires crackling against the howling wind carrying the smell of burning things to my nose. It smells almost like a campfire, but the distinct smell of my crystal also twinkles in the air. It always has a distinct smell to it, one I couldn't ever really define or replicate, but the memories from that familiar smell come flooding back to the forefront of my consciousness along with all the feelings I wish I could forget.

"It's okay, darling," Jance says as he holds me up. I lean into him. His chest is hard and warm and I cling to his clothing. My hands and body tremble, and it feels impossible to keep my heavy lids from closing—my energy pouring out of me with every tear, and I'm unable to stop the floodgates of emotions. "It's okay."

I look back towards the spot where I thought I saw a figure; if it was Deimos or not, I'm completely unsure. There's nothing there now, and I wonder if I saw anything there at all.

I'm too exhausted to care.

"You know I only said those things to get a reaction out of you, right?" he placates once my tears finally cease, and my sniffles were further and further apart.

"Okay," I say. The familiar numbness creeping over me.

Softly, his hand approaches my face and wipes the tears from my cheeks. "I went too far, I pushed you too much and didn't realize . . . I didn't realize how much weight my words could truly have on you. I'm sorry. I was wrong. You don't know how glad I am to have finally found you. To have you here. You're a part of this team: Arianyte won't touch you with me around."

My eyes blink heavily at him, too tired to care or believe him, too exhausted to hope for the truth in those words. They were words I've always wanted to hear, yet now that I've finally heard them, they're not as I'd imagined them.

CHAPTER 18

"No way!" Pacey squeals, snatching my Dezlar from my hands after I run into her room in a panic.

It's been over two weeks since she and I hit the Arianyte outpost and drew the acting leader of Arianyte to the house. I thought the entire situation was over; however, I was wrong.

Stunned, I stand there wide mouthed in Pacey's room, unable to register what's going on. "This isn't happening. What do I do?"

"What's going on?" Ardelle barges into his sister's room, confusion and worry on his face. "It sounds like someone is about to die in here."

Pacey jumps up from her computer chair and shows my Dezlar to her brother. "The fricking Emperor of Arianyte just asked Kara out on a date!"

My groan could be heard all the way from the Saturn colony base.

"It's not a date," I moan as I snatch the device back. The stupid thing is still being glitchy. "And he's not the emperor. That's his dad or some crap like that."

"Does it matter? The guy is in charge here. To me, that makes him the leader," Pacey says, looking up at her brother. Ardelle's face is emotionless, indignant—almost cold.

I grunt in frustration, head angled skywards. "Do I have to go? How'd he even get my number?"

"Absolutely! And he's the leader of Arianyte. He gets what he wants." Pacey makes her position clear. "I'm picking out your outfit and doing your hair and makeup. Ardelle, get out."

"This isn't a date," I reiterate, but she doesn't seem to hear me. It's almost as if she wants me to go on this *encounter* more than Malakyte does. Her brother, however, not so much.

Without a word, Ardelle leaves the room a tad huffy, if not a bit broodingly, and I'm left alone with my hyper matchmaker.

Looking over the message from Malakyte again, I try to decode it.

FROM: MALAKYTE ARDEEN
PLEASE DO ME THE HONOR OF ALLOWING ME TO TAKE YOU TO DINNER AS AN APOLOGY FOR THE OTHER WEEK. BE READY IN ONE HOUR. I'LL ARRIVE TO PICK YOU UP.

Stars . . .

"With all the things going on right now, why would he even be thinking about me?" I ask as Pacey rummages through her closet, chucking articles of clothing out like bullets from a gun. "This is odd."

Knee-deep in outfits I'm never going to be caught dead in, Pacey finally comes up for air. "Are you kidding me? Girl, milk it. Do you understand the type of influence you can have by getting on his good side? Maybe he can help you find Gav? You don't need to marry the guy, but you're smart. Use it. And looking hot can't hurt your case."

Before I can argue, the door opens again, but this time it's Sylo. He's holding a garment bag in his hand, a confused expression on his face.

"A SSPARROW dropped this off a second ago." Holding up the black bag, he sounds skeptical. "Why are you going on a date with that vampire dude?"

Pacey pounces over to him and snatches the garment bag from his hand.

"It's not a date!" I say again, folding my arms in defiance. Is he playing dress up with me or something?

I should say no, message him back with some excuse of food poisoning or cramps.

Pacey unzips the black bag as she lays it on her bed, and her gasp tells me any plans of getting out of this are long gone.

A catcall whistle greets me as I walk down the staircase and into the living room, something I expected would come after first laying eyes on the gown Malakyte left for me. My gown has two pieces, one made of lace and the other of satin and soft tulle. The lace piece is a sheer, floor-length, and long-sleeved black gown that's only lined black from the bust down to the upper thighs like a leotard. The entire thing would be completely see-through if it isn't for the beaded black-lace patterns hand sewn into the delicate sheer nylon. It contrasts against the pale skin of my arms and legs. Attached separately with a dainty belt is the flowing skirt. It's the satin that gives it volume, and the tulle breathes it to life. It billows softly as I walk down each step, bobbing like a cork in an ocean. The dress is all delicate edges, except for the striking silver collar that lunges all the way up my jawline and across my shoulders. Talk about a statement piece.

I have to make sure I hold onto the railing because the black pumps Pacey lent me are a little too big, and I also don't typically run around in heels while partaking in Resistance shenanigans. She styled my hair up beautifully, where on one side several tight cornrows are braided halfway back, adorned with gold jewelry, while the other half is curled and combed over to the other side. I want to hate it, I mean—how could I be happy about my mortal enemy dressing me up like his little doll and taking me out to dinner for his so-called apology? Yet, I do feel and look beautiful. I always attempted to do my makeup, have my nails done, and my hair somewhat presentable, but I don't dress up like this *ever*.

When I dare to look up from the stairs, my eyes catch on Ardelle's.

Ardelle sits isolated from the rest of the group, sitting in the same red chair Malakyte had the day of the lie detector test and glowering just as profusely as the Arianyte prince had. Although, when he looks at me, all his contempt bleeds right out of his face and is replaced with something else entirely. Maybe I'm mistaken, but for the first time it seems as if Ardelle has actually noticed me. His eyes are captivated and mesmerized by me, and even though the rest of the house walks up and ogles at me, the two of us don't break our profound gaze.

Jance approaches me with a smile on his face. "You look beautiful, kid." He brushes the side of my cheek with the back of his fingers, and I finally draw my eyes away from Ardelle. Since the field incident where I completely lost my shit and almost fried him, he's been a lot warmer towards me. I sort of like it. Jance is growing on me. Maybe others are, too? "He's outside waiting."

My gut roils.

"I don't want to do this," I confess with a half chuckle, my dangling earrings clinking together as I look down at the floor. "He's up to something, and I don't trust him."

"Then don't blow it for all of us, Sparks." Sylo chimes into our conversation that clearly everyone can hear.

I look back up at Jance, and his dark eyes are rich with emotion. Leaning in so only I can hear, he gives me some good advice. "Play the game. Whatever his angle is, find out what he's after and make him think he has it. Play your hands carefully. You're one hell of a fighter, kid, but this man is skilled in an entirely different arena of battle. Stay sharp. We'll be waiting for you."

Comforting.

Wanting a piece of me back, I swing my leather jacket over my shoulders as I walk to the front door. Malakyte's hover idles in the driveway, and I really, really don't want to do this.

Geonni would absolutely *die* if he ever found out about this. Trinity more, probably. I make a mental note to never tell them or another soul about this so-called date.

I step out into the chilly air, wish I had my smoke pen to place between my bright red lips, and go have dinner with the Emperor of Arianyte.

CHAPTER 19

In an eerie way, Malakyte is one of the most beautiful men I've ever seen. During the ride down the mountainside, I couldn't stop thinking about how he looks so young, perhaps a few years older than me, but how he speaks as if he's from another time. It must be a cultural thing. It's something about him; I can't put my finger on it. Though the car ride is as awkward as I expected it to be, I try to make the best of the situation. Taking Pacey's advice, I need to somehow coax this guy into helping me find Gav, no matter how I've got to play things.

We ride in a brigade of sorts, and by the time we reach the city alongside the Zarmenia River, the sun is beginning to set.

"I'll get your door," he tells me as he exits the self-driving hover, the doors opening upwards instead of horizontally. My sworn enemy takes my hand as he helps me out of the hover. My ankles wobble from more than the heels.

"I'm afraid there is no other route than to walk." Malakyte gestures towards the floating restaurant on the river several hundred feet ahead.

Thus, we walk together in silence, the clinking of my heels against the sidewalk mixing with the singing of squawking gulls. The perfectly manicured grass and landscaping are still green by our feet, contrasted by the red, orange, and yellow leaves on the trees as nature shows its beautiful hand. With all those colors accentuated by the sunset straight ahead of us, I couldn't imagine a more beautiful scene. The water reflects the orange-and-pink rays I'd die to tattoo right now. It's almost as if this is normal, and he's not the person I swore to destroy.

"I owe you an apology, Miss Ruzz," he finally says, hands buried in the pockets of his immaculate jacket. The front is rather simple, almost seamless, but when you get to the back, it literally looks like a spine made of string and fabric. His clothing is clearly tailored to his body because everything from his black trousers to the long-sleeved jacket fits him like a glove.

"Please, call me Kara." I clear my throat, nervously wondering where the line would be with this guy—and testing it. "And what exactly are you apologizing for? Accusing me for the second time of being a rebel, or barging into our house unannounced and forcing us all to take a ridiculous test when our word would've sufficed?"

Surprisingly, he laughs. "Not mincing any words, I see. I like your tenacity, I really do. It reminds me of someone I cared deeply for. Nevertheless, yes—all the above. Like I told you, I want to keep the city safe. That someone could infiltrate my systems in such a marring fashion places the city and its inhabitants at extreme risk. You fit the description of the assailants, but my assumption that it indeed was you who broke into the building was erroneous. Something I am tremendously grateful for, by the way. As I've said, you are special to me. I hope that isn't too forward."

Oh, it is. However, I neglect to tell him how bizarre it is that someone of his status even cares about me. It can't be for anything good, and I have a feeling it's more about the ancient weapon within my chest than the true heart of the person that beats there.

As we walk side by side, his face turns and looks at mine, eyes tilting down at me affectionately. I blush despite myself.

"You look stunning, by the way. I hope the gown wasn't too much. I thought it would be fitting for you. I'm glad to see my assumption wasn't far off."

"Is the dress a part of your apology too?" I force a smile so I don't say what I really want to. *That he's making me into his gorgeous little monster.*

He breathes in, and I feel the cold radiating off him against the thin material of the gown. "One of the many surprises I have in store to hopefully win your favor back."

"Whoever said you had it in the first place?" I tease, hoping he understands the context and doesn't get offended.

People like him get offended easily.

I'm relieved when he chuckles once again. "I'm assuming you've settled in well? They're treating you nicely?" I nod, and seemingly satisfied, he takes a right turn with the topic. "I want to warn you once again about Deimos. Do not underestimate him, and whatever it is he may say to try to sway you, don't believe it. I know your crystal is difficult to control, but you're one of the best weapons we have against him now. Be aware that he's clever and tricky and will come at you from every angle."

I think back to the creepy call I got and the day I was with Jance in the field. Deimos is up to something, that I know for sure.

"I've faced worse monsters," I say, and it's true.

He seems to contemplate that answer, picking apart every word and assuming the stories behind them.

"That's where you and I finally find a common thread, Karalevine. You remember how I told you my family is the head of Arianyte?"

How could I forget? Although, I nod and let him continue. The less I have to talk, the better, but he's not the worst conversationalist, I have to admit.

"Family can be arduous, almost grueling. My parents have been strictly governing this empire within the Milky Way for a long time, and they have a very strict set of rules they abide by. Some years ago, I violated those rules.

"Have you ever thought something was the right thing? Did nobody else around you seem to agree with that assessment? My situation was strenuous at best, and I admit I acted out of emotion rather than logic, but I thought I was doing the right thing. My parents along with my sister—their golden child—were furious with me. As next in line to take over the throne once my parents stepped down, they had extremely unrealistic expectations of my behavior. While my sister could go around causing as much chaos as she desired with no reprimand, they held me to a much stricter set of guidelines. Despite all my accomplishments across this galaxy, this one transgression proved unforgivable in my family's eyes. This empire, they see it as one thing—as a business with living assets—but it can be so much more than that. Their arbitrary rules are relics of an old age, and they can't see the potential that I see for it. I want to change matters, make each world I touch a better world. That's why I tell you this story, so you understand where I'm coming from, that you see me as more than some tyrant."

I'm truly floored by his vulnerability and openness. Is he the true cause of all Arianyte's evils?

"That's family drama, however. What family actually gets along, right? They actually marooned me on a planet that had zero off-world capabilities. They told me I needed to rethink my strategy for ruling. My own family, abandoning me in the worst way I could've imagined. I'd lie to you if I said that resentment and anger doesn't still linger within me, because it does. It's akin to abandonment. Once they finally deemed me worthy enough to rejoin the empire, my shame was a scarlet letter branded upon me for the galaxy to witness. Because my intelligence informed me the Starseeds were here, I bargained for Earth. My sister, she owned the planet before I did, not realizing what gems lay hidden within it. She's quite the villainess; in my story, anyway. I doubt she sees herself that way. We came to an agreement, and ultimately Earth is where I got to start over. It hasn't gone as smoothy as I intended, but I'm trying."

I wasn't sure what he was going to say to me tonight, but I didn't expect *this* to come from his lips. It humanized him more than I could've thought possible. Suddenly, he doesn't look like the cold, threatening, power-hungry alien that invaded and took over Earth. Right now, in the warm glow of the sunset, he almost looks human.

"So your parents abandoned you too, then, huh?" I ask, too ashamed to look him in the eye and reveal all my wounds.

"That doesn't make either of us worthless, Karalevine. I'm sure you ruminate on those thoughts as much as I do."

"Another thing we have in common."

"I'm sure you have a lot of preconceived notions of who I am, and what I do," he begins, and I take a deep breath that's a lot shakier than I wish it to be. "However, I'm likely not what you think. Yes, I came to Earth unannounced, my arrival a disruption to say the least—I realize that now. Some species are not accustomed to extraterrestrials making themselves known as I did. And perhaps I was a little overzealous with my demands. My family runs things the way they do, and I was desperate to impress them.

"When I initially asked for the concessions in exchange for healing this damaged planet—a planet that was one thousand percent headed for a complete climate disaster—I failed to see the impact that had on the Terran population. As the war raged on, I realized that, even though I could simply force my way in and enslave this planet, that would be what my parents would do. What my sister wanted me to do. It wasn't until the Terrans came to me with an offer of a truce that I put my ego aside and did what was best for the planet, not for me. I know not everyone agrees with the deal we made in the Devouring Accords, but Arianyte saved this planet. The air is breathable, and the water is clean, and the oceans are cooling once again. Life is returning to our Earth. And I think that's a beautiful thing, that those once thought dead and gone can be brought back to life."

It sounds nice when he puts it that way. I wonder if it is true for me too?

"But not without a cost of human life in exchange?" I challenge. He's failing to mention that fifteen percent of the population must be handed over to the empire every single year. One of those people is Trinity's mother and Geonni's wife. Little does Malakyte realize the anger he sows so deeply in his enemies by facilitating this trade-off. By taking best friends from little girls that grow up to seek vengeance on their behalf.

Malakyte shrugs. "Nothing is for free, unfortunately. That's the way the galaxy works with us. It's a give-and-take."

"Yet you require the Starseeds and Ringers to work for you for free," I say, and he smirks—almost impressed. *Almost.*

Shockingly, he takes my hand in his as we continue walking down the path towards the restaurant. It's as cold as ice, and I don't know how I feel about the gesture. If I absolutely despise it or feel sort of special.

"I paid Jance considerably to ensure all of you get everything you need. I instructed him specifically to purchase anything you asked for."

I shake my head, knowing he wouldn't get it—rich people never do. "Jance isn't my legal steward, though. He's not saving up money in a vault somewhere for the work I'm doing here to give to me once I turn eighteen. I am also putting hours of work in. I'm training and risking my life for this mission—for you and for Arianyte. I'm missing my real work. I can't tattoo as much because I'm too busy training and learning about this crystal that's inside of me, and I have—" I pause, a suspicion rising as the image of my destroyed loft flashes through my eyes. What if Malakyte's behind the raid? He found my phone number; he could've easily found out where I lived. I've been focusing on Deimos, but it as easily could be him. It's so hard to know when I apparently have so many enemies. He's been suspicious of me, and he'd even have motive to steal my drawings of Gavrielle, with his collection of Ringers and Starseeds, because it sounds like Gavrielle is not within Arianyte's grasp any longer. He could be anywhere. "I have rent I'm supposed to pay for the place I was living before you forced me into that house. And my landlord told me someone broke in while I've been gone, and I have to pay for the damages too." I glance at him, gauging his reaction. He keeps his eyes forward, nodding, contemplative, so I continue. "The risk to my life alone should be worth personal cato credits to me. And the other Starseeds and Ringers. If you're for compensation, then compensate us first."

He stops us, his personal SSPARROW soldiers also stopping a few feet behind. As his dark onyx eyes look at me, I can't help but feel flustered by his gaze. His full attention is intimidating. "You're right," he concedes, and I let go of my breath in relief. He sure isn't acting like a pompous, evil dictator. "I'll have back pay deposited into your account tomorrow morning. All of you. I'm also disturbed to hear about the destruction of your previous home. I'll ensure personally any and all repairs are done promptly. That worries me, and for your safety I'm comforted you're no longer living there."

Shocked at such an easy win, I smile genuinely. "Thanks. I guess that takes a notch off your evil-emperor status."

We both laugh.

"You're cold, Karalevine. Cold as ice."

144

"Not as cold as you."

The emperor shrugs as if to say, 'it's true.'

I have to ask him about Gav, it's now or never. "Can I ask you something? It's a little personal. I hope you don't mind."

"After what I just told you, ask anything you'd like. I haven't felt comfortable enough to open up this much in years. I guess you bring out the vulnerability in me. Perhaps that's why I found you so intriguing from the moment I first saw you."

I had that with someone once, but you took him away from me.

"So, I have this friend, and he and I were separated about six years ago. I haven't been able to find him and it's really important for me to track him down. You're the only one with the power to do that, and I was wondering if I could ask you to help me find him?"

Malakyte seems to consider my request, and moments tick by as I anxiously await his answer.

"For you, I will." I feel elation rush through me at his words. "Find Deimos and bring him to me alive. Then I will find your friend. Deal?"

I deflate a little, but I suppose he wouldn't straight out do me this solid without wanting something in return. So typical.

"It seems like a lot of children like my friend have gone missing," I press, curious what his explanation for the Hijacked would be. "You wouldn't have any information about that, would you?"

"I can't violate the Accords. Arianyte has no access to Earth's children. None. Whatsoever."

Such a diplomatic nonanswer. "Who would stop you, though?"

The ice returns to his eyes as he side-glances at me. "Arianyte keeps its word, my parents ensure that. Violating our agreements with the planets jeopardizes our credibility. And as I told you earlier, my parents dislike me breaching their rules. I wouldn't risk mutiny once again. I'm sure my sister would love it if I did. She's been licking her chops waiting for me to mess up. Does that answer your question?"

The vibe completely shifts and I don't know how to respond. We finally turn onto the bridge that leads into the floating restaurant. Malakyte stops us.

"I told you Deimos is strikingly clever. I wouldn't put it past him to be taking children and selling them on the intergalactic black market.

When a new species becomes sentient to its place in the galaxy, and space travel is accessible, the galaxy at large finds that species much more lucrative because it's new and fresh. I've seen it time and time again. We try stopping it, but there's only so much we can do when criminals work in the shadows. Unfortunately, that means Terrans are highly sought after, and children go for even more credits, more frequently. The dark proclivities of Earth's people are not unique to them alone, I'm afraid."

My stomach flips at that, all appetite seeping into the river.

"I have the entire restaurant cleared out for us tonight." He changes the subject abruptly. "As I mentioned, my apologies for my rush to judgment. I no longer believe you're part of the Resistance, and I hope that this gift shows my sincerest regrets."

He motions to one of his soldiers, and one scurries over to us with a long-shaped case in his hands. I'm a little apprehensive as the faceless soldier holds the case out in front of me.

I look to Malakyte a little hesitantly, and he chuckles, opening the case for me, his long fingers snapping open the locks.

My heart absolutely sings, and I swear my knees go weak.

Holy stars . . .

It's a sword. But this is no ordinary sword. Not by a space-mile.

My heart races as I look at the smooth, elongated edge of its blade. It's not too long or too short for me, but the perfect length. My fingers gently touch the cold handle, and it looks to be made of something similar to rose gold. However, it's no material I've ever seen. The longest part of the handle looks like filigree was melted onto it as I feel the soft, textured edges swirling around it. Anyone with eyes in their skulls can take one look at this thing and see it wasn't made on Earth. The weapon is as alien as the beast swimming inside my heart and the man standing beside me.

"It's so intricate," I breathe as my fingers softly caress over the sharp point of the blade's tip. Pulling it from its case, I'm surprised by its immense weight and stunning quality. I'm afraid I'll drop and break it, so I set it back inside its cushioned home, so mesmerized by it. Held in by this strange fillagree within the cross guard is a fat pink pearl. Or what *appears* to be a pearl. Something seems to swirl within it, a universe all its own with light and stars and shadow existing inside. Flashes of yellow, blue, and purple shine off it, comparable to the actual blade itself.

The blade is a strange black color and shines with an iridescent purple hue when hit by the light. I notice what appears to be cracks within the blade, as if this sword has seen many battles, but it's still polished and shiny and drop-dead gorgeous. It looks to be made of some strange black amethyst crystal.

Carved precisely at the top of the hilt is my Elendril symbol. *The Star.* Two triangles, one pointed up, one pointed down, with a third smaller triangle in the center. My words are hushed as I try to speak its true beauty out into the world, but no words come. Some ethereal, cosmic energy pulls me to it, calling me towards it like a moth to a flame, and my indulgent curiosity resists not an ounce.

The sword is speaking to me, and I am wide-eyed and all ears—dripping on its every word.

And in this moment, the vision I experienced that first night when I looked at Ardelle's crystal flashes into my memory. Why now, why the two feel so familiar and linked together, I don't understand. Brushing the vision and Ardelle from my mind, I turn to Malakyte, smiling widely and genuinely.

"This is the most stunning sword I've ever seen. Honestly, it's gorgeous."

His grin shows all four of his canines. "I'm glad to hear you resonate with it. That doesn't surprise me, because you see, it's your weapon. It's the Star's weapon. They were forged together, somehow. It was created specifically for the person who holds the crystal. For you. The others also have their own weapons. I had them delivered once you left the house, but I wanted to present yours personally."

My eyes snap up to his, the two of us side by side. He smells of citrus and cedar, a hint of wood, strong with a confident power—so much damn power.

And I'm not as disgusted by him as I truly should be.

Darkness loves darkness.

"Why?" I ask, my voice a whisper.

The prince faces me with a powerful stance.

"Because you deserve someone who sees you, Karalevine." He grips my chin softly, his icy touch sending a jolt of goosebumps down my spine as his words warm a part of me I hadn't realized was frozen over this thoroughly.

The cold, dark Prince of Arianyte unlocks a tiny piece of me, and I truly wish he hadn't.

It's a damn shame I'm a rebel spy.

The dinner with the Arianyte prince went better than I had expected, but all I could think the entire time was how bizarre and out of place this entire thing is.

He's the head of the alien occupation I have been fighting the last six years, and I was sitting and having dinner with him. The Resistance would absolutely lose their minds if they ever found out about this. As for me, it was simply surreal.

After Malakyte drops me back off at the house, sword in hand, I stand in my room still dressed in the gown he got for me. Staring at myself in the full-length mirror, I wonder why he sees me the way that he does. Pacey is just as beautiful, just as special. A wicked fighter and far more skilled with her crystal than I am with mine. Yet, Malakyte's focus on me is a treacherous dance I tiptoe around, a constant balancing act where I'm high up between two mountain peaks walking a tight wire with no net below. As alluring as he may be, shattering my expectations of who this person was supposed to be to me—my villain—I'm a lot less sure about that than I was before today. Am I wrong about the Hijacked? Are all the missing children being taken by some other force—like Deimos? I'm aware kids and teens get taken all the time, and it's not necessarily the aliens that do it; however, the number that has gone missing is staggering. Most of them are exactly like me and Gavrielle: homeless, forgotten, parentless. Nobody to come looking for them.

With a population that's so vulnerable to an entity like Arianyte, it's hard for me to think anyone else could be responsible. However, this alternate theory about Deimos is not out of the realm of possibilities, especially with the video footage Pacey and I found. Deimos was hauling children away, and all of this is making me question everything I thought I knew.

Changing quickly, I allow my questions to stay behind with the fancy dress in my bedroom closet, and I make my way downstairs. Everyone is quite curious about how it went and also hyped about our new weapons.

I stop abruptly as I catch Ardelle leaving Pacey's room. The adults aren't stupid; they put the girls' rooms on the complete opposite side of the house from the boys'. So, Ardelle sneaking around his sister's room—like he's up to something bad—is odd.

"What are you doing in her room?" I feign serious authority.

Shaking his head, he rustles his hair nervously. "Well, aren't you glowing. Arianyte turning out to be better than you had anticipated?"

If I were a betting girl, I'd say Ardelle is jealous. "Shocked that someone like me can actually go toe to toe with a guy completely out of your league?"

I can tell by his face that may have been a low blow. "I thought you hated the guy. He's the reason you're here, after all."

"You're the reason I'm here, *after all,*" I mock, crossing my arms defiantly.

Ardelle steps closer to me, so close I can smell his scent, one that's becoming more familiar by the day. Holy stars those arms are pure muscle, and his back is just as built—I've seen it. His energy is so opposite of Malakyte's. I thought I felt arrogance from Ardelle, but I'm starting to see it as something different.

"Maybe I wouldn't regret it so much if you weren't so . . . you. Why do you have to be so combative all the time? I swear, you're like one of those little dogs who thinks they're a big dog, but really, you're just a little dog."

I can't help but laugh incredulously. "Wow."

As I move to walk past him, I bump his shoulder for that little-dog-energy effect.

Ardelle catches my arm gently, stopping me. When I turn my head, our mouths are nearly touching. His eyes seem conflicted, torn between two different forces. Much like him and me, two completely different people from opposite worlds who would never truly see the other for who they really are. That's what I want, I realized thanks to Malakyte—I want to be seen.

Yet the energy that dances between us is the most palpable I've felt thus far. His powerful body towers over me, eyes tilted down to mine, and my heart ticks up only the slightest bit.

"Hey," he whispers softly to me. "You need to be careful. There are things happening that have you in the line of fire, and it's dangerous. Deimos is dangerous."

My brows knit together at his words and I do a double take, but his face is completely serious. Not sure if it's a genuine warning or if he's messing with me, I thank him awkwardly and continue walking downstairs. He follows me past the formal sitting room and into the kitchen, not saying another word until we see the others, but the chill of his words lingers.

Everyone is sitting along the massive white couch and ottoman while watching the giant curved television when we walk in. Something about the uprising with the Reptilians in the undersewers again.

"I'm straight up going to say it first," Sylo begins. He sits next to Pacey, her legs on his lap. "We need to piss off Arianyte more often. These weapons are *sick*."

Jance and Ahren sit side by side on the other side of the couch, which makes half a square shape, and Ardelle lounges in the center, arm stretched wide on the large fluffy pillows that form the back. Guess I'll sit next to him then, closest to Pacey. Saris saunters in after me with a glass of red wine in her hand and sits on the couch's armrest next to Jance, his hand automatically brushing against her back. I wish the two of them would just do it already; it's so obvious they want to.

"Technically we didn't do anything," Pacey makes a point to say. We both smile at each other, knowing the truth. "And they likely were going to give these to us anyway. They were just waiting for *the Star*."

Chuckling at her provocation, I plop down next to Ardelle, and his scent of cinnamon and sage and strength envelop me yet again.

"So, what did everybody get?" I ask, eagerly curious about each of the ancient Elendril weapons we've been given.

Ahren speaks first, his simple and minimal outfit making him look more like the dad of the house than Jance. "Ardelle got an amazing bow and arrow."

"No surprise there," I comment. The light of the TV bounces off his profile. He doesn't look at me.

"My weapon is the coolest," Pacey squeals, both her legs squirming on Sylo's lap as he tries to contain her excitement. "It's a literal sickle."

"Darlin"—Sylo looks over at her affectionately—"contain your excitement, because it's my weapon that's actually the coolest. Tell me, when was the last time you saw a rifle like this one? This girl is sleek and compact despite all her attachments. And do you see the second barrel under the main one? It shoots these amazing orange photon blasts in addition to these self-harnessed bullets. Absolutely outstanding, one hundred percent the best weapon here. I'll fight you over it."

That was pretty cool, but I think I'm with Pacey on this one. A sickle is awesome.

"What was Thumbelina's prize for all the chaos that happened the other week? We noted yours wasn't brought over with ours," Ardelle says, seemingly implying something negative.

Holding my chin high and refusing to let him make me feel less than him, I confidently say, "Yes, Malakyte gave me my weapon personally. It's a sword."

"Well, isn't that fitting?" Jance says before anyone else can. "You're very talented with that type of weapon. All you need to do is familiarize yourself with this blade, its weight and balance and how it moves with you. The rest of you also need to train with your specific weapons and make them your go-to weapon. Such familiarity takes time to acclimate to, so I fully expect all of you to dedicate time to making that a reality. We're all due to be working at the Titan Games parade in two days. The contestants are formally being introduced to the public, and Arianyte wants us introduced as well. We will be there to protect the parade contestants and public onlookers from Deimos specifically. Be prepared for anything."

The training has been rigorous, and because I don't want them to ask too many questions about where and by whom I was trained, I've been holding back. Tonight, Jance and I are in the basement gym alone, working on hand to hand.

"You're small," he tells me as we circle each other on the mats. "That's going to be your biggest disadvantage in combat, but you can learn how to fight smarter regardless of your size. You will be underestimated, but that's a good thing, kid. However, there are certain situations you need to know how to handle to avoid worse, more serious situations."

When Jance comes at me, I'm surprised by how fast he is for his size. I manage to dodge his first grab, but then I realize too late that he's behind me, and I feel his arm hook around my throat. Before I know it, he's pulled me down to the mat, and his large body is fully on top of me.

"Being down on the ground is the worst spot for you to be," he says.

Feeling a bubble of panic well up within my chest, I grit my teeth. "I know."

"Then get out of this hold."

I'm on my back, Jance has my arms pinned above my head as he uses the weight of his body to hold me down. My breaths are coming in short, uneven hitches, and I swear I'm no longer in the basement of his mansion, but inside the small bedroom I lived in when I was nine. On the bed, in the dark . . . completely helpless. Someone else entirely on top of my body.

Jance isn't touching me in any inappropriate way, but that's irrelevant—it's his position in relation to me that's triggered this flashback. Sensing something is wrong, Jance lets go of my arms and sits up, confusion etched into his brow. "Kid, what's wrong? Are you hurt?"

Shaking my head vigorously, I use my hands and shove Jance back farther. "Get off me," I beg, all strength in my voice whittled down to a pathetic whimper.

My Ringer's reaction is immediate, swinging his leg over me and taking several steps away.

You're okay . . . you're okay . . . I try not to let the walls come in on me. *You're safe, it's just Jance. Jance won't hurt you.*

"Breathe, darling. It's alright, just breathe," he says softly, remaining where he stands.

When I finally level out and have the strength to look over at him, his eyes are soft and full of sadness.

"I'm sorry," I tell him, and he begins to move towards me cautiously. I signal with a nod it's safe to approach.

When he sits down across from me, he softly takes my jacket and slides it back onto my shoulders. "Who hurt you?" he asks, and my chin quivers. "Tell me who it was and I'll make sure he never hurts you again."

My eyes snap to his, and the intensity there tells me he means it. He's serious.

"If I told you, you'd want to kill him."

Jance breathes in sharply and rubs his stubbled chin, and I can see the rage bubbling under his skin with the tightening of his body.

Finally, he says, "You know nobody here will ever hurt you, right? I want you—all of you kids—to feel safe here. But your comfort is a priority to me, do you understand? If I or any of the other adults do something that makes you uncomfortable, you tell me, okay?"

I nod, not knowing what to even say to that. I've never had an adult care about how I feel, not even Geonni. And though Geonni himself was never inappropriate, the Resistance is full of sketchy people.

Jance calls it a night and allows me to take my time going upstairs. I can't help but feel a closeness beginning to form with Jance; something I've never felt before with an older man. He continues to prove to me he's safe, and in a world where I've been hunted, abused, forgotten, and abandoned, safety is everything—safety is the very air I breathe.

CHAPTER 20

"You did good getting the UVB drive into Arianyte," Geonni says as the two of us walk through the green garden within the exposed courtyard inside the rebels' hideout. "We were impressed you managed to get it into the Main Outpost building. The amount of data we got is massive."

"And Gav?" I ask hopefully.

The sunlight bounces off Geonni's sunglasses as he shakes his head. "We've only had the data for a few weeks; we're not even done organizing it all. Give me time, Dynamite. I'll find your friend."

Dynamite. He's been calling me that since I was twelve—for obvious reasons.

He stops us as we approach a wooden bench hidden away off the main path in the garden, the sound of the fountain gurgling in the distance and birds chirping the only sounds. "There is something we have begun looking into, however, and I think it pertains to you. Please, sit down."

Geonni is wearing a Moss Green three-piece suit, a satin Grape Juice Purple undershirt with a white bowtie. Even his cufflinks shine with a pristine golden sheen. As we sit side by side, my curiosity blooms at what he's discovered. The info better be good because I risked my and Pacey's lives for it.

"Have they told you anything about something called an Elendril crystal?" he asks, and I deflate.

My gaze lowers to my lap, where I notice the acrylic nail on my ring finger missing. "Yes," I admit. "It's what this mark on my chest is called. So, you know all about it then? Who else knows?"

"Trinity, of course. A few of the higher-ups."

"Geonni . . ." I tap my nails together compulsively in fear of what could happen if this information got out. "Telling a bunch of people puts me in danger; it puts others in danger."

Geonni placates me with a shake of the head in the way he always does when he knows he's in the wrong but won't admit it. "I'll always protect you; you know that. And who cares about those others; they're working for the enemy, and they've got some of the strongest weapons known to the galaxy sitting inside their hearts. They're dangerous. We should kill them now while we have the chance. Steal those crystals and use them against Arianyte."

True fear shoots through me like a lightning bolt. "You can't be serious? They're just kids."

Shrugging, he doesn't seem like he thinks it's a bad idea. When I continue to glare at him, he waves me off. "I'm kidding, I'm kidding. No violence, I remember. But there is something you can do for me."

My belly does a flip-flop at that.

"Apparently, Arianyte has one of these crystal things hanging out in Arianyte Tower. The data seems to say it's within the leader's penthouse office in some super technological hidey-hole. Go get it for me, my little spymaster."

I had no idea how I was supposed to get inside Arianyte Tower to search for the remaining Elendril crystal when I caught a lucky break. Malakyte's impromptu training session demand happens to coincide with Geonni's request that I try and bring him the last crystal. The timing couldn't be more perfect, and I must find it. I cannot fail.

Although, this small bit of luck only gets me inside the building, and that's where my luck officially ends.

As I stand outside the imposing building of Arianyte Tower, the tallest in the city, I feel infinitesimally small.

Stars almighty . . . Cranking my neck back, I can't see where the matte black building ends and the clouds begin. Most of the building is encased in that matte black shell, almost like armor. The parts that do peek through are levels upon levels of whatever suspicious and illegal workings Arianyte engages in on the daily. Sky-hovers pitter around the tower like massive birds, scooting past giant advertisement screens from adjacent buildings.

The clanking of high heels on the black marble flooring greets me as I enter the tower, and an extra woman with white skin approaches me.

"Miss Ruzz, there you are." She grabs both my hands and brings them to her cheek, her teeth yellow against her skin color. What a strange greeting, must be normal on her home planet. "Mr. Ardeen has been expecting you. He wanted to inform you that he's running a bit late on a call, and that he'll be right with you. I'm to escort you upstairs to his quarters."

As the extra and I walk across the lobby floor, many other species of extraterrestrials scurry by on their way to accomplish their tasks for the day. The building is all sleek corners, harsh edges, and moody lighting as we approach a sophisticated elevator that's completely made of clear blue-tinted glass. It shoots us upwards at a smooth pace as I watch the lobby get smaller and smaller, the aliens below beginning to look more like ants by the time we reach the very top levels.

The elevator chimes a pleasant sound indicating 'Penthouse Level One' has been reached. I see, so Malakyte has several penthouse floors—he would.

The floor beyond is a white hallway lined with plants and alien greenery on both sides. Whatever official business that goes on below is separate from the penthouse floors because I can't hear or see any proof that the lower floors exist.

I'm taken down several hallways that look identical to each other until we stop at a door at the end of a hallway.

"Here we are," the alien woman announces as she uses a hand scanner to open a door. Maybe this will be Malakyte's office?

Once inside, I instantly realize it's far too basic to be where Malakyte does his work. It's an average sitting room, with a couple oversized chairs, a small bar and kitchen, and a television on mute mounted to the corner.

The assistant proceeds to tell me Malakyte will be right with me, but I know if I'm going to try and find this crystal, I can't get locked in here.

"What if I have to pee?" I ask as she's about to close the door, leaving me alone.

Looking surprised, she asks, "Oh, do you need me to escort you to a restroom, Miss Ruzz?"

Stars, no. "Actually, no. So silly of me; I actually am on my period. It's this thing Terran woman get once a month where—"

"I know of the Terran menstrual cycle, Miss Ruzz," she says, and I see the doubt in the woman's eyes. She's likely been told not to let me roam around freely.

"Great. Yeah, having to explain that to the Prince of Arianyte would be like, *super embarrassing.*"

I try to play it off shyly, hoping the blush in the cheeks comes off as innocent rather than suspicious. Sighing, I'm not sure if I've convinced her.

"Each door has a different code as a backup, so if you must leave, it's seventy-nine, thirty-two. The restroom is just around the corner to the left."

Smiling, I bashfully clap my hands together. "Thank you for understanding."

"Mr. Ardeen will be with you shortly."

Then I'm alone.

I let a few minutes pass before I cautiously open the door, peeking my head outside. My eyes bounce over the immaculate white walls and distinguished art pieces.

Utterly silent.

I stay close to the wall as I peer around each corner. If I were Malakyte Ardeen's office, where would I be? This penthouse floor is a maze, each hallway looking identical to the other, and I'm beginning to worry I won't know how to find my way back to the initial room.

I test a few random doors, all locked and equipped with the same handprint scanner my room was outfitted with. I can pick nearly any lock (yet another dishonorable skill the Resistance taught me), but I don't want to spend my precious time picking locks to doors I'm not even sure are Malakyte's office. Each of these doors looks the same, a light-colored wood with silver knobs, and that's too basic for Malakyte. From what I can tell of him and his style, he likes things to be exceptional in how they're presented. He may be the Prince of Arianyte, but he does have style.

After several tense moments of wandering around, it's clear I'm completely lost.

This is stupid. I should turn back. Geonni is going to have to suck it: I don't know what to tell him.

As I begin to turn back, I realize I've taken a wrong turn, and I don't know how to get back.

No, I knew this was going to happen.

I'll retrace my steps; surely that'll work. However, I end up finding myself just as turned around as ever, my anxiety growing with each passing minute. I don't want to lose Malakyte's trust again, and he'll suspect me if he finds me wandering around all by myself.

Then I stop in my tracks when something catches my eye. Well, well, well . . . what do we have here?

Standing fifty feet away is a shiny black door, completely different from every other door on this floor.

No time to waste.

I make it there in no time, pressing my ear against the black wood to ensure Malakyte isn't inside.

Nothing.

Bending to one knee, I pull my lockpick kit from my purse, a personal invention and gift from Geonni. Guaranteed to pick nearly any lock, including alien locks integrated with systems like this one. It's half a traditional lock pick and half a digital hack. It's never failed me, and today is no exception.

I'm in.

Swiftly, I slide inside and know immediately I'm in the right place.

The room is large, with a huge black desk sitting to the left of the space while a fancy rug sits underneath chairs and a coffee table to the right. It's all clean and modern, with bold black accents and odd shapes. But I'm not here for the décor; I'm here for the crystal.

I go to the desk first and notice immediately that the drawers all have fingerprint access, something my tool can't crack due to the different tech.

Moving on, I check behind every painting and wall fixture; nothing but bare wall hides behind them. The floor-to-ceiling bookcase on the far wall has more knickknacks than books, but I don't notice any hidden compartments or doorways.

Where the hell is it?

Chewing on my lip, I stand there, unsure where else to look. Geonni said the hack produced a tip that said the crystal was in a special hiding place within the prince's office. Looking around, I don't see any special place it could be. Scanning the room, I suddenly notice something I hadn't before, and I freeze in terror. Is that a damn camera up in the corner?

Oh shit.

Oh shit, oh shit, oh *shit*.

Turning, I check the opposite corner, and sure enough, another odd-looking device is mounted up there, pointing directly into the center of the room. I find a third and fourth in the other corners as well.

Well, that's rather odd. Why have four? Is he that paranoid?

I'm already caught and majorly screwed, so I sneak up under one with the help of Malakyte's desk chair and get a closer look at it.

There's no lens. Unless I can't see behind a lens cover or something? When I tap a tiny button on the side, a red laser shoots out from the center of the cylindrical shaft, stopping in the dead center of the room instead of on the opposite wall like it should.

What in Jupiter's rings?

When I examine the laser beam closer, it's almost like it hit an invisible wall right in the center of the room, hovering eight feet in the air. There's something weird going on here.

Hurriedly, I wheel the chair to the other side of the room, hopping on top and pushing the button on the other device mounted in the corner. It too shoots a red beam, and it does the exact same thing as the first one did. Except this time, a form in the center of the room begins to come into shape, and I quickly do the same with the other two devices. It's pretty clear at this point that they're not cameras.

When the last beam hits the center point, a full cube is lit up in red light, like the lasers had manifested it out of thin air.

Taking the chair and wheeling it directly under, I climb up, wobbling as I have to stretch super high in order to reach it. My hand hits some cold material, and the cube instantly glitches and shifts into a solid object. A hidden safe.

Holy alien shitballs.

This has to be what the stolen intel was referring to.

Though my excitement instantly deflates when I notice the most sophisticated fingerprint scanner I've ever seen on the safe, and there's no way for me to crack it open. I'm so close; I've got to get into it.

Think Kara, think.

Time is ticking by. Malakyte will kill me if he catches me in here; there's no doubt. No excuse I can come up with will get me out of this one. My heart rate ticks up, and panic begins to flare.

I can't exactly cut the guy's finger off and put it up to this scanner, now, can I?

I gasp, hopping off the chair so fast it swivels, and I almost eat shit upon my landing. Rushing over to his desk, I rip off a piece of tape from the dispenser sitting there. My smile is glorious as I bend down to his locked drawers, carefully placing the sticky side of the tape on one of the fingerprint scanners. Slowly, I press my thumb into it and softly remove the tape from the scanner.

My squeal is full of excitement as I lift the perfect impression of his fingerprint with a single piece of tape.

I return to the safe, praying to the stars this works. Folding the tape around my thumb for warmth, I press the sticky end into the safe's fingerprint scanner, and it feels like I'm pressing my thumb into jelly.

A light begins to emit as it starts to scan, a soft beeping noise follows, and for a few tense seconds, I don't even breathe.

Then the safe opens with a chime.

Malakyte Ardeen, the Prince of Arianyte, and all his fancy technology gets foiled by a Terran girl and a piece of old-world tape.

What a sucker.

And when I finally peer inside the safe, I freeze.

What the hell is this?

Sitting cold between my fingers is a large vial filled with some sort of blue substance.

And that's all that is inside the safe.

No Elendril crystal, only a stupid vial.

This entire thing was for nothing.

Screw this.

I throw the vial back in the safe, not risking my life over something Geonni didn't even ask for. It takes me a few minutes to figure out how to shut off the lasers and get the safe to become invisible again, but it finally vanishes back into its mysterious hiding place.

I peek out the door before making a quick dash back down the hall, my crystal's mark tingling with fear that Malakyte could be around any corner, ready to throw me back into confinement and completely erase my memory. There's still no solution for the fact that I don't know my way back to that room, and every second I waste running around out here is one where Malakyte can be walking towards the room I'm supposed to be in.

It's all a blur as I run down hallway after hallway when finally, I spot the elevator. *Yes!* I know the way from here.

"I'm almost to her room," I hear a voice say coolly from somewhere near, and I know it's Malakyte. "Yes, she's here alone."

Who is he talking to?

Who cares, you idiot, *go!*

Heart hammering, I make it to the final hallway and sprint towards the room. It's a long way to go, and Malakyte isn't far behind me. I slam into the door, fingers trembling as I punch in the code.

It's wrong.

I punch it in again, still wrong.

What was the code again? Thirty-nine, seventy-two? No, the seven came first. Seventy-three, twenty-nine? *Shit.*

Malakyte's footsteps clank nearer; he's got to be right around the corner.

Oh, my stars, how could you have forgotten the code, you damn idiot?

I'm dead, I'm *dead.*

Seventy-nine, thirty-two!

The door unlocks and I gasp, shoving my way inside before the door even opens. It takes everything not to slam it shut, and I throw myself onto one of the chairs and try to force my breaths to slow.

Two seconds later, I hear the scanner beeping, and Malakyte Ardeen enters the room.

"It's about time," I deadpan, uncrossing my legs as I stand to greet him. "I was beginning to think you forgot about me."

When he smiles, I see one set of his pointed canines. He looks good when he smiles like that.

"My apologies for burdening you with such a lofty wait. If it makes up for it, there's no forgetting about you."

Don't buy it; it's all bullshit, I order myself, but I'm finding that harder to do than I should.

"Well, I'm here now, and I want to see what you can do, Miss Ruzz."

After taking me to another floor that is basically a bomb shelter, Malakyte watches as I use my crystal's power. It's hard to hold it back, even harder to rein it in as he watches almost lustfully at my display of power. After an hour passes, all my power is completely stripped from me.

"I can't go on," I say, chest rising and falling rapidly as I take a seat on the hard, fire-retardant ground, the mark still burning from use.

Malakyte takes a seat next to me; he's closer than I would've liked.

"Drink this," he says, handing me a cold bottle of water, and I gulp it down desperately. "Why do you fear your power so much?"

I blink, feeling like his question came out of nowhere. He's got a bad habit of terrible segueing like he simply doesn't know how to talk to people. But I suppose the language barrier between alien species is a little rough.

"I'm not."

He gazes down at me skeptically. "I can see your hesitation every time you use your crystal. It's painfully obvious, I'm afraid. That hesitation can make the difference between life and death in many instances, and I'd hate for that uncertainty to cause you harm."

"Why do you even care?" I ask before I can think longer about the question. He's borderline obsessed with me and it makes no sense.

Shrugging, he nudges his shoulder against mine, his skin cooling the sweat on my body. "I like you, isn't that obvious? You intrigue me. You're so different from anyone else I've ever met before, and trust me, I've been to many planets in my life."

I can't help but blush, and it's crazy to me someone with so much power sees *me*, of all people. I want to hate it so much, but I don't.

Malakyte reaches his hand over and cups my chin, drawing my face towards his to look him in the eyes.

"Why are you afraid of your power?" he asks again, not allowing me any space to hide.

"Because I fear it makes me a monster." My voice is a hushed, too raw, too honest whisper, and I wonder if it's the first time I've admitted the truth to myself, let alone another person. "And I don't know if that's what I want to be anymore."

"Anymore?"

"I'm not sure you'd like me if you knew the things I've done," I confess, almost hoping it turns him off.

His skin is so smooth, a porcelain veneer that's practically poreless and such an odd color that he looks almost like a corpse prince.

Inching even closer, he says softly, "I'm the king of making poor choices in the past, and if I can learn to forgive myself, so can you."

Those dark eyes show something dangerously close to humanity, and it surprises me each time I see a small piece of his social mask fall, and he chooses to drop it for me. As his hand softly caresses my arm, I lean in, ignoring all the warning bells.

"Do you really think I can learn to forgive myself?" I ask vulnerably, and to my surprise, the Prince of Arianyte takes me in his arms and wraps me in a cold embrace. I should thrash and fight to get out of it, blast him to high heaven and race out of here and far away from this city. But instead, I lean into his firm chest and feel more heat than ever before.

"I think you can do anything you set your mind to," he tells me, and it makes me smile because I want to believe him.

CHAPTER 21

Never have I ever been paraded around like a show horse. The days of me being a forgotten and invisible orphan are long gone. Since being forced onto this Starseed team, I've become the one everyone is looking at.

Stars, this cannot be happening.

My mark tingles with nerves as my fellow Starseeds and our three Ringers stand beside a pop-up stage that's been erected near the starting point of the Titan Games parade route. We're deep within the city, surrounded by gigantic buildings that stand watch over the subjects of the alien occupation and were built off the backs of the unfortunate Terran Tributes. The day is sunny but ice cold.

The parade is an annual celebration thrown specifically to introduce the Titan Games' champions in person to the public for the very first time. If you make it into the games, you become an instant celebrity. The audition process alone is as intense as some challenges in the games, which are different every single year. It's a mash-up of the old-world Olympic Games and martial arts tournaments, and the entire world gets involved. It's held in Zarmenia every year, and the stadium Arianyte built specifically for it is as enormous as the games themselves.

I personally don't get the point of it. Why people risk their lives for one measly shot at incredible fortune and a ticket onto the Azurite Fleet, I wouldn't know. I suppose I can see the lure on that last bit. If you get the credits and the incredibly rare opportunity to actually get to the city that's inside the Azurite Fleet, you can go anywhere in the galaxy—and many people want off this planet altogether. It's never something I would do, but I suppose I can see why it's alluring. Plus, nothing entices the people more than to watch the violence.

We stand in front of Arianyte Tower. If the outpost Pacey and I hit was the brain of the city and Arianyte, this tower would be its heart. I shy away from my time in that sleek, mysterious building. A huge polished-stone driveway leads up to the building's entrance. We stand at the end of it by the street.

"Hurry up, now." A woman with snow-white skin, wearing a pantsuit I'd color with Dragon Fruit Fuchsia and hair to match, fusses over each of the Starseeds in turn as we stand in wait to be officially shown off to the entire world. Her lipstick and eyeshadow are also a watermelon shade of pink. The accessories on her body are all gold, including an elaborate headband that crosses her forehead and dangles in front of her Flamingo Pink eyebrows. An extra, from somewhere flamboyant.

She spends the next twenty minutes rearranging where we should stand in front of the stage and how we should pose until finally she has me standing between Ardelle and Sylo, with Pacey on her brother's other side.

Then Malakyte Ardeen arrives on scene.

I need to remind myself that he's the person I'm actively taking down and I shouldn't be excited to see him.

Unfortunately, Malakyte brought his wicked-horned comrade, Naresteé, along for the show today. The two of them are dressed impeccably, as usual. Naresteé sports a flawless ivory pantsuit that contrasts heavily with her blue-green skin. Malakyte wears all black yet again. An attached black cape billows behind him like a constant wave made of shadow, all that power and strength converging like he is the ocean himself.

Because we all knew we'd be revealed to the public today, we each dressed our best while keeping in mind we're also here as security detail, an elite group of fighters here for one person and one person only: Deimos.

Malakyte's eye catches mine as he approaches us, Naresteé on his heels looking annoyed as ever. Was it the constant stick up her ass that made her act this way, or merely her lack of personality?

"I'm happy to see you all sporting your weapons so eloquently," Malakyte says. Each of us carry the Elendril weapons on our bodies. Mine is strapped to my back by a wine-colored leather strap. My outfit is intricate, yet simplistic. I wear burgundy tights with lace-up, knee-high boots polished to perfection, but my coat is the real centerpiece. It's a long wool coat with a plated leather epaulet going up the center of my chest to my neck, spanning out onto my shoulders in a layered pattern that creates a wing-like effect. The leather continues as a short corset around my waist, flaring out the bottom of the coat as it goes from short in the front to long in the back. And of course, it has pockets.

Ardelle's bow and arrows are strapped to his back as well, his outfit battle-ready leather mixed with an asymmetrical rough-and-tumbled style that's also refined and put together. Sylo sports high-top sneakers that are studded with copper spikes, with his large, barreled gun clipped onto his hip. Pacey is a glam princess in her iridescent shifting overalls, paired with a see-through PVC fabric jacket that also shifts colors depending on the light and how she stands. Her hair is now Royal Blue, which matches the keychains, charms, and girly accessories she tied to the top of her massive sickle where the blade meets the long, intimidating handle. The blade of her sickle is also black, but it has a light sky-blue hue to it— exactly the color of her crystal. The other weapons were made of the same material as mine, yet anything that happened to be that black-metal material had a hint of each of our crystal's colors in it. They're all the same, yet different.

"I think we all look pretty badass," I say with a smile, the others nodding in agreement. It's sort of amazing to truly feel like I belong, and for the first time in my life I'm not a total outcast.

"Couldn't agree more." Malakyte spreads an arm out wide towards the makeshift stage. "Let's show the world how amazing my new Starseed team is."

Then the news cameras and Network influencers and anyone who's anyone arrive to snap pictures and yell questions at us. The entire event is a blur. Malakyte speaks enthusiastically and charmingly behind us up on the platform, and I try to keep my smile genuine, but the reality begins to hit me hard when my name is shouted for the hundredth time from the aggressive paparazzi.

"My Star, Karalevine Ruzz. My Archer, Ardelle Dawson; my Nature Princess, Pacey Dawson; and my Gunslinger, Sylo Torres."

I don't like how he's releasing our full identities, and I look over to Ardelle standing rigidly beside me. What if his parents see this? I mean, they're going to eventually. I'm surprised neither Pacey nor Ardelle has mentioned this concern; they must be worried. I am worried. What if some of the Resistance members don't know what I'm doing here? My cover can get blown extremely fast. The likelihood of that is shockingly high, and it's caused me anxiety since finding out about this ridiculous Starseed team reveal party. I'm clearly not the only one who's worried about being seen, but how can we say no to this? The two of us are trapped in this game, and we've got to play it, regardless of its dangers.

This has gone way, way too far. What the hell am I doing? I'm standing up here as a spy for the Resistance, while at the same time getting introduced to the world as a member of an elite Arianyte squad. Any number of slip-ups, mistakes, or walks into the wrong lie at the wrong time can get me killed. It's all I can think of while cameras flash and recording drones fly around, filming every angle of my face.

Even though he's irritating, I'm slightly comforted by Ardelle's presence next to me. He must've noticed me staring, needing to focus on something other than the literal mob before us, and he looks down at me. It's minute, but his mouth ticks up slightly. Pretending to adjust his stance, his arm brushes against mine. I barely feel it through the thickness of my coat, but the small gesture is clear. Despite the two of us being at each other's throats most of the time—at least in this moment—we're on this crazy ride together.

And he's not a complete dick.

I'm in my head the entire press conference, and when it's over and Malakyte is distracted, I take a rare opportunity I've been dying to take a crack at.

Narasteé is standing silently, her predatory stillness otherworldly. When I walk up onto the platform to meet her, she scowls with irritation.

"What?" she asks before I can say anything. I'm not sure what she does for Malakyte, but her body is built like a tank, and being this close to her, I see she's a beautiful, haunting beast. There's no doubt in my mind that she's deadly, and Malakyte's second for a lethal reason.

"I want to know where Gavrielle Abraxas went after you kidnapped him from the orphanage they named after you. Remember? That was the night I—"

"I remember what you did to me that day, you uncontrollable little monster," she hisses, sharp canines bared against her black lips.

I twitch my head at her abrupt attack, and even though she's trying to hide them, I can still see the scars I gave her on her neck. Did I end up inadvertently blasting Naresteé *twice*? Is that why she's this way towards me?

"Wow, you went from typical stuck-up bitch to a complete psycho in less than five seconds. Impressive."

Probably not the best way to find Gav, you idiot, I blast myself, letting my anger get the best of me. I hate her, I fricking hate this chick. She took him, she knows where he is—why won't she tell me? Why did Connar and Dimitri have to lose her? I could know where he is by now and wouldn't be stuck in this stupid situation. It's all so impossibly frustrating.

Naresteé looks down at me, those Black Cherry eyes ablaze with fire from within like a volcano biding its time to erupt. "You're nothing but a little pawn to him," her sweet voice informs me, and I'm assuming she's talking about Malakyte. "Enjoy the fanfare and the pretty dresses and attention for now, because someday soon, you're going to wish you were back in that gutter we pulled you out of."

She leaves, bumping my shoulder with hers as she goes.

"I'm going to find him," I say to her as she bounces down the steps, but she continues walking away. "And you're going to regret ever taking him from me. You better pray he's still alive."

She doesn't look back. My glower burns a hole in the back of her head, and I hope it'll spontaneously combust from mere hatred alone. She knows what happened to him, that witch, and is intentionally keeping it from me.

I'm left there, angry and feeling exposed on the top of the little platform, her words a demonic haunting inside my mind.

Cursing myself, I wish so badly—with so much boiling pain and hatred in my heart it's like ground meat—that Gavrielle was here with me.

CHAPTER 22

ARIANYTE DUBS THE SOLAR SYSTEM THAT'S HOME
TO EARTH "THE AURORA SYSTEM." THIS INCLUDES
ALL OFF-EARTH COLONIES, BASES, STATIONS, AND
SHIPS RESIDING WITHIN. ITS BORDERS END PAST THE
ASTEROID BELT'S EDGES.

"I'm going to be the first one to say that Arianyte is nuts for hosting the Titan Games parade with Deimos running around. Are they asking for a mass-casualty event?" Pace drawls as each of us approach the blockaded streets once the press has finally been shooed off.

"Don't talk like that. Arianyte might throw you in a dungeon for the day," Sylo says with a laugh.

I typically wouldn't find that funny, but it reminds me of *him*. "That is totally something Gav would say."

Pacey smiles sadly at me. "You're going to find him. I know it."

At least one of us is hopeful.

Pace doesn't let up, however, and her glossy lips purse in annoyance. "All jokes aside, I think with Deimos hanging around, it's a bad idea. Not to mention there's rumors the Resistance is hanging about."

"We were instructed to focus solely on Deimos," Jance reminds us all, which for me is fabulous because I do not want any interaction with the Resistance today. I highly doubt they'd even be here.

A SSPARROW approaches us, and it actually makes me squirm at its close proximity. Then I see Sylo run towards him and embrace the soldier. Seconds after, they proudly walk arm in arm towards us.

"Dad"—Sylo opens his arms towards the group of us—"this is my new team I told you about. The ones I'm living with."

"I've heard great things about you all," the man says, the mask not distorting his voice; there must be a button for that or something. He's differentiated from the other soldiers by the red lights on his uniform, matching the Arianyte logo painted on in several places like the back, shoulders, and back of the helmet. "I'm told you all will help my son become a righteous soldier like his old man. Couldn't be prouder."

This takes me aback. I know Sylo supports the SSPARROWs because of his father, but I didn't think he wanted to be one.

When I look over at my fellow Starseed's face, he's smiling, not with beaming pride or excitement but with unease. As if this is his father's goal, not his. This makes me wonder if he truly desires this path or not.

Sylo's dad continues: "They've assigned me to show you where you'll be stationed today. Our Champions will enter through block A-2." He points to a laminated map. "And they'll finish at block K-4. Once there, a SSPARROW squad will escort them to their private sky-hover to be transported back to an undetermined secure location. We want at least two of you on that escort, and traveling the parade route alongside them. I'll take my boy along with Saris at the parade's starting line. In addition, Kara, Jance, and Ardelle will take the first section. Pacey and Ahren will walk the route's second segment. You know your priorities. Don't engage with the fans, they're a bit unstable."

From what I could tell, Sylo would do almost anything to live up to his father's standards. Did he truly believe in 'Arianyte Strong'—a common slogan amongst the faithful—or did he only want his dad's eyes to look upon him with pride and admiration? The way he talks about him, you'd think Sylo's dad was a god or something. The way Sylo tries to pull it off is that he's the golden boy, but I think it's far from true. What does it truly mean to betray your own race by working for the alien occupation that demands literal human sacrifices? And I can't be called a hypocrite because I'm not doing this for real. I am an actress and this entire charade is my stage, which reminds me of Narestée's words and how soon they may ring true.

Given our tasks and knowing our jobs, we browse the parade route looking into vendor tents while waiting to be signaled that the parade is starting up.

I separate myself from the others, needing to decompress from the intensity of our reveal. Almost every other second, a person walks by and says hello or ogles one of us, and I find it highly annoying. All adults and Pacey and Sylo mingle with the SSPARROW soldier who is a father under that oppressive metal armor. They look happy, all of them smiling and laughing like nothing is amiss. It's hard to imagine that each SSPARROW has a family. They're someone's parent, someone's brother, sister, friend, or lover. It's hard to villainize them when I look at them that way, but how many times in history have atrocities been committed on the mere notion of simply following orders? When do their culpability and accountability begin and end for the things they're ordered to do by the people in power?

Ardelle's powerful body comes and stands beside me. I turn to look at him, but he continues to stare straight ahead at the others, lost in his own thoughts.

I go back to watching the others, too, seeing Jance's face panic for a split second when he doesn't locate me at first.

"It's the Ringer and Starseed bond that makes Jance so protective of you. Ahren is the same way with me," Ardelle says when we both see Jance's posture relax as he waves at us. I never see Jance falter or flail; he's as steady as they come, except when it comes to me. "Jance was going to have a kid once, so that could also be a contributing factor. It didn't happen."

My eyes widen in surprise as pain fills my chest. What a horrific thing to go through. No wonder he's so protective and always there.

Silence passes between us as we continue watching them. "What happened to them?" I whisper, seeing the pain on Ardelle's face, and I don't know why I'm confounded by his empathy. Perhaps because it doesn't quite fit in with the guy I've constructed in my mind.

"His wife and nine-month-old fetus were murdered."

My face is a porcelain portrayal of pure disgust. "What the hell?"

He fans a hand through his hair, grimacing when he instantly hits a wall of hair product he spent too long putting on this morning.

"Yeah, I know . . . It's awful. I don't know how the man survived after that."

My throat tightens and I feel prickling behind my eyes, unable to imagine the type of pain he must feel, and how that would never leave, no matter how many years went by. I'd know. It's easy to wonder why Jance was a jerk sometimes. The world especially forces men to hide how they truly feel, even if it's the most horrendous pain imaginable.

"They were going to have a daughter," Ardelle continues, and I connect the dots. Somewhere in him, whether it be our Starseed and Ringer connection or simply his instinct to protect, Jance sees his little girl in me. He's a father without a daughter, and I'm a girl without a father. If the shoe fit, I suppose I'd let it. Although, I fear it'll all get taken from me like everything else I've ever cared about has. Given my current path, it's going to.

"Are you worried that your parents are going to see all this footage of you and Pacey? Aren't they looking for you guys?"

Ardelle shifts on his feet uncomfortably, looking around as if they'd be behind the next performer on high stilts.

"I'm surprised you care, Thumbelina," Ardelle muses. "Malakyte has promised we'll be protected, but yes, their goons are everywhere."

I take a deep, concerned breath in. Their situation sucks. "But you want to go back home . . .?"

"If I can find a way to remove our crystals, then yes. And I'll find a way. Nothing is impossible."

This again. Why does he keep saying that if the crystal was gone then he'd be able to go home? It won't help their overarching problem, but he doesn't seem to see that. "What if nothing changes and you gave up the crystals for nothing?"

Ardelle faces me, the arrows in his quiver clacking against each other. It's as if he's never considered this before. "Then I'd have made a terrible mistake."

Silence falls between us. Air charged with worry and hope and sadness all wrapped up into one big mess. I see the pain in him, beyond this mask he's been forced to wear—to hide behind. What of my own mask?

"Go be with them," he suggests, feigning another look around, eyes constantly searching for anything or anyone out of place. "I'll keep an eye out until things start."

Instead of being the outcast I always am, I do what he suggests and don't regret doing so as I join the others.

I can't help but wear a stupid grin as we all laugh and spend time with the vendors before the parade starts. For those few moments, I don't think about Arianyte or the Resistance or Deimos, I don't care that I'm rubbing elbows with a SSPARROW sky-rat, I'm enjoying the moment.

Jance buys me a deep-fried gray alien, its bulbous head smothered in cinnamon sugar. He showers me with his attention, and a part of me loves that attention like a drug. The other part of me fears it like one would a plague. This isn't the first time I've gotten male attention. The last one who set his eyes on me, he destroyed me in ways I couldn't repair. Fundamentally broke the person I was, and the girl who came out of that bedroom was never the same as the one who went in it. So, despite how good Jance makes my daddy issues feel, I keep a watchful eye. Neither Jance nor Ahren give me that inappropriate creeper vibe. However, you can never truly trust anyone. People are going to be out for themselves in the end.

Ahren's eyes catch mine as he looks around the crowd. "Have you seen Ardelle?"

"I haven't in the last twenty minutes. I thought he'd be off lurking around, brooding over his hair gel. He couldn't have gone far," I say, watching as the first float appears from around the corner. He's disappeared again? He does this at night, too, lurking off when he thinks nobody is looking.

"It's time for us to work now," Jance says, but he looks at me for emphasis. "Stay close and be diligent, everyone."

We split up to our designated places, Ardelle still nowhere to be found. The parade passes us by uneventfully, each Titan on display as they pass the array of passionate fans who scream for them and for Arianyte. Waving to the crowd of adoring fans, the Titans smile from ear to ear, soaking in their newfound celebrity. Their gratification makes me sick. The Titan Games are a distraction—a money making, gluttonous, and exploitive tool of Arianyte to tighten their grip on the Terran public.

Once the final Titan contestant passes our post without incident, I find it rather disrespectful Ardelle ditched us. He isn't even answering our calls. So much for being Mr. Punctual.

I let Jance know I'm going to search for the little princess, and I slither through the crowd. Perhaps I'll drop in on the tattoo shop. I was thrilled to see Malakyte made good on his promise to pay us all, and we each woke up with a considerable number of credits in our individual accounts. To everyone's applause, I might add, and I made sure to give myself all the credit for this win.

Geonni's been giving me vague threats about replacing me with another apprentice since I'm never there anymore, but neither is he. Both of us have rebel work that's more important, but I've been concerned that he hasn't responded to my message about what happened at Arianyte Tower the other day with the whole Elendril crystal mission failure and all.

The people I pass are sporting masks of contestants poised to win the games. Kids chase each other with foam swords and shields and an array of Arianyte propaganda disguised as merchandise. They even have the Arianyte logo on lollipops, I mean, when does it end? Stars . . .

Excited that I see Sadie the dog sitting on her typical street corner, I quickly buy a burger and feed it to her. She licks her chops gingerly as if she hadn't eaten in days, and I get the insane idea that she should come home with us. I should probably ask Jance first, although I feel it's likely better to ask forgiveness than permission, so I nod my head forward and she prances along in step at my side.

I'm a half block from the tattoo shop as the parade continues down the street (still no sign of Ardelle) when suddenly I'm bumped harshly from the side. Immediately, my mind goes to Deimos, and I feel like an idiot for letting my guard down. However, I have no time for self-deprecation and I reach for my sword. My hand slows when standing there, barely three feet tall, is a little girl.

"Can you help me? I'm lost," says the sweet child's voice from beside me, her face partially blocked by a large white hat. I pat Sadie as she begins growling at the girl, trying to hush the dog's snarls.

"Sure, honey. Where are your parents?" I ask kindly, bending at the waist.

She raises her face to me, and my blood chills faster than if I'd been struck by lightning.

The sweet face framed by honey-blond curls and bright-pink ribbons, standing in a pair of pink overalls and snuggled in a white fur coat, is more frightening than any demon. A green blaze is emanating from within her soul, gleaming in shade Forest Floor.

My mind is slapped blank.

I cannot cut this girl down with my sword. Cannot blast her to high hell with my crystal. I cannot beat Deimos out of her.

What can I do?

"What's wrong?" she asks innocently, but her grin has my blood turning to ice like Malakyte's. I back up with panic, bumping into the snarling dog and wanting to get her terrifying face and the distorted features out of my mind.

The feeling of Deimos is back in full force, pulling at my gut relentlessly. That petrifying, helpless terror from the vision the night of the Capitol building is back, and it's threatening to tremble my bones to dust.

He's close.

Before I can answer, the little girl pushes a beautifully wrapped present into my hands. It's a white square box. The ribbon wrapped around it is a fluffy baby pink material tied in an enormous bow at the top. Stunned by the fact Deimos would do this to a little girl, I automatically take the present.

The little girl skips away, seemingly without a care in the world as her blond curls bounce out of view. Although, the dread that I feel from Deimos only grows stronger with every skip she makes. I whip my head wildly as I look around for him. Staying here around all these people, with what could be anything within this box, is an incredibly stupid idea.

I dart into the street, practically colliding with a parade float as I bolt right out in front of it. There is no time to call for help: the parade will end in minutes. Carrying the present close to my chest, I run, Sadie hot on my heels. There could be a bomb in this box, poison, or several deadly mechanisms designed to maim or kill.

Deimos is here, and he's playing one hell of a deadly game.

CHAPTER 23

The images of what can possibly happen are flashing into my mind as I swerve through the crowd. People are everywhere, each one a potential enemy I can't fight.

"Open it," says a woman in Mustard Yellow pants and Forest Green coat as she passes me. I jump in surprise, hating that a shriek escapes my lips when I see her eyes glowing green.

A man on a bicycle cruises by, coming from the opposite direction. "Maybe I want to play with you?" he shouts as he rides past, waving at me as he does.

"As my official introduction," says a teenage boy, but I turn and run, not waiting to hear him finish his sentence.

How many people can he control at once?

I round a corner but smash into a couple walking their dog.

"Running from me is rude," the man says, his horn-rimmed glasses reflecting the green glow. I fumble as I get back on my feet.

"You have until the parade is over to open my gift," says the auburn-haired woman holding the dog leash. The dog barks at me furiously, completely ignoring Sadie's exposed teeth. Its eyes, too, are glowing green. Deimos is acting like the monster he's been described as, and I don't know what his end goal is. Does he want to hurt others, or hurt me? Be a terrorist, or my personal tormentor? What threat level does he truly pose, and how worried should I be? His little puppets are thoroughly freaking me out, so if his goal is to give me nightmares tonight, he's likely achieved that.

"Many will die if you don't open the box."

Many will die? I can't let that happen, and the thought of it spurs my panic. Shouting at the woman and her dog, I spin and dart the other way. The hollering and cheers of the crowd throw me into even more of a frenzied panic. Their wide-open mouths and cartoon masks are everywhere. Anyone could be him, and I feel like I'm in a feverish nightmare. Where are the exits? How do I get off this topsy-turvy ride I never signed up for?

Quiet, I need to find somewhere quiet.

As my braids bounce off my back, I slither and shove my way around the numerous people gathered around the streets until I finally find a small alleyway off the parade route. It's only thirty feet long or so and has a brick wall at the end of a line of large trash bins. Here, I can take a breath and think for a second. Sadie remains by my side, looking up at me expectantly with her mismatched-colored eyes.

I'm about to ask her what I should do when the rustling of footsteps echoes from behind us, and I turn back in a rush, expecting glowing eyes to meet me.

But what I find instead is much worse.

Trinity stands with her hands on her hips, several other rebels nipping at her heels like little puppies.

"We thought that was you, Kara," one of them says, but Trinity and I are locked in on solely each other. I can tell just by her expression that she's not particularly happy with me.

"You looked mighty comfortable upon that stage, didn't you?" Trinity surmises. Her brown leather jacket is lined with thick lamb wool, and her long, braided hair rests against it.

"Nice to see you too," I say as they close in on me, eyeing me and the present in my hands suspiciously.

"What's going on with Arianyte, Kara? We don't hear from you for days after you failed to bring us what was in that safe, then we see this? Why do you look like a damn traitor, and why shouldn't we beat your little ass right here for what you've done?"

My hackles rise as I feel the threat in her words. What is she talking about? All I've done is risk my life for the Resistance. I'm their damn spy. I wish I could simply disappear from this parade from Hell.

"Trinity, I got the UVB drive into the Arianyte computers and almost got caught doing it. I risked my ass to find that safe and there was no crystal inside it. Why risk so much for something we don't even need? I've been giving Geonni updates as much as I can, but I'm being watched. So seriously, girl, I don't know what you're talking about. And don't forget, it was me who saved you from Arianyte. You're being absurd."

"You're up there smiling with their leader!" She points behind her with a sharp hiss, looking so convinced about her made-up assumptions. "And getting all dressed up to go out with him too. I'd think if the guy kidnapped my best friend, I wouldn't be looking at him with so much light in my eyes."

My body spikes with tingles as if a firework went off inside. How does she know about that?

Play it cool, this can look bad without context.

I shake my head vigorously, noting something tipping inside the present I'm holding. "Are you serious? It's all a part of the act. What do you want me to tell them, that I'm actually a Resistance member and I can't be a part of their little photo-op because the leader's daughter might get butthurt over it? Get serious. This is war. Be smarter than that. I'm getting close to their leader so I can get the information I need. If I was against you in some way, Arianyte would have raided the hideout weeks ago. You're being irrational."

"Or you're biding your time and collecting evidence on us," one of them suggests. A blond girl with long legs and a pissy attitude named Deeanna.

Ignoring her, I focus back on Trinity. "Is this because your dad thinks I'd be a better leader than you, and you're trying to drive me out with these ridiculous accusations?" This is truly where the tension lies, why she stopped being my friend. Geonni knows she doesn't have the gall to lead the Resistance, and so does she.

The others around her stiffen as Trinity goes dark. I back up a step. The dog, however, stands her ground.

"Pops knows who the leader is going to be once he steps down, and it's never going to be you. He knows who's going to bring mom home. They kept you as the lookout and threatened to kick you out for a reason. You're a hotheaded, dangerous *freak*. Nobody can trust you.

It isn't only me who thinks you're the dark horse that's going to bring all of us down."

Now it's my turn to darken, the glower over my eyes becoming storm clouds, and my mark tingles at the rage building within me. I've bled into this desperate desire to belong to the Resistance, but from the sounds of it, they don't want me here at all. They want to do what everyone does—abandon me. Even after all I've done.

"I've done what's been asked of me, at extreme risk to my own life. You can believe what you want to, but the evidence shows that I've been loyal. I honestly don't know why you're so upset."

"You're losing your grip. We all saw how you were acting at the press conference earlier, and we can't have the entire organization depending on you keeping your loyalties. It isn't just the leader you're eyeing all preciously, it's the whole lot of them." Trinity holds her hand out in a beckoning motion. "That's a fancy sword they gave you. That could feed the troops for months. If you're as loyal and committed as you claim, hand it over and we won't consider you an absolute traitor."

It's all I can do to not feel like I've been slapped in the face. I haven't had the sword long, but my attachment to it is unyielding, and the thought of them taking and selling it like it's some scrap metal angers me more than the fact that they don't trust me. Plus, everyone would notice it suddenly missing.

"I . . . I can't," I stutter out.

I won't.

It doesn't seem to be a good enough answer for her. "Give it to us and we'll consider you still part of the team."

They all press in on me, outnumbering me greatly. I have a 9mm, a flip knife, my sword and crystal, so the likelihood I can get out of this is relatively decent, but they're as close to an actual family as I've ever had, and I don't want to hurt them. Hell, I don't even want to fight them. It doesn't matter that Trinity has jumped to conclusions; she'll see the truth once she takes the time to see what I've done. She's not an irrational girl. I think she's just scared—scared I can bring everything her family worked and sacrificed for barreling down in a big ball of flames with one snap of my fingers.

"Trinity, I'm still me. I'm still the friend you grew up with the last six years. The one who went through all those grueling hours of training with you, who went out and attacked Arianyte food trucks with you so we could feed the rebels. You know me."

She doesn't show emotion often, but not even Trinity can control the quivering of her chin and the softening of her body, and a little bit of that anger seeps into sadness.

"I thought I did."

A black arrow suddenly whizzes right past Trinity's head, flying so close to her it slices through her hair with a dramatic whoosh. The two of us are standing kitty-corner to each other, so the arrow was never in danger of hitting me as it hurtles by and spears into the brick wall behind me.

Cursing, the group scatters like roaches searching for darkness. Ardelle is invisible within the crowd, and my so-called rebel friends are long gone by the time he appears through the bodies. Wrenching his arrow from the wall, I'm surprised by how heavy and thick it is.

"Who in Jupiter's rings were those people?" he asks as he approaches, taking his arrow from me. "And what is that?" He looks down at Sadie.

"Just some people I have history with." My voice is heavy, full of lead and defeat, the hurt I'm feeling something I'm far too familiar with. The people I sacrificed so much for abandoning me over a sword. That pain, there's nothing else like it. Its bite is more painful and venomous than a viper's. It burrows its way deep within and lays poisonous eggs that hatch into rage and wrath and the overwhelming need to seek revenge. To want them to feel this heart-wrenching collapse inside my chest as I watch them run from me with disgusted looks on their faces. Trinity is Trinity; she's always been fiery. I need to speak with Geonni about all this—immediately.

"What's with the gift box?" Ardelle nods to the present in my hands, and my stomach drops.

"Oh shit, is the parade still going? Tell me it's still running."

He looks behind him towards the parade route. "Maybe? What's the problem?"

"Deimos! That dickwad possessed some little girl to bring this gift box to me, telling me if I don't open it before the parade ends, he's going to kill a bunch of people."

"Get away from it," he orders, pointing at the box with the tip of his arrow. "That thing could be a bomb. Put it down and step away."

It could be anything, but if I don't do what he says . . . "I have to open it," I tell him.

"I'm calling Jance, just wait," he says as he reaches for his Dezlar and immediately holds it to his ear.

Shaking my head, I bend down and lay the box on the ground. "The parade is going to be ending at any minute. I can't be responsible for any people getting hurt or killed," I say, more to myself than to Ardelle. I wouldn't be able to face the guilt, not on top of the self-hatred I have for what I've already done in the past. He's yelling for Jance to get to us right away, but I know I have only moments. Deimos is likely watching me right now. I can feel his crystal as it controls the bodies of his victims, surveying me through their eyes. Will he be good on his threat?

Carefully, I pull the ribbon until the bow unties, softly falling to the ground without a sound. The box top is heavier than expected, and once I get a good grip on it, I plant my feet away from the box. Ardelle grabs the dog and is telling Jance that I'm about to open it. I can hear Jance's shouting from the Dezlar, but I ignore him.

In one swoop, I throw the lid off the box and dart away from it as fast as I can. I'm expecting loud noises and debris to come at me, but there's nothing. No poisonous smoke, no needles flying at my face, no bomb. There's nothing. Although relieved, my suspicion and curiosity both bloom.

I creep closer and closer towards the box. The inside is white and silky, but as I tiptoe nearer, I see spots and splatters of something red. My mark stings as my heart pounds loud in my ears. A warning bell goes off, telling me to get away, to run. But I can't—I need to know what's inside.

The object sitting at the bottom of the box is covered in blood. The white lace within is practically invisible and stained with red.

Perched atop a tiny white pillow is a bloodied human heart.

 182

CHAPTER 24

My knees buckle and I drop, unable to look away, eyes cemented to the bloodied human heart as it sits atop a cushion before me. I'm confused at best. At worst . . . well, at worst I'd say I'm feeling quite chilled with fear. Like Antarctic waters being pushed through my bloodstream at the pace of a freight train. Staring into the box made specially for me, I freeze in a dark, haunting trance of both my and Deimos's making.

What's the message that's intended to be sent with this? The crystals physically exist within our hearts so the logical conclusion is that Deimos wants what's inside mine. Deimos is a monster, and it wouldn't surprise me if he was the one who broke into my loft all those weeks ago. He did seem to be nearby and was watching me then. If he's capable of dropping a human heart just to send me a message, he's capable of anything.

Including the Hijacked.

Ardelle squats down in front of me on the other side of my thoughtful present. I finally avert my eyes from the heart, and the first thing I see is Ardelle's crystal mark, completely visible between his opened gray coat. The exact feeling that occurred the night I first laid eyes on his mark sweeps over me in a rush. I can't stop or slow it. I feel my edges closing in on me, a black tunnel vision on steroids. Then I'm gone before I can cry for help.

There's no time reference for how long I've been running across this reddish hellscape. My thighs burn as viciously as my eyes from the dust slamming into them. All I know is I continue to zigzag through rocks and dust and violent wind. It tints my white hair an ugly orange color, and my heart is a consistent drum of panicked siren songs. I can't go on like this forever.

What choice do I have when I can hear the multitude of bodies hunting me down close by? How many puppets does my pursuer have at their beck and call? They are his to command.

Finally, I allow myself a small resting period when I can no longer go on, hoping my scent got blown away in the dust storm. I pull out a flask of water and finish it gingerly, but it's not enough to quench my thirst. I lick my dry lips, tasting salt and dirt, and try to find any sense of direction. It's my lover's face who comes to mind, however—Erodis's face. I put a hand on my stomach, a new compulsion, a new hope—or so I had thought. If my pursuer knew of the newly conceived child within me . . . I can't even think of what would happen. Not only to me, but to their father, who does not know of their conception. Nobody knows. It's too risky. If they got captured, my enemy has many persuasive means of getting information out of people. I wouldn't blame them for giving in, but I simply can't risk this information getting out. Not while the galaxy itself is dangling in the balance.

But now, I feel like the life that has just begun inside me is already on its last star, because once I did what I did, after I betrayed this powerful man, I had no choice but to run. And of course, my team had to come with me. They'd be killed otherwise. Foolishly, we thought we could get out fast enough—but clearly we were wrong. Someone ratted us out.

And he found us.

Found me.

A sound from above jolts my attention to it, and I see it's one of the enemy ships coming in for a landing fifty yards away.

Knowing every second is a moment I cannot wait, I sprint away on long legs as plumes of red dust trail me. This is so bad. If he catches us, not only are the crystals going to be stripped from us all—killing us—but his promise to do unspeakable things before that certain death rings loud in my memory. A fate worse than the swift warrior's death we all deserve. My promise to protect the ones I love, the one growing within my womb—that promise is falling apart.

He warned me about this when he suspected our team was turning against him. The man who's been my puppet-master for so many years saw this scenario coming long before I did. He ensured I listened to every word of how he would torture my friends and family so brutally they'd be begging for death. That he'd let the females I love be violated by as many men who wanted them. That . . . I couldn't think of it again. The images, his sick, detailed descriptions of how he'd make them all suffer have me rolling through waves of nausea. Tasting bile. No, I wouldn't let him do that to them. This was my idea, my plan. They should never suffer from my mistakes and my utter failure.

But they're about to.

And suffer greatly, they shall.

I can hear footsteps closing in on me, their pounding boots my final death song. My long, pointed ears never fail me.

Skidding to a stop, I close my eyes and concentrate, listening to the surrounding sounds. Something is happening to the left of me, out there in the orange haze. A scuffle or rummage. Someone else is using their crystal, I can feel it. This isn't good.

He's found us.

But it's me he truly wants.

And suddenly, coming up on me out of nowhere from the orange is a group of puppet-soldiers. It's too late to run, there's nowhere to hide.

They rim the rock mound and pause at the crest. I go into a braced stance, reaching for my sword at my left hip but grabbing air instead of the ornate hilt. It's gone forever now. Notwithstanding, I'm the real weapon. One this galaxy has never known. The one everyone is searching for.

"Don't make this harder on yourself, Zariya," one of them says, but I can't tell which. They're all black shapes—nothing but bodies that stand between me and those I've sworn to protect. Protect them, I shall. "We've already caught three of you, we'll find the rest of you, and you're gunna come in. I don't wanna hurt you, but I've got orders. You either come willingly, or by force."

"Is he here?" I ask the ass-kissers, yelling above the howling wind.

I see their heads all turn to look at each other, and that tells me everything.

He's here.

Coming for his traitorous, runaway bride.

I suppose after what I did to him, I'd probably come after me too. I have checked none of the galactic news feeds since we discovered the tail on us, but the information I leaked has likely made it to every corner of the galaxy by now. Everyone will know what a lying, deceitful, puppet-master he truly is.

"He knows you're with child," another voice says, and I stumble back on my feet in shock. One of them takes it upon himself to use this moment to get the jump on me. Unfortunately for this person, my crystal instantly vaporizes him, and he fades away into the orange with the rest of the dirt, becoming a faceless drop in the bucket.

A dozen weapons point at me after that. "Now, now, let's not lose whatever dignity you've got left. He wants you alive. You can leave this moon alive with your child."

I laugh insanely. "Alive? I'm an animal going to slaughter. He's going to torture me."

Silence.

No empathy from this group, not for a traitor. That's exactly what I am. Traitor, liar, martyr . . .

"If he wants my heart, you're going to have to come over here and get me yourselves."

Collectively, their body language is hesitation, and that's my one and only chance. They're all dead within five seconds.

Zapped by my Elendril crystal before their clanking skeletons can hit the ground like heavy chains. All but their bones become a part of this soon-to-be mass grave. I don't like it. Killing is never something I enjoy, but it's about survival at this point—you do whatever you have to do.

I pace while future scenarios flash through me as fast as the ships I love to fly, and I continue to come back to the same terrible conclusion.

The only way out for us all.

A scream—blood chilling and anguished—rings out across the expansive landscape, and the wind carries it to my ears. I know exactly whose it is. Tears well up my eyes, and they burn like acid raindrops. How do I stop this? Is there any way to keep them safe at this point? No matter what I do, or how strong I've become, this devil will never die. There's no way of getting free from him. I am strong. My crystal is strong, but he's stronger. I can't win, I'd never win. The only way to be free of him is if I were dead. He wouldn't let me go any other way.

And what would become of this Elendril crystal inside me, then? Who would bear its burden once I was gone and those I led to their deaths became ghosts to haunt me for all eternity? What would he *make others do with all this power?*

I should have known this would happen. And to top it all off, he knows I'm with child . . . a child that could never be his. Reproduction takes a certain act, an act that hasn't happened between us. I know what he'd do with that information. He wouldn't kill them, or force me to miscarry, or simply rip my heart from my chest to take the crystal—that's too predictable. No, he'd keep me alive long enough to give birth, kill me then, or maybe keep me alive so I can watch him destroy my baby. Not watch them die a painful death, he isn't that depraved. But he'd delight in making me watch as he hones the child into a monster of his own image. No child has ever been born while their mother had an Elendril and their father was a carrier of a crystal too. The possibility the child would be born with a unique power is likely.

Or he could kill me, insert the crystal into the child, and raise it that way. So many terrible outcomes awaiting us both . . . How could that be a fate I would ever accept? To know that my child would become an arm of evil would be the cruelest of fates I could imagine.

We pass the crystals from person to person. Once a person died, someone is always standing in line to take the crystal for themselves. What would happen to the crystals if they couldn't ever be recovered, if they were destroyed while still inside of their hosts?

The screaming continues from out in the orange. I cover my ears and drop to my knees. I cry. I cry for everyone on this stupid moon. For my baby, for my lover, and for all the people I've let down. More than anything, my tears fall for what I know I must do now. This irrevocable act would be one of mercy and love, but that doesn't mean it won't shred my soul to its very core.

The galaxy will forever know it as an act of evil.

I let the crystal build now. Build and build and build. I pass my previous ceiling easily, the limit being shattered like a spaceship blasting out of the atmosphere. I don't stop. Instead, I pour in my heartbreak and wrath and fear and pain until it's an overflowing, bursting geyser of agony.

It's unstoppable.

My body breaks under the power's weight. There's a reason I've never gone this far—because it would have killed me. Blood pours from my nose, my ears. Pains in my stomach erupt like I'm being knifed, but I keep going. I can't think of what is happening to my baby right now, because it's already doomed.

We all are.

The physical manifestation of my rage finally shows itself in a ball of antimatter, typically pink, but it's now a raging white-hot circular mass floating between my hands. I create my own wind now, so much power manifesting that my hair sizzles when it blows too close.

Tears continued to fall like rain on parched land, sizzling right off my cheeks like water on a hot platter. My only solace is that my relentless pursuer is here. He's on this forsaken moon along with the rest of us. And if we are going down, he's burning inside this hell with us.

With all my might, with all my emotions and pain and rage, I ravage this place. Plummeting this ball of raw power into the orange dirt at my feet, it barrels straight down like an unstoppable cannon. Pummeling down, past rock, past earth, past crust and magma—I push and I push and I push, farther and farther into the moon. It's not hard, not with fury at my back. Once I hit the core, it'll be over for us all. For all I know, it's gone all the way through.

And all I can do is scream.

CHAPTER 25

OFF-WORLD BASES WILL IMMEDIATELY BE SCHEDULED FOR CONSTRUCTION AND INSTALLATION. THESE BASES WILL BE OPERATIONAL ON EARTH'S MOON, THE PLANET MARS, THE MOON NAMED TITAN OFF THE PLANET SATURN, AND THE EUROPA MOON OF JUPITER.

I wake to utter chaos, screams shattering my ears as fear completely overtakes me—but are they my screams or *her* screams?

I'm standing in the same position I was in before my consciousness flipped over to the vision—exactly like last time. It seems no time has passed. Ardelle is still squatting across from me, and the heart looks exactly like it did.

It takes me a few seconds to come back into my body, but when I do, I whirl backwards— disoriented and panicked. I realize quickly that what I saw isn't real or happening in this moment, that I'm back in my body, at the parade, in the alleyway with Ardelle—but holy stars, the terror is so *real.*

"Thumbelina?" Ardelle's voice raises with concern as sirens begin to wail throughout the city and screams from the parade-goers erupt around the streets. A massive boom seems to rock my very foundation, the loud noise causing past triggers from the domestic violence at my many foster homes to flood to the surface, which makes my panic even worse. I'm scared. I've never been so scared.

Someone's bombing the parade, I realize, and we need to figure out who and stop them. We need to find our friends—our family—and make sure they're safe, but I'm frozen in a panicked vise that I can't break free from.

Ardelle grabs me before I can run away. Where I'd go, I don't know. I'm so scatterbrained and shocked and freaked from the vision, the heart, Trinity—everything.

"We were on a moon . . ." I whisper, grabbing onto Ardelle for dear life, and he feels my trembling. Our eyes lock in an unbreakable stare, and he's looking at me as if he can't believe what I'm saying. "He's coming for me—for all of us. There is nothing I—she—can do. The orange . . . there's so much orange."

I'm losing my mind.

"Thumbelina . . ." he starts, likely thinking I'm insane. I know I feel insane.

Get it together, get it together, I urge myself, needing to calm down. *You're safe. You're fine. That is not you, you are not that girl. You're Kara and you're safe.*

Even Ardelle understands I'm not okay, and he holds me tightly against his hard chest, wrapping his arms around me in a secure, safe embrace. I'm too emotionally weak not to lean into him, to not clasp my arms around his body and bring him as close as physically possible. The dog, sensing my panic, nuzzles herself against my legs.

"Hey, it's alright," he says to me, hand cupping the back of my head to ease my trembling body. "Deimos isn't going to hurt you. I won't let that happen. None of us will. He's only trying to scare you."

His other hand gently caresses my arm in a steady rhythm, and his thumb moving up and down gives me something to anchor to—like he's done this before. The smell of him brings me back even further, his expensive cologne and cinnamon-sage scent familiar enough to bring on memories. Memories that are real, that are mine—no one else's. They're not the greatest memories, I'll admit, but they're *mine.* And that's what I need right now, to cement myself into this reality, this time and space, not whatever this girl Zariya was experiencing. I can't focus on that right now.

This vision was even more realistic and immersive than the last one, although I didn't think that would have been possible. This woman's emotions felt like my emotions. I could feel the life inside her body as if it were my body. Her pain and fear and fury were all my own. The power she wielded—my power, my crystal's power—it felt exactly the same, but it was different somehow too. The power she exercised could have been ten times the amount of my biggest manifestation of power. I can't even fathom the pure force of her.

Whoever she was running from, that person had her scared shitless and out of her mind. Was she about to kill everyone on that moon? She was doing just that, and herself along with them. Who was chasing after her? Who had such a powerful girl so afraid?

Deimos has made it clear today he wants my crystal and is coming after me, so what if the person chasing Zariya was after the same thing? Could he be the one chasing her? And now he's coming for the crystal again? I've got no idea when in time this happened or the alien's age, so it could be him. The two feel incredibly similar. When I'm in this vision, I feel an incredible sense of dread, which I also feel when Deimos is near and using his powers. Also, both times when the visions have been triggered, Deimos was lurking close by. Yet, so was Ardelle. It's like I look at his mark and that's the trigger, but why? I don't have the pieces to this puzzle, and it's beginning to feel more like an endless maze than anything.

What am I saying? These visions aren't real, and I'm losing my mind.

Another bomb racks the city, more screams follow. Ardelle separates our bodies so he can look down at my face. True concern is written there. It surprises me.

"Are you alright?" he asks softly. "You were scaring me for a second there."

I breathe in heavily and blink the wetness from my eyes, but I nod even though it's far from the truth. "I'm okay."

Before he can say anything else, I step away from him, immediately missing his warmth and the sense of security he gave me. "We should probably go see what's going on. Deimos is likely bombing the place. We can't let him hurt people."

"It could be a trap to lure you out," Ardelle suggests, and he's not wrong, given what message Deimos left for me.

I put the lid back on the box and pick it up, fear turning into anger.

"I'm not afraid of him."

Complete and utter bullshit, but what else can I do right now?

And so we go.

As the two of us plus the dog run into the craziness that's Zarmenia City right now, we run in the direction people are running away from. It's hard not to feel like we're running up against a stampede because people are moving recklessly and irrationally, knocking over anyone that gets in their way.

After taking a few corners, the crowd thins, and we're left on a street that's eerily empty and quiet. Trash and food lie scattered everywhere, as if something had zapped all the bodies to another dimension. Decorative and dog-shaped balloons lie alongside masks and spilled popcorn. No floats remain this far back, but the businesses along this part of the route had locked their doors and shut off their signs.

A man darts around the next corner, dressed in familiar clothing, and my breath hitches in my throat.

"Hey!" Ardelle yells at the guy, a clear member of the Resistance. I can't tell who it is from here, but he continues to run without looking our way. Several other rebels appear and dash in the opposite direction. Ardelle is already going for the first guy, using his crystal to stop the kid in midescape, and so I decide to go after the others, knowing I'll let them get away.

Sadie follows me as I'm still holding this stupid gift box, the heart bouncing around within it making me nauseous, and I try not to think about whose body this heart belonged to. Thank the stars the rebels are gone once I round the corner. If any cameras are watching, which they likely are, I don't want to be caught directly letting them go. Why are so many of them here? They can't be the ones setting off these bombs, could they? Surely, Geonni or Trinity would have tipped me off, right?

I continue to walk along the deserted streets, making sure to stay far away from where Ardelle is in case he caught that rebel. I don't want the kid to blow my cover. That's the last thing I need right now.

It's been silent for the last ten minutes as I walk alone but for the dog along the parade route when I come across a horrific sight.

Jance and Saris stand side by side at a bombing site, and Ahren is on the ground attending to injured patrons, several of them children. SSPARROW soldiers are also standing and assisting people, along with several extras. Malakyte stands in the center, pointing and delegating resources around the parade route, his soldiers standing ready to take orders.

Bodies lie littered around the street like the discarded candy and soda pop that's been left all over the city. These people are clearly long gone, their bodies bloodied and broken beyond repair. Their eyes are still open, still slick with tears, as if they died only moments ago. Alone and afraid, and I want to cry for them. I want to do more than that for them, but there's nothing I can do.

I silently approach the group helping survivors, feeling extremely numb. If Deimos hadn't been messing with me, I would have been a lot closer and able to help at the very least. Was this all by design? All a ploy to keep me out of play while the bombs went off? As I approach our Ringers, I don't know how to ask who did this because I don't want to hear the answer out loud. This is not the type of rebel I want to be.

Saris sees me first, her eyes lighting up, and she immediately interrupts Jance's conversation with a SSPARROW nest leader to alert him. My Ringer's neck snaps over in my direction, and he immediately runs to me after seeing the look on my face and knowing. He knows, without me having to say, that something's happened. Malakyte also stops midconversation, but he stays where he stands as Jance and I close the gap between us. I set down that horrendous box and jump into his arms, their powerful grip on me automatically allowing my defenses to fall. I'm safe now. I have my Ringer. The celestial artifact bonds us closer to each other every day, and the more I stop fighting it, the more comforted I feel by him.

"You're alright?" he asks, looking me over for wounds. There are none, at least none he can see.

When I nod, I tell him where Ardelle is. Pacey and Sylo are still missing, apparently. Then I inform him of what Deimos did, Malakyte approaching as he hears the story. I leave out the vision because that isn't relevant.

Silently, Malakyte opens the box's lid with disdain and disgust, looking down with a frosty expression.

When the prince and I lock eyes, I see the words there before he speaks them.

Deimos is dangerous, Deimos is cunning.

"From what we can tell of these bombings, it appears the Resistance is involved," Jance informs me, his voice sullen. "Apparently, they've already taken credit for it over the Network feeds."

This seriously surprises me, and I look up to my Ringer with a shake of my head. "That's so unlike them. They've never been violent like this, not with the public."

"They're rebels," Malakyte reminds me, his voice cold and cruel. "They don't have morals."

I want to argue how that isn't true, how they do, and they simply want freedom and justice and autonomy—but I can't. Not without looking like a sympathizer and blowing my cover.

"I need to find the rest of these kids," Jance tells Malakyte, his booming voice not asking for permission.

Ahren decides to remain behind and help with the wounded until medics arrive, so Jance, Saris, and I comb the parade for the others. It doesn't take us long to find Ardelle where I left him, a few SSPARROWs taking custody of the rebel he caught.

Thankfully, we find Pacey and Sylo together. They had led a large group of people to the safety of a parking garage.

We inform everyone of the current state of things. Everyone holds their own opinions about how and why.

"Wait, whose dog is that?" Sylo asks, and I immediately look up to Jance. The dog's head tilts adorably to the side, so I do the same for maximum effect.

"Ours, apparently," my Ringer says, and my heart has enough gas left in it to soar. "All that matters is we're all safe now."

Are we, though? Any of us?

Am I?

From the events of today, I don't know if I'm ever going to feel safe again.

CHAPTER 26

I've been taking out my frustration in the indoor pool for the last hour, the water a place where I can completely disappear, almost as if I'm on a whole other planet.

There are only so many laps I can swim, though, and no matter how hard I force it, I cannot outswim what's coming for me.

Deimos.

He's after me, after my crystal—after my heart. Why not the others, though? What's so different about me? Is it merely the power of my crystal?

I float flat on my back, staring up at the arches and recess lighting in the ceiling, contemplating what I should do. Could I take Deimos one on one? Would the others risk their lives for me? Sure, I've got a few years of training on me and an incredible weapon, but Deimos has decades of experience at a minimum. Or maybe I'm simply being insecure and shaken from the parade—what he intended for me, I'm sure.

Something soft whacks me in the face, and I scream, my body thrashing in the water as I orient myself. The sound of mocking laughter hits me once the water pops out of my ears, and I see Ardelle standing by the edge of the pool, shirtless and looking as hot as ever. The *V* that's created by his hip bones as it disappears into his swim trunks drives me wild, and I'm not even staring at how his arms are shaped to absolute perfection.

Stars, he's so hot.

"What the hell, dude?" I splash him as he continues to laugh. I swim over to find the inflatable beach ball he chucked at my face, and I throw it back at him, but he dodges it easily.

Smiling as he looks down at me, he says, "I tried getting your attention the old-fashioned way, but you didn't hear me."

Swaying my legs to stay in my place at the deep end, I fold my arms and look to the side, still annoyed.

"Come on, don't be mad at me. It was hilarious."

"You spooked me," I say. "I'm a little on edge, okay?"

Ardelle jumps into the pool, landing right beside me.

Water waves around us as his head breaches the surface. Despite the heated water, his close presence gives me goosebumps all over. I imagine what it would be like to wrap my legs and arms around him, to simply feel those strong arms around me for one second—to feel protected.

But Ardelle isn't exactly my safe space, I remind myself as I shove that ridiculous daydream out of my head.

"Deimos still?" he asks, and I nod. "Don't let that creep get in your head; that's what he wants. Plus, for whatever reason, I don't like seeing you like this."

By the look I give in response, he can automatically tell I don't believe him, although I wish I did.

"Hey, I'm being serious." He swims nearer, and now we're practically touching. I'm treading water, and I've been swimming so hard for the past hour I'm utterly exhausted. His face says he's being genuine, and his eyes are soft as he looks me over. "You can put some of your weight on me; I don't want to dive down there to rescue you when you eventually pass out from exhaustion. Come on, Thumbelina, I don't bite."

After an annoyed noise escapes my throat, I reluctantly place my arm on his shoulder, but it doesn't do much. He squints at me, telling me without words that we both know how ineffective that'll be.

"I'm fine," I claim.

Before I can stop him, he snatches me up into his arms, and I yelp.

"Stop being so difficult, you're fine," he says, cradling me in his arms. "Relax, Thumbelina."

"I'll relax when you stop calling me that," I deflect, not allowing myself to sink into him, although it feels right to. I wouldn't have ever imagined this scenario several weeks ago.

Ardelle starts swimming around in small circles, and after a minute or two of this, I finally allow my body to relax.

"Trust me yet?" he asks, and I look up at him from my place next to his peck. It's not a bad view.

I contemplate my answer. "I don't trust people easily."

His chuckle vibrates through me. "I didn't notice."

"Oh, shut up." I slap his chest softly, hoping my tone indicates playfulness. I realize that I must not hate this guy as much as I thought, because the first telltale sign of me liking a guy is when I start to rag on him with my incessant sarcasm. At least this one can throw it right back at me, for once. "You aren't exactly Mr. Cuddly, yourself."

His circles become faster, the water splashing around us softly. "You know you adore me; don't even try to deny it."

"Your humbleness is legendary."

"All a part of my charm, sweetheart."

"Sweetheart?" I choke, laughing as if I'm some super villain about to spill out their evil manifesto for the world to hear.

Ardelle bends his head to my ear and whispers, "Yes, sweetheart," and I blush absurdly at the seductive tone there. "That's what I said."

Stars, help me with this boy because the butterflies fluttering around in my stomach feel far too good for my own sanity to bear.

Lately, I've been afraid. So afraid of losing those I've considered family for years, knowing how painful it is to be the one left behind. Whether it be by force or by choice, I'm still left abandoned, and it ravages me all the same. Who is my family now, I wonder? Am I losing one and gaining another? Or am I simply losing what I never truly had in the first place?

What's so wrong with me? Sure, I can be headstrong and intense sometimes, I suppose, but it's like at some point, in some way, everyone leaves me.

And I don't understand why.

What am I doing so wrong? What about me is so repulsive and abhorrent that it repels people? I know I'm not the biggest people person but am I that unbearable?

Feels like it, sometimes.

I can't have that. Not with the Resistance, anyway. Whatever it takes, I have to make sure that they know I'm on their side, especially Geonni. If I can't convince him, then I'm as good as out. They're the ones I clung to so hard after losing Gav; it's losing a family all over again. They may not be the perfect family, but they're all I've known for the last six years. I don't want to lose them.

The city streets are quiet this morning as the sky transitions from night to pale gray. I puff on my new smoke pen, not able to live without it after the parade's events two days ago. I pull my coat close to ward off the chill, both from the cold of winter and from the memory of the parade. I snag a breakfast burrito from a street vendor along with actual coffee, something I could never have afforded before, and make my way towards the rebel hideout. Thankfully, I'm trusted enough by team Super Starseeds that I can go into town without the tracker. The risk of even coming here is gigantic, but after my encounter with Trinity and the crap the Resistance pulled, I have to show up in person.

A lot happened at the parade, and I still don't know how to digest any of it. It's clear now that Deimos has it in for me, and his message is hauntingly clear. In the nights since the parade, the nightmares about him have been horrible, and my eyes are dark and the circles under them even darker. Jance even had to come into my room last night because my crystal turned on during a nightmare and he was worried (reasonably so) that I'd blow the house's roof off. Apparently, my crystal level was so high that it woke the whole house because we can feel each other's powers. I worry I'm getting too out of control for them, and they're going to do exactly what the Resistance is doing now. Everybody wants me, they want to use my power for their own purposes, but when they realize it's so unpredictable and out of control, they want it gone, they want *me* gone. I'm too much to handle, too explosive and erratic. Maybe I'm only good enough in small doses?

I've tried so hard to avoid the Resistance kicking me to the curb; it was why I wanted to pull a power move and kidnap Naresteé. It was all to show the Resistance that I was good enough. All it did was prove to them that I'm not. When will the other Starseeds and Ringers figure that out too? I'm not going to be good enough for them in the end, either, because at some point the truth will come out.

That I'm a lying, dirty rebel—let's hope that last part sticks.

Then there's the vision—*Zariya.* She too has been haunting my dreams. I'm her, like I am in the visions, and I'm running. I'm running and being chased down by a dark silhouette. Faceless, nameless, nothing but darkness at my heels. A part of me thinks I'm being delusional, but another part makes me wonder if I'm seeing something that's actually real. It feels so real, like I'm there inside her body experiencing everything from her thoughts to the howling wind and all her pain. Her anguish bleeds into mine, and ever since that second vision I've been feeling her ghost inside my mind.

More so than any other point since my massive screwup at the Capitol building, the last few days have weighed the heaviest on me. I'm not sure I know what I'm doing anymore, and as I walk into the place I called home for so long, I don't feel so at home.

I feel like a stranger instead.

The usual happens: I'm taken up the stairs, searched for recording devices, and patted down quite aggressively before being allowed to see Geonni. A wave of relief floods into me when I see that Trinity is not present. His office is messier than usual, and I take a seat across from him, Titanium Gray light pouring through the large window behind him.

"So, we're suicide bombers now?" I greet, truly disgusted by the blatant and deadly attack at the parade.

Geonni's gap between his two front teeth winks at me, but he isn't happy with my words. My stomach tightens. This is only Geonni—I'll be fine. He won't kick me out . . . I'm almost sure of that. Almost. "Our goal wasn't to hurt innocents, it was to hurt the occupation. Which it did. If those who support the aliens will think twice before supporting them again, then I'd say that's a day well spent."

"You were always about protecting the innocent people of this city and the rest of the world. When did that change?"

Grabbing onto a chipped coffee mug that says 'Probe me' with the cartoon alien in an inappropriate pose, he sips and continues holding it close to his mouth. "It's been almost eight years since Martha was taken as a Tribute," Geonni begins. "Did you know that people of color, LGBTQIA+, and the chronically poor are twenty times more likely to be chosen as Tributes? I'm sure you've suspected because you fight for everyone, Kara. However, despite your lack of economic resources, you still have privileges others cannot even dream of. Additionally, Arianyte is doing more and more behind the public's back, bribing and convincing the Terran officials so they can keep it on the downlow as long as Arianyte continues to funnel money, goods, and alien tech to them and their businesses. They are the ones getting more dangerous, as you have said yourself. More oppressive, not only to people like me but to every single Terran on this planet. Isn't it one of your passion projects to stop the Hijacked? Because while you've been up in that mansion, thirty-seven new children have been reported missing."

That's so many. "Of course, it is, but not at the expense of other human lives, Geonni."

"You had no concern for other human lives when you pitched your idea for kidnapping the second-in-command. Or for the person whose hover-van you stole, who is still locked up, by the way, because of you. Not to mention the countless others you harmed after losing control in your quest for revenge and finding your little friend. You used to understand that whatever it took to rid Earth of Arianyte's grip was worth it. My daughter has a good heart. She's tough, but she's too soft. You, you were always my little monster, always ready and willing to do anything to get back at Arianyte. Have I changed, or have your feelings and possible allegiances changed since you've been deep undercover?"

That isn't fair.

"I got to their data, did I not?" I say, fighting for my life here. "I found the hidden safe, but the crystal wasn't inside. My cover would have been blown if I took that vial. I explained that in my message to you. Who knows what was inside of it; it could be the guys secret sex potion for all we know. Not worth it."

That doesn't seem to be good enough for him, and he practically slams his mug on the desk, its contents sloshing around. "You have done a lot, that was how we knew exactly where to strike the parade route to effectuate the most damage. Thank you for that. However, it's a whole other thing altogether when we see you rubbing shoulders with the leader of Arianyte. Publicly and privately . . . Why didn't you tell me about any of this? The reports you gave me on these other Starseeds are weak at best, and that's information we need in this war. I expected more intel than this."

Unable to help my palms from sweating, I get a fluttering in my chest from nerves. It's almost like Malakyte's lie detector test all over again. But why do I feel such a pull for my Starseed and Ringer companions? Are Geonni and Trinity right, am I losing perspective?

"What more do you want, Geonni?"

His answer is as simple as it gets. "More intel."

"And proof I'm not a damn Arianyte spy?" My voice shakes slightly, half from anger and half from fear that he might actually say yes.

"I don't believe you're a spy, Kara," Geonni begins, aimlessly organizing papers on his desk as he talks. "What I worry about is that you're getting sucked into this way more than you ever intended to. You're a kid, and it looks like things are getting over your head."

I laugh incredulously, tapping my pointed nail on his mahogany desk. I'm not getting sucked in. I'm still a rebel. "So, you think I'm simply too young and dumb to realize that I'm being taken advantage of?"

"I think the occupation is very good at manipulating and twisting reality."

I open my mouth to argue, then stop before I say something that only proves his point. When I don't reply quick enough, he goes on.

"All I'm trying to say is that I care about you, and I don't want to see you getting sucked into this without having a way out. The two of us want the same thing, we always have, it's why I trained you personally for all those years. Don't throw it all away for them."

What Geonni truly means is that he doesn't want things to get so bad for me that I rat on him to save my own ass. How do I defend myself without making it seem like I'm brainwashed by Arianyte?

By doing something stupid.

"How do I prove to you that this is all part of my plan? That I'm the one who's playing them?" I ask, leaning over the wooden desk and taking the 9mm pistol, the one he always has sitting next to him. I've always loved this old-world gun. It's so different than the pistols nowadays.

It's coated in Gunmetal Gray chrome with an eagle head etched into the grip. I'm completely aware how reckless this is, but I'm too scared of them ditching me to care. Gavrielle was like family to me and losing him broke me. Foster families that I thought could be my actual family, bringing me back to the orphanage, broke me. I can't lose the Resistance too. Even if I am not agreeing with this new scorched-earth strategy of Geonni's, he's right. We do want the same things.

Lacing his fingers together and leaning on his elbows, he muses aloud, "We are planning on making an example of a Terran government official tonight. From that data you got us, we found that these specific people have been accepting extensive bribes from the occupation. We need to set an example so that other Terran officials know if they turn a blind eye in exchange for their own selfish gains, we view them as dangerous and guilty as Arianyte themselves. You can come along and help. I'm sure your powers will be of use if we need a quick escape. Depending on how that goes, we can talk about what I found about your friend."

He found something on Gavrielle?

"Just tell me now," I demand, my heart beginning to tick up in hopeful excitement.

He shakes his head. "We were able to steal an immense amount of data: I'm still combing through it all. Prove to me you still got that smart head on your shoulders, and by then I'll have a definitive answer for you."

"But—"

Geonni holds his hand up, scarred palm facing me. I stop short. "Be ready at midnight tonight; we'll pick you up halfway down the mountain. We're going to give the city of Zarmenia a lot to talk about tomorrow morning."

CHAPTER 27

The middle of the night has always whispered its eerie song to me, as if those reckless enough to meet it head-on deserve to be told some of its secrets. It's only fair. I'm not sure I have all the answers as to why the night calls to weary souls such as mine, but its eyes are surely watching with judgment as the five rebels and I creep on silent feet through the property grounds and up to the mansion of a high Terran official.

The acreage of the grounds is expansive, most of it surrounded by the luscious pine and fir trees that are prevalent within the mountains surrounding Zarmenia. Hopefully, we'll get in, make a strong point real quick, then get out. I can't get caught tonight. The consequences would be too dire and the blowback too vast to even consider. They have not apprised me of the details on our way here. Geonni, Trinity, dumb and dumber—Dimitri and Connar—picked me up a few miles from Jance's house.

We sneak up along the poolside on foot while avoiding the armed guards posted all over the property. The main house sits large and long across from the pool, which is wrapped up for the winter. It's shocking that the people that are supposed to be leading the Terrans are living with such creature comforts while most of the population is struggling to eat and survive. It really makes me sick.

"Are we still planning on sneaking inside the back door?" I whisper, looking over at Geonni for answers.

Nodding but saying nothing, Geonni pulls out a black circular device that's about half an inch thick and concave in the center. Several lights are embedded around it, and he wiggles it for emphasis. That must be the new antilock device that I've been hearing about for ages. He must've finally figured out the prototype, his endless tinkering paying off.

One by one, we each duck around wrapped pool furniture, statues, and bushes as we tiptoe along the pool area and up to the porch. An attached cabana with its own kitchen and dining area gives us more cover in the dark night, the moonlight casting a friendly shadow as it deepens the darkness around us. The back entryway to the main house sits before us as we all squat down, hiding within the shadows cast by the lantern lights nailed to the house walls.

Geonni places his antilock device alongside the electronic keypad, and it attaches itself there so he doesn't have to hold it. My anxiety intensifies as I peek behind my shoulder and see a guard lurking several yards behind the pool house. We cannot get caught. I'm tense as I elbow Trinity and point my head towards the unassuming house guard. They aren't SSPARROWs, but they're certainly armed. Looking out into the dark, she squints but sees what I see. She comes in close to her dad's ear and cups her hands around her mouth as she delivers the message of haste.

With Geonni's Dezlar screen on its lowest light setting, he taps on it. Looking over at it, I can see that it's now connected to the entire security system network of the house. He's hacking their system, and that's totally something Pacey would be stoked about. After a few seconds, the lights on the circular antilock device gently pop to green, and a shifting sound breaks the silence, indicating that the door has been successfully unlocked. Hopefully, the security system will be disabled too. If we open this door and it's not . . . well, we better be ready to run.

As I check back to see where the guard has gone, I no longer see them. I can only hope that's a good thing, and as I bring my attention back to our break-in, Geonni slowly and carefully opens the door.

Sitting crouched, we all wait, and nobody dares release a breath. We're nothing but shadows, all dressed in black with our faces covered—we're nothing at all.

When no blaring alarm alerts anyone to our presence, it looks like the coast is clear.

It's even more of an eerie quiet inside. The automatic sensation of being in a place you don't belong comes on so thick and intense it's almost overwhelming. I want out, the sensation in my body leaving me tense and stiff. We're each instructed to find any physical evidence of the Terran's indiscretions and bribes. I doubt heavily that they're going to be leaving that information lying around on their kitchen table, but whatever Geonni wants.

Feeling like every single step sounds like a stampede of elephants, I separate from the others. My heart races, and a rush of adrenaline pummels my body. This is insane—I shouldn't be here.

It's dark, but the house is impeccably clean and decorated with many cultural artifacts, art, and massive vases that only fancy people can afford nowadays. The furniture is large and grand and more ornate than the furniture at Jance's house. Yet, with all its rare items and grandiose statement pieces, there's a part of the house that feels cold. As if it's missing some integral part of what a home truly should be, that life and energy that welcomes you upon entry. What the house that I live in now has—*love*. If I wasn't so afraid of making noise, I would chuckle to myself because I didn't realize until this very moment how much I've come to like it there. That I'm actually living in a place that feels like a home. *My home*. How had I missed that?

Leaving the living room area, I trek down a long hallway lined with dozens and dozens of pictures, all in elegant filigree frames. Unable to help myself, I look at the photos and see the people who live here. The people who exchanged their power and influence for more power, more money, more of all *this*—and betray their species as a result. Why there is even a Terran government after the Devouring Accords, I don't know. They're allowed to dictate how their Zones are run at a local level with regard to day-to-day functions and allocation of Zone funds. It's a small amount of power, yet they're drunk on it. Also, you have to ask what Arianyte wants from these Terran leaders in order to bribe them. Bribe them for what? I believe that's the deeper question Geonni is trying to answer here, one I would like to have answers to as well. Arianyte wants something only the Terran government can give them, which puts everyone in more danger. I agree we need to set an example for the other Terran leaders so that they know accepting these bribes and being corrupt is unacceptable and has consequences.

Then my stomach flips, instant nausea overtakes me, and my mark tingles from what I see.

Not only do I recognize the adult couple that lives in this house, I recognize their children. How had I not put it together? How did I not realize the connection?

I step back, heart hammering and eyes rapidly looking from photo to photo. There they are as children on Christmas. Their school photos, sports photos, party photos, holiday photos . . . Turning around, my feet clank down the hall as I wildly look at the other photos.

No, no, no . . .

We've broken into the house of Emily and Richard Dawson—Mr. and Mrs. Devil Incarnate—the parents of none other than Ardelle and Pacey Dawson.

CHAPTER 28

TERRANS WHO DESIRE TO APPLY FOR LEADERSHIP OF THEIR RESPECTIVE ZONE SHALL BE CHOSEN THROUGH THE APPLICATION PROCESS AND CHOSEN BY ARIANYTE LEADERSHIP ONLY. APPLICANTS MUST RESIDE WITHIN THEIR ZONE FOR A MINIMUM OF TEN YEARS PRIOR TO APPLICATION REQUEST. IF CHOSEN, THEY SHALL RETAIN THE LIMITED SCOPE TO GOVERN THEIR ZONE PER THE DEVOURING ACCORDS.

Shit.

"I see you've discovered whose house this is," Trinity coos as she makes her way towards me. I'm hot under my tight black coat, but more so from the realization that they played me—*again.*

Hissing in a whisper, I say, "You knew these are the parents of my teammates."

Trinity shrugs at the accusation, not seeming to give a crap, her smirk is all in those honey eyes of hers. She's still upset with me, I see.

"It's all about loyalty, babe." Her voice is laced with as much pride as a hunter snaring its prey, all signs of my old friend long gone. "We're here to set a very clear boundary to the rest of these traitorous Terrans. They've gotten away with letting Arianyte run wild for long enough.

We're also here to test you, our little spy master, to make sure you've truly kept your head in all this."

She pauses, throwing her small flip knife up into the air and catching it in the same hand. Doing it repeatedly, each throw a potential bomb that can blow this entire operation up.

"We want you to walk up those stairs and execute them, then your loyalty will be solidified. We'll never have this conversation again."

For one of the first times in my life, I'm stunned into utter silence. That silence becomes its own blaring noise, a constant static behind the increasing thumping of my heart. My eyes naturally look away from her to the pictures on the wall. Birthdays and Christmases and family portraits, all smiling and happy and normal. Something I would've killed to have, clawed up mountains to attain yet have never been that fortunate. On the outside they truly look like the perfect family, exactly like Ardelle and Pacey described them as being. Nothing is out of place, everything is picturesque and perfect—but that's not the whole truth. Somewhere in this house, these two adoring parents abused their children for years under the disguise of curing them. Yet their children have no disease or affliction. They have Elendril crystals—and they are powerful. I also see plaques and awards in their honor nailed to the walls, their wealth allowing them the privilege of making mass donations and providing a ton of financial assistance to charities all over the world. They've done a lot of bad things, yet they're not irredeemable to the point that them being murdered in cold blood is justified.

And how could I ever walk back into Jance's house again and look either Ardelle or Pacey in the eyes, knowing I was the one who killed their parents? I've done so many bad things, made a plethora of terrible choices, but this is a line I will not cross. Plus, all Ardelle can talk about is finding a way back to his parents. As toxic as they are, getting back home is his goal. I couldn't leave them as orphans. I know all too well how it shatters your soul.

"I'm not killing anyone," I say softly, my voice weaker than I wish it would be. "I'm all for messing around or scaring them—no love lost there—but we're not murderers like this, Trinity. Holy stars, what happened to you?"

Trinity deadpans, "I'm only trying to be more like you, Kara."

Such a low blow . . .

She isn't wrong; however, the lives I took were always in defense of myself or others or a complete accident from my crystal's uncontrollable power. I'm not a killer, I don't set out to kill, I never have—I never will. I may have dark tendencies and have my issues, but I'm not this bad. Am I?

Her father approaches us from behind me and I shudder at his footsteps.

Geonni says, "We got our paperwork. Phase two is complete and I've sent the boys back to the hover. Time for phase three." He looks at me, still in his sunglasses. It's apparent the two of them set this up because I can feel Geonni's expectations in the way his body looms over mine. His vibe. This is not the man I used to know, and I suddenly feel an incredible sense of loss. Is it me that's truly lost perspective, or him?

All I can do is shake my head. "There's got to be something else we can do besides kill these people. Stars, Geonni, this isn't going to bring Martha back."

It all comes back to Martha for them, as it should, but this isn't right.

"Nothing else will make as much of an impact." Geonni's voice is stiff and cruel. This isn't the man I spent the last six years with. "I want to trust you, I do. But if you're willing to spy for us, you could be convinced to spy for them. They have very persuasive techniques to make you think betraying us is a good idea, and none of that is your fault, but if I'm going to have you in my ranks, I need to know whose side you're truly on. Not bringing me that vial you found in the hidden vault and the public display at the parade has me on alert. After all, we know what you'd do in order to find Gavrielle."

The leader of the Resistance shoves his titanium handgun into my hands, and I take it despite not wanting to, its metal cold. He motions towards the stairs, where I need to go. As he grabs my shoulders and turns me around, I feel like I'm outside of my body. He walks me towards the base of the stairs. They want me to go up there by myself and do what? Shoot them both in the head and have their guards rain down on me while the rebels just take off and abandon me here with the fallout? This is so messed up.

Geonni whispers in my ear from behind. "Do this, and you'll be leading at my side. If you don't, then you're out."

My eyes go wide. The moonlight peeking in through the windows makes me feel like I'm in some awful dream. The prize and the betrayal are all mixed into one promise. Get everything you want most, or everything you fear most.

All you need to do is pull the trigger . . .

He shoves me forward, and I almost trip as my boot slams into the first stairstep. I'm numb, as if I'm walking through a house underneath a frozen lake. Geonni follows behind, his body forcing me to take one more step. One more step to my friend's parents, one more step towards belonging and leading the Resistance, another to finding Gav, and one more step towards cold-blooded murder.

CHAPTER 29

In every person's life, there are pivotal moments that define them from that moment forward. A precipice that either takes them down the road where they discover who they truly are or the path where they fall to the depths of their worst nightmares. Tonight will be one of those moments in time where I'll likely look back and be full of regret.

Geonni leaves me at the top of the stairs, watching and waiting for me to do the evil deed. Not even a floorboard creaks as I make my way down the hall and towards the master bedroom. I wonder which room is Ardelle's, if his sports equipment is as neatly organized or if he color codes his closet the same way as his closet at our house or if he completely left behind who he was here. He's really been there for me since the parade, after Deimos and his cruel present. Ardelle thought I was so upset because of that, and I was, but it was the vision that truly twisted my gut and got me acting the way I did. And Pacey—stars, Pacey . . . How could I do this to her? And if either of them ever found out I'd done it—that *I* pulled the trigger . . . Some things are unforgivable. This is one of those things.

Although doubt in my resolve not to commit this act is wavering from the fact I still can't remember Gavrielle's face.

As my stealthy footsteps finally make it to the main bedroom door, I look back at the leader of the Resistance, his promise to finally—after all this time—elevate me to his side. To be the hero inside the Resistance like I've always wanted. The one place I've fought to be, the one place I want to belong. Yet, is it worth it if this is the cost? On the flip side,

Geonni holds the power to also shatter me in the worst of ways. I'm sure he knows my weaknesses, my fears, my desperate and pathetic need to belong to something. Both father and daughter are using it against me. They're using the fact that I want to belong so badly to this group that I'd be willing to do almost anything to ensure that I don't feel that rejection. The abandonment that's burned into my soul from repeated brands. I'm not stupid, I see it, but am I willing to endure it?

When all I've wanted could be moments away . . .

My hand wraps around the matte black doorknob, round and soft and silent as I twist it. The pristine white door with beveled and embossed carvings opens with little more than a soft click. Poking my head inside, I see the two unassuming bodies lying together on the bed. The room is grand, ridiculously large and ornate and bathed in nothing but moonlight. The bed itself is up on a literal pedestal, framed by a large wooden four-poster bedframe and sitting under a massive chandelier.

My heart is thrashing like a wildfire.

I fully step inside.

It's a surprise my ragged breaths alone don't wake them, my breathing so panicked and uneven I can't control the fact that I sound like a tired dog.

As I make my way across the room and towards the side of the bed, the gun in my hand feels like a hundred-pound death sentence, but not in the way you'd think. I can feel my kneecaps literally bouncing like a ball as I walk towards them. Taking a life this way, it's an exchange. You may not physically die; your body may still pump with blood and remain seeded with life—but you die too. You die inside. At least, you should.

I raise the gun five feet from the bed. It shakes so badly I have to hold it with both hands just to make sure I get a decent shot. Emily, their mother, faces me. I can see Pacey there, older and far colder even with her eyes closed. Their father lies on his side facing away from me, but he has Ardelle's broad shoulders. This could all be over in the span of seconds.

"*All you need to do is pull the trigger . . .*" Geonni's voice says.

Then much of what I want will be mine.

And if I don't, I say goodbye to any chance of finding Gavrielle or belonging with the only family I've ever known—aside from Gav. I know they're complicated and not perfect, but I've been with them for so long and I don't know who I am if I'm not a part of the Resistance. They're my identity. My two worst-case scenarios. It's ironic that this one action— no matter which way it goes—will result in two massive changes to my reality.

Knowing what I must do and having decided, I take in one long deep breath, then release it slowly.

I take aim, and I fire.

CHAPTER 30

Three shots ring out into the silent night.

Bam! Bam! Bam!

I dash from the bedroom faster than lightning, ears ringing like bells. Geonni waits for me at the top of the stairs, one arm stretched out and hand beckoning me to hurry. He's no more than a dark silhouette, moonlight backlighting him from the window at the corner of the stairwell.

I can't think as we both fly down the steps, through the living room and kitchen, and out the back door. Trinity is gone, and we make it through the house unimpeded. Our luck ends there.

Geonni flies out the door first, and before I can follow, he's whacked in the head with the butt-end of a rifle, knocking him straight to the porch. With the gun still in my hands, I shoot the guard's foot and his cries fill the space the gunshot leaves behind. The heavy ringing inside my head worsens with each shot I fire.

Kicking his rifle from his hand with ease, I manage to knock him out with only a few strikes to the head, but I'm instantly pounced upon by another guard that approaches out of the shadows. We both punch and duck, but I'm too small, too fast for the guard to grab and he's down and out quickly. The training Jance and the others have been putting me through has definitely changed how I fight, and it's not left unnoticed. Geonni watches me from where he's been knocked down on his ass, his sunglasses sitting beside him, crushed.

He stares at me, his one blind eye a second moon. Reaching my hand down for him, he grips it tightly as I use my full body weight to heave him to his feet.

As the two of us run past the pool, we're almost home free when a voice stops us dead in our tracks and my stomach flips.

Richard Dawson stands in the doorway, pistol in hand, and very much alive.

Exactly the way I left him and his wife.

When it dawns on Geonni that my gunfire shots were a mere fallacy, I can see the rage building there.

I don't wait for the storm raging in his eyes to manifest on me; I bolt. Geonni follows as more guards converge.

They shoot live fire rounds over our heads, several barely missing their marks. We zigzag between trees, their bark spraying out in every direction as bullets rain down.

Shouts erupt from behind, hollers for us to stop and that SSPARROWs are coming. They can't catch us. And if I'm forced to use my powers, the description alone would identify me, despite the mark being well hidden behind thick clothing. It's too identifiable, but as the guards get closer and closer, I fear I may ultimately be forced to use it.

As Geonni and I reach the long driveway that leads to the gated entrance that these idiots left open, we're so close to freedom that hope dances inside my chest, my crystal mark burning from pure adrenaline. Escape is near.

Then, the guards must've guessed our planned route out, and the gate begins closing.

"Go!" Geonni roars, running ahead of me.

Pushing my legs hard, I sprint towards the closing gate.

Headlights manifest from the left, and the hover Trinity drives slams to a hard stop before the gate's entrance.

Windows down, she and the two boys are howling at us to run faster.

The double-door iron gate is already halfway closed.

Ahead, Geonni clears the gate's threshold, the back of his long coat whipping behind him. He throws the back door to the hover open and dives inside, and I have the sudden rush of fear that he's going to order them to leave me behind.

But I have more pressing concerns.

I'm too far away—I'm never going to make the gate. If I use my power to blast it open, I'll be found out. It'll surely get back to Malakyte, and if I don't blast it . . .

The gate closes right as I reach its ensnaring bars. I'm so close I can't stop in time and I ram into it, its cold metal bars far too close together for me to slide through. Geonni and I lock eyes, my chin quivering with desperation, all pride leaking from me like a broken faucet.

Don't leave me here, I silently beg him.

And when he turns back around into the hover, my trembling knees give way.

My punishment for not being his assassin.

It's more brutal than I could have imagined.

I fall then, knees scraping against cement as I cling onto the bars. I shake the gate, shake it so violently my neck whips and thrashes.

It doesn't budge.

The guards are right on my ass, and they'll be here any second.

Then Geonni reappears, a grenade in his hand. And it's lit up red.

He doesn't have to tell me to get out of the way before he throws the bomb. Diving into the grass beside the gate, I land on my stomach and cover my head with my arms. The explosion is so loud I lose all hearing as smoke and metal and dust envelop me.

My feet shudder and I wobble. I need to get out. Get out through the gate. My sense of direction is topsy-turvy, and as I stand, a high-pitch rings in my ear.

The gate . . .

The hover's lights guide me back, and I stagger through the smoke and rubble, tripping several times over mangled pieces of metal gate and asphalt chunks.

A rough grip snatches me up before I make it ten feet, and I'm thrown in the back of the hover, arms and hands pulling me inside.

As the door slams shut, Trinity guns the hover into high speed and flies off the estate, guards trailing behind us in vain, their bullets bouncing and popping off the hover.

I'm lying horizontally on top of Connar, and he awkwardly helps me sit upright between him and Geonni. As I try to catch my breath, I set his pistol in his lap. Looking at him, I try to explain what words could not. That I couldn't kill them, not in cold blood and not like that, but that it doesn't mean I'm not loyal. The backs of my eyes sting at the look he gives me in return, a look that tells me he's going to keep his word. He saved me back there, saved my life when he easily could have left me, and that's the last bit of grace he's going to offer me.

I'm out of the Resistance, I'm never going to find Gav . . . and the family I've worked so hard and tirelessly to belong to has forsaken me.

Exactly like I feared they would.

CHAPTER 31

THE ARIANYTE EMPIRE DECREE #45

FACTORY FARMING IS OUTLAWED IN HIGH-POPULATION
ZONES AND THE TREATMENT OF FARM ANIMALS WILL
BE HIGHLY REGULATED FOR THE HUMANE TREATMENT
OF EACH SPECIES.

Once we get clear of the security guards and any inbound SSPARROW that may have been coming our way, Geonni forces Trinity to stop the hover.

Without his sunglasses, Geonni truly looks the part of an unhinged, out-of-control rebel that's trying to ruin the systematic structures of our world. Where had he fallen so off the rails? This wasn't what we were trying to do—we weren't murderers. We didn't kill our own kind. What has Arianyte done to drive Geonni so far, or has it been years of being beaten down by the occupation that finally made him snap?

Though he stares at me with a mixture of sadness and contempt, I truly don't think he believes I am against him, but it's clear he no longer believes I'm one hundred percent for him either. And for Geonni, you're either all the way in or you're all the way out.

"You're out," he tells me, his voice as cold as the night air.

"Dad . . ." Trinity tries, but he holds a hand up to silence her protest.

No one else speaks, yet the tension is palpable, and I don't think they ever expected him to actually kick me out. I didn't either. For so long, everyone in the Resistance knew that their leader believed I would be the one weapon Arianyte could never stand against. The caveat? If only I could control that raw power that lived within—that destroyed. What everyone didn't realize was that it wasn't my power that was the destroyer of everything—it was me. It's always been me.

Without a word, Geonni opens the hover door and gets out so I can leave. When he gets back inside, he's about to close the door on me but hesitates—perhaps questioning his ridiculous and rash decision-making. A small spark of hope blooms in me then, that maybe he's regretting it all and he'll take me back. We can work something out, there's got to be something I could do.

Then the hover door slams in my face.

Then they're gone.

Gone for good. Taking all my hopes of finding Gav with them. My family no more.

I am a rebel without her Resistance, standing alone on the side of a dark road and wondering how my choices brought me here.

I'm not too far from Jance's house, so I begin walking that way. It's not like I could call any of the others to come and get me; there'd be too many questions as to why I'm out here in the middle of the night, covered in debris and clearly depressed.

What I can't shake the most is who Geonni and Trinity have become. I thought the suicide bombs at the parade were ridiculous and outrageous, but tonight? Geonni always used to be so rational and cared about the public's view of us, and if he did kill, it was for good reason, not personal gain or whatever the hell this was tonight. To trick me, to goad me into crossing a redline like cold-blooded murder without any regard to the consequences that would have on me, is plain evil. Then to kick me out for refusing, that's even worse. I miss the person he was, the person who took care of me and taught me everything I know. Where had that man gone? What more could Arianyte take from me that they haven't already? I guess I should've known.

The winding road up the mountainside shrouded with trees may be a new path against my feet, but I've walked this lonely road many times before. I walked it when I was six, a year after my first foster family got rid of me. After that, I was seven, so hopeful and full of joy as my second foster family promised it would be different this time. Then, when I was nine, it became a road I chose to go down for once. After everything that specific foster father did to me there, at that house, in that bedroom—I'd never be the same again. Yet, that road led me to Gavrielle.

Those few years we spent together at the orphanage were the best of my life because he brought me back from the brink and showed me life could be worth living. Nobody understands why I fight so hard to find him. He saved me, and I abandoned him in return. And tonight, I chose others over him. I chose Ardelle and Pacey over him. Chose my relationship with the Starseeds and Ringers over him. Even when I do the right thing, I'm still hurting people. Maybe that old saying, 'Hurt people, hurt people,' is true. That's not what I want to be anymore.

I angrily kick a rock in frustration, and it ricochets off the side of the mountain and rolls into a ditch. I feel a lot like that rock; in fact, I'm a little jealous of it. The easy thing to do would be to crawl inside that ditch and never come out, but as defeated as I feel in this moment, I know I can't give up. The Hijacked need someone to fight for them; Gav needs someone to fight for him. With all that's happened, I'm unsure of Arianyte's position now. Malakyte seems so reasonable, and he did say he would help me find Gav if I bring him Deimos. Do I believe or trust him? No, absolutely not. But what other option do I have right now? If I'm tasked with finding Deimos anyway, I may as well try to get Gav out of it. I'm likely naïve, but I have to hope for something right now. Putting my faith in Arianyte is stupid, sure, but I should put finding Gav before any personal need for revenge at the moment. That's the responsible thing to do, for once. Although, it's a desperate and unrealistic fantasy for me to rely on Arianyte to bring my friend back to me, it's literally my only hail Mary.

And since I'm officially out of the Resistance, they can reveal my true identity at any moment. I need to get out ahead of it. And I know exactly where I have to start.

"What's wrong, Kara?" Pacey asks as the two of us switch off holding the punching bag. It's my turn to keep the bag still. "You've been so withdrawn all morning. I thought you were tearing up a bit at breakfast and you were so quiet."

Am I being that obvious?

"I'm fine," I say, bracing myself for her first kick.

Pacey's long legs are powerful, and that initial kick to the bag jars me and causes my footing to slip. "You're clearly not. It's okay to not be okay, you know."

She's right, of course. I'm not okay. Yet, I can't tell her that, because then she'll want to know why. Yes, I want to confess what's been going on, but I don't have the strength right now, and I want to tell everybody together, so I don't have to spill my guts and shame repeatedly. For now, I'll try to enjoy this time with Pacey. Soak in every bit of what this feels like, what it feels like to fully belong to something.

"It's just one of those days," I tell her, hoping it'll pacify her curiosity.

"Well," she kicks hard then punches twice, "if you want to talk about it, I'm here for you. You don't have to shoulder these burdens alone anymore. We're all here for you, even my jerk-face big brother. He cares about you, Kara. He's just—"

"A jerk," I finish for her, and the two of us laugh together. He's down in the gym with us, sparring with Sylo on the mats. Unable to stop myself, I watch as Ardelle's body not only towers over Sylo's in height but also in sheer mass. He's wearing a black undershirt that's drenched in sweat and shows off all the muscles of his arms and back.

I swallow, mouth dry.

"I see that look," Pacey snickers, her kick literally knocking me out of my distracted daydream. "Don't be sad, okay? Ardelle told me this morning that he's worried about you too. It won't take long for Jance to come snooping, you know. He's a dad like that."

That's true, Jance is. But that's the part of him that I love. I don't want to lose that.

I've betrayed them, lied to them—why wouldn't they cast me out? It's what I deserve.

I'll hold onto them as long and as hard as I possibly can until then.

The nightmare wakes me, my skin covered in a thin sheet of sweat as my chest heaves rapidly. Heart racing, I dig my fingers into my hair, brushing the long strands out of my face. Stars, that was a bad one. Even my crystal is searing hot as I take a drink from the cup of water at my bedside.

It doesn't help.

This dream is a premonition . . . my fate.

In it, I'm shunned, all of the Starseeds and Ringers throwing me out with hatred on their faces.

"Get out, we don't want someone like you here," they all said. *"You're a disgusting liar."*

Stars . . .

I get up out of the bed, panic building in my blood. I flip on the light to the bathroom as nausea rolls over me. I can't handle this. I'm so weak, so pathetic that I'm losing my shit at the mere possibility of them casting me out. Why? Why do I even care? I hated these people from day one, I loathed them—they were the enemy.

Then they weren't . . . they became something else to me, something more.

Now, the Resistance is gone. My sense of purpose, gone. My family, gone. Gavrielle and all likely hopes of finding him—gone!

Gone, gone, gone . . .

And these people are all I have left.

I should leave. I should pack up all this nice crap Arianyte paid for, the clothes, the makeup, all of it—and bail. Run away. Get out of the city and start fresh somewhere else; stars know I can't safely return to my loft. I have enough credits to leave the city. I could tattoo in another major city, in another Zone.

Dammit.

No, the Zone checkpoints. I'd never get past them, not with the facial scanners. Malakyte certainly has my face in the system.

I pace around my room, the only light a small wax warmer Pacey lent me, saying the light from that and the television helps the nightmares not suck so bad.

They aren't working.

Desperately, I leave my room and cross the length of the house. I don't know what I'm doing, why I'm doing it, or what I expect the outcome to be—but I'm frantic.

And I don't know where else to go.

It's the dead of night, and when I knock on Jance's door and crack it open, he shoots right up out of a deep sleep. His room is one of the biggest in the house, with black walls, black furniture, and black bed sheets.

"Hey, kid," he says, voice still sleepy as he looks at his watch. "Come in, what's wrong?"

I hate when people ask me that because when I'm truly not okay, I don't have the strength to keep up the façade. Jance sees it, sees my silence and my watering eyes in the darkness. He swoops his bedsheets over and sits up in his bed, feet touching the floor.

"Come here," he beckons, and I don't hesitate. Before knowing him, I would never have trusted another man in this situation.

Ever.

But it's Jance, and I do trust him.

Geonni wasn't ever a creep, but I kept him at a distance, my wounds too fresh from foster homes at the time we met for me to risk this type of closeness.

I collapse in his arms as he wraps them around me in a safe embrace. "I can't do this," I tell him. "I can't."

He thinks I mean one thing, but I mean something completely different. And I want to tell him so badly that I'm sorry and I'm stupid and I'll do anything, just don't leave me. Don't abandon me too.

Jance must sense that there's more to this when he asks, "What's going on, Kara? You can talk to me. It's okay, darling."

I consider spilling everything to him right here and now, but his embrace is so comforting, so safe that I'm not willing to lose it. To be thrown off him in disgust at what I've done here. Stars, I've messed up so badly.

He gently brushes his hand along the back of my head, waiting for me to calm down as we sit together.

Finally, he says, "You're going to be okay. I won't let anyone hurt you. I'm your Ringer. I care for the others, of course, but you're my priority, and I'm always going to protect you first. Do you understand? I have your back, I always will. You are mine."

He places his branded hand over my star mark, both symbols side by side—together.

You are mine.

I'm something to someone?

His words get me crying again, the tears falling not from sadness as much from cruel irony. Why is it that the father figure I've craved my entire life finally shows up when I'm lying and betraying him? That I've found this amazing person who cares about me, and I'm messing around in crap that could get him killed, sent off with the other Tributes to go work in a slave camp for the rest of his life, or worse. I'm not only playing with fire regarding my own life, but his as well. All of theirs.

Yet, Jance sits and continues to hold me, his deep voice a soothing melody that I cling to because I'm weak and fragile and need his strength because mine has evaporated. I can't be strong all the time, at every moment.

I'm not strong enough.

And that's why I need to tell him, tell them all what I've done.

Before they find out in the worst-case scenario, and any slim chance I have at keeping them would be long gone.

The reason we're out in the arctic cold is because Sylo's crystal is disturbing, and the only dead bodies we could find were ones of animals in the woods.

Yes—*dead bodies.*

And it's not only me who's completely disgusted by this game of necromancy.

Pacey's face squishes with repulsion. "Gross, why are we bringing a dead deer back to life?"

Jance shoots her an unapproving look, his large body wrapped in a tan coat lined with creamy wool. "Even Sylo has a right to practice his crystal. His and Kara's crystals aren't as accessible as the two of yours."

"Yeah, babe," Sylo says as he stands above the dead deer, his eyes bright with excitement. "My ability to control the dead is a lot more complicated than your ability to control nature. I know it may appear creepy and possibly a bit scary, but it's not as frightening as your brother's glowing red eyes when he uses his. If that's not zombie-esque, then I don't know what is."

Ardelle crosses his arms in response, leaning against a tree. For me, I'm soaking up every minute I can get with them all, because today is the day I come clean and confess my crimes.

As the poor fawn reanimates and comes to life before our eyes, pieces of its body missing and coated in dried blood, not even Ardelle can keep the shock off his face.

Pacey screams as Sylo has the deer begin to chase her around the wooded area. It moves all wrong, the bones on one of its legs broken and bent at all the wrong angles, and its stiff frame is resistant to Sylo's commands. Its eyes glow orange like his do, reminding me of Deimos's cruel puppet powers. Sylo's crystal is a lot like the green devil's power, yet Sylo is only able to control those who are dead. Ten out of ten, the worst of all the crystals, hands down.

Each of us gets a chance to work with our crystals. Mine explodes and burns down quite a few trees as my fried emotions cause an extreme lack of control. Pacey is able to weave those trees back together with her brother's help like they were of one mind. Training together like this also gives each of us a better feel for the others' crystal signatures. It's so interesting that I can feel the difference between Sylo's magic and Ardelle's. Out of everyone, it's Ardelle who gives me one of the strongest pulls, deep inside my stomach, when he uses his magic. Although he's been distant and disinterested most of the day, I've caught him watching me several times. His eyes dart away, as if I suddenly caught him doing something horrendous. Yet those Royal Blue pools of water never stop finding mine.

Stars, do I really want to risk losing those beautiful eyes? I run the risk of losing them completely and having them gaze upon me with hatred if I don't confess, but I also risk all that if I do.

Collectively, we agree that we are done for the day and begin our trek back towards the house.

My heart begins to race at what I know is going to be an incredibly difficult conversation ahead. However, if I don't do this now, I'm never going to rummage up enough courage again. The Resistance can drop the bomb that I have been working with them to undermine Arianyte at any point, especially with some of them in custody. The only side they'll know is the one being told to them, so I must get out ahead of this. If I lose these people—my fellow Starseeds, my Ringer—I'd never recover.

It's been exceptionally hard the last few days realizing that I truly lost the Resistance, that I don't have a place to return to. I'm no longer with them, so I'm no longer a spy for them. And I feel naked and exposed and alone more than ever. Yet I did what I did . . . so I have to take accountability for it.

"So, guys . . ." I begin as we collectively walk downhill towards the direction of the house. It's an average winter day. No snow has fallen but the chill in the air is stark, and the wind blows even colder. The sky is a washed-out Sidewalk Gray color, and all the pretty leaves from the trees have all been blown bare and are now soggy versions of their previous selves on the forest floor. I walk in between Ardelle and Pacey. Jance hovers closely behind us, and I look down at the ground pretending to carefully watch where I'm walking, but it's really because I can't look them in the eye as I say this. "I need to come clean about something."

Okay, rip the band-aid off.

"I . . ." I hesitate, knowing I'm insane for offering this information up. They could easily send this information straight to Malakyte. Yet, if I keep hurting the people I care about with my actions, then continuing this huge lie is only going to further that pain. I'm trying to be better, and that has to begin with actually *being* better. "Well, I've been doing a lot of thinking, and I realize that there's something I haven't been completely honest about."

Jance says from behind me, "Anything you say stays right here with us, so whatever it is, it's okay."

After I barged into his room last night, he continuously tried to get these words out of me, but I wasn't ready then. I wanted one last night of some sense of normalcy. His strong, dependable nature is something that's grown on me these past weeks, and it's so hard not to let him get closer to me. He wants to, he's trying to—and I've kept him out. I've kept them all out, and I don't want to anymore.

"Okay. I guess I'll start from the beginning."

Again, Ardelle and I lock glances, and the memory of that first night and him pointing his arrow right in my face flashes in my mind.

"When Blondie over here brought me in, I was really, really scared. The SSPARROWs were being awful to me. They were hurting me and telling me I was going to be Reconditioned, and I thought a lot of bad things were about to happen to me. And so, in order to get out of it, I lied and said Deimos was controlling me. He wasn't. He never did. It was only a guess that he could control people from what I saw when I was watching him use his crystal from the rooftop."

The silence that follows my confession is much longer than I had anticipated. Mouth dry, I keep my eyes glued to the forest floor, watching as my black boots dodge puddles and large rocks. Part of me wants to fall into a puddle right now and never come back up.

Ardelle is the one that speaks first. "I knew he wasn't doing that. Your eyes never glowed green when I was up there."

"Why did you lie for me then? I know Malakyte asked you about it."

He shrugs, hands in the pockets of his black leather jacket that has a high collar and a crisscross lace-up detail on either side of the zipper and sleeves. It looks so good on him. "I didn't want to make things worse on you—despite your actions, I thought you deserved a second chance."

My chest tightens at his explanation. The sloshing of footsteps on wet ground is the only sound between us as we look at each other, his eyes drowning with emotion, yet he keeps his face impassive.

"I actually think that was a pretty smart move, to be honest," Pacey chimes in, coming close to me and lacing her arm around mine. "Arianyte can be terrifying. I definitely would've peed my pants if I was in that situation. Ardelle said they strapped you down and were torturing you. Stars. Who cares if you told a white lie? It's not like Arianyte and the SSPARROWs don't lie."

"Hey, not all SSPARROWs," Sylo clarifies.

My cheeks blush at her vocal defense of my actions, but I'm sure that's not going to last when she realizes that I lied to her about breaking into the outpost. I'm not sure why they aren't asking why I was up on that roof blasting my crystal if I wasn't being forced to by an alien madman, but I continue on before they think too deeply on that detail. I'm sure someone is thinking it and wondering for themselves.

Pace and I both hop over a small stream at the same time, arms still linked. The others follow behind, completely unaware of the massive bomb I'm about to drop.

"I'm glad it's not as big of a deal as I've made it out to be in my head, but there's more," I say, my heart going faster with every word.

This is the big drop . . . *I've been working for the Resistance since day one and have been actively lying and spying on you and Malakyte and Arianyte in order to relay information back to the Resistance so I can find my long-lost friend and get revenge for Arianyte kidnapping him.*

Simple.

But before I can spill my guts, Jance walks up on the other side of me.

"Kid, none of us have walked in your shoes, and none of us can fully comprehend what you had to do to survive out there on your own. I'm sure you had to do many things that you're not proud of in order to survive alone out there." He isn't wrong. "Whoever you were before now, and whatever you did, it doesn't matter. Each of us was a different person before coming together but being a part of this family has changed us all, I believe, for the better. We're stronger together; we make each other better people. All of us understand that life can deliver blows that leave us worse off than we were beforehand, but if we commit to being better every single day and not letting those events or bad choices define us, we can move forward from them. You don't need to confess anything to us, all you need to do is commit to being a better version of yourself and giving yourself grace and forgiveness for whatever you feel is weighing so heavily on you."

When I look up at him, Jance's espresso eyes are warm and tender and full of something I've never seen before. Something I never saw in Geonni's eyes—it's love there. Some type of love, something like a father would have for a daughter, and it really floors me. My first instinct is not to believe it, asking myself what he's doing or trying to gain. However, it really doesn't feel like that's the case, that I can trust in him. Is he purposely giving me a way out? I can feel that deep pull and connection described to me when it comes to the Ringers, especially after last night.

I finally understand that it's more than a normal connection. It's deep, and hope blooms inside my chest that, yeah, I lost the Resistance—those I thought were my family—but family doesn't abandon each other; they don't ask you to murder for them. Perhaps, if I can do this right for once in my life, the people here can be the family I've always wished for, the family that's good for me and lifts me up and makes me a better person. The family that can truly love me for me, and I don't have to hide my mark or my powers or who I am in order to be good enough. A family that'll see past what I've done . . . maybe.

"But Jance—"

"You don't need to fall on the sword, kid," Jance interrupts before I can say much more. "I promise you that none of us are perfect. You don't need to be. It's okay."

I get his words, that's fine and all, but he doesn't realize what I've been doing. Although, the others seem to share his sentiments—even Sylo doesn't seem to care about what secrets my past holds—almost like their own closets are full of skeletons too.

I decide to take Jance's words at face value and not reveal what I was doing with the Resistance. I have a little more confidence now that if Trinity or Geonni or someone else in the Resistance were to rat me out, Jance would come to my defense. Maybe Pacey, too. The dumb part of me hopes that Ardelle would as well.

CHAPTER 32

For being almost midnight, a frigid winter night, the city is still bustling as Ardelle and I walk towards our mysterious destination. Small amounts of snow silently fall, their individual stories wisping by us, stark against the dark night. Then they melt against rooftops, warm cheeks, and forgotten things left unattended in the cold, their lives coming to an end as they melt upon landing.

We each snagged a cup of coffee from one of the late-night shops, half to warm ourselves, half to stay awake. Something had possessed Ardelle to insist only the two of us go on my training mission for tonight, and I have no idea what he's dragging me into. I simply try to keep up with his ridiculously fast stride.

"Hey! I don't have your legs, remember. Can you at least tell me where we're going?" I moan as he forces me to make little dashes in order to keep up. His cologne, hitting me harder than my decadent cup of coffee, does not escape my notice. Neither does the fact that he had gotten his haircut today. His overgrown mop of dirty blond hair is now buzzed into a smooth fade, the remaining length styled dapperly to the opposite side of his hard part. It looks amazing on him, like overnight he became a man. When I first saw him, I looked twice, maybe three times.

"Nope, wait and see."

Turning down a street, then another, we find ourselves alone on a darkened road. It's a little bit creepy out here. Not to be paranoid or anything, but my intuition feels like we're being watched.

"You nervous about something?" Ardelle asks, noticing I've nudged as close as I possibly can to him without actually touching.

I chuckle lightly, brushing off my paranoia. "Creepy neighborhood is all. Maybe all we've been through the last month has gotten under my skin, you know? Ever feel that way?"

"It has been a lot," he agrees. "But, I wouldn't think you'd be super affected by any of it."

I take a big swig of my coffee, then I laugh out loud, my breath bursting out in front of me like cannon fire. "Where do you get the audacity, dude? Stars . . ."

He looks down at me, an unforgivable expression on his face. "Come on, Thumbelina, you're our resident wild child. Nothing gets to you."

"You must have forgotten about how badly I needed you after opening that little present from Deimos."

Ardelle makes a grumbling noise that sounds like a reluctant agreement. "I suppose so. You're hard for me to read, apparently."

"Ardelle, you're like the king of unreadable. I never know if you hate me or you're simply tolerating me because you don't like me. But they do say what you don't like in others is a direct reflection of what you don't like in yourself. So, take that."

Pretending to be stabbed by some type of fake weapon, Ardelle staggers, and without thinking, I grab hold of him to make sure he doesn't fall. Surprisingly, he pulls me into him once he stands upright and I'm enveloped in his warmth.

I tingle despite myself.

"It's not you, I promise. Well, maybe in the beginning it was you," he confesses.

"No, it absolutely was me. I'm not what you normally engage with. I challenge you and your preconceived notions of who people like me are. I don't fit the mold you expected and it kills you to be wrong."

Sipping his coffee gingerly, he ponders my words. "Are you reading some deep psychology books in your spare time?"

"What spare time?" I say, both of us laughing at the truthful irony. His face is looking straight ahead as I look up at him, and I see the little boy from the photos in his house and know for certain I made the right choice. "I've just lived a lot of life, I guess. I can read people."

"And you don't think you misjudged me at first?" This time, Ardelle presses back at me.

I shrug. "I did."

How could I not have?

A soft chime rings out into the air, and one-handed, Ardelle pulls his Dez from his coat pocket, reads the message there, and responds. For a second, I swear his brow is furrowed in a scowl, but then he looks back up at me, a bit confused.

"This way." He abruptly snatches my arm, leading me down an even more sketchy side street. I eye him suspiciously as we walk, and it's almost like his eyes are darting all over the place.

Once we arrive on another main street, I'm about to say something when he stops us outside an old building with a dramatic arched entrance.

"We've arrived," he announces, ushering me forward as my heart leaps at the building before us.

"This is one of the last remaining bookstores on the entire continent," I breathe in awe, my breath pluming out before me against the dark night. "Which is lovely, but it's closed. Exactly like all the other shops around here. It looks like the zombie apocalypse on this block. You're not going to make me break into this place or something, are you? You know books aren't being made anymore. Everything is digital, so these are precious commodities."

Looking as cocky as ever, Ardelle fishes into his fancy coat and pulls out something I haven't seen in ages: an actual key. Like a key–key. With only a look of satisfaction, Ardelle hands me his cup of coffee, inserts the key into the lock, and softly opens the door.

"Where in the almighty empire did you get that?" Brows raised, I look at him skeptically.

Smiling, a shadow of a dimple appears on his cheek in the darkness of this deserted street. Damn that face when he smiles . . . "Let's just say there are perks to being a hero of the city."

I snort so loud it echoes.

"You would."

Opening the ancient door with a loud creak and ushering me inside, Ardelle finds no hesitation from me. It's a magnificent building. Old, from before the war, yet perfectly preserved. It had a glow of sparkling gold to it, even at night, as if a fairy came through every so often and sprinkled magic across its floors. The bottom floor has a circular hub at its center, where worker bees would be scanning items and checking out customers. Surrounding the hub are rows upon rows of shelves stuffed to the brim with books. Signs everywhere read: 'Fiction,' 'Romance,' 'Extraterrestrial Studies.' Looking up, gazing at the rows and levels of multiple floors, I'm stunned. To me, they could have gone on until they touched the stars.

Pillars of gold frame the bottom stairway leading up to the other floors where thousands of books hold their enchanting secrets. There's another floor above that, then another, and another. Tall windows look down upon this area, feeling much like those of a cathedral or castle. Golden stained-glass frames it like an old sixteenth-century doorway, and moonlight shines inside, blanketing the entire space in a pale glow that carries a magic all on its own. The only lights that remain turned on are randomly placed miniature lamps with old-world violet shades.

I ogle wide-eyed, a smile brighter than the sun plastered on my face as I open the closest book and sniff it as if it were the last piece of food left on the planet.

"Didn't take you for a book nerd," Ardelle says from behind me as he unbuttons his coat in the color Temperance Gray.

"Didn't take you for someone who could read," I laugh.

His face looks around, taking it all in. "I chose this place because I used to come here to get away from my parents. From all their punctuality and endless assessing. I could be who I truly was here, I could escape."

Not wanting to open that can of worms, but knowing how important it is that I do, I say, "Yet you're determined to go back? To put Pacey back in that situation?"

"You've never wanted to stay with someone who isn't exactly good for you?" he asks, and I immediately think of Geonni and the rebels. Yes, yes I do. When I don't answer him, he continues.

"Her nightmares have stopped since being at Jance's," he tells me. "While we were on the run, she would have these night terrors where she'd scream bloody murder. I swore I'd never bring her back home until I knew for sure Mom and Dad understood what they were doing to us wasn't okay."

It feels like Ardelle is proving my point for me. I think back to our night breaking into the outpost, how she told me about her sexuality and how her parents and Ardelle likely wouldn't understand. "Pacey is a unique individual. I don't know your parents, but from what you describe of them, I can't see her being her true self with them no matter what."

He nods. "You wouldn't even recognize her a year ago. She gets to be herself now."

"So why are you trying to draw her back into that situation? She doesn't want to go back. She's told me that," I press.

Conflicted, Ardelle glides his hand through his hair. "I don't know. Family is complicated."

"I don't have a real family, as you know," I say, knowing that I can't truly help him. "But I've been a part of many. Most I didn't fit into, many I watched from the outside looking in, wishing that I did. You're lucky to have Pacey, and despite what I think is a dysfunctional set of parents, you're lucky to have them too. But the mental health and physical safety of you and your sister are what come first. If your parents can't love you both for who you are, there's something fundamentally wrong there. No amount of changing who you are will be enough to please their unattainable standards."

Ardelle looks at me almost like I've decked him in the face, but slowly his face softens, the shadows becoming less harsh.

"Well, we didn't come here to talk about me and my family problems."

I cringe, not really excited to see why he brought me here. So instead, I go searching for the art books to shake off the heaviness of this conversation.

When I hear his heavy boots following me as I saunter across the white marble floor, I wait for his rebuke.

"We're not here for the books either."

"Yawn, yawn, yawn. You can't take a girl into this place when there's no customers or people and expect her not to take advantage of that. Living with your sister should've taught you about that one."

Taking my one chance, I ditch him as I sneak into a cardboard cutout of a castle entrance in the children's section. The space leads to another exit, one I promptly skate through before he squeezes himself through the tiny castle.

"Thumbelina." I can hear the annoyance in his voice through the many layers of books and children's displays between us, but I only giggle as I take off and lose him between pages of knights fighting dragons all to gain the princess's love.

Once I find the stairs again, I take them two at a time, with small but powerful strides.

On the second floor, I take off deeper into the building, knowing it'll take Ardelle a while to find me up here.

I make it through the young adult and science fiction sections before his grumpy attitude finally finds me.

"Took you long enough." I slam a hardback shut for emphasis.

Arms crossing, Ardelle deadpans, "You're so clever."

I walk up to him and place my hands on my hips. "You should have known better than to pin me down. Especially in a place like this. But, you've got me now, so what are we doing here? By all means, grace me with your sophisticated presence."

Without speaking, Ardelle leads us up two flights of marble staircases. There, we find two green velvet chairs sitting across from each other on either side of a petite golden antique table. We sit face-to-face.

"Okay," he breathes, grabbing my hands and placing them in the center of the small table, palms up. My body tingles like a schoolgirl's would, surprised at his touch. His hands are warm, solid, strong. When he lets go, I'm slightly disappointed. Only about ten percent or so. Does he see my cheeks blushing? My lip biting? It's painful how beautiful he is, especially with that haircut, and I have to force these thoughts away. Stupid thoughts. That would only lead to disappointment: he would never choose a girl like me. *Focus, Kara.*

"Jance told me that when you've been training with your crystal, the energy output is enormous and uncontrollable. He seems to think you've done the work to bring the energy out, but now it's a blazing inferno after years of you pushing it down. We're here specifically to force you to control your abilities. There's a lot of vital information in this building, information that doesn't exist anywhere else in the world on some shelves. If you blow this place to high heaven, there's a lot to lose. Your choice. Now, show me what you can do."

"But—" I begin, horrified and contemplating any excuse I could think of to not go through with this.

236

Shrugging, his sapphire jewel eyes pierce into mine. "Like I said, there's a lot to lose."

Mouth hanging open, I look away. I'm rendered speechless.

As we sit in the dark building, tense minutes pass us by and the silence becomes too unbearable. "I'm not doing this. I'm going to kill you."

And I've already hurt enough people.

"You won't."

"I will."

"You've been practicing with Jance for weeks and you're nowhere closer to controlling your energy output. This forces your hand."

"But what if—"

"Don't overthink this," he interrupts, hovering his hands over mine. "Concentrate on condensing the energy. Imagine another force pushing it down into a small ball. You have the power, it's all there, you simply need to tone it down and control it. It doesn't control you, it's not your enemy, and it doesn't make you a monster. If I can master my abilities, so can you."

His words surprise me as much as his insane request. It's nice, for once, to have someone simply understand what I'm going through with this thing. How difficult this burden is to bear. How I truly feel like a monster, like this crystal is a living, breathing beast calmly waiting for its time to come out and eat its fill. It's been gluttonous lately. It's also a persistent reminder of what happened at the orphanage. A reminder of what I'm really capable of.

"You make it sound so easy," I whisper, staring down at my hands. There are no sounds in this building, the wooden bookshelves and floors holding their collective breaths to see what I will do. No kids playing or crying, not one person chatting or bells dinging as people come and go. It is only Ardelle and me, our soft breaths and hushed voices the only sounds.

Ardelle's stare is getting more uncomfortable by the minute, and I realize he won't let me out of this. But I want to learn more control, so I make the choice to try.

Focusing my attention on the center of my hands, I let out a shaking breath. It is easier to bring the power up now because instead of pushing it down deep every day, it bubbles under the surface. Which feels like a dangerous game to play, since my emotions flare wildly in crazy situations, and that leads to the crystal becoming unstable. I have to keep an even keel at all times now, or else it would erupt. My training blew away the many years of walls I've built to keep my power down. However great my progress, it's still wildly out of control. I really hope Ardelle knows what he's doing. It would really be a shame if I blow this place up.

The heat fills up my chest, and that familiar rush I've begun craving soaks into me like a drug would. My lashes flutter as the mark stings in succession. I release another breath and ease into the sensations.

My hands shake from so much energy brimming right there that it hurts not to let it burst out like I typically would. My monster is tasting its freedom; it wants out of its cage.

"Imagine it as a small ball," Ardelle instructs as he sees me struggling, his voice a serious whisper. His hands are directly above mine. "See it in your mind's eye. See it as easy and natural. You have control of this, Thumbelina, not the other way around. Remember that."

My chest swells, the power at a threshold. "Ardelle, I'm going to destroy this place." I'm feeling my control slipping. "I don't think I can do this."

"You won't destroy anything," he says, sounding so sure. "You've got this."

Wishing I had his confidence, I regrettably realize I am past the point of no return. I built the energy up too high to not release it now. The feelings of melting insides that Jance and Ahren had warned about tickles at the corners of my thoughts. Sparks of pink begin shooting around us, but they're not confined to my hands. Ardelle demands that I condense them, to bring them closer between my hands. I try imagining them being pulled down in between them. It takes some force, and I feel my entire body dripping with sweat under my winter leather jacket and scarf.

"They're coming in closer. Keep going. You're doing phenomenal. I know you can do this." The air is crackling with static electricity, lifting the finer hairs on both our heads into the air. My hands are trembling now, partially from fear but mostly from power. It surges within me like a star, and for all I know, the sun itself is shining within me now.

I gasp, the energy slipping from my hold. Ardelle jumps to his feet, his hands hovering over mine as his pupils glow red hot. I sense him then, that distinct sensation of his crystal shooting to life. Ardelle's gravity magic is holding my antimatter in check.

He's visibly straining to keep the energy contained, and I can see it wobbling this way and that, thrashing at its cage. He scrunches his face in concentration, but he's holding it. *We* are holding it—together.

Once it stabilizes, I watch the ball of pure solid antimatter energy. It's gorgeous, far from the destructive beast I've come to loathe. The coloring is vivid Bubblegum Pink and Fuchsia Tart, blending into a stunning magenta that lights up Ardelle's face and the surrounding area. Now that we condensed it into a ball with the diameter of a basketball, it looks to be made of an opal-type glass. The colors of the pinks and purples swirl around each other like creamer just poured into black coffee. White-hot flashes of lightning bounce within it, creating a beautiful, silent symphony of colors within a storm of pure antimatter.

"Wow . . ." I breathe, mesmerized.

When I dare to look away from it, my eyes immediately lock onto Ardelle's. He has already been watching me, and my power surges and the ball grows bigger—responding to my emotions. To Ardelle. He smirks in response, sensing how he makes me feel. Stars . . . how embarrassing.

The books and the giant risk of this situation all blur around the edges as the two of us remain locked in a trance. There could've been a battle raging around us for all we could tell. For whatever reason, my mind pops into the strange visions I've had of the alien warrior begging me to stay with him. The two men remind me of each other, somehow. Strong, protective, brave. This is the only moment that I've felt a connection between the two, despite them both having the same crystal symbols, but something clicks together here unexpectedly.

Then my concentration slips.

It snaps.

My brain tries to grab back onto it, but I can't. I see Ardelle straining as the ball veers left and right wildly. I have to focus, rein it in.

Clearing my mind of any thoughts of Ardelle or vivid visions, I remember the tools that Jance gave me for this exact situation.

Imagine my power seeping back into my body and release out of my shoulders in a fine mist. Visualization is key to control. Jance kept driving that into my brain, and I find it working as the ball of energy steadies. It becomes smaller and smaller until Ardelle can sit back down in his chair and control it with little effort.

Then the energy zaps back into me, causing an electric shock between Ardelle and me. We're both shot backwards into our chairs, each tipping over onto the hard marble ground. My shriek is the only thing that explodes into the air, echoing out onto the dark floors beyond. The energy of the crystal has evaporated, plunging us back into darkness. The dragon is calming and seeping back to its depths—for now. No deaths, no explosions, and most importantly—all books remain intact.

And I feel more alive in this moment than I have since before Gavrielle . . . since that awful night. This was a new night, a new memory formed and made, and it isn't terrible.

I feel invincible.

What starts off as a giggle quickly turns into a full-on fit of laughter. To my surprise, Ardelle starts laughing too. The sound of the two of us bounces off the books as moonlight shines overhead.

I roll to my side after finally gaining control of my laughter. "I can't believe I controlled it. Well, with your help." My voice sounds stunned as I watch him walk over to me.

"I was fairly certain you could do it, but I did have my doubts," he confesses as he holds a hand out. I remember the last time he offered his hand, and how I swatted it away with defiance and loathing. But after tonight, I guess he deserves a little more credit. I take his hand, and he lifts me up to my feet with ease.

"So that whole bit of confidence you had back there was all for show?" I push him jokingly.

"No. I guessed I'd be uniquely suited to help tame your power. Although, the bookstore was my idea. Despite the fact you're a clear book nerd, anybody with a brain could see the information within this building is invaluable. It's a good motive for you to do everything you possibly can to keep it from being destroyed. I'm glad you were able to keep it together.

"It was a solid effort, Thumbelina. You will be able to get this down; just keep working on it until it comes naturally. I'm thinking that eventually you'll be able to do incredible things with your crystal, besides destroying everything around you. That ball could become an impenetrable shield; it could become rain and decimate large numbers of enemy soldiers. You have an amazing imagination; your art is enough to prove that. Use it to get creative with your powers."

I look at him, so surprised that he even gave me that amount of thought. "A shield? Yeah, right."

"A hat, then? It could become anything, Thumbelina."

He isn't as awful as I initially thought, but stars, that nickname. "Do you really have to keep calling me that?" I demand. Ardelle's smile is genuine and mischievous. "What?"

He shrugs, throwing on his coat and scarf. "What about Ankle-Biter? I almost like that one better; it's awfully fitting."

I punch him in the shoulder, and he pretends to be hurt. "Absolutely not!"

He turns to run from me, hiding behind an eight-foot-tall bookcase. "Fun-Sized? Tinkerbell? Bite-Sized? I really like Bite-Sized."

I take the nearest book and chuck it at him, and he dodges it by slipping back behind the bookshelf. "Hey! Those are precious commodities, Bite-Sized!"

"Stop it," I whine as I go after him, but of course, he sneaks around to the other side of the bookcase when he hears me coming. "You're dead as soon as I catch you."

"You got to catch me on those little legs first," he shouts from the other side of the shelf. The urge to push it on top of him is overwhelming.

"I'm faster than I look."

"Okay, Thumbelina. Whatever you say."

CHAPTER 33

After training for the last three weeks since the parade, twelve hours a day, and trying to fight off nightmares of Deimos, the smells of the Zarmenian Christmas Carnival gives me new life. It's entirely Christmas themed, one of the few remaining old-world holidays we celebrate on the continent. Even the Extras get into it. Jance says it's more nostalgic than it is about the religion Christmas sprung from because after the existence of aliens was proven, religion became irrelevant. Most people believe in reincarnation, matrix theory, multiple dimensions, and all sorts of stuff that was coo-coo before the aliens arrived. Yet, they taught humans a thing or two about the true nature of reality.

There are Santas and elves, reindeers and Christmas mouses, little people building toys and gingerbread houses, and foods of all kinds. People here seem happy as they play games in booths, shop out of tents, and eat goodies they can't get anywhere else. The rides are also Christmas themed, with winter wonderlands and gingerbread men painted on the sides. The flashing lights twinkle red and green, icy whites mixed with berry blues, rich golds, and reds.

I can't help but feel happy to be here, too, allowing myself to feel good despite what the Resistance has done.

We practically skip through the entrance, each of us wrapped up in our winter hats, scarves, and gloves to ward off the chill.

As people walk by, I search their faces. A habit now, looking for green glowing eyes that may watch me from vacant expressions. Though, I also think of Gavrielle, if he is a face in this crowd, if he is looking for me too.

A sweet voice raises up as we all take in our surroundings. "Kettle corn!" Pacey shouts like an anthem. Anything other than the protein-packed clean diet we're all bullied into eating every day. Bring on the junk food.

"Let's go, I see some right there," I say, craving a giant corn dog with extra mustard. All of us get some type of unhealthy snack. Jance is probably dying inside over it, but none of us care about his overly strict rules tonight. It's our collective day off.

"Jance needs to relax and take Saris on a ride or something," I tell Pacey as we wait in line for food. Jance looks around, worried and stressed.

Pacey starts giggling.

"What?" I ask.

"Yeah, no, he really needs to take her on a ride." Her perfectly drawn-on eyebrows bounce.

Oh stars, gross!

I make a disgusted face and sound, doing all that I can to get that image out of my mind.

"I think he's worried this place is a soft target," I say as I watch kids jump around people dressed up as alien elves. It definitely is.

"Why the worried faces over here?" Ardelle asks as he approaches us. "This is a carnival, sticky fingers and smiles are mandatory. No sadness tonight," he says specifically to me. Oh yeah, I suppose I've still been sad over Geonni's abandonment.

I smile at him a bit condescendingly, and he bares his teeth at me playfully in return. His hair is styled in a hard gel perfectly to one side of his part. His outfit is simple, a black-on-black fully lined sheep's fur jacket with a matte leather on the outside, paired with blue jeans as a throwback to the old world. A group of teen girls in line behind us continue to gawk at Ardelle. He wears his cocky smile as confidently as any prince, and I'm a little annoyed at myself for feeling a twinge of something unpleasant when I see him winking back at them. I don't actually *like* this guy, do I? The butterflies flopping around in my belly say *maybe*.

"If it wasn't so cold, we'd be a lot happier," Pacey says as she hunches down and curls up against her brother. The girls in line give her death glares. Pacey doesn't dress for the occasion, going toe to toe with the winter weather and giving it the middle finger in a neon-yellow nylon dress that shifts colors in different lightings, but at least she's wearing thick white tights and a Bubblegum Pink fur coat that's long fur ruffles in the soft breeze.

We get our food and bring some back for the others. We eat, we visit the animals and play some carnival games.

"See, they rig the game," Jance points out as we stand before a carnival booth, and the look of the worker is skeptical. It's the game where you try to get a softball, which is connected by a string, around a bowling pin and knocking it down on its way back. The bowling pin sits on a plain, circular wooden platform, while the ball is attached to the ceiling, dangling around the pin like a pendulum.

"Show us again?" Jance asks the man running the suspicious game. The game master places the pin on the platform, swings the ball, passes the pin, then, on the way back, hits it dead-on.

When it's my turn, I bring the ball back super high, hoping for the most momentum. Letting it go, the ball swings past the pin, and on its swing back I think it's going to hit, but it misses by a hair.

"How come he can do it?" I ask. I'm with Jance on this one. Rigged.

Unenthusiastically, the man snatches the pin back up into his hands. "Experience."

"We'll give it one more go." Ardelle appears out of nowhere and hands over his Dezlar to deposit the cato credits. Jance gets called away by Sylo and Saris and doesn't get to watch as the game runner places the pin back onto the platform and Ardelle takes the softball. The ball casually falls from his hand and grazes past the pin, and in a swoop, swings back, looking as if it's going to miss it. Then, as if a phantom wind nudged it along, the softball knocks the pin over. I see the residual red glow fading from Ardelle's pupils as he glances sidelong at me for the briefest of seconds, and when he looks back up to the man the red glow has vanished.

Bad boy. After my own heart right there.

The man places the pin back upright, sighing unexcitedly. "You won. What'll it be?"

He bumps me softly. "Whatever the pretty lady wants, sir."

It's impossible to not smile up at him. "I'll take the biggest triceracorn stuffy."

As we walk towards the others, I say to Ardelle, "I didn't think such a guy of your stature, with such perfect morals, would stoop to such criminal levels for little old me."

That cocky smile still hasn't faded from the moment he won that game. "Well, Thumbelina, maybe there's more to me than you think?"

"Oh my, my, my, where did that thing come from?" Pacey muses as we meet up with her, Jance, and Saris—Ahren and Sylo currently checking out the animals. My cheeks are blushing as red as a Santa hat as I approach holding a stuffed animal half my size. "Wow, big brother, good job." Pacey doesn't even have to ask to know; the smile on my face tells enough.

"What do you suggest we do now?" Ardelle asks with a twinkle of mischief in his eyes, avoiding her question yet walking around like a prized peacock. Jance glances over at him, sensing Ardelle already has some idea up that wicked sleeve of his.

"No," Jance says sternly, glaring at Ardelle. It doesn't sound like there's room for negotiation.

"Come on, it'll be fine. One ride," Ardelle suggests, his voice as smooth as whipped frosting. But Jance isn't so swept up in Ardelle's sweet persuasion as I am. Plus, it seems hard to imagine Jance on a carnival ride.

"No," Jance reiterates, more sternly.

"Well, I'm not going on one of those death traps, either," Saris says, lacing her arm around Jance's as if he'd protect her.

"Ice cream?" Jance asks Saris, her typically stone-cold face smiling a tad bit.

"I thought you'd never ask."

I glance back and smile as they disappear into the crowd, leaving me with the siblings.

"Guess it's me and you two weirdos," Ardelle says, putting one arm around each of us as we walk on either side of him.

"Such a joy," Pacey says in clear sarcastic vexation.

The warmth of his arm around my neck feels nicer than it should when he says, "Don't sound so excited, sis. I'll get you riding that one ride with the gravity trick that you threw up on that one time. You know the one that spins really fast? And it was because I was unknowingly making it way worse for everyone in there. You remember that?"

Pacey's face looks aghast. "Yeah, you psycho. I was six, and it felt like you were crushing my body. Half the kids threw up on that ride, half were choking and the other were crying; it was a disaster."

Ardelle laughs at the memory.

"You must have been such a pain-in-the-ass brother to grow up with," I say unapologetically.

"Oh, I was," he says unabashedly, and I look up at him as we walk aimlessly forward. His eyes, stars, they're so focused on me. Every time they meet my own, I wonder if his body heats up the same way mine's beginning to.

Being here, with the two of them, feeling accepted and finally in a place where I could belong, I allow myself to smile. To really smile. To feel the one thing I want most . . . like I'm a part of a family. My forever family. The Resistance was like a family, the closest I ever had, but there was always a separation between them and me. Me having this mark with an incredible power and them being regular Terrans . . . it always made me different. However, now that I am here with the other Starseeds, there is no me and them—we're all simply together.

Truly, for the first time in my life, I belong here. I genuinely feel that. There's nothing I won't do to protect this.

Nothing.

"Well, I'm going to get myself an 'Out of This Galaxy' slush," Pacey announces as she slips out from under Ardelle's arm, "but that Ferris wheel is looking like it's about to let people on. Why don't the two of you get to know each other better?"

Shoving us towards the Ferris wheel's line, she giggles manically as she glides away into the crowd, leaving the two of us alone.

Why my cheeks redden all of a sudden is beyond me.

Say something smart or interesting, I order myself.

"That was—" I begin when he also starts to say something at the same time.

"No, you go first," he says politely as we step up onto the metal platform, next in line for the ride.

Biting my lip nervously, I say, "Thanks for this guy." Holding up the stuffed animal, I pet its soft head with my long nails.

His smile is broad, and he looks happy for once, that heaviness that always seems to follow him around like a raincloud cleared away by sunshine. He seems . . . himself. "When I caught you napping, you were snuggling a pillow. Thought you could use something real to cuddle with."

"What's realer than a stuffed animal?" I say without thinking, feeling that electricity bounce off the two of us.

His eyes dance with amusement, almost excited to play this dangerous game. "Something strong, warm . . . something that's arms can hold you back."

I bite my bottom lip, and his body shifts, edging closer, the lights from the Ferris wheel reflecting off his eyes.

"I can imagine that's a lot better than a stuffed animal." The blood rushing within me is a tsunami.

Ardelle places both hands on each side of my arms as he closes the final step that separates us. Once he bends down to whisper into my ear, my heart begins to race. "It feels like home, and desire, and never wanting to be anywhere else."

My small intake of breath betrays me.

"Next, you two, come on board," the ride operator says. The entire line of people including the operator is watching us intently, likely uncomfortable by our display. Ardelle pulls back, taking his warmth with him, and the two of us return to our senses and step onto the ride.

I'm already craving his touch, and I'm feeling awfully stupid for playing the most treacherous game at this carnival.

CHAPTER 34

The Ferris wheel's lights are flashing blue-and-white orbs with a snowflake at the center. Ardelle holds my hand to steady me as he lowers me onto the blue seat. It wobbles as he slides in next to me, his scent enveloping me in a hug. We slowly ascend backwards, our bird's-eye view growing better with each passing minute.

We crest the top, and the seat swings as the conductor breaks to let more people on. Grasping onto his arm, I try to push my nausea down.

His chuckle doesn't ease the death grip I have on him when I explain. "I almost died on one of these death traps once, leave me alone."

"What? The fearless Thumbelina has a weakness, and it's the dreaded Ferris wheel? And all this time I've been using my irresistible charms in attempts to break you down when all I needed to do was get you on this ride? Stars . . ."

The punch I throw is playful, but I make sure it has a little kick in it for good measure. "You can't really believe I'm fearless. That's too much of a compliment for you to give."

"I don't think you truly see yourself the way others do, Thumbelina," Ardelle says, not a tone of sarcasm present.

My snicker is bitter when I say, "Nobody truly sees me."

The way his brows knit together make his eyes look sad. "Why do you say that?" he asks as we crest the top again, the wind pulling my long strands of hair in all directions.

"Because it's true. We all hide parts of ourselves, and maybe because I spent so much time in the orphanage and foster homes or wherever, I got used to being what people wanted me to be. At some point, even

I forgot who I actually was, and I started wishing someone—anyone—would see past the mask that I wore. Maybe give me some insight into what I've become, you know? What I had to do to survive has made me into someone I don't recognize. I want to be better; I'm trying to be better, to find a way back to the girl I was before everything happened with Gavrielle. Isn't that the goal? To be accepted, that's what everyone wants, right?"

I think of Malakyte, actually. How he seems to see me . . . *Of all people.*

Ardelle's mouth opens to reply, but he stops himself. Those sapphire eyes are pools of awe and pain and something like the notion of understanding. Almost, but not quite. He still holds back, hiding behind solid walls. As do I. My sudden vulnerability causes me to instantly retreat behind that mask of protection so that it doesn't hurt as much when his rejection comes snapping back at me like a viper's fangs.

"Being seen means risking being rejected for all that you are."

He's not wrong.

"But then we're never seen, and we're never truly free," I whisper, the honesty in my voice too raw to say outright. "And you know . . . sometimes I just wish that someone would try. Try to get past my defenses for once. To look at all these wounds and not see baggage, but battle scars. I had a person who did that, and I let him get away. It's been the biggest mistake of my life."

Ardelle's hand comes up and brushes pieces of my hair that have gone flying all over the place from the wind behind my ear. Both of us feel the energy that passes when he says, "And that doesn't make you afraid? Afraid of letting someone in that close?"

Behind my eyes the prick of tears stings, yet I can't avert my eyes from his. I've lost count of how many times we've crested over the top, the world outside us disappearing into a bokeh of twinkling lights. His Dezlar beeps but he ignores it, taking my hands in his and shifting his body so we face each other, knees touching and bodies close.

"Maybe it just makes me stupid," I confess, feeling the utter terror of true vulnerability rattle through me. It's like free-falling off a cliff with the biggest jerk I've ever met, of all people, responsible for pulling my parachute. Ardelle doesn't have to be a jerk if he chooses not to be, and I have a funny feeling we aren't as different as we both initially suspected.

Inching even closer to me, I can smell his cinnamon breath on my cheeks. "I think it's the bravest thing I've ever seen. Thumbelina, being closed off completely, it keeps people away. I know because I've been doing it for years. I did it with you. Sure, perhaps we're safer that way, but like you said, nobody truly sees the real us. We always have to hide. Maybe I'm done hiding who I am? Maybe I want to be the person I am without feeling the pressures to be what everyone else wants me to be?"

His Dez beeps again, and this time he seems to hear it, and something like fear flashes behind his eyes, almost like something's clicked into place and he's only now realized it.

It's like I'm seeing Ardelle in a completely new light, and he's no longer that arrogant asshole who's constantly flipping crap to get a reaction out of me. Is he trying to say that is his mask? That it's not the real him? But instead, the person I'm seeing tonight and the last few weeks is the true Ardelle Dawson?

Because I'm weak and stupid and have no self-control, my eyes slip to his lips—heat rushing into me fast enough to turn the cold outside my body to steam. I crave his strong arms around me, need it almost like a drug. To know what it would feel like to have him affectionately holding me and keeping me safe seems almost like a dream.

One I want to drive headfirst into, despite myself.

The tension from before we got on the ride ramps back up, the pull low in my stomach strengthening like a volcano wanting to burst.

Another buzz from his device. He ignores it still.

Our lips are so close the wind between them barely has room to sing its sweet, deceptive song. My hands lace and tighten around his, feeling as his other hand moves to the smallest part of my waist while he pulls me onto him.

His face moves in closer still, my fake lashes brushing up against his cheekbones.

I realize I want him to kiss me; I want him to touch me and place his hands all over me.

His Dezlar begins ringing now, and his eyes close in annoyance as the two of us part. Disappointment floods me as he pulls it out from his pocket and reads it.

"Is it Jance?" I ask, assuming my overprotective Ringer wants to know where we're at.

However, Ardelle's face looks grim as he stares down at his device, brows knitted together with what looks like genuine fear on his face. "What's wrong?"

He looks back up at me, a flash of panic there for a moment, but he shuts the device off and puts it back inside his pocket.

"How about when this ride ends, we get out of here? You and me?"

I'm a little taken back by his suggestion. "Without the others? Where would we go?"

"Yeah, of course, just us," he says with a soft chuckle. "And it doesn't matter. We can go anywhere. Let's ditch this place."

I shake my head. "You're ridiculous." But I can't help but smile as I say it.

Ardelle offers his hand to me, and I don't think I can resist saying yes to him and this adventure.

"Okay, yeah. Let's ditch. You're such a bad boy, Ardelle. You better cut it out or you may become my type."

"Baby, I've always been your type."

My cackle rings out into the icy night air. "You think way too highly of yourself."

Ardelle opens his mouth to answer when the Ferris wheel suddenly and abruptly brakes. I'm slammed into him forcefully, our heads clank against each other, and I curse loudly. Our cart whips forward from the sudden stop, and our momentum brings us backwards way too far. Anxiety floods through me as I shout in fear, and Ardelle holds onto me as our cart whips back and forth, his crystal the only thing steadying it.

Something's wrong . . .

Screams flare up from all over the park as the lights collectively flicker out till there are barely any lights at all.

The entire Christmas Carnival has been cast into an eerie darkness. The rides are forced to a dramatic stop.

The once lively area surrounded by the laughter of children and playfulness of the holiday has become one of blackness as the screams rain down from the other side of the carnival. Something terrible is coming.

CHAPTER 35

Screams continue to escalate across the carnival. Their cries reverberate off each other in a horror-filled symphony that makes my bones clatter together like trembling chains. Ardelle holds me close.

We are stuck at the crest of the Ferris wheel, and from this altitude it appears the electrical glitch that's spread throughout the park has forced many other rides into a similar unnatural stop.

"Ardelle," I breathe, my senses attempting to level out from his assault on them—to focus on anything other than his strong chin and perfectly shaped mouth. Contrarily, that awful, terrible gut twist that's come to haunt my dreams pulls all thoughts of Ardelle's mouth far from my mind. "He's here. I feel him. Deimos is here."

He plunges into his coat pocket and looks at his Dezlar once again, but when the light doesn't shine back onto his face, I know that it's dead too.

The entire park is dead.

"I feel him too," he says, eyes now scanning the park with careful attention. "He must have launched some type of short range EMP attack, because if our devices are dead along with the rest of the park, that can only be an EMP."

Stars . . .

A shriek rings out from below. We see a woman being chased by a colossal figure three times her size. It has scales for skin and a thick tail sailing behind it like an anchor.

A Reptilian.

"Oh shit," I gasp.

It doesn't take long for terror-filled pleas to rain down on us like sleet, chilling us both. Dozens and dozens of Reptilians fan from out of nowhere, their stocky shapes attacking anything in their path.

"We have to help these people," I say.

My legs wobble as I try to stand, and so does the cart. Ardelle grabs onto my hips tightly before I fall to my death, and I try my hardest not to make a comment about how my ass is directly in front of his face.

"Sit back down, Thumbelina. We need a strategy before going balls to the wall. Those Reptilians down there are over three times your size, double mine. Think about this."

"But Pacey is down there all by herself," I argue, knowing she's his weak spot.

"Pace is as much a helpless little princess as Jance is. She's fine for now. I do agree we need to find a way to help, but we've got to be smart."

Leaning on him, I slowly lower myself back down. He's right.

"So, what's the strategy then, sir?" I say mockingly, but he doesn't seem to listen as his eyes focus on something beyond me. I turn in time to see four to five dozen people, many children, running for their lives in our direction. Behind them, a large group of armed Reptilians make chase. Delightedly, I might add. Their bloodlust is palpable.

"Their eyes aren't green," I observe, "they're doing this of their own free will. Deimos isn't controlling them." At my words, I can see his mind ticking away behind those eyes in the shade Lapis. "Why would

Deimos be here with them if not to control them? He'd have a literal army at his disposal. Unless he can't control that many at once? That is a lot of minds to keep track of. Although, he seemed to do it just fine at the parade."

"Well, remember what the news said the other day?" Ardelle reminds me. "The dark territory of the outer Zarmenian undersewer tunnel systems has been lost to Arianyte for months. The occupation has been trying to reclaim it. Reptilian leaders have been organizing and fighting hard against Arianyte to keep their independence. That could be why they're here and Deimos is simply tagging along for the ride. You know he gets off destroying anything Arianyte, and they put on this Christmas Carnival thing every year as a solidary pledge."

Then I wonder something I should've asked myself from the very first moment.

"How did Deimos know we'd even be here?"

Ardelle stiffens, eyes locked down as children cry out for their mothers and fathers to make it all stop. He looks anguished and horrified.

"We're about to find out."

His words make me shudder.

For Ardelle and me, things look like they're about to get worse.

Below, about six or seven Reptilians assault people on and off the Ferris wheel. Those who stuck around or who are too high to jump off the wheel are screaming and fighting back. Throwing purses, Dezlars, and wallets—chucking anything to keep the monstrous aliens at bay. Someone even throws a valiantly won stuffed alligator, which simply bounces off a Reptilian in brutal irony, but there's no time to laugh.

"We have to help them. How do we get down? I mean, I could probably climb down," I suggest, looking at the wheel's spools and wondering if I could make it.

"No," he says quickly, "that's too dangerous. If one of them gets to you—no, I won't risk you getting hurt. I can use my crystal to get you down safely."

My teal eyes go wide. "It'll trigger Deimos to come this way. He'll feel it."

Ardelle nods, having thought of this. "Once you're down, I want you to run and find the others. Find Pace if you can, but don't tell her where I am. I'm serious, make her go with you. I'll draw Deimos to me, and you run."

I'm shaking my head before I can stop myself. "No," I tell him, defiant. "I'm not leaving you here. I'm not leaving you to him."

"Yes, you will," he snarls back at me, his voice as angry as I've ever heard it. Ardelle brings his hand up to my cheek. "Look at me."

His voice is low and deep. My mark tingles at his command, and I do as he says. He's trying to tell me something with this look, with those eyes that are blazing with fire and passion and pain.

"Ardelle—"

"He's after you," he interrupts. "I'm not messing around here. We got lucky at the parade, but that heart was a clear message. It was a threat. He wants that to be your heart in his hands. Your crystal inside his body. I told you to be careful, remember? I also told you I won't let him hurt you. We're not prepared for this fight, and we're highly outnumbered. Our weapons are at home; this was our one day off. Also, the likelihood SSPARROWs will come to assist is unlikely if we can't call out. Using my crystal is going to attract him like a moth to a flame, and he'll come. I'll be able to draw him away from you because you're the only one he wants. Let me do this for you, please."

"Well, he could want your crystal too."

"He doesn't."

"How do you know that?"

"Thumbelina, please." His voice is pleading, rushed.

"You don't owe me anything," I say, my mind spinning as to why he'd take such a huge risk.

Ardelle places both hands on my shoulders and angrily says, "Thumbelina, I—"

He searches my face and takes a deep breath.

"You're going to have to trust me."

Now, I have no other choice than to put my life in Ardelle Dawson's hands.

CHAPTER 36

"**S**o, you want me to let you throw me off the side of a Ferris wheel?" I end my question with a cynical laugh.

Hurt flashes in his eyes, but he shrugs and smirks.

"My crystal will manipulate the gravity surrounding your body so that you lower slowly. You won't fall. I know I haven't been the nicest to you and I've judged you unfairly, and I know this isn't the time or the place, but I'm sorry for that, Thumbelina. I was in such an awful place before you came home, before you woke me up and brought me back to life."

His words throw me, but we're glued to each other and there's no breaking it apart.

"I'd never put you in danger, Thumbelina. Trust me."

He makes me realize I had judged him too. I had thought he was this certain person with whom I couldn't connect and had nothing in common.

I was wrong.

"I trust you."

His nose brushes against mine and butterflies find their way into places they don't belong, places they've never been.

We can't stay like this any longer. The outside world is screaming and crying for our help—literally.

The people are running around like chickens with their heads cut off. Hordes of butt-ugly Reptilians with weapons of all shapes and sizes are chasing people. Their skin is a grayish green, lighter and darker in certain places, with visible scaling. Their tails are long and thick like an alligator's. They swing around and trip people at every turn, whipping and bashing their bodies to the ground, shopping tents and carts going with them. Popcorn and fried foods soar through the air like birds. I can smell the blood being spilled, the wind carrying it into the sky as it mixes with corn dogs and cotton candy and cries of children screaming.

"You won't let me fall?" I ask, my eyes searching for reassurance.

Despite the crazy scene unfolding around us, he brings me in and cups my cheek with his hand, his thumb softly brushing my bottom lip. "I'll never let you fall, Thumbelina. And even if you do, I'll always be there to catch you."

Stars, I'm in trouble . . .

A moment of silence passes, and I suddenly feel regretful about all the time I wasted hating this guy.

With his brawny arms, he holds me steady as I stand, the cart wobbling beneath my feet. The rush of his crystal's power floods into my belly with a familiar touch, a signature that's specially his.

The red-ember glow inside his eyes burns until it's fire incarnate.

I gasp as I'm lifted into the air, instinctively trying to grab onto something until I ultimately trust he will not let me fall. Lifting me up and over our cart, my stomach does flip-flops as he begins my descent down to the carnival grounds. Chaos reigns down there, brutal, deadly chaos—yet there's nothing but those eyes. Marbles of sapphire and the glow of red spheres hold me transfixed and oblivious to what's going down below me. Something unspoken passes between us as he holds my life in his hands. Whatever fracture that cracked our relationship at the beginning is now mended through honesty and vulnerability on both ends. Through trust. He lowers me as carefully as anyone has ever handled me, and I feel the gentle tug of the gravity envelope me like the most tender hug. Almost the same way you'd hold a baby duck, softly with all the care in the world.

My feet gently touch the ground at last. As I regain my balance, he lets his crystal fade. Our eyes still refuse to unlock. That mouth I wish would kiss me curls upwards in a smirk, and I can't help but smile back—and mean it.

"Watch out!" a girl from the wheel shrieks, shattering the moment between us like a hammer smashing through a mirror.

I see it coming a moment too late.

As if in slow motion, a Reptilian charges me like a linebacker in a china shop—and I'm the china.

"Thumbelina!" Ardelle shouts, fear spiking through me as I'm pounded from the side, and we tumble, my world getting tossed as if I've just been thrown inside a hurricane.

I don't even have a chance to scream.

CHAPTER 37

We somersault, the Reptilian body massive against mine as we roll once, twice, three times from the force of his hit. We finally come to a stop, and thank the stars, I land on top. I punch its flat face wildly the moment I catch my bearings. Because toe to toe, I'm no match for this thing. Its long, wet teeth drip with saliva while they snap and roar at me. It thrashes furiously at my fingers, and I dig my pointed nails into its eyes with all the ferocity that I have. It feels disgusting.

Its clawed hands wrap around my waist, practically covering my entire midsection as it violently throws me off it, nails digging into the skin there.

"You smell delicious," it purrs with a hissing texture, dark-green blood dripping from the corners of its eyes. "I don't need to see you to eat you."

My attacks are having no effect here. I skitter back in a half-attempted crabwalk, looking for any way out that doesn't involve my crystal. Deimos will know my crystal's energy signature and come running. He's likely already sensed Ardelle's and is heading here now. My heart's pounding. Using it would be like lighting off a firework that said, 'Here I am, come get your new crystal, asshat.'

It's up on its feet now, slowly creeping towards me. Searching for a weapon, any weapon, I find nothing but stuffed toys and dropped soda cups—I left my triceracorn stuffy on the Ferris wheel, I realize. Most of the people in this area have fled, and I do not know where Ardelle is. The wheel is twenty feet behind me.

I can't win this fight with brute strength. Jance told me that's always going to be my biggest weakness.

He's right.

Given that, once I rise to my feet, I run towards the Reptilian.

He doesn't expect me to come at him. Quickly pivoting right before he goes to grab me, I shoot behind him, swiftly kicking hard at the back of his knee with the heel of my boot. His scream fills me with adrenaline, and I move even faster. My goal is never to win this specific brawl, so the moment my pointed ears hear the noise of shattering bone and cartilage, I dart away. It can't kill me if it can't catch me.

I know Ardelle told me to leave him, but as I look back towards the wheel, I hesitate. He's fighting six Reptilians. Even Ardelle's broad shoulders are nothing on these aliens, and they are double his size, standing a clear foot-and-a-half taller than him. He's holding his own with no weapon, using his brute strength to kick and punch the enormous bodies that surround him. I've never been so attracted to someone as I am while I watch him move like a pure predator, with grace and speed and power.

"Go!" he yells at me. My feet seem to be held in place by invisible hands sprung from the earth like a zombie.

Ardelle bends to the ground suddenly, his hand splayed before him as his fingertips touch the dirt. All at once, he thrusts the six aliens into the air with his magic, each sprawling in different directions like miniature tanks through the air. Wasting zero time, his long legs make it over to me quickly, never stopping as he grasps me by the arm and continues running.

"I told you to go," he growls, looking straight ahead and pulling me along like a ragdoll.

How could I describe why I couldn't leave him? Do I even know?

Opening my mouth to give him some type of answer, I gasp instead. We both skid to a stop and freeze like a couple of deer only now realizing they are being hunted and have been in the shooter's scope the entire time.

We never stood a chance.

Standing before us is a nine-foot-long catlike alien that fits every definition of the word beast. Its fur is midnight blue and spiky at the top, fur sticking out sideways along the inside of its wolflike ears. Its thin tail whips and snaps, the light on the tip that's shaped like a yellow teardrop glowing in the dark. I swallow nervously at its paws, its claws razor sharp and covered in blood. And those teeth . . .

"Ardelle . . ." I breathe as he slowly positions himself in front of me.

"I see you've met my little pet," a malevolent voice says from our left, and my heart plunges at the man who's grinning back at us.

CHAPTER 38

THE ARIANYTE EMPIRE DECREE #7

ALL CURRENCIES WILL NO LONGER BE OF ANY VALUE. THIS INCLUDES CRYPTOCURRENCY AND NATIONAL CURRENCIES. THE NEW GLOBAL CURRENCY WILL BE KNOWN AS CATO CREDITS AND SHALL BE DELIVERED, SHARED, TRADED, AND USED DIGITALLY THROUGH THE NETWORK.

Shoving me behind him, Ardelle and I stagger away from both beasts. Both extraterrestrials' eyes are glowing with the green Elendril crystal.

Jupiter's rings . . .

"You're a sick piece of shit, you know that?" I spit at Deimos, trying to run up to him, but Ardelle holds me back.

"Oh, we've got a wild one here, don't we?" Deimos mocks, voice light and excited and dripping with contempt—much different from how I expected him to sound. Deimos looks even scarier than he did in the shadows by the Capitol building. A sharp hairline of pure white hair contrasts with his dark-green skin that's weathered and wrinkled. His large, elongated ears frame his face, oversized enough to give him the dramatic look that's borderline comical. The black bodysuit with green piping shows that despite the alien's age, he is all muscle and certifiably not one to mess with. And those creepy black eyes never get easier to look into, especially when they glow green as they do now.

My gut is absolutely twisting.

"Who'd you kill for that heart, huh? Why didn't you just come up to me? So scared of a small girl like me, you had to hide behind a child?" I gesture to myself. Ardelle's jaw clenches. He stands directly in front of me, his body my shield.

Deimos's laugh is incredulous. "Perhaps I merely wanted to give you nightmares instead. Did you like the gift I left you? I thought it was quite . . . clever."

My head shakes in disgust at him, but he merely smiles a white, fanged-toothed grin.

"Since you're so pretentiously offended by my methods of introduction, I'd like to formally say hello, dear Karalevine. I've heard so much about you. You are a pretty thing, aren't you? I wonder if your heart looks as pretty as your face?"

"You don't scare me," I say as confidently as I can muster, but of course it's a flat-out lie. The fear may pour off me in waves, but I refuse to show an inch.

"I should."

The extraterrestrial cat-beast roars, giving us zero time before it charges, long teeth bared, glinting in the moonlight and eager to taste flesh and blood. My shriek blasts out into the frigid night air as it pounces right for the two of us.

The creature's paws are as big as my head and pivoting quicker than a moon fox. As its tail wags with bloodthirsty anticipation, it draws Ardelle and I away from each other. The two of us are separated instantly, leaving me alone with Deimos.

Ardelle has only seconds to jump out of reach of the beast's jaws. The sound of them snapping shut just as his leg escapes certain amputation shakes my bones like a jackhammer. It bends down on its front two paws, back end in the air in a pouncing stance. When it leaps, its jump is a massive arch that covers the distance between it and Ardelle faster than I could have ever thought. He stops it with his gravity somehow, feeling the crystal's power surge through me as he uses his magic to stop the monster. Those teeth are inches from his face, but he holds them back.

As saliva drips eagerly from its mouth, the sheer power of the monster's body breaks past his magic's defenses. Its enormous claws reach out and he doesn't jump out of the way fast enough and claws slice his upper thigh. His shout of pain causes me to take a step towards him, but I'm held back.

Deimos takes his opportunity while Ardelle is fighting his pet, and I dodge his first advance, quick as a dart.

"It's not wise to watch someone else when your opponent is standing right in front of you, you know," Deimos coos, and he's right. I'm being stupid, but I can't look away.

Ardelle heaves the beast aside with his power, throwing it a few yards with a painful roar, but it'll only give him several moments of rest. Blood pours from his leg, and I panic because that's the location of his femoral artery. If it's hit, he'll only be alive for another few minutes.

In my peripheral, I see Deimos slowly walking towards me.

"What do you want?" I ask Deimos as Ardelle and I lock eyes from thirty feet across the carnival grounds.

Deimos waves his hands around dramatically. "I thought my gift to you made that clear. Apparently, since you're not as smart as I've been led to believe, let me spell it out for your pretty little head. I want your crystal—it doesn't belong to you. I'm going to take it, and there's nothing you can do to prevent it."

CHAPTER 39

The green-eyed devil comes barreling down on me.

He's average height and build, but efficient. He fights in a style that's so foreign it throws me off. He lands the first blow to my shoulder, and I bounce backwards, feet tripping up.

As I catch my balance, he doesn't let up. He comes in to strike a second blow, coming in hot like a sky-rail train. But I'm faster. Dodging, I swivel my torso and elbow him hard in the chest—striking hard enough in the sternum to purge the air from his lungs. I use this precious time to place distance between us, looking for Ardelle. He somehow has spikes from a pop-up tent hovering in the air in front of him, pointy ends pointed at the alien beast.

"We can't play cat and mouse forever, kiddo," Deimos purrs as he calmly walks towards me again. The delight splashing on his ghoulish face shoots a shiver through me.

"You're never getting this crystal. If you get close, I'll fry you. Stop killing people for it; it's a waste of your time." We circle each other, the roaring of his beast raging behind me.

"Who says I'm killing because of you? You're an important piece in this game, kiddo, but you're not everything. You must love all this attention you're getting, being *the Star* and all," he mocks, and I step back, feeling the words like a blow to the gut. "But it may surprise you to find out that my motivations have little to do with you at all. You're simply in the way."

"Screw you."

He's saying this on purpose. I can't let him get to me.

He claps delightedly. The man is insane. Those dark eyes look me up and down, and I grimace in disgust. But there's something about this guy . . . he seems so familiar. We need to stop talking about me and start talking about him. I haven't forgotten Malakyte's promise to me—bring Deimos in alive, and he'll find Gav. I won't let this psychopath impede finding Gavrielle.

If he wants me to be so upfront and honest, I will be. "Why are you stealing children, huh? What's in it for you?" I ask, and by the widening of his eyes, I can tell he didn't expect that question.

"Interesting. They've got you very convinced, don't they?"

It's a risk, but I take a step closer to him—knees trembling. "This is about you, Deimos. Was it you who broke into my loft too? Turn yourself in, tell me where the Hijacked are, and maybe your death won't be as brutal as you deserve."

Deimos's smile is wicked.

"Now there's the girl I know," he purrs.

What?

Deimos pulls a dagger from his belt and is on me within a second. He's lightning fast, and my eyes widen as the dark blade glints green off the moonlight—an Elendril weapon.

I'm too slow, and it slices through my jacket sleeve and cuts my shoulder, the blade as sharp as my sword. Deimos licks my blood off the dagger's edge, tasting it gingerly. I cringe in disgust.

"Very interesting . . ." he muses as he smacks his dark lips together. My stomach curdles at him savoring my blood. "I think there's a lot you're unaware of, kiddo. Growing up as an orphan likely left you with a lot of unanswered questions, huh?"

His words send a spike of anger through my blood as my mark sizzles. "How do you know about that?"

His pink tongue and mouth are a stark contrast to his dark-green skin as he laughs out loud, mouth wide. "Kiddo, you'd be shocked at what I know about you. But that matters not. This isn't personal, but that crystal doesn't belong to you. It's as simple as that. I'm going to use it to bring down the monster who took everything from me, no matter what it takes or who must die to bring that to fruition. Getting your crystal is a step in that direction. I have nothing against you, per se. You're simply unlucky enough to be wrapped around what I need. And like I said, it doesn't belong to you."

Shaking my head in disgust, I say, "I was born with this. You're the last person it would belong to."

"I never said it belongs to me. I simply stated it doesn't belong to *you*," he claims, shaking his head at me. "If you knew the real truth, you wouldn't be on the side of the enemy like this. You'd be with me, by my side once again."

I furrow my brows and kink my head in confusion. What does he mean by that? I've never met this psychopath. Deimos is saying some crazy things . . . like being on his side *once again*? What does that mean? Is he simply insane?

Why does my gut say no?

As I look at this man, who is so alien in so many ways, I can see he truly believes what he's saying. His dark eyes linger on me, on my body, my hair, my face. It makes my skin crawl.

I suddenly remember the last vision I had, the terror of being hunted by some madman. It feels exactly the same as Deimos. The connection is unmistakable.

"Who's Zariya?" I demand, taking a shot in the dark and hoping it'll catch him off guard. His lingering gaze widens in surprise and it's all the ammunition I need to strike.

Throwing all caution to the wind, I charge for Deimos. Once I reach him, my knees bend, and I dip low. I thrust my elbow up towards his chin, my other hand giving me the extra power I need to make the hit hurt. Some bone cracks in his face, and I spin my leg down, tripping him onto his back.

Deimos recovers quickly, however, and this time he comes at me and there's no room to avoid him. From out of nowhere, the dagger comes flashing at my face, and I duck in time to miss getting a facelift. The curved iridescent blade jabs towards me, and I spin, but not fast enough to avoid a slash across my chest. It's a light cut, but he's aiming for my heart—and getting closer each time. He continues to charge, and I dodge and duck, heart pounding in my ears. The rush of adrenaline from a real battle is like a drug to me. My breaths become more and more shallow. I need to breathe, Dammit. *Remember your training.*

Deimos is fluid in motion, with not a single sign of fatigue in his movements. The others were right about him; he knows his shit. His form is perfect, despite the alien fighting style. He wields his weapon like it's an extension of himself, his body and blade one fluid entity bent on ending my life. The blade cuts me again on my outer thigh, and I only know because I feel the sting. My eyes widen as the blade comes straight for my chest, and in a sloppy, dirty move, I call forth my crystal's power, the mark glowing like a beacon ready to save me.

The crystal's energy pulses out of me. Deimos yelps in pain as his body blasts twenty feet across the carnival. He hits the ground hard, rolling several times in the loose dirt before being stopped by a cotton candy truck. He lies there, still and smoking like a barbequed piece of meat. This is exactly why I didn't use my crystal, because he's no use to me dead.

"*Kill him . . .*" that voice says, the same one that I heard at the Arianyte outpost building. I don't immediately dismiss it, but killing him isn't the goal. I need him alive.

The spout to my power shuts off. My knees wobble, and it feels like I've run ten miles from that small attack alone, but I don't let it show. I look over my shoulder. Ardelle is valiantly fighting the alien animal still.

"Damn," Deimos mumbles, tapping his lips, as if he can't feel them. He's already back on his feet? "I haven't felt that power in many years. Too bad Zariya could do ten times better than that pathetic attempt at an attack, even on a bad day. Is that's your best, kiddo? If it was, I fear you're in more trouble than you realize."

"Who is she?" I ask again, mind spinning with all the possibilities. *She's real then?*

For a moment, he merely watches me with a long, creepy stare. "You really don't remember, do you?"

Clenching my jaw, I imbue my growl with irritation. "Remember what?"

Deimos lets out a mocking, disbelieving sound.

"Zariya Ethoria killed herself along with most of the Starseeds and their Ringers while on a moon orbiting outside the Deenary System. Decades ago. She cracked the moon in half with that Elendril crystal inside your heart, killing everyone, including herself. I would know, because I was there. I watched it explode from space."

My entire vision flips on its head.

How is he describing the exact situation I saw in those visions? What the hell is going on?

"No . . . no. You were the one trying to kill her," I accuse, heart pounding, my entire body shaking but not entirely from the fight. It was all real, the visions, her death—every bit of what I saw was *real*.

Deimos chuckles, but the laugh doesn't touch his eyes. "Not even close. Whoever is telling you this is lying or doesn't know shit. But I see Zariya in you; you have her spunk, it makes me like you. She and I were close, so I would know. Honestly, with reincarnation and everything, I'd argue you are her. You were born with her crystal, so that means your souls are one. If you're the same soul, then aren't you the same person, essentially?"

My mind flashes to the old extraterrestrial woman who stopped me by the tattoo shop. What did she say about past lives . . .?

"I'm curious what your new family would think if they found out you killed them all in your last life together? I'd simply be guessing, but who's saying they may think twice about letting you sleep in that comfortable bed if they knew what you are truly capable of?"

Fear hits me hard and it's deadly serious. This battle is turning into a completely different type of fight. "I'd never hurt the ones I care about. Screw whatever the circumstances were," I spit faster than lightning. "You're crazy. I've never hurt—"

"Hurt anyone? Really?" the alien mocks, a fluffy white eyebrow lifting. Even he knows I am a dangerous killer. But I've changed, I make better choices now. I'm different.

Tasting blood from gnawing on my lip so hard, I question myself—I question everything I thought I knew about this.

About *me*.

"You are aware of extraterrestrials' deep knowledge of the soul, are you not? How most races, if not all, have abolished religious pretexts and are under the mathematical certainty of reincarnation? We live in an amazing world, kiddo. Our souls are immortal. The body may die and change and grow old and weak, but the soul always remains the same. Everyone knows this to be true. Assuming they're all correct, that technically makes you the Killer of Worlds, Karalevine Ruzz. Or should I call you Zariya? Personally, I'd go with Killer of Worlds. That has such a fancy ring to it, don't you think? I mean, who blows up a moon with their bare hands?"

Rage bubbles inside me, turning my blood to pure frenzied agony, but more so, fear. Fear of the truth I know to be real. "I didn't hurt anybody."

Deimos bounces on his feet. "But you did. You destroyed the moon. They call you the Killer of Worlds; you can look it up. You'll find it referenced in the Akashic Records Database. Arianyte has tried to erase the records about it, but kiddo, you are legendary."

Did the others know of this? Did he say Arianyte knows about this event? "I don't believe you," I say, unable to think straight. "You're lying." It's the only explanation. It. Can't. Be. Real.

Deimos shrugs.

"I wish that were true. She'd still be alive if I were lying," he says, sounding genuinely sad. "But she's dead. And now you have her crystal and I'm going to bring it home for her. You're too dangerous to leave in the hands of the enemy. You must be put down before you become the weapon they've waited decades to obtain.

"Either let me have the crystal, or I'll spill the truth to your Starseed family all about what a dangerous little monster you really are. We'll see how much they want you on their little team after that. I know how much that'll hurt you. How you long so desperately for a family. Wouldn't dying be better than having them all abandon you like trash? It's happened so many times before that I'm not sure you can take one more hit."

My chin quivers and I can't say a word in rebuttal. They'd be happier without me anyway. The Resistance sure is. If this is all true—which, who am I kidding? It is—that'll mean only one thing. That on some level, my spirit—my soul—is capable of an atrocity. Yet, when I saw the vision of Zariya, I could feel her rationale. All her pain and terror. She had a baby inside her and she ended all the lives on that moon instead of being captured. How desperate would a woman have to be to make that dreadful decision? So desperate not to go back to whoever this person was that she killed them all.

I killed them all.

Nausea rolls through me like a stampede of bulls, and I retch, but nothing comes up. This can't be happening. Of all the things, this would be what they'd all abandon me for. Jance, Pacey, Ardelle—don't even get me started on Sylo and Saris. All of them would be in such fear for their lives they'd demand I get far away from them.

They will abandon me. They will.

For sure, this time. Because I've committed too many crimes against them for any rational person to think letting me stick around is a good idea.

I've done too much, told too many lies, kept too many secrets.

The beast Ardelle is battling shrieks in pain, its roar a slap to my senses. I look over at the sound to see its body skewered by a pole Ardelle had shot into it. Looking over at him is my fatal mistake. Deimos is on me like a viper, and I'm elbowed in my lower ribs so hard that I hear the bone snap before I feel it. My scream rings out as it feels like all the breath from my lungs has been sucked out of my body.

I manage to connect a good punch to his face as a reflex, but he comes back at me with a punch of his own, twice as hard. Deimos grips my shoulders and slams his head into mine, and I see stars. My feet peddle backwards, and he somehow gets a hold of me from behind and wraps his arms around me, clenching my back to his chest. He lifts my feet off the ground easily, squeezing my arms against my body in an unescapable hold. Deimos smells of spices and earth and blood. Every time I buck and struggle, his arms tighten harder on my cracked rib.

It's excruciating.

"Who's giving you this information about Zariya? Who?" he yells into my ear. His voice is rough as he shakes me, purposely pushing into my ribs with his forearm. Screaming, I can't breathe, and I see black dots peppering my vision as I get extremely light-headed. I'm completely helpless, and it brings up more shame than I'm prepared to feel right now.

"It doesn't matter. That crystal is mine now—it's coming home. Say goodnight, Killer of Worlds," Deimos says, holding me with one arm as he plunges his dagger directly over my heart.

CHAPTER 40

I'm a dead girl.

This ugly squid is the last thing I want to see before I die, but I can't escape him.

Or my past.

Deimos has me, and I watch helplessly as his dagger—almost in slow motion—nosedives towards my chest. There's no time to cry or beg. There's only enough time to die.

Then gravity takes hold.

Ardelle's gravity.

It's like Deimos hit an invisible brick wall, the point of the blade literally centimeters from my heart. He shakes as he tries to overcome Ardelle's magic.

It all happens within milliseconds. Then Ardelle pummels into Deimos from the side like a bull, completely clobbering Deimos to the ground.

The dagger plops beside them as they roll several times. Meanwhile, I try to regain some breath as I rest on all fours, the pain of my ribs blinding and making it hard to breathe.

"What are you doing?" Ardelle roars at the alien. It's the first time I've ever seen him lose his composure, and his eyes are furious. Almost like . . . like this is personal for him. Maybe he cares about me more than he's let on? More than even I assumed?

Deimos lands on all fours, posed like a cat ready to pounce. Confusion and malice glaze his haunting eyes, his white hair disheveled.

Deimos licks his lips, white teeth a sharp contrast to his dark skin. He says to Ardelle, "I'm just playing the game, kiddo."

Ardelle's breaths are loud, his tank of a chest rising and falling unevenly as he snarls at the alien. He's covered in blood and scratches from his fight with that giant alien cat, its body still twitching as it lies skewered over by the hotdog stand. Ardelle spits, most of it blood, but I'm still puzzled at the look he's giving Deimos. For his part, Deimos looks almost amused by Ardelle's anger.

Then Pacey's voice rings out from close by.

"Ardelle!"

She and Sylo are running towards us, both filthy with dirt and blood, some their own, some not.

Sensing the threat of facing not two, but now four Starseeds, Deimos rises to his feet with worry on his face.

Ardelle walks and helps me to my feet, the pain turning into a dull ache as my adrenaline pumps. We stand beside each other, him taking my hand. He eyes Deimos with so much conviction as if saying: 'This is what I'm protecting.' I can't help but feel a tightening in my heart at this silent declaration. Having him choose me, have my back in this fight—it's everything. And it proves to me that my feelings aren't simply one-sided; they're real and he feels them too.

Shaking his head and shifting his feet, Deimos seems annoyed by it all, but he's about to be way more than annoyed as Pacey and Sylo arrive on scene. The four of us stand together as one unit.

Starseeds against Starseed.

I wish the Ringers were here, however, given our training, I believe we can handle this. It's what we've been preparing for.

It's time to get this asshole.

And get Gav back in the process.

But what if Deimos talks about me? Gives away this secret? Tells them everything?

Deimos eyes his dagger fifteen paces away in the dirt. I truly wish I had my sword right now, but I have an even better weapon to pull.

Ardelle's the first one to pounce, engaging Deimos in hand-to-hand combat right at the start. Ardelle trumps the alien in size, but Deimos is also sleek and fast and stronger than he looks. They kick, block, punch, and stagger. Ardelle's moves are smooth and strong, and he gets a good elbow strike to Deimos's nose. Eggplant-colored blood pools out immediately, and Deimos spits and wipes it from his chin. They continue blow for blow, Deimos getting a hard kick in Ardelle's ribs. He staggers back. The two are evenly matched, and I can't tell who's gaining the upper hand.

"He will not be able to keep this up for much longer," I say to the other two, our eyes glued to the fight. "We need a plan. Remember, Malakyte wants him alive. Oh, and don't look him in the eyes. We can avoid his powers by avoiding eye contact."

I wince as Ardelle grunts, Deimos striking him hard in the gut.

"Sounds like we need some help," Sylo suggests, not looking concerned even though there's blood dripping from his nose. "Why don't we use his own army against him?"

I look over at Sylo, confused, until I see his eyes begin to glow. The power of his crystal pulls at me. From the shadows, three Reptilians rise from their graves, their bodies not even cooled or stiff from rigor mortis.

Pacey and I look at each other, both mortified.

"I can use my crystal to bind him," Pacey says as she turns her back to the dead Reptilian puppets, teeth clenching.

Fidgeting from the pain in my side, I tap my nails together rapidly as I develop a plan. "I have an idea."

After going through the plan quickly, the three of us gradually spread out, walking slow enough as to not draw Deimos's attention away from Ardelle. Once we're evenly spread apart in a circle around the two fighting, I begin to raise my crystal's power up. The magic slides into my veins like heroin, rushing me with a beautifully numbing embrace. The painful revelations of today disintegrate, along with the pain in my ribs. I'm numb from pain and full of euphoria.

That's Sylo's signal.

From out of the shadows, three Reptilians that were once dead now charge forward into the fray with orange spewing from within their lifeless eyes. They face me as their thick, stocky bodies run up behind Deimos, clawed hands out in front like they're ready to grab him and bring him into the undersewers with them. Thankfully, Ardelle is facing the three Reptilians as they barrel down towards the two of them, and I can see him struggling to keep Deimos from turning that way. Even taking several hits on purpose to keep Deimos's back to Sylo's zombies long enough for the surprise attack to be effective.

It doesn't take long for Deimos to realize something's up. The alien looks around, his instincts on alert, but Ardelle doesn't let up. He knees Deimos right in the side, causing the green alien to dry heave from the pain. As the Reptilians charge upon Deimos, Ardelle ducks and rolls out of the way with enough time not to get trampled.

Deimos is shocked as the stampede of Reptilians literally walks over him. My laugh is loud and ridiculous as I watch Deimos flail around and struggle to get back on his feet. The zombie Reptilians have no brain function, so their movements are slow and hardly formidable, but that was never their point.

My crystal's power sings a treacherous siren melody that leads me down to the depths of a numb eternity. It's better than any drug, more delightful than the strongest adrenaline rush. It's *everything*.

"*Yes,*" it purrs at me, knowing it's about to be released. It speaks to me psychically, or maybe it's simply driven me to insanity. I'm not me when this power is released. I am hungry for the power and will do whatever it takes to feel it. Just one more time—consequences be damned.

It explodes.

The rush is like a million needles in my veins. It hurts and is the best all at once, and I target all my rage at him. I slap all his laughing and taunting right off his face the moment he realizes he can't get out of the way fast enough to block my incoming attack. Both his arms raise in an X over his face as he gets hit straight on.

Ardelle is smart enough to get out of the way.

Now it's Deimos's turn to scream. And he does.

There's no pity to be had. Not from me. I delight as I continue to blast him, no longer caring about frying him up like a piece of meat.

"Thumbelina, that's enough, you'll kill him," Ardelle yells, but I'm not ready to stop. It overtakes me, it makes me someone else. Rarely do I get to let it out this fully. Risking burns or worse, Ardelle staggers closer to me with a look of concern on his face. My power rushes wind around us; my hair whips in every direction. I glance over at him, and it's the look in his eyes that snaps me back into my body. To my senses. What I'm doing right here, right now, is exactly the type of thing that's going to cause them to see me differently, to fear me—fear this power. If there is any validity to what Deimos said about our past lives and about what Zariya did—what *I* did—then acting this way will only make that story seem more believable. I have to rein it back in.

Now.

But it's like taking the most beautiful feeling you've ever experienced and completely shutting it off in an instant. Because I have more control now, because I've trained with it on smaller levels, it responds better to me. Although, it too doesn't seem to be ready and bites and snares and scratches at me as I rein it in, causing my body to feel highly uncomfortable.

Like it's alive within me and doesn't give a damn about the consequences.

But I do.

My knees buckle once it stops, and I feel so weak, like every ounce of energy has been zapped from me in that moment. Rushing to catch my fall, Ardelle holds me upright in his arms.

"I didn't think I could stop," I say breathlessly, the magic and power seeping out of me with every passing second. It's the worst hangover I've ever felt. Like a part of me has died by not feeling it as much as I could have.

I try hard not to resent that feeling—to push it away.

Ardelle brushes the hair out of my face, slick with sweat. He rests his hand on my cheek and I lean into it, needing something to anchor to as I completely come back into the feeling of my body. All those numbed emotions flooding back in, and the pain from my snapped rib spikes.

"But you did stop." He inches closer to me, bending down so were face-to-face. He whispers, "I know how hard it is to stop. To not want to."

This surprises me and my eyes go wide, the understanding and sadness reflected in his own eyes. To know that I don't struggle in this alone. That the consequences of using these crystals affect us all, but more importantly, we face it together.

Pacey uses her own crystal to find massive roots within the ground beneath us. Springing from the dirt, long, thick tendrils wrap themselves around Deimos and pin him to the ground. He's steaming again, forearms burned and leather melted into his skin. He took the full brunt of the crystal he wants so badly, and he faced the consequences of it. Somehow, his clothing protected him because he should have been dead from that attack. His ears and hair are both singed and burned, however, his burns aren't that bad. I wonder if he designed his clothing to specifically withstand an attack from me, from this crystal?

As the rest of us approach him, he's flattened on his stomach, Pacey's roots tied all around his body.

It took all four of us, but together, we captured the infamous Deimos.

CHAPTER 41

THE ARIANYTE EMPIRE DECREE #55

ARIANYTE'S AZURITE SHIP WILL PERMANENTLY REMAIN IN EARTH'S ORBIT. ONLY AUTHORIZED PERSONNEL AND CURRENT RESIDENTS OF AZURITE ARE PERMITTED ABOARD. ANY PERSONS WHO ATTEMPT TO BREACH THE FLEET WILL BE MET WITH HOSTILE FORCE.

"You're all being used," Deimos says, almost unemotionally as Ardelle ties him up with rope he found from one of the demolished shops. "The moment you realize it, it'll be too late. The hand of Arianyte is always the one that bites. You don't realize what's at stake."

Ardelle slaps him on the back of the head, his giant ears bobbing slightly. "Shut up."

"Where's Jance, Saris, and Ahren? Does anyone know?" I ask, worried they haven't found us yet.

Ardelle looks around. "They've got to be around here somewhere. We'd know if something bad happened to them. The connection would tell us. Unfortunately, our devices are fried thanks to our friend over here so there's no calling them." He glares at Deimos incredulously. "Be aware to avoid eye contact, he can try to be sneaky and control one of us."

"It's only that perfect body of yours that I dream of controlling, pretty boy," Deimos coos, pointed canines flashing a cocky smile, his pink tongue rolling over his pointed tooth. He's just being a cocky ass.

I can't help but feel rage towards him, towards the bombs he dropped on me during our earlier conversation. It's so obvious to me now what he's trying to do. He's the villain, the bad guy who's manipulating everything and everyone around him to get what he wants. What he wants directly opposes what I want, which isn't a good thing for me when what he wants is my heart. I sort of need that to live.

Now, if what Deimos says is true about our past lives together, I can't imagine what they'd do with me. If I'm the sole reason we all died back then and that, according to him, Zariya—me, my actual soul—destroyed the moon and killed everyone on it—they'll completely lose faith in me. They'd fear me. They'd think I would hurt them. Lose control or worse, do it on purpose. This crystal, the direct link between Zariya and myself, the bridge between our two lives, has been speaking to me. For whatever reason, it wants me to know about this event. To tell me something important. Are the crystals alive in some way? Do they have their own sentience that only the user can know of and understand? I'm beginning to believe so, and if that's true, are the others noticing or experiencing the same phenomenon? The million-credit question is, what is the crystal trying to tell me? And why?

All questions I can answer later because Deimos is going to be handed over to Arianyte, and that means I have a shot at finding Gav. That's a win, despite my fears that Deimos can drop this bomb at any moment. However disturbing this squid's claims are, however mind-blowing and wild these past-life visions are, I cannot let Deimos take all the good things I've gained away from me. That includes finding Gav, my Starseed family, Ardelle . . . I've got to protect these things at all costs. Deimos can't take these from me.

I won't let him.

I need to do something. I need to stop him before he destroys everything for me. They can't know about Zariya; it'll create a domino effect that'll lead to me losing them.

"Aw, what's the matter?" Deimos taunts as he watches me step away. "Got anything you'd like to talk about, perhaps?"

I whirl on him, teeth bared and triggered. "Shut the hell up."

He laughs in my face. "Oh, my. We are testy, aren't we? What's the problem? You've finally caught me, no doubt fanged-toothed Malakyte will reward you all. I'd check it for poisonous snakes, if I were you."

"You're the true snake, Deimos." Yet it's my voice that's filled with venom.

His eyes shift to Ardelle, who stands behind me with his arms crossed. Sylo and Pacey stop their conversation and flirting as the tension between Deimos and me intensifies. Ardelle's face is as still as a carved statue. It's odd that Deimos's stare lingers on him a beat too long, all of us watching the wordless conversation. As the seconds tick by, it's clear it isn't only me who's still furious with the wicked puppet-master.

This green-eyed devil needs to go.

Ardelle's gaze shifts to me. "Don't let this squid affect you; he's biting at straws."

"Squid," Deimos whispers as he drops his head, chuckling to himself. "At least I'm not a liar and a murderer of those I love."

And that's when I snap.

I ignore the pain in my side as some invisible force brings me over to Deimos without hesitation. If Malakyte hadn't promised me he'd find Gav in exchange for this piece of shit, I'd do to him what Geonni wanted me to do to the Dawsons. It would be different: he's a monster who terrorizes thousands of people and is likely the one responsible for the Hijacked. I didn't want to admit he could possibly be the one stealing children, but after watching him prance around with so much arrogance and self-righteous bullshit, I can't deny it any longer. Whether that be for credits, more power, or weapons—it doesn't matter. He's the one who's taking them. I have been mistaken about Arianyte this entire time, focusing my anger and rage on them for taking Gav, when in all likelihood, they were searching for us to bring us all together. Like we're together now. Arianyte brought me my family, and Deimos is trying to tear them away from me.

I won't let him.

As I approach the alien, I don't hesitate to snatch him up by the collar of his frayed bodysuit and punch him hard in the cheek.

Sylo hoots loudly from behind me, a laugh mixed with a curse. I can feel Ardelle come up behind me, a shadow looming to keep me under control.

I don't want to be kept under control. I want to shut this guy up, so he'll know to never utter one single word about what Zariya did decades ago. It has no bearing on this life now—none. It's stupid and pointless and I won't let it ruin everything.

Deimos utters my name softly, head down again. "I'm curious, do you know what it feels like to be stabbed in the back by someone you care about?"

My brows knit together in confusion, but before I can question the cryptic phrase, Deimos's arms whip out from behind his back, his bindings falling to the ground at our feet.

His dagger is somehow back in his hand, glinting in the starlight as it makes its way from behind his back to being buried in my side to the hilt.

It all happens so fast.

Then chaos ensues.

CHAPTER 42

Their voices are underwater.

Blood pounds in my ears and pools in my lap.

Screams. So many screams.

They're my own.

They're my own.

"Thumbelina!"

"Oh, my stars . . ."

"Forget Deimos, let him go. We need to get Ahren. I know he'll know what to do. Find him, now!"

"They've got to be by the hover. Pick her up and let's take her there. It'll take twice as long to bring Ahren back to her."

"Kara, hold on, it's going to be okay."

"Thumbelina, keep your eyes open."

I don't want to wake up, I don't want to face the music.

I only want to remain in my dreamland where there's no pain. Where I'm warm and safe and—

"Thumbelina!" Ardelle's voice snaps me out of my shock, then reality barrels down on me like a hover-train.

I remember now that Deimos stabbed me, but Ardelle acted too fast for him to pull the dagger back out. It's still there, protruding out my side, angled in between my hip bone and ribs. I can't look . . .

"Ardelle . . ." My voice is weak and scared. "Take it out. I want it out."

"No," he says immediately. "Whatever you do, don't take it out. It's the only thing keeping the blood inside your body. You take that dagger out, you're dead."

Shit.

I'm on the ground, lying back in Ardelle's arms. Pacey is beside us. Sylo stands off to the side looking more panicked than anyone. Deimos has run off.

"She needs a hospital. The SSPARROWs will be here soon, they'll take her," Sylo suggests, but all I want is for Ardelle to promise he won't leave me alone.

Ardelle shakes his head, hovering his hand over the knife in my body. "We can't wait for that. Babe, this is going to hurt like hell, I'm sorry."

Before I can ask what he's going to do, I scream as Ardelle uses his gravity powers to push against the wound, stopping the blood flow immediately to a slow trickle.

"You're okay," his voice soothes through my cursing and screams. He slowly and gently slides his arm underneath my legs, his other arm supporting my neck as he tenderly lifts me off the ground. *Stars, the pain.*

"I'm sorry," he breathes. "We'll head to the hover. Ahren will know what to do."

Every step Ardelle takes as he jogs towards the parking lot is a tiny little stab, Deimos's dagger inching its way in deeper and deeper. My nails claw into Ardelle's forearms, my body tense and tight and trembling.

"It's okay, Thumbelina. We're almost there," he says to me. "Stay with me. Keep your eyes open."

Keep them open . . .

I'm tumbling and twirling and shifting, forcing myself outside my body. I can't be here, I can't do this. I drift into a deep part of myself, the place I go when truly terrible things are happening. It's been a long time, but the door to that place opens and I go inside, walling myself off with layers and layers of steel barricades.

I'm lying flat now. Then I smell bergamot, coffee, rum and cedar—and I know that smell. Its familiarity along with his deep voice brings me back.

"Jance?" I mumble, my mind spinning so wildly it feels like I'm falling.

Strong hands grab my own, anchoring me. "You're okay, you're okay. Be still. I'm here."

I'm lying across the three men in the back seat of the hover as it flies at full speed. My head rests in Jance's lap; Ahren hovers over my middle, appearing stressed as he examines the blade sticking out of me, and Ardelle caresses my legs.

"Can you help her?" Jance demands as Ahren starts digging in some emergency medical kit.

Ahren nods. "If she's not too far gone, my magic can heal this, yes. However, I need to get inside the surgical suite. I need to know what I'm healing, take images and see inside this wound; otherwise I'm going in blind and if I miss something critical, it can kill her. Sylo, drive faster. As fast as you can go. This is serious, we just need to pray blood doesn't enter her chest cavity; there's broken ribs here as well I'm concerned about."

Their voices sound so far away, so distant. I don't really hear them.

Ahren digs out a small cylinder with an orange strip along the top and digs it into my thigh with a click. I hardly feel anything, but apparently its some type of drug.

"I don't want to do this . . ." I begin to say. I don't want to do any of this, but then the drugs hit me like a baseball bat, and I'm spinning and rolling and flying all at once. "I can't breathe."

"It's alright, you're safe," Jance's deep, textured voice repeats. I stare into his eyes. They're so dark and beautiful and warm. But then they are glowing a pink-and-purple hue, such a beautiful color, the sphere a jewel within those dark eyes. It takes me a bit too long to realize what he's doing, and I clamp mine closed. No . . . no, he can't do this. He can't go into my mind. He'll see everything. He'll know I was a spy for the rebels.

"Kara . . ." he whispers tenderly. I'm so emotionally raw. After every blow Deimos hit me with tonight—it wasn't just to my body. It was to everything I thought I knew. And I'm in this position because of him, but also because of *me*. "Darling, open your eyes. I don't want you to be in pain. I can make all this pain go away, you won't feel anything. I'll take care of you, you can trust me."

Ardelle squeezes my leg and holds them tightly. He's here with me, he didn't leave.

"It's okay, Thumbelina."

It's not okay. Letting Jance's magic into my mind means letting go of the last minuscule bit of control I have left. My own thoughts. My own experiences. He wants to dive into a place that has always been only mine. A place no one could ever touch—until now. Which means he can do anything he wants to me and I'd be none the wiser. Anything that happens, he could simply make me forget it. We've gotten close, but not to this level. He doesn't get that type of trust—he hasn't earned *that*.

Tears streak my cheeks, escaping under clenched eyes. Jance wipes them away.

"I won't hurt you," he whispers in my ear, but I shake my head and gnaw on my lip. "My magic links into your mind, not the other way around. You see and feel what I put there, but I can't see into your mind or thoughts. Those are all yours. Trust me. Trust me . . ." He brushes my face, a tender touch that almost makes everything worse. Struggling, I feel Ahren touching the knife just slightly, and it pulls, making me want to scream. I may already be.

"If you allow me to block your pain receptors," Jance continues, "this becomes a much better experience. Darling, you're very hurt. Ahren has to do things to make you better, and it's not like in the movies where he magically heals you in a few minutes. I can put you to sleep with magic; and I'll take all this pain away. And I'll be right here to watch over you. Please, Kara, I'm begging you. Let me in, darling. Please. I won't hurt you. Please. I want your permission."

Knowing with each ticking second I slip closer and closer towards death, I look at Jance's pleading eyes. Black as a friendly raven. Black like straight coffee, extra sugars.

When I last gave all of me over to another man, he promised it would be okay, too. He said he wouldn't hurt me, too. And I've never trusted one fully since. Do I have much of a choice? It doesn't feel like my options are very good.

Nodding yes to him, I give all of my control over to my Ringer, and it's more terrifying than the possibility that I may die tonight. Scarier than the knife currently bleeding life out of me with every sharp turn as we speed through the mountain side. Maybe we'll get there in time, maybe we won't.

"It's okay," he assures me again as his thumb brushes the tears off my cheeks for a few seconds. The pink glow returns, and he glides into my mind like a soft mist. I barely feel him there, and my body relaxes. Ardelle pets my legs, soft and steady, lulling me into Jance's peaceful embrace. I don't realize how much pain I'm in until he takes it away. Now all the pain dissipates like smoke in my hands, vanishing completely. A feverish euphoria replaces it. Everything feels like it's going to be okay. It's . . . it is . . .

"Shh, you're safe," he soothes. Beautiful images of valleys filled with wildflowers flash gently inside my mind. I'm unsure if his voice is inside or outside of my mind now. It doesn't really matter—I'm already gone.

CHAPTER 43

It's the nausea that hits me first. It's a wall, overwhelming and unclimbable. The constant beeping of my heart rate from some machine gets louder and faster as I become more and more aware.

I'm in bed, I think. My bed. There's softness surrounding my body, and I'm warm and wrapped up in soft blankets, but stars, the pain is excruciating.

When I try to move, there's so much pain that I moan in agony, waking the figure at my bedside.

Ardelle's eyes blink sleepily until he realizes I'm awake, and he snaps up.

"Don't move, don't move," he says softly before he calls for his Ringer, his voice urgent. "Hey, hey, it's okay. Ahren is coming right now. Ahren!" Ardelle calls again, more forcefully.

"You're alright." He takes my hands, and I squeeze them tight against the pain.

I try to say his name, but my voice is too dry and hoarse to get more than a whimper out.

Footsteps rush up to my room, and soon both Ahren and Jance appear, faces tired and stressed. Dark circles encase both sets of their eyes.

Ahren darts straight for the bedside table that's become a pharmacy of drugs and needles. An IV bag filled with fluids hangs above me. He quickly puts on gloves and picks up a huge needle and vial.

Jance squeezes between Ahren and Ardelle, practically pushing Ardelle away.

"Hey, kid. You're okay," my Ringer tells me. "Ahren was able to heal you, but it doesn't happen right away or all at once. It's accelerated, but your body is still healing. You're out of the woods, thank the stars. It's just going to be rough for a few days, but you're going to be fine."

"What's your pain level, Kara?" Ahren asks, and I roll my head on my pillow and glare at him incredulously.

My voice is rough and my tongue sandpaper when I say, "A damn one thousand."

The drugs Ahren shoots into the IV line is strong and my eyelids can only blink heavily as he smiles back at me.

"At least you haven't lost that spunk."

"Ouch!" I whine as Ahren presses down on my stomach with the glowing wand that can see all of my insides, and it hurts like hell. A week has passed since the carnival, and I wish they still had me sedated.

"Almost there," he says softly, releasing the pressure after he got the image he wanted. It's enough to make me want to puke. "This is looking phenomenal. I'm pleased with your progress."

For being near fatally stabbed by a seven-inch dagger a week ago—same.

It still sucks so much ass, though.

Jance brushes hair out of my face as he sits next to me in my bed, an overly attentive shadow. When the nightmares come, it's comforting to have him here. I don't tell him to leave, and he never does. He's been such a steady presence for me, and without a doubt, I couldn't have gotten through this without him. He, Ahren, and Ardelle have gotten me through this, and I feel immensely closer to all of them.

"When can I train again?" I ask Ahren, the anger at what Deimos did to me boiling up again. Every time I think of it, it makes my blood steam— he will not get away with this. My pride is more wounded than my body.

"Perhaps in the next week or two," he concedes, but Jance doesn't seem happy with that projection. "Let's get you walking again first."

"Ow!"

They don't leave me alone often, but the first chance my room is empty, I reach into my side table drawer and find my Dezlar. It's dead, of course. The EMP messed with it, but I was told Pacey was able to get everyone's back up and running again. The memory of that night is black and patchy, but seeing the dried blood on the device shoots fear through me. I was dying, my mortality finite and waning before I even lived. I would never be in that type of situation again, I promise myself. It's also not the fact I almost died that haunts me either. What Deimos said about Zariya, about our past lives . . . about what she did. What I did . . . I can't deal with that right now, and I am thankful for the haze the medication gives me because I don't know how I'm going to keep these secrets from everyone. To keep the worst from happening.

Remembering the unbearable pain of being abandoned by supposed family after supposed family has left me with a familiar pain that lights up in my chest, a pain only this specific thing induces. The wound from Geonni and the Resistance is still such a fresh, bleeding, festering crack within me. Hands trembling, I know I cannot take another hit like it again. For all the effort I put in to trying to change, to trying to be this new and improved version of myself, one more fracture will break me completely.

It's a threat to my very existence.

CHAPTER 44

THE ARIANYTE EMPIRE DECREE #29

IT IS THE RESPONSIBILITY OF ARIANYTE TO KEEP PLANET EARTH IN LIVABLE, VIABLE ORDER. AIR QUALITY, WATER QUALITY, OCEAN CLEANLINESS, CORE TEMPERATURE, ANIMAL SPECIES CONTAINMENT AND SURVIVAL, GLOBAL INFRASTRUCTURE, SPACE INFRASTRUCTURE, SPACE TRAVEL, SPACE COLONIZATION, MOON-BASE COLONIZATION, OFF-PLANET COLONIZATION, SUN HARNESSING, TERRAN SURVIVAL, HEALTHCARE, EXTRATERRESTRIAL INTEGRATION, AND OVERALL PLANET INFRASTRUCTURE SHALL FALL SOLELY ON ARIANYTE IN ACCORDANCE WITH THE DEVOURING ACCORDS.

Moving my body sucks space-balls.

"I really can't keep going," I protest, leaning heavily against Ardelle's arms as he holds both my hands, walking me in circles around the gigantic couch.

Holding my weight with ease, he smiles so confidently it makes me sick. "One more lap," he tries, but my face tells him I'm done, and the compromise is to make it to my spot on the couch, where I've been vegging out for the last week.

If it wasn't for Jance, Ardelle, and Ahren, I don't know if I would have made it through this. Pacey, too; but with all three men hovering over me like hawks, it's been hard for her to squeeze in. Jance has been taking the night shift, sleeping in my bedroom with me due to the night terrors that have been plaguing me relentlessly since the IV drugs—the good ones—haven't been keeping them at bay. Had I been told I'd allow a grown man in my room with me a few months ago, I would have slapped that person silly, but Jance isn't creepy like that, and to be honest, I need him there. Just for a bit longer. He's safe and comforting and if I'd say I was attached to him, I'd be underestimating what's going on there. He's shown me repeatedly that I can trust him, and as scary as it is, I'm allowing myself to because I need someone to trust. After allowing him to use his Ringer abilities on me, it's been even easier to trust him much more than before, and it's nice. But I'm sure Saris is missing him, so he'll be leaving my room shortly. It'll start getting weird if he stays much longer now that I'm not physically needing his constant assistance.

Ardelle has been taking days, helping me more than he needs to and rarely leaving my side. Many things he's seen have been so mind-shatteringly embarrassing, it's hard to look him in the eyes. Let's say it's far from cute and attractive. I'm currently searing it from my memory bank as I think back on it, not wanting to be reminded of how this super hot guy has seen me in such vulnerable positions. Yet, his days revolve around me and my care, making sure I'm healing as well as I can. He's taking care of me, and it's really cemented our relationship.

It's been almost two weeks since the carnival, and according to Ahren I'm practically healed, but the new tissue his magic regenerated is tight and not very malleable. That includes organ tissue, and it sucks balls right now.

What doesn't suck is my relationship with everyone here. Even Sylo has come around, and the tension regarding our differences in opinions has subsided, at least for now.

"I got you . . ." Ardelle lowers me on the couch, gently sitting me propped up on blankets and fluffy pillows. Once I'm settled, I snatch up the stuffed alligator he'd replaced with the one we lost from the carnival and hold it close as I snuggle up against Ardelle. I haven't been able to let the stuffed toy go, and I felt like he knew me well enough not to get me some basic stuffed animal like a teddy bear.

The television is the only sound between us. Sadie snoozes in a ball on the floor, having welcomed herself and fitting right in. Ardelle seems nervous, contemplating something as I side-glance over at him.

"Something on your mind, Blondie?"

He smiles genuinely, shifting his arm so it rests behind my head, his hand softly caressing my shoulder. "So, I've been noticing you drawing a lot lately since you can't get up and do much."

I look down, wondering if he's noticed me trying to draw Gavrielle, what I'd assume he'd look like now. "Yeah, it's a little boring around here," I admit. "I've got to keep my mind busy somehow. It's not like I can watch much more of this." I nod to the television, coverage of the carnival still on full blast. Somehow it was leaked that Malakyte's elite Starseed team couldn't do a damn thing against this attack, and we're called as useless as a sloth.

The more I'm in the public eye, the riskier my cover becomes. Despite me being out of the Resistance, I doubt that little detail would matter to someone like Malakyte. I've still got to protect my secrets with my life.

"Ignore that crap, they're vultures," he tells me.

Silence falls between us again, not particularly awkward in nature. I catch him staring at one of my tattoos. It's the one of a girl's face. She's a warrior, her eyes are covered by a moth that transitions into a detailed mandala that goes all the way up my arm. She sports a fierce grin, surrounded by flowers and more mandala art. I got her because I wished one day I could be as strong as she is.

A girl can hope.

"This is one of my most recent ones," I say. "My tattoo mentor did it for me . . ." I can't exactly say that person is also the leader of the Terran Resistance, can I?

"What's wrong?" he asks innocently.

My sigh is heavy as I make up some story about how my relationship with the tattoo shop manager is on thin ice since I'm unable to work very much.

"I'm sorry." Ardelle sounds genuine. "I think I may have something that'll help you feel better, speaking of the tattoo shop."

Shooting up from his seat, Ardelle scuttles out of the room. He pops back into view a few seconds later.

"I went over there the other day once I noticed how stir-crazy you've been getting, and your store manager was happy to help me out."

I gasp with an excited rush of emotion.

Ardelle's smile at my reaction makes me tingle. "There's the Thumbelina I know and love."

His word choice doesn't escape my notice . . . but I'm sure it's just a figure of speech.

An affectionate look from him makes me hope I'll forever be the object of his attention. On that first night I looked at him, I knew he'd make me stupid.

Damn him.

"You got my tattoo machine for me?" I ask in awe as I reach for it, covered in dried ink splats and graphic stickers, looking as old as dirt. Hugging it gratefully, I suddenly realize something. "But who am I going to tattoo?"

Running his hands through his messy hair, he smiles too broadly to be inconspicuous.

"Oh, so you want a free tattoo. I see how it is."

"No, it's not like that," he placates playfully. "It's a win-win for us both. I've got this awesome idea I know you'll love."

"What is it, then?"

After describing his idea to me, I agree to draw it up and do it. Only because he wants it on his back and that requires him to be shirtless.

I've been drugged; I have no inhibition right now.

He comes up next to me and snuggles under the blanket, his arms around my neck as I lean into his chest and close my eyes.

I could stay here forever.

And I must've dozed off because when my eyes open, the room is full of people.

Malakyte Ardeen, specifically.

Shocked by the Prince of Arianyte's appearance in our living room, I try to sit up more but Ardelle keeps me down.

"Karalevine." Malakyte's voice is stiff as he strides over to Ardelle and me. It's still not my preferred name, but it's better than *Miss Ruzz*. He's dressed in all black, but there's an icy edge to him today that hasn't been there previously. "I'm glad to hear you're doing better. I did try and warn you about Deimos."

He did.

"We were unprepared for the attack," Jance says as my answer, and thank the stars. Everyone is either in the living room or the attached kitchen, probably wondering why Malakyte is here. Is it the drugs, or is the prince looking at Ardelle and me with contempt?

"Deimos has been attacking targets all over the city, succeeding in causing chaos and sowing fear. I need everyone but my Star out there searching for him. Will she be ready for the Titan Games finale? We suspect that it's going to be a high-level target, especially because the Terran leaders are coming to watch," Malakyte asks Ahren, whose eyes are as sleep deprived as Jance's from my around-the-clock care.

"The finale takes place in two weeks?" Ahren asks, and Malakyte nods. "Then yes, she should be completely back to normal by then."

"The finale should be postponed," Jance interjects boldly.

"Fabulous," Malakyte says, completely ignoring Jance. "We've got a handle on things, I assure you. The public still has confidence in this team, and thankfully the press didn't find out about your injuries. Although, I'm personally more than disappointed by this team's failures. Stop embarrassing me and catch this terrorist before he does inexplicable damage."

We all look towards each other, uncomfortable with his words. The coverage of the carnival plays in the awkward silence, a potential prequel of what's to come if we fail again. The chances of finding Gav get slimmer with each mistake we make, and I cannot let it happen one more time. I'm sure Malakyte won't uphold his end of the bargain if it takes us a million times to bring the alien terrorist in. Each day that passes, I become less and less convinced that Malakyte will hold good to his word. Which makes me sad, I realize, because I want him to be the type of person who would help someone when they needed it.

I can feel the air shift before Ardelle says, "Of course, the press discovering our failure is of top importance, never mind Thumbelina's life."

Malakyte's glare snaps to Ardelle.

"I'd like a moment alone with my Star."

Malakyte isn't asking.

Glancing at Malakyte, Ardelle hesitates, then leaves a kiss on my forehead as he goes. Once the room is empty aside from the Prince of Arianyte and myself, I actually find myself missing Malakyte a tiny bit. How, I have no idea. It must be the drugs.

Malakyte takes a seat next to me, his chill causing me to wrap the blanket closer to my body.

He apologizes for the cold and goes on to tell me about the last few days, plans for the Titan Games finale, and his demeanor completely changes back to the guy from our *encounters*.

"I was so disconcerted when I heard you had been injured so severely. Had Ahren not been able to help you, I was prepared to step in."

"Step in how?" I ask. The frigidness of his body intensifies.

Malakyte leans in and whispers, "I'm a very powerful man, Karalevine. I have my ways of assuring your protection, even from death. Did they tell you I was here the day after it happened?"

My eyes widen a bit, surprised. "No . . . they didn't." The Prince of Arianyte came to see *me*? It's flattering, almost.

His eyes, however, turn to slits.

I turn my neck to face him directly, the two of us as close as we've ever been. It could be the drugs (it's likely the drugs), but I swear I see playful mischief dancing in his expression with the way he tilts his head at me. He bends his head down, and my eyes go wide again when he brushes his icy lips against my neck. I suck in a breath at the frosty touch, the hairs on my skin raising to the ceiling. A soft chuckle escapes his lips at my reaction. This should repulse me . . . but it lights me up.

Stars.

All that I could do with this man by my side . . . I'd be unstoppable. Plus, he's dangerous and I like that. I shouldn't, I really really shouldn't, but I do.

Despite the chill, heat rises within me, and I wonder for a brief second if he's going to kiss me—if I'm going to let him. He leans into me and I meet him. What would those icy lips feel like against mine?

Then Ardelle's face pops into my head, and this doesn't feel right.

This can't happen.

I inch backwards, and his head jerks back as if I'd slapped him or something. Looking at him, I say, "I'm on a lot of drugs right now . . . I might do something stupid I'd regret."

"Perhaps you can say that you want to be mine?" he says, taking my hand and placing it on his frigid cheek. He's so beautiful, and I briefly imagine what that would be like. The power, the money, how I could have anything I'd ever want . . .

But my heart seems to pull me elsewhere, towards someone else, despite the thought of such a powerful man's lips on mine thrilling me beyond measure. It doesn't feel quite . . . right. As if the two of us are puzzle pieces that fit, but you sort of have to pound them in to get those pieces to fully come together. They don't fit perfectly.

"I can't," I say, and I feel him retreat in more ways than simply pulling his body back, dropping my hand. "I'm sort of a bit of a mess right now," I try to placate him, let him down easy, but I think he knows why I'm rejecting him.

Faking a smile, he takes my hand again and kisses the back of it. "Just watch, Karalevine. The villain gets the girl in this story."

Once he leaves, I sit alone and wonder if I've just made a fatal mistake.

CHAPTER 45

"Stop moving," I growl, gripping Ardelle's bare shoulder with one hand and my tattoo gun in the other. I sit on his bed, and he sits shirtless on the floor before me. His room is a typical guy's room, with a dark-blue comforter on his bed, two gamer chairs facing a gamer's computer setup, and a television in the opposite corner mounted to the wall. Posters on the walls are of comic-book superheroes (of all things), all types of weapons, and his bow and arrows are stacked neatly in the remaining corner. Altogether, his room is neat, like any rich boy's room would be.

Ahren's cocktail of pills is something, and I'm struggling to tattoo a straight line as it is without Ardelle moving around and doing unnecessary crap like breathing.

"I think that's you, Thumbelina," he chuckles, and I slap him on the back of the head in playful retaliation.

"Hey, if you want wobbly lines, keep cracking jokes. You're at my mercy, remember?"

Once his breathing returns to its normal tempo, I start again. The sound of the tattoo machine instantly puts me in a meditative state where my mind goes blank and I can work methodically as I follow the outline created by the stencil I drew up.

"I think the outer space idea you had is great." He fills the space of silence left behind by my concentration. "I really think it'll make the whole thing pop."

"Yeah, cause you're so pale, the main pieces wouldn't show up otherwise."

His lips make a sound of disbelief. "Okay, speaking of the girl who's white as the snow outside. At least I could tan if I really want to."

"Tanning fades tattoos," I say like it's the most painfully obvious fact in the world. Which it is.

"This attitude of yours is ruffling my feathers, Thumbelina," Ardelle teases, and I can feel his quickening heartbeat under my palm. Below my hand is his bare back, the defined, sculped, hard muscles rippling beneath my touch.

Focus . . .

Now it's my turn to laugh. "Consider yourself lucky I don't tattoo a duck on your back, Mr. Feather Boy. Keep being mean to me, see what happens."

"I like it when you threaten me like that." The tone of his voice, the slight seriousness in it, causes heat to rise inside my chest. Wiping the ink off with a paper towel, I clear the tickle in my throat.

"You say that now," I rebut, letting the tattoo machine's buzz fill the room again, "until you've got a fuzzy duck on your back dressed up with an arrow and quiver."

Ardelle shakes his head. It's about the only movement he's allowed. Suddenly, I feel his hand touching mine as he reaches back and laces our fingers together. I'm grateful he can't see how insanely hard I'm blushing right now.

"I was so worried about you . . . at the carnival. My carelessness left you vulnerable. It was me who tied his bindings wrong; I don't know how he got loose. But I failed you that night, and I'm sorry. Seriously."

The tattoo gun stops as abruptly as the topic swap. "I don't feel like you failed me."

"You almost died. If Ahren wasn't able to heal you like that—"

I cut Ardelle off. "Then you guys would have taken me to a hospital. Deimos didn't get what he wanted. He didn't win by any means."

"I don't care about Deimos, Thumbelina. I care about you."

Breathing deep through my nose, I consider what he's saying. There are vague memories of him running with me in his arms to safety. The pain of his gravity magic stanching the bleeding. That's it. Everything else is a blur.

The buzzing comes back swiftly because I don't have the words to respond adequately.

Eventually, we shift the topic away from that gruesome night, and after another hour of playful banter flying between us, I finally finish the tattoo.

Ardelle stretches for a moment before holding up a small mirror to check out the tattoo in his full-length mirror.

"Dang, Thumbelina," he breathes, and I tingle from the sound, even if he is calling me by that stupid nickname.

"You like it?"

The smile on his face is enough to tell me that he does. The fact he can't stop looking at it is a good indicator too. "Are you kidding me? Of course, I like it, it's amazing. It's perfect."

I pick up the paper stencil that I made, looking at the 2D version of the masterpiece I just created. Funny how a few purple lines could turn into something that looks so three dimensional on skin. I took each Elendril crystal mark and tattooed them one on top of the other, so, together, they create one solid symbol. I colored each mark corresponding to the colors we each emit when we use our crystals, and against the dark space background they look like they're glowing. "Perhaps it's too perfect. The Elendril symbols fit and overlap like puzzle pieces. My star is six sided, you have six circles, Sylo's diamond shape has six corners, and Pacey's symbol fits right in the middle over my mini triangle like it was made to be there. If I'm remembering Deimos's mark—that asshat—his would fit right over Pacey's mark." I point onto the stencil, in the remaining spaces between my star and Pacey's blue symbol.

"You're right . . ." He walks back over to the bed and softly takes the small paper from my hand.

"It still looks incomplete." I point to where I imagine Deimos's mark to be. "There's still room for one more mark, right here." Judging from what I remember of Deimos's and Gav's mark, and some educated guess at what the sixth mark within Arianyte would be, I fill in our missing fifth and sixth marks.

They fit perfectly.

"Yes," he breathes like a memory just came back to him after being lost in a junk drawer for two years. "That's crazy. It's like the crystals are all one." He looks at me, eyes bright and twinkling.

"Yes," I say breathlessly, looking into his eyes. "They've got to be."

We stare at each other for a few minutes, the growing pain in my side magically gone for the first time without drugs. Except maybe one with blond hair and piercing blue eyes . . .

The most addictive of all.

I almost lose it when he crawls onto the bed with me and brushes his knuckles along my cheek. The smell of him brings back memories of the Ferris wheel, of how he made me feel before the moment went to shit.

His lips are too tempting, and my eyes slip to their perfect shape. The top one tilts up only slightly, practically begging to press against mine. This time I don't care that he sees, and I'm not embarrassed. I take my time looking back up, but when I do, I see my own desire reflected back in his eyes. So stupid blue, it isn't fair.

The soft touch of his knuckles slowly transitions to him brushing the nape of my neck. His fingers curl into my hair. I lean into that touch, moving slowly and sensually as lightning sparks between us. So much so my mark tingles from it, and my cheeks flush. Pressure grows deep within my core, blood rushing to my head and to places I'm more unfamiliar with.

Ardelle doesn't wait for the interruption surely on its way, and when his soft lips finally touch and melt into mine, I explode with decadent gratification. He kisses me slowly, testing how our lips fit together. Like when you wade into a cool pool of water, you never go in fully the first time. But after getting this first taste of him, I can't wait for more. I push our kiss harder and faster until I'm tasting every part of him. Our hands are wrapping around each other, and though it hurts to move my body with his, I do it anyway. Almost losing your life means you're no longer afraid to live it.

The feel of his skin, his bare chest on top of me, is too tempting for me to keep my hands away. He's a marble statue of some mighty warrior who came to life specifically to torture me. I'm all over him. His chest, his shoulders, his arms and back. My nails claw his skin and he grins at my playfulness. To finally get to do what I've been fantasizing about for weeks is more satisfying than I imagined. The rings on his fingers are cool as they touch my body, my arms, my waist, my thighs. I melt into him.

As our tongues touch slightly, my crystal can't help but flare. I feel it tingle, and he chuckles against my lips. The swell and tinge of magic blooms in the air. It isn't just my crystal that's swelling from his touch. All of me is bursting to life. The way his thumb caresses my cheek and his fingers twist in my hair are maddening, but nothing compares to when his tongue glides against mine in a tender way that makes me melt into his powerful arms. My heart wants to dissolve under him. Actually, it wants to burst with bubbles that make me float to the moon and stars. When his scent envelopes me, it strikes me as a little like home. It causes my skin to completely cover in goosebumps. I tingle with his every touch.

"Down kitty . . ." Ardelle whispers as our lips finally break from a kiss that I wish would last forever. My swollen lips tingle with the taste of him. Cinnamon, sage—Ardelle. "I don't want to hurt you," he says, referring to my injury. It's hard for me to care about that right now, when for the first time, I don't feel either drugged out of my mind or in so much pain I wish they'd drug me out of my mind.

I feel awake again.

Alive.

"I'm fine," I protest, but he moves back slightly.

I lie under him on his bed, legs somehow wrapped around his waist as he sits up shirtless before me.

Ardelle leans in and kisses my forehead. I hold onto both his arms and relish in his closeness.

"I don't want anything to ruin this," he says to me, his voice a vulnerable whisper.

My face softens. "Nothing will," I promise.

Although, I try my hardest to shove away the very real threats that linger far too close for comfort.

"Where did you come from?" he asks me, voice mesmerized and primal and full of desire.

I dare a glance at his crystal mark, the other tattoos along his chest and arms telling story after story. While most of my tattoos are random additions I slapped on myself when I was bored, Ardelle's are mostly illustrative, each an entire piece meant to expose tiny parts of his soul he's too scared to reveal any other way.

"I've always been here, Ardelle," I say, my mind snapping back to the man Zariya was so in love with on that moon. His name . . . I think, blinking through the haze of drugs, his name was Erodis. Zariya loved him then—I felt that love as I lived through her eyes. And if Erodis is Ardelle and Zariya is me, then we've been in love far longer than the two of us ever could have realized.

"I've always been here."

I lie flat on my back on Pacey's bed as the sound of her lightning-speed typing clanks in the air.

"So," she muses out loud, "what's with that stupid grin you can't get off your face, huh?"

The utter playfulness in her voice tells me she already knows.

Snatching one of her fluffy pillows, I chuck it at the back of her head. "No idea what you're talking about."

Yet, the smile she's referring to cannot leave me.

"Interesting, because there's someone else in this house who's suspiciously acting the exact same way, and I couldn't help but wonder..."

"La, la, la, la!" I try, but our laughter ends the entire charade. "Yeah, okay, so I've kissed both siblings. Are you happy now?"

Pacey finally turns her chair to face me, and I sit up, smiling so hard my cheeks hurt. Her eyebrows are raised at me as if to say: 'and?'

"I mean, sorry, he's a better kisser. What do you want from me? He's just more my type. You're definitely the best girl-kiss I've ever had though, hands down."

Pretending to wipe something off her shoulder like it's nothing she hasn't heard before, she champions her new title.

"He likes you. He's told me."

Her words cause a blast of emotion through me, and the feeling is so good, it's scary. "Yeah, I guess he's grown on me too."

"Well, we know what's got to happen then?" she begins, grabbing the closest thing on her desk, which happens to be a digital pen. Pointing it at me, she says, "Hair, nails, and getting you a banging outfit to get you feeling like your old self again."

That smile grows even wider.

CHAPTER 46

Why does walking into this massive arena feel like a walk to the gallows?

I'm as cold as a snowman when we arrive at the Titan Games arena. Not because of the snowy weather, but because of the sense of dread straightening my spine as stiff as ice. Weeks after my near-death assault from Deimos, my body has healed, almost like it never happened. There's not even a scar: Ahren's magic healed everything. I've never felt better.

Physically, anyway.

"Even if you had stage-four cancer, my magic would have healed you," Ahren told me one night. Too bad it didn't take away my internal wounds, because as we walk underneath the threshold to the arena's side entrance, my trembling is as intense as the crowd's roar.

"There are at least one hundred thousand people here," Pacey says to no one in particular, her voice in awe. As the biggest event on the entire continent, the Titan Games finale is the climactic ending to the three brutal challenges that await each of the Titans. Each year, all three challenges differ from years prior. You never know what you are going to get. They're often brutal, vicious, and deadly.

And people cheer for it.

Bringing Pacey close, Sylo agrees. "Dad said the logistics of the games has been a nightmare thanks to Deimos and now the threats from those rebel scumbags. This place is bigger than two football fields; they could be hiding anywhere."

Am I a rebel scumbag? I think to myself. *It's almost a badge of honor—if I hadn't been kicked out, that is.*

However, the mention of Deimos's name makes me shudder. Yesterday, I used the tattoo shop as an excuse to go and find that psychic alien I met on the night I struck the Capitol building. She seemed to know things. Information about me, about Deimos, and I needed final confirmation all this is real. So, I walked into her shop yesterday, being met by her stringy gray hair cascading down her hunched shoulders like a bunch of matted rat's tails. She only said one thing to me, repeating it over and over again until I was so spooked I ran out of there in a cold sweat.

"She burned the world to ashes and stones, the womb burned to screams and moans, and the prince rages from oceans to shores, to hunt her down till her bones are no more."

I pretty much have been white as a ghost ever since.

The setting sun disappears behind us as we're enveloped in a dark hallway crowded with SSPARROWs. The inner workings of the arena are housed in thick concrete, a maze of multiple levels housing thousands of seats, where lucky patrons sit propelled up above the massive bowl-shaped stadium to watch the action. Above, sitting somewhere perched in their special section, are our Terran leaders. Ardelle and Pacey have to know their parents are here, and their faces reflect their nervous energy. Towering even higher than the exclusive box for the Terran government are the giant lights covering the entire arena in a blanket of artificial sunshine. The open roof allows soft falling snowflakes to peek in on the games, free of charge.

We are decked out in full battle-ready attire. Pacey had done all the girls' hair in elaborate up-styles and braids, with hair jewelry and accessories. Each of us looks like a ballerina badass. Pacey and I also have full faces of makeup done up to match our hair, because doing otherwise is a cardinal sin. Nobody said you couldn't look good while kicking some ass.

"You shouldn't have worn that outfit," Jance scolds. I'm wearing a loosely fitting, short-sleeved gi made of dark-blue organza that flows and moves with ease. A red bow tied at my waist and the deep V in the front makes it slightly revealing, but the accessibility of its movements and the giant pockets won over the chilly wind. I had my sword tied to my back and a 9mm strapped to my ankle above where my pants bunch together. I topped the look off with my staple leather jacket. "It leaves you too open."

"My best asset is my speed, but I can't go fast if I'm weighed down by constricting clothes and armor," I argue, swerving between bodies and trying not to hit anyone with the sword's hilt. Ardelle and Pacey are having similar problems with their weapons, all of which are garnering us a lot of looks. We don't need to see all the eyes on us to know we're being watched.

"Stay close to me" is his only response.

Once a SSPARROW captain finds us through catcalls and gawking, he takes us through a secession of concrete hallways and stairs. The flickering florescent lights make my eyes sting. I feel Ardelle take my hand as we walk towards the back of the group, his jacket's exaggerated cuffs hiding the fact that we're holding hands. Not that our connection isn't plainly obvious. It makes me smile and feel safe in a very unsafe-feeling place.

We reach an elevator and step in after the soldier puts in a code.

The floor we exit onto differs greatly from the ones we entered through. It looks like a high-scale corporate building, with white walls, golden accents, and fresh green plants lining the hallway. The hallway has a few doors on either side, mostly clear glass or wooden.

The soldier opens both wooden doors simultaneously for us as we reach the end of hallway.

Sitting at a long rectangular table is my favorite squid in the galaxy—Naresteé, who's hauntingly beautiful as she sits at one of the table's ends. Those blood-red eyes now throwing daggers at me trigger a flash of anxiety. Her last words echo back to me—what did she say again? Something about being a pawn? Am I not always somebody's pawn?

I'm going out on a limb here, but I don't think she's very happy to see me.

Yet, neither is Malakyte.

I swallow hard, looking away from Malakyte's face, uncomfortable, and try to smile at him as we all file inside. Is he upset because I denied him? He stands at the opposite end of the table, shuffling through paperwork. It's the first time I've ever entered a location where he hasn't been watching for me, staring at me.

His rejection stings more than I think it should, but I deserve it.

Ardelle glances between Malakyte and me, confusion plastered on his face. He's always been aware of Malakyte's attention on me. I didn't tell him Malakyte tried to put the moves on, but it's obvious he notices the shift.

After we all take our seats at the table, Malakyte addresses us, voice melancholy. His charming façade seemingly shattered.

"I'm happy to see my Starseeds together and healthy," Malakyte starts, although it doesn't feel genuine. "My intelligence has informed me on a plethora of details during these last weeks, and a pattern has presented itself as of late, revolving around our sweet little Star."

The entire table turns and looks at me, my cheeks beginning to sizzle as my smile rises and falls awkwardly.

Shitballs, does he know something?

Has Malakyte found me out? What does he know? He always seems to know everything; what if he put together that I was with the rebels?

"We've realized, quite obviously, that wherever the Star goes, Deimos follows."

I let out a breath in sudden relief.

"Well, yeah," Ardelle echoes, voice a little condescending. "He almost killed her for her crystal. He's after it."

Malakyte's dark eyes meet Ardelle's, and again, the chest-puffing between them is obvious. "Precisely. Because of that, we set a mouse trap. We made it public knowledge you all would be attending this event, hoping to lure him here."

There's not a second for us to speculate what Malakyte is talking about because a side door to this small office blasts open. Three SSPARROWs burst in, holding a struggling alien male with a black hood over his face. He's bound at the wrists and ankles.

Deimos.

There's no need to see his face to know it's him. My mind instantly goes to his dagger hidden inside my gi. Now, it sears against my skin, as if it were calling out to its owner, wanting to go home.

I jump straight up, as if I'm on fire. Jance's hands are quick as he grabs my shoulders to stop me from toppling us both over, along with our chairs.

"We caught him mere moments ago on a lucky tip. Our little problem child came right to us today." Malakyte's cocky attitude seems to return with that statement. "We caught him inside the tunnels beneath the arena. Security is tight, but he probably used his devilish mind games to gain access, I'm sure."

"Flaunt it if you got it, asshole," Deimos says in return as he speaks through the hood over his face. "Is the kiddo feeling better? I sort of did a number on her the other week."

My fear fading, it takes about point-five seconds for me to charge at him, but Ardelle snatches me before I can strangle him.

Deimos's cackle continues as Malakyte says, "I'm sorry to use you as bait, Miss Ruzz, but it was unavoidable. After the last few incidents, we wanted to ensure his capture. Along with the security of today's event, of course. Don't feel inadequate that we were able to capture him when you were not; my people are vigorously trained, and I realize the team has a few kinks to work out. And like I said, we got lucky." Does this mean he won't help me find Gav since it wasn't us who brought Deimos in? Malakyte goes on. "We've been tracking Deimos heavily these past months, learning his habits and movements. Unfortunately, we discovered some additional disheartening information."

I feel Ardelle stiffen as he holds me, the air shifting dramatically.

"What other information?" Jance demands.

Malakyte glares at Ardelle.

Holding onto Ardelle even harder, I ask, "What's going on?"

"Why don't we let Mr. Dawson explain everything." Malakyte picks up a remote from the table and points it at one of the televisions mounted to the wall.

I look up at it, confused at first, not understanding what I'm seeing. It's security footage, or drone footage, I can't tell. I look over at Pacey, because the hover-van that we first saw when we hacked the Main Outpost is now on the screen. She recognizes it too. Deimos comes into view on screen. He opens the back of the hover and begins unloading children. My stomach aches for all those innocent children. Every one of them could be Gavrielle. Could be me. But then, my whole world turns upside down when another figure comes into view, a figure I know so well.

Ardelle.

CHAPTER 47

I push myself off Ardelle, more in shock than anything else. I wouldn't believe it if it wasn't for the look in Ardelle's eyes—a look of utter and complete regret reflects back at me.

In the footage, I watch as he helps Deimos unload the children from the hover, each one of them disappearing off camera somewhere, somewhere awful, most likely.

Malakyte points the remote at the television again. "This was taken during the parade."

I gasp as I see Ardelle and Deimos talking to each other. There's no sound, but what causes my shock is what I see him holding in his hands.

The gift box.

Ardelle is holding the gift box Deimos gave me.

I almost puke.

Malakyte changes the footage again, and I shake my head, not wanting to watch. "This is the morning of the carnival, I'm afraid."

My eyes are welling with tears as I watch the two of them again engage in conversation, but this time, there's audio.

"You're sure she'll be at the carnival tonight?" Deimos asks Ardelle in the video, and Ardelle nods back yes.

"I'll make sure of it."

No, no . . . this can't be happening.

Averting my eyes, I turn away. The sound of Pacey's voice asking what's going on absolutely crushes me.

Her brother betrayed us all, that's what's going on. Stunned, I cover my mouth with my hand.

Realizing we've all seen enough, Malakyte turns off the video footage.

Heat boils inside my chest, and I can't even look at him. His guilt is written all over his face.

"I can explain," he tries.

"You almost got me killed!" I roar. Jance comes to stand behind me. "You set me up, didn't you? Why? That's how he knew we were there— you told him. It was Deimos who kept messaging you on the Ferris wheel while we were—" My laugh is as bitter as dirt. Everything makes sense now. All the pieces fall together. This was all an act to get close to me, to hand me over to a killer. "Did you intentionally leave his bindings loose? Were you trying to get me killed? Was that all a part of this grand scheme the two of you cooked up?"

"No! Of course not," he tries. "Thumbelina, it started as one thing, but when I got to know you, I realized what a mistake it was. I only helped him because he said he could get Pacey and me home by removing our crystals. I swear, I promised me you wouldn't get hurt. He promised he just wanted your crystal, that he could remove it without hurting you. I didn't think—"

"No, you didn't think!" I yell, tears kissing the brims of my eyes. "You didn't think about anyone but yourself and what you wanted! And I can't believe you'd be dumb enough to believe a single word this piece of shit says."

I turn my back on him, unable to look Ardelle in the eyes a second longer. I also don't want him to see the pain he's causing me, because my heart is shattering.

Deimos laughs before Ardelle can answer, and I stalk over to him, ripping the hood off and baring my teeth at him. "Is it true?" I demand, not knowing why I even bother.

Deimos's large, dark eyes search mine inquisitively. "Pretty boy here wanted the crystals gone. I promised him they'd be gone. The kid's as dumb as he is good looking. What can I say?"

Ardelle sold me out . . .

The rush to my head is so intense I wobble.

"What were you thinking?" Jance's voice is as enraged as my own.

I answer for him. "He doesn't care about anyone but going back to his rich-ass mommy and daddy. You put your own sister's life at risk by messing with this psychopath, Ardelle."

"I know," he pleads, but I can't even look at him. "I tried to get us out of the carnival. I chose you, Thumbelina. I did. There just wasn't enough time, and I did everything in my power to keep you safe. I told you to run and to let me handle him."

I make a disgusted sound. "Screw you, Ardelle."

"Thumbelina—"

"Don't!" My voice cracks with heartbreak. My body trembles and shakes. How could I have fallen for this act? How could I have let him touch me and take care of me these last weeks and fill me with a hope that I've never felt before? My entire life I've been an outcast, and only Gav has ever welcomed all of me and didn't run away; he loved me for me. That's rare and beautiful and why I fight for him, but with Ardelle, he showed me that there's hope for me in ways I hadn't previously considered before. That, despite differences, regardless of having belief systems that don't align or pasts that are on completely different roads, I can still fit in somewhere beautiful. Still belong. How could I have been so stupid? "You don't get to call me that anymore."

He looks as if I've just stabbed him in the heart, his own eyes filling with tears. He tries to say something, but he stops himself. Looking over at his sister, I see her cheeks are slick with tears, her face red and shocked.

"Unfortunately, these are direct crimes against Arianyte. Take Mr. Dawson into the catacombs until the games have finished, then transport him to confinement."

"What? No!" Pacey cries as she lunges for her brother. Ahren holds her back, but she fights the Ringer tooth and nail. "You can't take him. He's one of us!"

Four SSPARROWs escort Ardelle towards the door, his body sunken and defeated. He looks at me as the soldiers walk him past, our eyes meeting once again, both tear-filled. Possibly for the last time, because I never want to see his face again.

I give him *nothing*.

He didn't even get what he wanted in the end, so it was all for nothing. It was all a lie by Deimos to manipulate Ardelle into giving the alien access to what he wanted.

Me.

"Your Dezlar has been hacked," Ardelle says to me before the SSPARROW shoves him through the door.

Then he's simply gone.

Like he was a ghost this entire time, a fantasy.

I'm hollow and stunned.

Pacey continues to struggle but falls to her knees in tears. I go to her, not even knowing what to say, but knowing I need to be with her. She was betrayed too. We all were.

As I put my arms around her, she latches onto me, crying hysterically. Ardelle is her rock. He kept her alive this entire time, and I honestly don't know what she's going to do without him. She doesn't have a Ringer, she doesn't trust Ahren because he's a doctor, and she's alone. I know what that's like, and I refuse to allow her to feel like that.

"It's going to be okay," I say, but I don't believe my words.

She wipes the tears from her face, eyes red and her chest splotchy. "Take me home, now. I'm not serving the person who's going to hurt my brother."

"Pacey . . ." Ahren says softly, bending down to meet her. He knows the dangerous line she's walking.

"I apologize for having to confine your brother, Miss Dawson. It pains me as much as it pains you." I highly doubt that. "However, your brother broke my laws and actively plotted against myself and my Star. Not to mention, he was thwarting you from keeping your crystal as well. Ardelle is on record agreeing to give all three crystals to Deimos, which would make this terrorist virtually impossible to defeat. There must be consequences for his behavior. I'm a man of my word and will continue offering my protection to you, Miss Dawson, but only if you continue to do as I ask."

There's a convincing threat beneath those words, and Pacey doesn't argue further. She knows she's screwed without Arianyte's protection from her family, and she has no one else with the resources to ensure they don't find her.

"What's going to happen to him?" I ask Malakyte as I stand.

He shrugs casually, like this didn't just shatter our entire world in a matter of minutes. "I'm unsure, but I will reiterate that crimes against Arianyte are taken seriously. I do not offer second chances. I am genuinely sorry to bring this information to you."

Malakyte walks up to me and places a comforting hand on my shoulder. I lay my hand on his, my head still shaking in shock. How could everything with Ardelle be a lie? After everything we've overcome, how could he do this to me?

To my surprise, in front of everyone, he whispers in my ear, "I'm always here for you, Karalevine."

I blink, trying not to blush. Did I pick the wrong guy? My mind is spinning, and I can't think about this right now.

When I don't reply, Malakyte reaches for me and cups my chin in his hand, feeling like an ice sculpture come to life. His thumb caresses my lip affectionately, and despite the chilly touch, I blush. It's not hard to see the real Malakyte Ardeen in those eyes, a guy who is misunderstood and held to an unimaginable standard. Someone like me. Perhaps my hatred for Arianyte has blinded me to him? Or perhaps my heart is simply stupid and found its way into the hands of someone who didn't recognize its value.

"I see how much pain Ardelle's lie has caused you," Malakyte says, looking at me as if the others in the room have all but vanished. "And I've realized in this moment if I were to continue lying to you, it would only make me as much of a traitor to your trust as he is. I'm certain my discretion doesn't rise to the level of betrayal you've just experienced; however, I couldn't sleep at night knowing how you'd be hurt by my keeping this from you. From you all." He finally acknowledges the others, each of their faces drawn back in mortified or confused expressions. What are they seeing that I'm not?

I don't want another secret revealed, but without saying another word, Malakyte begins to unbutton his jacket. It's sleek, black, and fits over his muscled chest perfectly. His long fingers unbutton the shiny fabric, exposing a slightly blue-tinted, hairless chest. The shadows of his pecks frame a symbol right above his sternum bone. The Elendril symbol sitting at rest is dark blue due to his cold, blue blood, unlike everyone else's mark that reflects the red blood within our veins and looks more like the color of a maroon-colored bruise when it's not in use.

The mark is six ovals, each separated out evenly and no doubt lines up perfectly with the points of my star, and they each have some intricate design within them.

I stare at it, mentally placing it on top of the design I tattooed on that lying, deceiving jerk Ardelle two weeks ago. The design fits right where I expected it to, but as surprised as I am to see it, I don't care that he's a Starseed. I only care about Ardelle and his betrayal. But as I stare at the mark there, my head fills with bubbles and the edges of my vision darken as the familiar sensation of being pulled down overwhelms me, and I'm at the mercy of the blackness once again.

"Much of your disregard for me and Arianyte teeters on dereliction of duty, Zariya." His voice denigrates, berates, intimidates. I try not to let his scolding affect me, but I look anywhere in the small room within the bowels of the Azurite Fleet than in his dark, lifeless eyes. With only the soft plasma lights setting the room in a blue glow, he appears all of the ice prince his reputation perceives him to be. What a foolish girl I was to think I could change him—save him. "Not only are we publicly bonded, but you also replaced Naresteé as my second-in-command. My subordinates are asking me why the leader of my most elite unit, as well as my partner and soon-to-be wife, is so incredibly out of control. Moreover, they're asking why I haven't punished you for these absurd lapses of judgment. I'm blinded by you, by your potential, your beauty. As my future mate, I'm always finding myself simply vexed by your behavior."

Will I be punished? Will Malakyte punish his future bride so blatantly? My instinct is to leave, but I can't. He's made sure of that.

"Your tenacity has continually attracted me to you. It's why I've let so much slide in regard to your behavior. You and I, we are on the precipice of a colossal power shift.

We're going to rule everything together. The Milky Way is our playground to conceive endless possibilities side by side, to birth a new empire. When my parents step down, you and I will have the power to solidify our autonomy without their preposterous restrictions. We will build Arianyte new again, you and I. This moment is imperative for me, you know this. Any indiscretion on my part can spook my parents into holding onto their power, but we know it's about time they pass the torch. They want me to rule with my equal, as they have ruled together as one. You are that equal, Zariya. With your power at Arianyte's helm, none of the other races will challenge this empire's rule again."

Drunk on all the possibilities of power, Malakyte—my betrothed—has gone mad. He was not always like this. Sure, he's always been intense and serious, but together he and I laughed, had fun, stole private moments that were genuinely precious, until he became something else. Unreasonable, controlling, manipulative, gaslighting me at every turn to make me the exact version he preferred. I'm becoming a shell of my former self, and I'm debating if she's still in there, or if Malakyte has sucked her right out of me.

I'm trapped in this room with him, trapped in a thousand different ways. Yet, there's no scream I can make, no fight I can contest, no escape I can find. The door is open. The door is never locked or bolted, yet he manages to keep me inside, forever his prisoner and puppet.

"My advisers told me taking a girl from the gutters of Azurite and making her empress would be reckless. That you can take the girl out of the gutters, but not the gutters out of the girl. You're acting like that gutter girl right now. I thought you could overcome that part of yourself. Because I built you up better than that. I took you from nothing and am about to make you a queen. Every girl's dream is to be you right now. Yet, you dishonor and disrespect me by running your mouth like you're the one in charge here."

His finger brushes my cheek, and it takes everything in me not to shrink away from that frigid touch. The old me would have bitten it off, but I don't think she's here anymore. My lips remain sealed.

"I just want to be with you, Zariya." His voice is soft now, tender almost. But I know him well enough to know it's like lightning on Planet Ornoth—there one moment and gone the next. "With all the privileges I've given you, I've trusted you to do what needs to be done—discretely. You assured me you wanted the security of what Arianyte can provide. Without that crystal living within your heart—the one I put there—you'd still be nothing, a nobody girl with no power or future to speak of. You *owe every success you've ever gained to me. So then, why are you doing this to me? Have I not given you everything you've ever wanted?"*

His face gives away all that fury and savagery. He's such an oxymoron, looking so young and beautiful, and if you caught him smiling just right, he could even look glamorous. Who could resist his lure? With all his power and prestige and charm? How had I not seen the evil in those onyx eyes? No, only ice and thunder live there. A monster dressed in flesh, cold-blooded literally and figuratively, Malakyte Ardeen is my soon-to-become husband, soon-to-become Emperor of the Arianyte Empire. And I am the soon-to-be bride by his side. His empress.

I'd rather die ten times over again.

But if he becomes emperor, the galaxy itself will die along with me.

Some part of the girl I used to be comes forth, defiant and brave. Perhaps she does exist deep down. If she hadn't, then I wouldn't have been able to do what I did.

Today, my delightful husband-to-be has tied me to his favorite torture device, a device that I've used on others many times. Perhaps karma has arrived to collect her debts at last.

I deserve every single thing that happens to me after all I've done for Malakyte in Arianyte's name. I cannot complain.

Zapper bugs suddenly cover my entire body, crawling up my brown pant legs. They come from the lower sectors of the Arianyte Mothership where I spent most of my childhood after my home planet was no longer habitable. My crystal buzzes and prickles in response. Each one of their many legs I feel crawling up my legs, my lap, onto my chest and arms. It's an illusion, *I tell myself.* The chair creates a person's worst fears; the neurolight glowing blue by my temples allows it to create an image of my worst nightmares. They used to crawl on me while I slept. *I refuse to light up, or scream, or cry. I won't give Malakyte the satisfaction of it.*

He clicks the wireless mechanism off and stops my hallucinations. To my dismay, it caused my entire body to be covered in a sheen of sweat, my white hair dampened at the nape.

"I don't enjoy this," he whispers.

He lured me here, his cronies strapped me down into this chair. "I need you to understand the serious predicament you've put me in. How, in this Milky Way, you convinced some of my loyalist supporters to question me? Nobody questions me, do you understand? Not even the future empress. If word gets to my parents that I'm not following every single one of their rules, they will not concede power to me. They've ruled for too long, they're relics. Everything I do is systematic. This galaxy is a fragile, desperate thing. It needs to be told what to do. When to eat, when to sleep, and when to live and die. Systems don't function any other way; I don't function any other way. Now, when there's a problem with that system, I send you and your team to retain that balance. That's why I gave you all the Elendril crystals. You do my bidding. I, in turn, make you a queen. How you feel about the process, or how it's done, is irrelevant. As it should be for you. Going around, parroting some unjustifiable nonsense about how the races have a right to stop us from using their young for the Silent Breath is paramount to treason. Just do your job!"

I flinch at the vehemence plastered on his face. A face that haunts my dreams, and definitely isn't the face of the person I used to love. Strapped to this chair, I'm not sure how I allowed myself to get here. How I allowed him to put me here.

"If I find out you're doing anything like this again, or any of your 'crew' is complicit in your plights, I will ensure they get the idea in a much clearer way than what you're getting today. Don't worry, I won't do anything to you, my sweet Zariya. I'll need you looking as beautiful as ever for the ceremony. But you'll watch as I do despicable things to them. I'll make the men watch as their women get violated. Torture their minds until they don't know which galaxy they're living in anymore. Make them remember an entirely different life than the one they've lived . . . make them forget you, forget their own names. That's always a fun game my sweet Narestee loves to play. I have no qualms about letting her spin her plots and stories as she sees fit. What's important now is that we get past this and move forward so we can start fresh once we're crowned and power has been established."

Swallowing against a cardboard throat, I weakly say, "I understand."

I absolutely loathe myself for saying it, and I'm clenching my teeth so hard they may crack.

He kisses me on the cheek. Smiling as if a lover had given him a thoughtful gift, he looks at me adoringly. Removing the neurolight panels from my temples, he softly releases the binds at my wrists and ankles. He kisses me again on the forehead, his lips as cold as ice.

"Also, don't you think it's a little inappropriate to be socializing alone with that gutter-found teammate of yours when you're engaged to the future leader of Arianyte? Erodis-something? His place on your team is purely a professional one. Stay away from him, Zariya. I don't like the way he looks at you. He makes me look bad."

Then he disappears into his shadows, where he thrives and belongs.

Chilled to the bone, I finally allow myself to release my breath. I was so wrong about Malakyte. So wrong about thinking he wasn't the veritable monster I see before me. *It shocks me how wrong I could be, and how it took me so long to see it. To see what he was doing to* me. *But I see it now, and I see it clearly.*

I'm a statue of utter fear.

It's too late to undo what's coming . . .

There's no stopping all I've set in motion. When I accidentally found the files I ultimately confiscated from Arianyte's systems, the stars themselves shined their light upon me. I thought, this could be my way out. I didn't have to marry him if I leaked this information and caused his parents to retract their retirement. Perhaps it wasn't as much of a blessing as I initially thought. Those files, those documents, are currently traveling through the digital space between worlds. They'll soon be exposed for the galaxy to see.

And I will open their eyes wide to the truth about Arianyte.

I knew Malakyte wouldn't take it well, but he's becoming much more unstable than I ever expected the closer we get to the wedding and coronation. He's torturing me for mere rumors. My stupid assumption that I was exempt from his abuse because I was going to be his empress was clearly a gigantic mistake. It's obvious I've actually been the most abused person in his life; I simply hadn't seen it for myself until it was far too late. What is he going to do once he realizes what I've done? What we've all done . . .

I place my hand over my stomach, sensing the new life growing there, knowing we'll all burn for this.

CHAPTER 48

I jerk as I come back into my own body, the scene before me dissolving back into the arena conference room. At this point, I'm used to this crazy shit. Another vision had been triggered, this time not by Ardelle's crystal but by Malakyte's. I believe this most recent vision was before they ever got to the moon. Or so I'm guessing . . . but the timeline isn't as chilling as the scene itself.

Or what it means for me and every other person in this room—including Ardelle.

Nobody seems to notice I zoned out as Malakyte and the adults talk about Ardelle, while Sylo tries to comfort Pacey.

I pale, going ghostly white as I look at the cold-blooded alien standing mere feet from me, conversing as if he isn't putting on an entire act.

I'm floored, but not surprised. This is Arianyte, after all. And Arianyte has always been—will always be—*my enemy.* They just did a better job at concealing themselves this time. My heart has absolutely betrayed me, and it's hard to know how I can trust myself when I clearly have such terrible judgment in men.

Holy stars, this is bad.

It's all coming together now.

Deimos was right . . . stars, he was right.

I know it now; I feel it. The crystal has shown me the truth, the awful truth.

I try and recall more details of the vision. The Silent Breath? What was that? Why was Zariya trying to stop it?

This is all insane. Absolutely *insane.*

This entire time, Malakyte has played us.

He was the person chasing Zariya and the others on that moon.

He was the one Zariya was petrified of.

It's always been Malakyte.

Did he set Ardelle up? Was our connection a threat to Malakyte the same way Erodis was a threat to him because he loved Zariya, and she was in love with this other man? Ardelle did what he did but . . . what if Malakyte knew it all along and has been biding his time to get Ardelle and me apart? But stars, Ardelle almost got me killed. Dammit, I don't know what to believe and I can't trust anything anymore; my entire world is upside down.

What do I do?

My body quakes.

I have to calm down, get myself together. Breathing slowly through my nose, making as little noise as possible, I relax the way Jance taught me to. In, one–two–three–four . . . out, one–two–three–four . . .

It really wasn't Deimos who chased down Zariya, it was Malakyte Ardeen—it was Arianyte this whole time. And Deimos's stupid tales of past lives and galactic battles and wars, how we were right in the middle of them before I took us all out of the game. All of it was real, and once the others figure this out, too, I'll be alone all over again. How many more people will I have to lose before this is done?

But they're in danger if I say nothing . . . and isn't the ultimate act of love sacrifice? Didn't Zariya do just that?

Movement to my left catches my attention. Deimos remains sitting on his knees, bound at the wrists and ankles. The look of wonderment in his eyes is surprising, to say the least, but he had been watching me when no one else had been. Deimos sees the truth.

He sees everything.

We lock gazes, and something happens between us that's so unexpected. We have an . . . understanding. Somehow, he sees that I know the truth now. He can tell by the way I'm glaring at Malakyte, how quiet and still I've become.

Instead of seeing the malevolent man with the glowing-green eyes from my nightmares, I see an old man who's weak and helpless and going about everything in the worst ways, but also someone who seeks the ultimate release: revenge. And I understand him, better than he realizes.

Then suddenly, almost like I have bees buzzing inside my head, I feel a fuzzy, pulsating sensation that sounds like it's coming from within my bones.

"*Hello, kiddo,*" Deimos says, but I realize all too late that his voice is coming from *inside* my head.

CHAPTER 49

"*Calm down*," Deimos orders, voice bouncing off the walls of my mind. My body stiffens when I realize what's happened way too late to do anything about it.

He's got me.

Dizziness floods me, and it feels as if I'm standing inside a pool full of jelly. I can feel him inside my mind and body as I attempt to fight him out.

It's no use.

"*Get out of my head!*" The words rage from inside my mind. He's cut off my ability to scream or cry out or speak at all. Nobody notices what's happening.

Annoyed, he placates me telepathically. "*Your fear is permeating off you. It's pathetic. If I wanted you dead, kiddo, you'd be dead. I knew your little healer would fix you right up. But the crystal doesn't belong to you. It belongs to Zariya. However, who it belongs to least of all is Malakyte Ardeen. That little prick is deadlier than you realize, and if you want your boyfriend to live, you'll play along. So shut up because you're mine now whether you like it or not.*"

Pausing before answering, I try to keep my mind as clear as possible so he can't hear more of my thoughts than necessary.

"*Screw you. Screw you. Screw you!*"

Deimos wastes no time.

In an instant, I feel as if my body has no more weight to it. I feel myself grabbing my sword, sliding it out of its sheath faster than I could ever manage on my own.

Then the blade is at my neck.

"Don't touch her," Deimos says as he rises to his feet awkwardly with the bindings. "Or she dies. Uncuff me, *now*." He gestures to Malakyte, whose face is stone cold. Malakyte nods to one of the SSPARROWs, and the cuffs clank on the floor.

Deimos and I walk to the double doors, the sword still at my neck. I have absolutely no autonomy over my own body and despite everything, I look for Ardelle—then realize he's not here.

Jance and the others all tense as we walk by, Jance's eyes filled with pure fear.

Deimos backs the two of us out the doors. It turns out Deimos can't control every function of my body because my tears crest as he closes the doors.

My finger comes up to where the two doors meet at the highest point, and I'm having to stand on my tiptoes to reach the top portion. For the first time in my life, the fire of my crystal calmly, effortlessly releases from my pointer finger and gently melts the two doors together along with the outside hinges.

The doors seal shut.

Deimos controls my crystal way better than I ever have, almost like it was his own.

I'm taken towards the elevator door, and he stops and turns towards me.

"Do the others know you've got my knife hidden under that fancy outfit of yours? Or are you lying to them about that too?"

I can't reply.

Deimos chuckles a bit, pleasure passing through the glow in his eyes. A glow that's reflected in my eyes. "Let me fix that for you."

Like a light switch, he brings back my ability to speak.

"I'm going to kill you" are my first words. "I'm going to slit your throat with it, so you better do whatever you want with me now because the second I'm able, you're dead. Especially after you manipulated Ardelle like that. You took advantage of his pain and his suffering, and you used him to get to me."

Pursing his lips, he contemplates my threat. "I think I'm actually the one in the position to throat-slit, if we're playing semantics and all. And pretty boy made his own choices. He didn't hesitate to install my spyware on your Dezlar: it's how I've been following you around. The kid sold you out. He didn't even tie my binding that well at the carnival. I thought he did that purposely so I could escape. The dagger show was because of your mouth. You're lucky I still wanted you alive."

When I don't reply, he walks up to stand within an inch of my face, bends down, and whispers, "But semantics are just that, right, kiddo? I can do anything I want to you. Nobody is here to stop me, not even you."

Hands of dull green with sharp black nails trace my jacket's sleeves. If I could shudder in disgust, I would. He presses his hands to my hips, barely touching the soft, flowing fabric, finding the dagger hidden underneath.

It must call to him, just as my sword calls to me.

My arm lowers, and my sword comes off my neck at last. It slides back into its sheath with a smooth glide and a click.

"Now, I'm no pervert, so I'll have you reach down your shirt to get my dagger back for me," he says as my hand dips through the front of my gi and down to where the dagger is strapped. My fingers curl around it, the hilt warm from sitting against my body.

Deimos snatches it out of my hand. "Thanks, kiddo. I missed this. I'm rather attached to it, you see. I'm really grateful you brought it today."

I scowl back at him, watching as he twirls the dagger around in his hand. He clearly sees me glaring. "You're still upset about all that? Oh come on, it's getting arduous." The cold, black alien metal touches my cheek as he presses it flat against it, causing chills to shoot through my body all the way to the tips of my pointed ears. "I'd think that we'd let bygones be bygones by now."

Sadly, he's taken away my eye-rolling function, otherwise they'd be rolling for days.

Why do I crave Ardelle's presence right now? I should hate him . . . but I'm so scared and need him here.

The dagger travels down my neck, shoulders, arms, and hips. He tickles it against my stomach, the spot where he got me last time. Now, we're here again, and he's ensnared me to where I cannot move, or fight, or even cry for help. Not that the help could get here. The bangs and slams and shouts against the doors tell me those in the room are trying, at the very least. I don't know if it's sick or not that their effort warms me while I'm a body locked in ice.

"You know the crystal belongs to Zariya, yet I've been racking my brain about how you could have known her name. Then it hit me as I watched you moments ago—her crystal lives within your heart. It wouldn't surprise me if it spoke to you. Showed you things. These are very special artifacts and all.

"Zariya was very special to me. Precisely why I've chased Malakyte's pompous ass around the galaxy in search of you. Zariya was also special to him, but he was not precious to her."

The alien lets me blink out the tears of fear that rim my eyes.

I don't want to die here—alone.

"There was a moment where I thought what we were doing was the right choice. Back then, getting us out of our horrendous situation and into one of power and influence seemed like the most advantageous to survival. It wasn't until I realized I had led her into a trap, a trap I could not save her from, that I began to understand what a terrible mistake we made. Then, when I couldn't save her . . . that's when I vowed to avenge her.

"Now here you are, parading around completely ignorant of what's happened a lifetime before you drew breath on this wretched planet. The irony. You're blessed to not remember how badly it fell apart."

Deimos bends down, a vein bulging in his large forehead, while the whites of his eyes are tinged yellow and red, and I imagine fury burns within those dark pools. "Oh, you're trembling," he says indignantly as he takes my hand. His face looks mad with indecision, and I can see the war going on behind his eyes. Some part of him doesn't want to do what the other clearly does.

Waving the dagger in front of my face, he stands and turns from me. "I can take my daughter's crystal back from you right this very moment," Deimos says in such a soft voice that I barely hear him. In fact, I'm not sure I heard him correctly. I couldn't have.

"What did you just say?" There's no way that could be correct.

He scoffs. "You heard me, kiddo," he says solemnly, turning back towards me. "I should kill you and take back what was once my daughter's. I taught her how to use the weapon you can barely wield. Exactly like I've got you in my control now, I assisted her, helped her control the beast within. Not just anyone can handle this specific crystal. It is a living animal. It's no surprise you have no control, but it's a little pathetic that you've had it your entire life and can barely manage a simple blast. Zariya had mastered it within three years, but she was so much more than you'll ever be. My daughter was a Killer of Worlds!" he shouts, coming back to face me as the dark blade's edge presses over my heart—over the star. The blood dripping down my chest tickles as the blade pierces my skin. I tremble, flashbacks of the carnival barreling into me as if they were a baseball bat repeatedly whacking the back of my skull.

I'm brushing past the breaking news here, and I know it. There's no way—no way in hell this monster could have been Zariya's *father*. Then I look closer, at the green skin, the white hair, the giant pointed ears, all of it matching her in such a way it's almost funny. How did I fail to see this earlier?

But that would make a lot more sense if it were true . . .

Now, Zariya's deranged father wants what was hers all those years ago, which is now beating within my chest.

"You don't know what it's like to watch your only child burn before your eyes. I knew what she did, why she did it. Who forced her hand."

Deimos looks towards the sealed door—to his real enemy.

"And that wasn't me," I say, fighting his hold with all I have.

"But you have all that's left of my little girl." His voice is a venomous snarl in my ear.

When I open my mouth, he snaps it shut.

"Shut up," he orders, and I'm done talking. "If I had more time, I'd have killed you today. Consider yourself lucky."

Then I'm released. All my fear and terror, all the trembling that my body couldn't release on its own, is all instantaneously released. The fear causes my knees to buckle and I fall to the floor.

The doors to the elevator open with a chime and a silent glide. "Oh, I almost forgot," Deimos says as he turns flamboyantly towards me. "My old friend Geonni let it slip the nature of the deal you two made, even though he kicked you to the curb. Yeah, I know you were involved with the rebels. I'd be careful with that little tidbit of information if I were you."

I scowl at him. "Why would Geonni tell you that?"

Deimos hunches his shoulders until they were practically touching his ears. "Maybe we've been on the same team this entire time?"

What?

"How do you think I knew about the Capitol building and the meeting? You got me that information. Thanks, kiddo, couldn't have done it without you. And also at the parade, my surprise gift to you was done systematically to keep you from stopping the rebel's bombs. Geonni wanted you safe as well, so I obliged. And today, the codes they stole from the drive you planted are the same codes that got me in here. Ah, kiddo, don't look at me like that," Deimos fawns as if he cares one wit about me.

How could Geonni have kept this from me? This whole time.

When do the betrayals stop?

Deimos continues because I'm speechless. "But that boy you were so valiantly searching for—well, kiddo, I hate to break it to you, but Arianyte killed him years ago. Sorry to be the bearer of bad news. Looks as if all this was for nothing. Hope you weren't counting on him being alive."

My world tilts sideways, and my blood pressure drops to the soles of my feet as Deimos steps into the elevator, watching me with glittering eyes, arms crossed like he enjoys telling me that Gavrielle is dead.

Dead . . .

Dead.

The weight of his words doesn't hit me when the overwhelming urge to tell him exactly who Gavrielle was to him bubbles up.

"That boy, the one you're gleeful about being dead, well, he was your Ringer, asshole." I seethe, tasting my tears and rage and hate as it all falls like a river from my eyes. And for the first time, a look of genuine horror flashes on Deimos's face. The elevator doors shut.

And I scream.

CHAPTER 50

INHABITANTS THAT VIOLATE ARIANYTE LAW DO SO WITH
FULL KNOWLEDGE OF THE TERMINATION OF THEIR RIGHT
TO COUNSEL. ARIANYTE RECKONERS SHALL ADJUDICATE
AND DELIVER JUSTICE BASED ON THE CIRCUMSTANCES
IN WHICH THE CRIME ARISES, IN ADDITION TO ANY
EVIDENCE PRESENTED IN THE DEFENSE.

Jance and the others finally bust open the doors, and I think they expected to see me injured and bleeding again, but when they all surround me, they don't see that it's my heart that's been stabbed this time.

I'm picked up by Jance. The events of the last thirty minutes are too much for me to handle, and I retreat deeply within myself. Missing Ardelle, hating Ardelle. Malakyte—damn Malakyte . . . and now Gavrielle.

Gav is dead . . .

I'm unable to cope. I'm unable to do this a second longer.

I'm somewhat aware of Jance and the other adults arguing with Malakyte about something, likely our positions here. They've brought us into one of those side rooms. Someone gave me a soda and some chips, and I force myself to sip on the pop at least.

The pain is so overwhelming and intense I almost wish Deimos had killed me. Ended it all, because my capacity to deal is nonexistent. I don't want to die, but I don't know how to handle this amount of pain and guilt and anger, and all I want to do is make the people responsible for it pay. Doing the right thing didn't work. Being a good person—it only led me here. To this terrible, awful shit show. I might as well do what I came to do at the very beginning and get my revenge. It's the only thing left for me now.

I never should've doubted my initial instincts. Arianyte is the true enemy. Malakyte manipulated me into believing otherwise.

So did Ardelle . . .

My heart absolutely shatters at the fact it was never real for him. I was nothing but a means to an end, so he could return to where he's comfortable instead of facing the fact that he doesn't belong there. He belongs with all of us . . . with me.

Malakyte says that Deimos needs to be caught and we need to do our jobs. Additionally, there have been several rebels scanned upon entry to the arena. However, my request for a few moments alone was granted by the dear leader, and for that I'm relieved.

Once everyone spreads out to search for Deimos, I'm left alone. I want to cry, to scream and throw things and blast this entire stadium to bits, but I'm so numb I can only sit here . . . wondering how Malakyte killed my friend. Was he the one who physically did it? Or was it Naresteé who did the deed? A SSPARROW? Who killed Gavrielle?

I thought I could handle the truth. Thought if I found out Gav was dead, I could take that blow and somehow be okay . . . but now that it's real and solid and sure, all I want is to explode. Like a glass rose chucked on concrete, I have been shattered into a million pieces.

I slam my fist into the table as my chest tingles. He's dead. Gone.

And I wasn't there to make it right with him, to beg his forgiveness for leaving him behind—for blasting him along with all the others. Stars, I'm a monster. I always have been.

Was all this chasing ghosts for no reason at all? Having gone through all the stages of grief back when I lost him initially, I didn't realize how the immutable fact of him being dead would drill such a super-massive black hole into my heart. Is revenge my only option now? What justice can I get a dead boy who nobody remembers but me? My drawings of him and his mark were stolen, so the only reminders I have for him are my dandelion tattoo and teal tips; but I can't look at them without tearing up.

I've forgotten his face. That sweet, kind, beautiful face. Those gorgeous violet eyes that I envied so much and I was never able to recreate with my inks. A boy that never got to grow up into a hauntingly beautiful man that would no doubt have every girl on their knees, begging for a mere chance to be looked at by him the way he looked at me that afternoon. That person's future was stolen; and I was the one to blame for it all.

I don't deserve to be standing here. I don't. I hate every single part of myself.

"*Some justice is better than no justice,*" said the almost-empress as she took everything from the filthy wicked prince.

I'm losing my mind. I'm a blazing bomb of fury and wrath and I am going to burn down everything, and I mean everything, to get that boy whatever form of justice I can.

As I sit and contemplate all that's happened in this short period of time, something suddenly doesn't make sense. The Malakyte in the last vision looked almost identical to how he appears today. How is that possible?

Keeping my crystal's energy down is an enormous struggle right now, something I'm still trying to get a handle on when a knock sounds out.

The door opens and a dark head of hair enters unabashedly. "Don't worry, we'll catch him," Malakyte says as the door closes behind him. He must have been able to sense my crystal simmering. He sees me looking for the others, and I don't see them. Good. They'd only try to stop me.

It's time to be alone with the leader of Arianyte. The one who's responsible for killing Gavrielle.

Perfect.

Strapping my forearm guards back on, I say, "Are you sure you want me on the job still? It doesn't seem like I'm very good at capturing your fugitives—or spotting them."

Malakyte's smile is practically playful. "We all have growing pains, Karalevine. Deimos is formidable, he always has been. As far as Mr. Dawson goes, he fooled us all."

"Call me Kara," I insist. Our exchange is formal and awkward, but how can I fake this when I know the truth?

330

My head barely meets Malakyte's chest, and as I look up into his Coal Black eyes, I take a step back.

"If only you realize how special you truly are, you wouldn't worry about those like Mr. Dawson. He's insignificant. There's so much we could accomplish together. Not merely here, in the Aurora System, but the Milky Way. So many planets teeming with life, ready to be taught all that exists out there. Arianyte gives life, and yes, we ask for something in return, but I believe order and peace and the expansion of life is a small ask for all we offer. You could be a part of that, with this." He slides the fabric of my clothing over to expose my mark. "You could rule the galaxy with that power."

Malakyte Ardeen is a smooth talker when he wants to be.

And I don't buy it for a second.

My fingers curl around my sword's hilt as it sits on the table, its textured metal cold against my hands. Before I can draw my blade against him, the door blasts open with a bang.

Deimos stands before us in the doorway, looking like hell incarnate with eyes ablaze like emerald fire.

Immediately, my eyes clamp shut as I dart to the opposite side of the table, bumping into several chairs. Malakyte doesn't move an inch.

"Don't worry, kiddo, you and I have already had our fun," Deimos says as he closes and locks the door behind him, but not before I see the bodies of the SSPARROW guards on the floor outside. "Mr. Malakyte is who I'm here for this time."

Deimos lands a hard right hook on Malakyte's left cheekbone.

I peer over the opposite side of the table as Malakyte is hit again, and again and again.

"You knew, you piece of shit. You knew he was my Ringer, and you had him murdered," Deimos roars, mere inches from Malakyte's face. "And we both know you're not above killing children, so I'm not sure why I'm surprised. Your little master plan, playing puppeteer, hoping that you can get another shot at my Zariya. It'll never work. She'll never fall for your act again. This new version may not be the sharpest tool in the shed, but she's not stupid."

Deimos shouts, pointing at me. "She knows about the raids you ordered on the orphanages, the towns, and cities you tore apart looking for her. She knows about the moon, what happened there, what you drove my Zariya to do. But did you know you actually found Kara? Instead of picking her up, you took my little Ringer instead. So close . . ." he mocks. Malakyte's mouth has been paralyzed, but all the rage in his eyes shines now that Deimos has stripped his façade. He remembers Gavrielle. He knows who Deimos is talking about.

"What was his name again, kiddo? Gav . . . something?"

The smart thing to do is to not answer and avoid all culpability. But I was just about to kill the prince, so, I'm throwing caution to the wind. I'm going to do what I intended from day one—get my revenge on Arianyte.

Gavrielle is dead. Ardelle betrayed me. The others will eventually find out what happened in our past lives together and abandon me; so why does any of it matter? If I could slay the dragon now and blame it on Deimos later, then I'd do what I had to do. Because it was Malakyte who took Gav from me all those years ago, who's left me with this rotting hole of empty space.

Consequences be damned.

"Gavrielle Abraxas."

Deimos's eyes turn to slits as I say his full name. He turns back to Malakyte, who's watching me with eyes that could burn a hole to Hell. I've crossed a line I can't come back from now. Everything is going to change from this point forward.

"A twelve-year-old fooled your 'elite SSPARROWs,'" Deimos says with air quotes. "You were so close to getting what you wanted for so long because she was there! She was right there. You took the wrong kid, genius you. Plus, you took her little friend, or whatever. That type of thing leads to grudges. You should know all about grudges. Didn't you come to Earth specifically to find the reincarnated version of Zariya? So you could, what, get revenge on her for blowing your opportunity at ruling Arianyte? Or is it some pathetic attempt to manipulate her into loving you again? You've got issues, my man. Get a therapist."

Turning towards me, Deimos shifts his focus. "You could zap this miserable icicle into a pile of snow with a flick of your finger. I know you probably don't view me as the most trustworthy character, and I can understand that. Think for a moment about what I know about this asshole, about all the things he's done to you. Not just to Zariya"—he looks back at Malakyte—"but to you, Karalevine." He adds a flamboyant *A* to the end with a click of his tongue.

"I can feel your anger, just below that pretty face of yours," Deimos continues poetically, inching his way in slowly and methodically, manipulating my mind like a virus. "Your power is so close to bursting. You'd sneeze and end up taking out a fourth of this stadium. I'd take this one and only chance to end the horror of what this grandiose piece of space shit has done for many, many decades. Don't let the young face fool you, he's older than me by eighty years."

Older by eighty years?

The stars only know how many lives I would save by taking this single one. Millions? Billions? Considering he's been out in the farthest reaches of the Milky Way, swindling naïve, desperate planets into exchanging their autonomy for tech and medical advancements and horrors they can't even comprehend. It's easy to see how Malakyte slithers within a planet's systems, offering to solve all their problems in exchange for a little 'unity.' If the people of Earth only knew the truth about Arianyte, only knew what they were truly giving up, they wouldn't make the deal. Not if they knew the true human cost of it. The suffering.

My suffering.

"He's the reason my daughter is dead. He's the reason you've lived the rough life you have. The reason Gavrielle Abraxas is dead."

Deimos unsheathes his dagger fast and abruptly, deciding for me. I have only seconds.

"Wait!" I scream, and the tip of his blade stops a mere inch from the center of Malakyte's chest. The mark here is lit up yellow in what I could only assume is pure fear.

I'm breathing heavily now, my huffing the only sound in the room. "Just . . . wait," I say, grabbing the drink from the table and taking a sip to wet my mouth. "I have a question to ask him first."

It had been bothering me since the moment I woke up from the last vision. Malakyte mentioned it only one time in that vision, but I know it means something important. Zariya was pushing back on Arianyte because of something very specific, and I want to know what it is—what she cared so much about she risked her life to expose. I had a sneaking suspicion it's very pertinent to what's happening here on Earth.

"What's the Silent Breath?"

CHAPTER 51

I don't know how long I've been running since I left the room
where Malakyte and Deimos remain, one alive, one dead.

The sounds of the roaring crowd mixed with the booming
vibrations of Titans battling to win money, fame, and glory blasts my
senses to their absolute max.

What just happened in that room has left me shocked, nearly incapable
of comprehension, causing me to run out of there like a bat out of Hell.

This changes everything.

I'm a girl hell bent on getting her vengeance, but now that I have
obtained it—it doesn't feel as good as I thought it would. I thought I'd
feel rejoiced and elated, but all I feel is fear and shame.

Now, I need to get the others and we need to get the hell out of here.

Before it's too late. Before Malakyte's body is discovered and his loyal
sky-rats suspect I had anything to do with it.

Although, as I make my way in a haze through hallways and spaces
lined with restaurants, bars, and merchandise shops, I have no way of
knowing where Jance and the others could be. Night has fallen upon the
Titan Games, and the stadium is a bright beacon amongst the city's many
buildings. Giant screens sit mounted on four places along the bowl's
circumference, showing close-up glimpses and point-of-view shots of
the competitors as they fight for their glory.

Where are you guys?

My mind panics, my heart races.

Did I make a horrendous mistake?

Where are you?

Did I just facilitate the murder of the Prince of Arianyte?

I run through the arena hallways in a daze.

"Hey!" an unnatural voice shouts from some twenty feet away. A small nest of SSPARROWs points at me, ordering me to halt.

So, I bolt.

SSPARROWs on me already? I swear I hadn't been out of the room that long, perhaps ten minutes maximum. How did they figure me out this fast?

None of this makes sense.

There are so many people along this platform high up in the stands, and there's absolutely no way I can use my crystal here, not even if my emotions were steady and safe. It doesn't take long for the SSPARROW soldiers to catch me. Flashbacks of that first night come flooding in as their metal bodies force me down to the ground. I feel violated and ashamed and enraged. Cold metal wraps around my neck and my hands are bound together before me. It's exactly the same as the night of the Capitol building. Except, it's only the shocked, Titan Games fandom watching wide-eyed with disbelief as I'm lifted up like a ragdoll and carried away.

I don't know where this moment will lead, but it cannot be any place good.

CHAPTER 52

I'm taken through a series of dark corridors, the slopes in the concrete floor going down, down, down underneath the stadium. So deep, in fact, that the thundering roars from the elated fans in the stands don't permeate the thick concrete walls. There are no windows, no hint of fresh air or natural light, nothing but what looks to be hallways upon hallways of cells once we reach the bottom level. It smells like stuffy mildew, the air moist and cold. Roaches scurry as the SSPARROWs forcefully escort me down the darkest hallway towards the only door.

A panicked cry gets lodged in my throat, and I can only whimper as I'm forced towards it.

Once through the door, there's yet another smaller hallway that leads to another door, this one made of iron and with strange alien symbols engraved on it. One of the SSPARROW soldiers holds his hand up to the door, pressing on certain spots in sequential order, sliding his finger along some predetermined pattern before it hitches and unlocks.

I'm shoved through roughly, the blinding white lights making my eyes water and blink rapidly.

"Thumbelina?" a hoarse voice gasps through the brightness. As my eyes adjust, I see Ardelle, eyes red with regretful tears, blood drying around his nose, temple, and mouth. He's strapped to one of the vertical, stand-up prisoner confinement panels that are lined all along the curved, circular-shaped wall. One right next to the other. Each one is equipped with metal leg and ankle cuffs, with a connecting wedge leading directly to a central drain.

For blood, I realize. My own goes ice cold.

"What are you doing in here?" he bellows as his muscled arms and legs thrash against their titanium shackles that don't budge an inch. He's collared, just like I am, our magic crystals useless.

This time when the SSPARROWs strap me down, I don't fight them. The fight in me has all but gone out.

Perhaps out of pure spite, they shackle me next to Ardelle, whose body continues to hammer against the metal at his ankles and wrists. The metal wall is cold against my back as I'm now strapped in beside him.

Ardelle tries to speak to me, but I don't have the strength to look at him. Not only because of what he's done, but because of what I've done too.

Stars . . . I've messed up. Maybe the room had hidden cameras I couldn't see? However they knew, Arianyte knew what I did.

I'm caught.

Ardelle and I aren't the only ones brought into the room beneath the stadium. One by one, our other Starseeds and Ringers get brought in. Sylo and Pacey come in together, then Saris, then Ahren and Jance. The latter demanding what is happening. Nobody answers—but I know what's happened. Each one of my friends—my family—is strapped to the vertical stand-up prisoner confinement panels to Ardelle's left. The room is empty on my side, and I think that's a fitting irony.

They're all collared.

Since we're all here, I'm prepared to explain what happened when the door flies open yet again. The SSPARROWs strap four grown men and two women down with us. People I know as members of the Terran Resistance's high rankers, including Geonni, Trinity, Dimitri, and Connar.

This is . . . perfect.

Geonni seems surprised to see me despite the sunglasses hiding parts of his face.

My explanation just got a lot more complicated.

Shouting suddenly erupts from the hallway outside. A colorful array of curses, threats, and words that even I wouldn't say come raining down as the door bursts open once more. It takes four grown men to drag Deimos into the last slot directly beside me in this collective prison shit show. They've collared him too.

After they fasten Deimos down like the rest of us, the room is dead silent. How am I supposed to even start? How do I tell them what happened? What I did . . . more so, what I allowed to happen. It happened—there's no changing that.

The leader of the Arianyte Empire—Malakyte Ardeen—is dead. With my assistance, Deimos killed him.

That's why we're here.

And now I have to come clean. By the looks of it, I'm going to have to confess to a lot more than my part in Malakyte's murder.

"You're the Terran Resistance, aren't you?" Pacey asks Geonni and his five subordinates.

Geonni's laugh reverberates throughout the metal walls, its echoes going on for days it seems. "Of course."

"What more did you do, Ardelle?" Saris demands, assuming we're all here because of him—rightfully so.

"Saris, he messed up, but he did it for Pacey and him," Sylo defends, although I can see the pain and anger on his face as he looks at his friend. But arguing ensues anyway, fingers being pointed at the rebels, at Geonni, at Deimos, at everyone but the person who deserves it.

I got my revenge, and now I'm going to pay for it.

"It's my fault!" I yell over angry voices and the room suddenly falls into a graveyard hush. My eyes can look nowhere but at the textured metal flooring while my heart pumps a mile a minute. With a desert-dry mouth and the awkward silence looming, I speak again. "I . . ."

The door flies open, and my neck snaps up, mouth dropping to the floor.

I'm eye to eye with a dead man.

CHAPTER 53

THE ARIANYTE EMPIRE DECREE #13

ARIANYTE RECOGNIZES THE REINCARNATION
METHOD AS THE ONE SPIRITUAL TRUTH. TERRANS AND
EXTRATERRESTRIALS ARE FREE TO WORSHIP OLD-WORLD
GODS, DEITIES, PROPHETS, AND INSTITUTIONS; HOWEVER,
THE REINCARNATION METHOD WILL BE THE ONLY
SPIRITUAL PRACTICE RECOGNIZED BY ARIANYTE.

Malakyte Ardeen should be dead.

Body slowly stiffening, and in normal circumstances, cooling by the hour—but in his case, warming by the hour? Whether his cold-blooded body cools or warms after death is the least of my concerns, because him being alive is a whole magnitude worse than him being dead.

Why isn't he dead?

Now it's my blood that's running cold.

I can't help but look at Deimos with horror as he stands strapped to the wall next to me. The expression of fear covers his face as well.

"This has to be his crystal's power," Deimos mutters so only I can hear him. "He's kept its powers secret for many years, and this is why. He didn't want people knowing he could bring himself back to life. I checked his pulse. He was dead."

"You look surprised to see me," Malakyte purrs, those icy eyes on fire as he blasts them directly into mine like laser beams.

"What is the meaning of this?" Jance demands.

The slow way the Prince of Arianyte turns to face Jance causes my skin to prickle with goosebumps. How did I not see the darkness sitting right there this entire time? It's emanating off him like a billowing cloak.

"Well, I suppose now that we're finally together after all this time, this façade is no longer necessary," Malakyte says coolly as he paces the circular room, the metal grated floor hitching from his weight. He doesn't look like he was just murdered. Which he was. Deimos killed him. I saw the blade that nearly ended my own life plummet into his chest. I don't understand how this guy is breathing. As cool and as slithery as ever, with a brand-new black suit and attached cape, long black tourmaline hair combed away from his face and down his back in a sleek waterfall, Malakyte is brand new, practically glowing.

So Malakyte's Elendril crystal can bring him back from the dead? That's just perfect.

I've made such a grave, terrible mistake. Being a part of Deimos's little murder mission was a bad idea, and now everyone is about to pay for it.

"I bet you're so glad to stop the fake, pretentious, loving benefactor act, aren't you? Pretending to care must have really been a struggle for you," Deimos growls, the hatred pouring off him in waves. I can feel it seeping through his every pore.

Malakyte doesn't even look his way. Like Deimos is so far beneath him there's no fuss to make.

"I've gathered you all here in this way due to the unfortunate incident that occurred once I gave orders for you to search for Deimos. He, in fact, was biding his time to get me alone, and when he did, he not only revealed his true motivations, but the motives of my Star as well. Miss Ruzz, why don't you tell everyone why we're here?"

Every pair of eyes shifts to me, and I glare at Malakyte with hatred in my soul. He's doing this to hurt me. That's likely why he brought the Resistance members here. He believes I still belong with them.

"Kara," Jance says from a few bodies to my left. "What's he talking about?"

I close my eyes, searching my mind for any small grasp of something I could use to squeeze my way out of all this, but I can't think of anything that would make a difference or a bit of sense. Not enough to save me.

They're all going to die here today.

At best, everyone in this room will certainly curse me for all I've done here. And in the end, I've made no difference for Gav, or the Hijacked, or anyone. So much for getting them help, so much for revenge, so much for being anything other than a complete and utter failure.

"Deimos and I tried to kill Malakyte," I say. The gasps and whispers bounce off the metal walls. Even the SSPARROWs seem to look at each other like what I just said was utter insanity—because it is.

Jance shakes his head, the collar clanking against the wall behind him. "No, you…" he stutters, and for the first time, Jance is rendered speechless.

My eyes and voice are cold as I say, "He killed my friend, Gavrielle. The one I told you about. And he's also been playing us all from the start. He's evil, and he's trying to gain as much power as he can so he can make himself King of Arianyte. We're nothing but his pawns." I could guess as much from my vision, and from the conversation he and I had before Deimos drove his dagger into his chest.

It apparently didn't stick.

"How would you even know this?" Sylo barks, the others too stunned to speak.

Blushing, I know I cannot confess to the visions without looking crazy; it's already evident to them all I've lost my damn mind. "I can't say."

He makes a repulsed sound. "Jupiter's rings . . ."

"It looks like the two of you liars belong together, after all." Malakyte stands before Ardelle and me. "Yet, there's still more to your story, isn't there, Miss Ruzz?"

No. My eyes say to him. *No.*

Yes, he pushes without a single word, his cruel eyes demanding my confession. I see him then, the Malakyte from the vision, the cruel man who tied Zariya down and tortured her for mere rumors. Long gone is the man who took me on a sweet date next to the riverside and promised a better future. Was that person ever real?

"Miss Ruzz has been playing us all," Malakyte tells my Starseed family. "She's been in league and actively sabotaging Arianyte by working as a

342

spy for the rebels. Seems like my initial instincts about you were right after all. I should've listened instead of being manipulated by you."

Ardelle's breath hitches beside me as he turns towards me as much as possible. "Is that true?"

My eyes close against the pain in his voice, and a single tear falls to my cheek—his answer.

"You've been lying to us this whole time?" Pacey demands, pain in her voice. "Look at me!"

I do, and I see tears welling up in her eyes for the second time today. "That night . . . when you told me about Gavrielle and that it was all about finding him, that was a lie, wasn't it? You tricked me into doing all that for them? For the rebels, knowing what could've happened to my brother and me?"

"No, Pacey, it was about Gav. It was just about the bigger picture too." I try to save face, but she's disgusted with me.

As she should be.

I'm disgusted with myself.

Her head shakes from side to side. "I don't believe you. I don't believe a thing you say anymore. I don't even know you. Is Kara even your real name?"

My heart cracks from her words, and my tears—genuine tears—fall like rainwater from my eyes.

"Yes, of course it is. I'm sorry, Pacey. I didn't think it would go this far. I tried to tell you guys that day in the woods." I turn to Jance, whose eyes are red but there are no tears there—only pain. "And you told me it didn't matter. I left the rebels and wanted to come clean. I was done with them after the parade. After they wouldn't end the violence. That wasn't who I wanted to be anymore, so I left. I tried telling you guys, and you told me it didn't matter."

"It would've if you told us *this*," Ardelle snaps.

"Correction," Trinity interrupts while my mark flares, "we kicked her little ass out because she wasn't strong enough to do what needed to be done. Like killing your parents, for starters." She nods towards Ardelle.

Before he can ask, I clarify, "They wanted me to assassinate your parents to prove my loyalty to them. I refused. They kicked me out for that refusal. End of story. But I was glad after: I didn't want to do those things anymore. I genuinely changed."

Ardelle practically growls at me. "You were going to kill our parents?"

It's the first time I feel straight rejection from him. "No, Ardelle, *I refused*."

"If you changed, then why did you try to kill Malakyte?" Pacey's voice is dark and condescending; this is a judgmental side of her I've never seen. "You knew Ardelle was already in this terrible position. If you're no longer this vengeance-seeking rebel, then why do this? Why do this to us?"

How do I explain? How can I salvage this so they can all stop looking at me like I'm the monster in the room when, in reality, the monster is standing in the center of this room smiling as if this is the best day he's had in years. The harder I try to stop his manipulative gaslighting, the more I'm looking like the bad guy and he's appearing like a victim. It's all backwards.

"He's . . ." I start, but can't find the words to depict the beast that Malakyte is. He's manipulative and cunning and smart and he knows what he's doing; he knows he's tearing us all apart.

And he's relishing it.

"Don't even start," Sylo says before I can speak again. "It'll be nothing but lies, anyway."

"I see," I say, my head lowered and voice turning bitter. My defensiveness boils up at their rejection. "So, Ardelle can betray you all, lie to you, and almost get me killed, but when I make a similar mistake . . . you all look at me like *this*? Now that doesn't seem fair, does it?"

Anger, true anger, flares within me at them—at all of them. And even though this collar is around my neck and stopping my powers from manifesting, it doesn't stop them from building up underneath the surface; they just can't come out.

"Kiddo makes a point. You all are quite the group of hypocrites," Deimos concurs, and I turn to him in surprise, my solitary ally—the man who tried to kill me.

"We had nothing to do with this," Sylo says to Malakyte. "Let us go and keep her."

My anger spikes at those betraying words.

"Are you going to have him call your sky-rat daddy to come and get you too?" I say venomously. If they're going to betray me so easily and throw me away like I'm trash, then screw them. Screw all of them.

But that's not how I truly feel . . . not by a space-mile.

"We never should have taken you in." Sylo's voice is cruel, and it hurts worse than Deimos's dagger did.

"Sylo, stop it," Jance barks back.

They continue to argue, and I look over at Ardelle. He watches me. He lied, I lied, he betrayed me, and I betrayed him . . . maybe Malakyte is right, and we deserve each other. But I can understand why Ardelle did what he did, why he believed Deimos even when he knew he shouldn't. He wanted to go home . . . and I wanted to be a part of one.

Although I see anger in his gaze, there's sadness there too.

"Honestly, as entertaining as this all has been," Malakyte interrupts unapologetically, "there's still plenty more you need to learn about your sweet Star."

CHAPTER 54

Geonni, Trinity, and the other members of the Resistance are about to get their minds blown.

Along with everyone else.

The final nail in my coffin is barreling down on me, hammering away until I'm buried and gone and alone.

Deimos chimes in. "You really don't want to tell them the story, mate. Doesn't make you look very good."

Malakyte looks at his Dezlar as if he's bored out of his mind and has somewhere to be. "Haven't you all wondered why you were born with the galaxy's rarest weapons?" he asks, eyeing each of the Starseeds. "No? Yes? A little convenient, don't you think? To be born with such prodigious powers, powers many people would kill for. We can argue whether that's fair or not, but admittedly, there is a reason."

"We don't care," Saris says. "Let us go, Malakyte. Whatever's happened, we can work it out. They're kids, for star's sake."

"No," the prince says, his head tilting to the side as he assesses her. "No, I don't think they've learned their lesson yet. This is no charade; this is as real as it gets. I am tired of giving chances to my own subordinates as they betray me again and again. Now you will listen to me, Ringer, as the truth finally procures the light. Deimos, you are right." He turns to the green alien beside me. "I am so very sick of pretending."

The blood in my veins goes cold as I look over at Ardelle, my eyes pleading with him not to completely hate me after this.

His fingers reach for mine, stretching as far as they can. I try reaching for him, but our fingers miss each other's by centimeters.

Malakyte sees this, and I swear I see rage in those depthless eyes. Jealousy.

"Forty years ago, Arianyte's most elite squad took helm under my guidance," Malakyte begins. My stomach turns to lead, and I've never felt more powerless. "This squad was extraordinary, something the galaxy had never seen before. Every member was fused with six of the seven Elendril crystals, along with each of their divine pairings. Starseeds and Ringers, all together and united with Arianyte. It was one of the biggest power moves ever made in this galaxy . . . and with that move, Arianyte became mainstream. A brilliant plan executed by none other than myself. It was perfection.

"Under my guidance, Arianyte's espionage activities were unstoppable. Each Starseed and Ringer was worth a thousand of my SSPARROWs. We took conquest over many planets over the years, which lead the King and Queen of Arianyte to finally appoint me as their successor and relinquish power to me with one final condition: that I rule Arianyte with a bride at my side—my empress. The leader of my squad was Zariya Ethoria—"

"Don't you say her name, you piece of shit!" Deimos's voice is deep and guttural, as if Malakyte held a knife to her throat at this very moment. Hearing her full name out loud pings something inside me, some emotional string being tugged on. There's this part of me that truly sees Deimos now, the way his face contorts in a mask of pain and rage at the mere mention of his dead daughter's name. Knowing what it's like to lose someone you love and care for by Malakyte's hand—it's heart-wrenching. There's a hole that's left behind. It's raw and rotting, with maggots and dirt and other gross things that enjoy living there, and eventually they will crawl towards the light and try to wreak havoc on your life. So, I see him—when I never expected to.

"Zariya Ethoria was a force upon this galaxy." Malakyte says her name with emphasis just to twist the knife into Deimos even further. "She was an obvious choice to be my bride, for none other than that reason. She and I loved each other once . . . I love her to this day, despite the events that led up to her demise. Over time, an idea infected her mind like a plague. It corrupted her impressionable young psyche. This plague took root in the minds of many of my most loyal servants, and eventually my entire team. My elite soldiers—who were practical gods—were destroyed from within. By Zariya."

There's no restraint in the muscle that controls my eye roll at the end of that. Sure, I don't know all the details of this story he's telling, but it's so obvious what he's doing right now. Narrative is a powerful thing, and if you control the narrative, you control everything.

I'm in trouble.

"My brand-new bride betrayed me. Her and the entire team fled the Arianyte Azurite Fleet after a data leak of vital, confidential information. Attempting to escape with the Elendril crystals that were not theirs to plunder. Along with the crown to Arianyte, I might add. The new Empress of Arianyte, a runaway bride. Absolutely ludicrous. See, I gave those crystals to each of them per an agreement that they serve me and Arianyte with our security needs. The crystals are some of the most remarkable, magical technology I've ever seen. Once placed near a person's heart, a crystal merges with the body of its host. Then almost like a parasite, it integrates within that organ and the body so completely that connection cannot be undone. Only death can remove it. I'll admit both entry and removal are quite gruesome to witness, even more to experience. Whatever it took to secure Arianyte, that's what was done. Whatever was needed to safeguard the smooth operations of planet integration, my old Starseeds secured it. I gave them power, strength, riches—everything. Still, they betrayed me, and that agreement was void. Meaning those crystals belonged to me then, as they belong to me now. I own every single one of your bodies, because they're conduits for my weapons. I can take them out whenever I wish, and contrary to Deimos's lie that Mr. Dawson naïvely believed, there is no removing the crystals without death. Therefore, I'd be very careful how you speak to me from this point on."

The room goes silent, the tension thicker than quicksand, and I look to the other Starseeds, a bit of 'I told you so' twinkling in my eyes. The wool is slowly being lifted from each of their eyes, and perhaps they're seeing that I had a good reason for doing what I did other than pure vengeance.

Braver than any of us, Pacey's the first to speak. "So, are you saying we're a reincarnated version of your last squad or something?"

My heart ticks up. Her instincts hitting the target spot on. She's the smartest person in this room, and everyone underestimates her.

Ardelle looks at me funny, as if he's trying to tell me something with his eyes.

I scrunch my brows at him, not understanding.

"That's exactly what you all are, Miss Dawson," Malakyte confirms. "You couldn't have the Elendril crystals otherwise. I'm guessing sweet Zariya assumed she'd be destroying the crystals upon the obliteration of her team's bodies. But these crystals are mysterious and magical. The essence of those crystals' magic stayed with your souls and came back with you once you were reborn into this life. It only matters that these crystals were not destroyed. It's physics. 'Energy can't ever be truly destroyed, only transformed.' Or so the Terrans say."

"But not that asshole?" Sylo nods towards Deimos. "Or you?"

"I was there for the entire thing," Deimos confirms bitterly. "I know the actual truth, the authentic story of what this pompous little prince did to my family and friends."

Malakyte's wicked smile is as incredulous as I've ever seen. "You talk so affectionately for a daughter who's named Killer of Worlds, don't you think?"

My stomach flips at that name. Everyone in this room is going to hear, 'Killer of Family and Friends' instead.

"Zariya did what she did because you were going to torture and kill us all," Deimos snaps back.

Malakyte instead shakes his head like Deimos's words are blasphemy. "I loved Zariya. I would never have hurt her."

"He's lying," I spit, then I describe to the room what Malakyte promised to do to Zariya and the other past Starseeds in the most recent vision.

The dark prince's brows raise, his expression trying to remain passive, but I see the slip there. I don't even know the person I'm looking at right now; I was so foolish to think that I did.

"How would you know this?" Jance asks.

It's coming out anyway, so I might as well admit to it all. "My crystal. It's been communicating with me somehow, showing me visions of this past life we all lived together. This story is real."

Sylo's dark head of hair shakes as he looks at Saris with a skeptical expression.

"She's telling the truth." An unlikely voice chimes in, and I look over at Ardelle. "I've been experiencing the same visions. Of an attack on a barren planet or something. I'm in another body, but I have my crystal and we're all being chased down and rounded up, and then the planet . . ." He stops, looking me in the eyes. I see the past-life version of him—Erodis—looking back at me now. He knows what happened. It's all visible in his eyes.

He was having visions this whole time too? He knows what Zariya did?

That's right, the night I first experienced the visions, Ardelle seemed to be zoned out as well, but I thought . . . I don't even remember what I thought, but it wasn't this. My crystal was about to blow and I wasn't paying much attention to him.

"That moon was blown to smithereens. It's how you all died." Malakyte's voice is flat and dead on the inside. Much like myself.

"So, you killed them all, that's it?" Sylo barks, as disgusted as I would be.

"Oh, it wasn't me who killed them, it was her," Malakyte says, pointing a boney finger directly at me.

I feel the power inside me boil, clawing my insides. A pipe ready to burst. Confirmation of what I already knew, of the scene that I saw from Zariya's perspective, that she killed everyone on that moon.

Everyone but one.

Him.

Zariya's sacrifice was for naught.

All of theirs were.

It made absolutely no difference in the grander scheme of things. Malakyte's crystal must have kept him alive, just as it kept him alive today.

Jance scoffs, not believing at first, but he picks up on the body language of the others in this room who know the truth, who know what happened. He realizes it then, as do the others, that Zariya—me—killed everyone.

"My daughter was strong enough to blow up a moon, and she did it to rid the galaxy of this monster—this tyrant. She was trying to save many more lives by sacrificing a few." Deimos tries to defend his daughter's name, but it's an arduous task.

Jance asks, "Why don't we remember any of this, if this actually happened?"

Malakyte has the answer for that too. "Every soul that incarnates on Earth goes through what's called the Veil of Forgetfulness. It's a part of Earth's systematic function. You simply forget. But Deimos and I haven't died, so we still remember."

"You look no older than the children," Ahren chimes in. He's been so quiet, watching speculatively with his doctor's eyes.

Malakyte smiles and doesn't reveal his secrets to looking young, but he's very aware that I know that dirty little secret he keeps so close to the chest. He's probably wondering what else I know, what the crystal has shown me. I could know anything, and that's where I have my only upper hand.

"Why are you telling us all this?" Jance asks. "Why not keep us ignorant?"

The prince shrugs, lips pursing. "Because of your little Starseed over there." He motions towards me. "She had to make things difficult, asking questions she has no business even wondering about in that pretty little head. It would have come out, and my charade would've ended in a dissatisfactory way. My Star is a little troublemaker, seems to be a pattern for her. I'd be careful. We never know when she'll lose it and blow up an entire planet this time."

My eyes slit at his words.

Ardelle fights his bindings once again—they don't budge. "He's trying to pit us against each other, because apart we're weaker than we are together."

"Bro," Sylo challenges, "your girl killed us all in our past lives. She can easily do it again."

"I'd never!" I yell, hating that they'd even think that, but it's not a surprise.

Sylo's face goes impassive. "Maybe not on purpose, but on accident— yeah, I could see that."

My body deflates. I'm not the villain here.

Am I?

Nobody comes to my defense, so maybe I really am.

I can't believe I ever thought Malakyte could be the salvation I so desperately hoped for, would bring me Gav, and make a positive change in the world. I'm so gullible and stupid. He fooled me, Ardelle fooled me, and hell—I fooled myself.

"The girl hasn't been associated with us in months," Geonni lies, finally speaking. They must've snuck into the arena the same way Deimos had, since they're working together and all, but why are they here in the first place?

As if remembering they are here, Malakyte's dark muscled form turns to the leader of the Resistance and smiles, those fangs glinting in the bright lights.

A terrible feeling comes over me, my instincts flashing warning bells. The amusement dancing on Malakyte's face reminds me of the look he had in the last vision when he was with Zariya.

"Let's see if that's really true or not?" he says in a lighthearted tone, shrugging as if this will be a simple game of truth or dare.

With a flick of his wrist, his SSPARROW soldiers unhook Geonni from his restraints and throw him into the center of the room, but that isn't Malakyte's only order.

"No!" I scream as they unhook Jance, and four SSPARROWs force him down to his knees in the center of the room next to Geonni.

As both men face me, Malakyte takes a live ammo pistol from one of his SSPARROWs. The pistol glows cyan across the barrel, and Malakyte points it at the back of Jance's head, then moves to Geonni's. Back and forth he points the barrel, taunting me with their lives.

Smiling manically, he looks up at me. "Choose."

CHAPTER 55

The room erupts with chaos and mass objections when he places the weapon at the back of both men's heads, switching between Jance and Geonni.

Both sides of the room are screaming, the rebels on my right and my Starseed family on my left, everyone thrashing and slamming themselves against the iron bonds.

Malakyte's eyes meet my own. He's serious. He means it.

My punishment.

Choose.

"Do you pick the man who took you in off the streets, taught you everything you know? The person who bred your hatred for Arianyte until it turned you into this . . . well, this stunning individual. If they pointed your indignation towards anyone else, I'd be very attracted to you right now, but I digress. Do you pick him, or do you pick your Ringer? The person who you've no doubt felt a connection with. A connection that goes beyond what most people can understand, a bond that's said to be unbreakable, but, I promise you, the bond can be broken. Which one will it be, Karalevine? Say the name of the man you're willing to lose. Choose now, or they both die."

Both men look up at me. They remove Geonni's sunglasses, no doubt for effect, to cause me anguish from the mere fact I have to look into his eyes. Jance's eyes are a volcano's worth of emotion, but not for him and his own life.

For me.

If I choose to save Geonni, Jance wouldn't care, not because he doesn't value his own life, but because he values me more. I don't need his words to tell me that, I can feel it from him.

Nobody has ever cared for me like this.

Ever.

"Stars, Kara!" Trinity screams at me over the commotion. "You've known this other guy for like what—two months? We've been with you since you were twelve! Say this other guy's name, Dammit!"

I open my mouth, but I can't speak.

Malakyte presses the side button that shows live ammo is triggered, the gun turning red.

The room jumps up again, all their voices overwhelming my senses.

"Kara! Don't let him do this, he's your Ringer. If you lose him you'll never be the same," Saris pleads.

While Malakyte holds the gun to the back of Jance's head, my chest is like a nuclear bomb as my crystal screams, the power building and building, but the valve is closed off. Yet, is that tiny ember enough to spark hope?

No. There's no hope here.

And I can't make this choice.

I won't.

But then they both die.

I close my eyes, the tears streaming out, but I can't look at them anymore.

Geonni's voice breaks through the shouts and screams. "I'll gladly die for this cause, for what I believe in. She'll bring you down one way or another. You can kill me, but killing me won't quench the fire within this Resistance's soul." Malakyte cracks his neck in irritation as he scoffs. "Kara, I'm sorry I kicked you out, I am. Trinity, I love you. You know what to do."

Trinity shakes her head wildly, tears sleeking her freckled cheeks.

"Choose me, Kara." Jance's voice cracks. "It's okay, just promise me you won't blame yourself for this. Remember what I've told you. I meant every word. You're mine. It's okay."

No . . . no I can't.

"Choose now or they're both dead," Malakyte shouts, his voice cruel and dark and booming. "Now!"

Jance yells, "Do it, kid! Do it now."

I want to break apart.

So much chaos. So many people screaming.

Dammit!

"Jance!" I shriek. The shot rings out, echoing inside my ears and within my soul—leaving it empty and hollow and stunned. My sobs are uncontrollable, my body tingles, and my crystal skyrockets and sears. The power begins to feed on me; and I welcome it.

The silence that follows is the true meaning of horror.

CHAPTER 56

Don't open your eyes, don't open your eyes, don't open your eyes.

I can't see what's waiting for me.

My Ringer—Jance—gone.

Gone.

He wanted me to pick him, but I didn't think this through enough. I didn't—

Trinity's scream snaps me out of my titanium cocoon. My crystal's power feeds on my insides because the collar isn't letting it escape. Maybe it's a good thing it's on me because if it wasn't, I would have blown this entire room up after what's happened.

When my vision goes from blackness to reality, I am not prepared.

Jance looks at me with an expression I've only seen once, that night at the carnival when I almost died.

He's alive.

My elation is short lived when Trinity's screams bring my eyes to the body lying beside Jance.

I instantly avert my eyes the second I see red pooling along the grated floors. Ardelle tells me to look away—to look at him instead.

Geonni, the leader of the Resistance—is dead.

What . . .?

"No rebel leader can live in this city, not with me around." Malakyte's words are cold, matter of fact, sterile. I'm not sure what just happened. "Take the Ringers out of here, leave my Starseeds. Keep the rebel's daughter. I want to interrogate her later. Execute everyone else."

Malakyte's orders are callous as he hands the gun back to his soldier, who takes it like nothing happened. Like Geonni's blood isn't pooling on the floor in a giant puddle underneath him.

Trinity is absolutely losing her mind as her comrades are taken away, along with her father's body. Only his blood is left behind.

I almost puke.

We all yell and try to prevent our Ringers from being taken, but it's useless and we're powerless and the rage that's within me is so overwhelming and raw that I want to kill Malakyte with my bare hands.

Kill him again and again and again until he stays dead forever.

He killed Geonni . . .

Malakyte leans into one of his SSPARROWs and whispers. With the cries in the room he likely thinks nobody can hear, but I can. "Make sure they're all removed from the city before the Titan is crowned. I don't want what's in the catacombs to destroy my property; they're too valuable. Have my sky-hover ready for Naresteé and me as soon as I'm finished giving my speech."

His dark eyes shift to me. I seethe at him, teeth bared. He tricked me, pulled the trigger on the person I didn't want to be killed. I wanted neither of them killed, and as Jance and the other Ringers are taken away, I look away from Malakyte and into my Ringer's eyes.

Then Jance is gone.

I scorch all my hatred into Malakyte, my entire perception of him flip-flopping into somebody I don't know, someone who's worse than even my wickedest nightmares.

"I'm going to kill you," I tell him.

Malakyte's smile is soft, like he finds me contemplatively amusing. He approaches me, the ice wafting off him. He bends down, slowly and gingerly, and his cold lips kiss my cheek. I recoil and shift my head away, but there's nowhere for me to go.

"You've already tried that."

The dark prince disappears through the door, along with all his loyal soldiers.

The room is now empty except for the Starseeds and Trinity, the latter wailing so loudly and painfully that I can't help but feel for her. The only part of her father that remains are his sunglasses left sitting in the pool of blood that's smeared all over the floor. This is the last thing I wanted . . . and I think Malakyte made a terrible mistake killing the leader of the Resistance. This will lead to war. Geonni will be a martyr for his people, inciting mass rebellion—and Malakyte clearly doesn't know the man's daughter, either because if he did, he'd realize the hell that's going to rain down on him soon enough.

"You're going to kill yourself if you don't get it together," Deimos seethes from my right, sensing the crystal building, but my emotions are so far out there, and I don't think I can stop them. The blood left behind from Geonni has my name written in it.

The purple spark tickling around at my fingertips is the sign I know something has changed. Pacey's audible gasp is the second.

Somehow, some part of my power slipped past the collar.

Ardelle is the first one to speak it, hope lacing his words. "Wait, her power is manifesting outside the collar? Can she get out of it?" he asks Deimos, and the green alien thinks for a moment.

"I've never seen it done, but if anyone can, it's someone with this crystal. If we can see the manifestation of magical abilities, then there's a slim chance."

There's so much pressure in my chest, it's unbearable. I can't do this.

I've lost everything. Gav, Geonni, the Resistance, my Starseed family . . . It's over. I've lost.

I've failed.

"It's only coming from your hands, isn't it?" Deimos asks, his voice calm. I nod, ashamed that our one chance of escape and saving the others is dwindling by the minute. "Zariya had a similar issue, but I taught her how to control that power to where it could surround her body to create a shield of pure energy. If you could do that, you can shatter that oppressive tech around your neck. It's the same energy coming out of your neck that's coming from your hands. Guide it up your arms, through your throat, and out the collar's latch. Break it. Incinerate it."

Closing my eyes, I try to ground myself against the cold metal at my back. The heat within me rises, shooting up like a rocket inside my chest. I can feel the energy sparking at my fingers again, but it's a speck of what I could normally do.

"Now bring it up your arms," Deimos guides, and despite the source of this guidance, I listen. Retracting the energy back into my body creates a sharp burn both locally and inside, and a painful gasp escapes my lips.

"She can't do this; it's hurting her," Ardelle warns, but I can't stop now. The energy is too high, and it's not like he cares, anyway. If I don't get it out somehow, it really will burn me up from the inside. This is the worst feeling I've ever felt. Like my insides are melting.

"Not if she keeps going, it won't. Get it up there. All it needs to do is tap the collar and it'll be over," Deimos counters, and I feel it crawling up my arms like a giant spider whose eight legs are red hot knives slicing through my flesh with each spindly step. "You're doing it. I can see it moving up. Keep going," Deimos orders, and it's the encouragement I need in this moment because it hurts like a bitch.

By the time it reaches my chest, I can't stop the tears, the pain, the emotional breakdown of what I've done to the people I care about. Tears are all I have, and it surprises me they aren't pure antimatter too.

I thought I was doing this for Gavrielle. It's what I told myself, at least. However, Gav was simply the pretext that I used to justify all the terrible things I've done. Truthfully, it was about me. How I didn't want to face myself, face the awful veracity that I blew him up and left him there. Arianyte or not, I let my friend down. Nobody else can be blamed, no one else can liberate my soul of that one notion of truth. For all my justifications, for all the good I've tried to do in the name of justice and saving others—including him—I'm a selfish fraud who couldn't face her own demons.

"There's blood coming from her nose," Ardelle urges, but I don't stop. "Thumbelina, stop, it's killing you."

Maybe it should. If I couldn't forgive myself, then nobody else could.

"No. She'll make it, just keep going," Deimos counters, but their words make no difference now.

My vision is blackening, and my body is critical. My blood is practically boiling under my skin when at last, my crystal's power taps the collar.

I hear nothing, can't see the collar obliterate into dust—I only feel my power explode.

Like a phoenix rising, spreading its wings after being chained and beaten down by death—it flies.

The head-high is unlike any other. It numbs all the pain inside me, Geonni's and Gavrielle's death, along with everything else.

I'm free—in more ways than one—*here*, I'm truly free.

My next conscious thought is about everyone else's safety. They are all at enormous risk. I could have already killed them. The fear of that scares me so much I immediately try to shut it down, but the valve's pressure has gone up to such an intense level that stopping it is impossible. I know nobody is in front of me, so I hold onto that one thought and pound my power straight ahead.

Go straight, go straight, go straight. I try to order my power with all the will that I have.

When it finally stops, there's nothing but silence; and I'm more scared to open my eyes now than I was after hearing the gunshot.

Who will be left alive, and who have I destroyed?

CHAPTER 57

"Thumbelina," Ardelle's voice stirs me, but everything hurts and I don't want to wake up.

"Get up, kiddo, we've got to go," Deimos says impatiently.

I'm no longer vertical. My face is pressed against a cold hard ground. My body feels like it's been run over by a stampede of elephants, and I moan in pain as I roll myself to my side. The restraints where I was shackled are simply gone, like they were never there in the first place. My crystal must have dusted them away.

I flinch as my hand falls into something wet and cold, and when I realize whose blood it is, I'm filled with nausea so intense it makes me dizzy. I can't bear to look at Trinity.

Then I see the bodies everywhere.

SSPARROWs must have entered the room at the last moment because several of their bodies lie half inside and half outside the room, smoking and black like charred barbeque—the door to our freedom melted open.

It takes me three tries to get to my feet, every breath I take feeling like my lungs are full of glass. I could be dying it feels so bad.

Methodically, like I'm a robot, I step over the smoking bodies and find the small side room they used to watch us from the cameras and grab the keys that unlock everyone's restraints.

I free Ardelle first, then he takes the keys and frees Pacey and Sylo, then Trinity.

"Are you okay?" Pacey asks me, and I nod silently. But I'm really not. Honestly, I'm surprised she's even talking to me. I don't answer. I only stare blankly as I watch Trinity pick up her father's sunglasses from the pool of blood.

Ardelle seems to hesitate when Deimos is the only one still shackled and looks back at me for approval.

Glaring at Deimos, I say, "If I catch you even thinking about stabbing any of us in the back, I'll do to you what I did to them, got it?" Nodding my head towards the smoldering bodies on the ground.

Deimos nods an accepting yes, then Ardelle releases his collar and shackles, and Deimos chucks the collar to the floor. It clanks loudly against the heavy silence.

"Let's go get this asshole," Deimos says as he walks out the door, patting me on the back as he goes, but even that hurts like hell. "But first, I want my dagger back."

CHAPTER 58

"We've got a problem," I tell the group as we strap our weapons back on, having found them in the side room. My voice is dull, numb, but I know I have to continue on, despite my body begging me to stop. "I heard Malakyte telling one of his soldiers about something in the catacombs causing casualties, and to have his sky-hover ready for him the moment he finishes his speech for the winner. I think he's got something up his sleeve and it doesn't sound good. He wanted us all taken out of the city because of it."

Before anyone can answer, Trinity chimes in, her eyes red and full of rage. "We have intelligence that says Arianyte has been planning something big for the Titan Games finale. It's why the Resistance is here."

I look over at her, pouring my apologies and condolences into my eyes as much as I can, because it's too soon and too raw to speak it, and I think she agrees because she nods in thanks and understanding. It's too raw for her too.

"Well, that doesn't sound good," Sylo says as he clips his gun's holster on his hip. "What about our Ringers? We've got to get to them too."

I speak up first, knowing what must be done. "We need to find out what Malakyte's got hiding under the arena, then we find our Ringers. That's what they'd want, and it's the right thing. Besides, from the sounds of this, if we don't stop what's coming, finding our Ringers will be pointless. We'll be dead."

Nobody argues, and with Trinity in hand, we run through the rat-maze that exists under this stadium.

Through the constant sound of dripping water, the deeper we run into the catacombs beneath the arena, the moldier the smell becomes. Rats scatter as our feet pound the dark wet concrete, each of us running at high capability, winding down the seemingly endless twists and turns. My body thrashes with every footstep, every deep breath. I continue on.

"My Dezlar is picking up some massive energy spikes straight ahead to the left," Pacey's voice cuts through as she glances down at the device, the light illuminating her face in the dark tunnels. We take the turn and follow a descending ramp until we reach the bottom. We all skid to a stop, each of us left stunned.

"Oh, damn," Sylo breathes as his chest pumps up and down from the run.

I step forward, but a hand on my shoulder stops me. I shake Ardelle off in irritation. "Well, I see why he wants to get out of the city now," I say, inspecting the array of what looks to be a dozen round blue glowing pods sitting within a wide-open room at the bottom of the incline.

"These aren't just bombs," Pacey relays as she buries her nose in her Dezlar, watching it pick up whatever energy is coming from the pods. "They're dripping with radiation signatures. We shouldn't even be down here." She walks up to the bombs, Ardelle protesting as she pokes one with her finger. It bobbles like a water balloon on its stand. "According to my readings, these are veclear bombs, twenty times more powerful than a nuclear blast, but, of course, that all depends on the amount and comparison models, but, in general, they're way more powerful. If these go off, forget the stadium blowing up, the entire city will be leveled. And it gets worse."

"What's worse than that?" Sylo asks, and I'm wondering the same.

Pacey glances back down to her Dez and then back up at us. "The radiation fallout alone will carry however far the wind takes it, but ultimately, it'll spread. It can cover half of the continent if the conditions are right. An environmental disaster. This is bad. Like bad–bad."

"Told you he was a psychopath," Deimos mumbles before anyone else could say anything.

Unnerved and in disbelief, Sylo blanches. "Why would Malakyte do something like this? There's no way my father would have been a part of this. He's here, he'd . . ."

Ardelle shakes his head and places his hand on his best friend's shoulder. "Bro, I don't think your dad is involved. This is Malakyte. As Thumbelina knew all along, this guy is sick, dude."

"Still regretting you brought me home, now?" I ask Sylo, and he averts his eyes in shame. Whatever.

"Well, we're all about to be dead if we don't figure out a way to stop this. Spread out and look for the timer," Pacey orders and nobody disagrees—even Deimos looks. "It's got to have a trigger console attached."

Each of us fans out into the small underground chamber, bending over the glowing blue orbs to search for a control mechanism. Fear is seeping in when Trinity screeches.

"I think I've got something."

Running towards her, we circle an unassuming pod seven rows down. Attached is something that looks a lot like a Dezlar pad, a transparent screen with plastic edges for gripping. Pacey slowly picks it up, examining it.

"This is definitely it," she says as she pulls some kind of cord from inside her bra. We gape. "What? Any self-respected hacker should keep one of these handy." Her self-gratitude is clear in her grin as she connects the device to her Dezlar and begins tapping on both screens, her acrylic nails clicking away.

As we wait, I can't help but feel Ardelle's gaze on me from across the group. I do my best to pretend like I don't see him staring right at me. What does he want? It's done.

Practically choking on air, Pacey gasps. "Oh, shit."

"Language," Ardelle barks, shaking his head like a foul word is way worse than the bombs sitting before us. Had he ever cursed this entire time that I've known him?

"Okay, well, does everyone want the good news or the bad news first?" Her nostrils flare gently as her giant eyes look up at the group from her spot on the ground.

We all eye each other wearily and we're all too afraid to answer.

Coughing awkwardly, she says, "Alright, good news is there's no ticking clock—yet. No anxiously deciding which colored wire to cut, because honestly, I couldn't handle that sort of pressure if—"

"Pacey," Ardelle pushes, essentially telling her to stop rambling and get on with it.

The grimace on her face shows her embarrassment as she continues. "The bad news is I can't stop it from here. Someone is holding a manual trigger button. It's wireless, and I'm guessing we know who has it."

"Shit," I hiss as I walk off from the group in frustration, Ardelle following me.

Deimos chimes in. "Malakyte one thousand percent has that trigger. And if we don't hurry and hurry fast, we're going to melt down here. Say bye-bye to each other now if we don't come up with a plan, an effective plan, immediately."

"I can try to disable it from here, but I don't know if I can, and it'll take some time. If I had my laptop, I'd have a lot more confidence that I could hack the system and implant a trojan or something to glitch up the signal, but with only my Dez, I . . ." Pacey tries to placate, to salvage something.

Her brother shoots down her suggestion faster than anyone can even consider it. "You're not staying down here when he could set them off at any minute." Making that very clear, he turns back to me. "Thumbelina, please, listen to me for just one second, I have to speak with you."

Stepping feet away from the others, I place my hands on my hips and face him, neck cranking upwards. "What?" I snap.

He tries taking my hands, but I snatch them back before he can secure his grip.

"I know how much I messed this up, and I'm so sorry. I was obsessed with trying to get home, to find a way back to our family. And yes, I was working with Deimos because he made me believe that hope was possible, that I could end this curse for Pacey and myself, and we could return home like nothing ever happened. The irony is you made me face the truth: it *did* happen. They abused us; they hurt us because we didn't fit their perfect expectations. Years of being someone else made me forget who I truly was, and I hadn't seen how much of myself I had been locking away because of that. My parents are still holding me captive. Pacey was able to let them go because she's stronger than me. She found her true self and flourished, but I couldn't. I was stuck in their expectations and mental shackles, and I didn't even realize how trapped I had become.

Until you. With your ridiculous colored hair and your filthy mouth and everything you do, you cracked my façade wide open and, finally, woke me up to what I was doing How I've been unable to free myself of my parent's chains. I thought I wanted to go home, and it took me too long to realize that I already *was* home. You are my home, Thumbelina, long before I ever met you."

We both know what he means: a lifetime ago we were each other's homes, and a part of us knew it all along. He saw the visions, too, saw how much Zariya and Erodis loved each other. Some part of our souls remembered that, somehow. Does that make us Soulmates? True mates? Destiny? Whatever it's called, it's real. And so is the pain we've caused each other.

Ardelle continues when I say nothing. "Deimos told me to get close to you, to bug your phone and see how you fought, and at first it was about fulfilling my obligation to gain access to the devices he promised could remove the crystals, I won't lie to you anymore. That is what I did. But then it became so much more. I was a dick to you because I felt this unimaginable pull towards you, these enigmatic visions were transfixing my every waking moment to you, despite you not being in them. So I shoved you away, because I didn't want to feel that way. How could I do what I was doing with Deimos and act on my feelings for you? There's no way I could, so I pushed you away. I didn't see you then, I wouldn't let myself." He grabs my hands a second time and I don't pull away, even though I should. "But ultimately you broke through. I began looking at you differently without the judgments of my upbringing. I saw you fight for others, like the friend you lost. I saw how you love and protect the Hijacked because they represent more than simply lost children—they represent *you*. I envy your good heart. Even though you pretend to be this hard, tough, reckless girl who doesn't care what anybody thinks, you're so much of a better person then you give yourself credit for. You aren't a bad person. I see all you've been through, yet you still manage to get up every day and fight for what you believe in; and I love that so much and I see you, Thumbelina. *I see you*. Even when you claim to the outside world that you don't want to be found and you push them away, I will always see you."

The tears want to come, but they're all dried up. I wish my heart was as empty because even though I want to hate him, I can't. We hold eye contact, the blue light of the bombs lining the sides of his face. For the first time in hours, I don't feel absolutely lost alone in the dark; I feel his light guiding me back to redemption.

Back to life.

"As touching as this all is," Deimos interrupts boldly before I can reply, "we can't stay here."

"He's right," Pacey says. Standing, her body language is confident. "But I can. I'm going to try and disrupt the bomb's signal from here. Don't even, big brother." Ardelle is already trying to tell her she can't, but she isn't having it. "This is my choice, my decision. I can handle it, and you can't stop me. Let me do this."

Eyes alight, the two siblings stare each other down. All Pacey has wanted this entire time is to not be seen as this helpless little girl by her brother, but as a capable member of this Starseed team. Which she is. It's her brother who struggles to see her strengths, her capabilities.

"Then I'm staying with you," he tells her, and she hunches back down and gets to work.

"I'm staying too," Sylo says, and I look at the others.

"The rest of us will go back up top and do whatever we can to find the Ringers and get that trigger from Malakyte before the entire city blows up," I suggest, and nobody objects.

I make my way back through the pods to Pacey while the others briefly plan. "Take this." I hand her my Dezlar device. "If you manage to shut off the trigger, then I need you to open the folder named 'Malakyte' and get this file out to as many people as possible. You'll know it when you see it. Good luck, and I'm sorry about everything."

I mean every word.

"We're seeing each other again, Kara, so don't even start," Pacey says, and I nod as we hug each other tightly.

Leaving her, I race after the others as they take off ahead of me.

"Thumbelina," Ardelle calls out to me, and I glance back to see him standing there, looking like a silhouette with his bow and arrows poking out from his back and the blue orbs lighting up behind him. "Kick his ass."

Unable to help myself, I throw him the only bone he is going to get. "Language," I mock, and his beautiful, stupid smile is the last thing I see before I turn, dash towards certain doom, and refuse to look back.

CHAPTER 59

It only takes Deimos, Trinity, and me ten minutes to find our way out of the underground tunnels and up into the public area of the stadium. We find a back room that the contestants use. It's level with the arena floor, and I swallow dryly as we watch the winner being crowned.

Standing next to the man who won the games is the snake in the stadium, wearing a ridiculous three-pronged crown made of blackened bone that spikes into the air.

Malakyte.

The four megascreens that capture close-up shots of the contestants in the heat of the games now have Malakyte's asinine face upon them as he speaks to his adoring crowd. Naresteé stands to his right, looking as unamused as ever.

My blood sizzles as Malakyte's voice booms over the cheering crowd and he beams into the microphone. "My newest Titan!" he roars theatrically and the crowd's response is like thunder clapping down. "What an epic showdown, but alas, we have our winner. May your new wealth and invitation to the Azurite Fleet make all your dreams come true."

The leader of Arianyte continues to fawn onto the worshipping crowd, and I can't help but pity them for falling for his act.

"The Ringers couldn't have been taken out of the stadium yet, but it's too big to search in its entirety," I say. "Somehow we need to get Malakyte to tell us where they are and get that trigger from him."

"Sure, why don't you go up there and ask him nicely," Deimos says, his voice as sarcastic as ever. Dammit, he's right.

I nervously bounce on my feet, clicking my nails together while trying to figure out what to do.

"Stop that." Deimos is audibly annoyed by my nervous tick. "How do those others live with you? Stars . . ."

His comment reminds me, and although the timing is horrendous, I need to know for certain. "Did you break into my loft?"

Deimos looks at me, surprised by my question. That reaction tells me everything, but he says, "No, that's a bit high on the creep meter, even for me. It must've been Malakyte. Something important must've been taken since you're asking at a time like this."

"It's nothing."

Shifting my attention back to the present, I sense something off about Trinity.

Aside from her father being murdered before her eyes, I know her enough to see something else flashing through her mind as she glares down at her Dezlar.

She glances over and tells me, "Dad was on the fence after making you leave, questioning if we were doing the right thing or not by coming here today."

My stomach begins to turn, that nervous feeling creeping up my spine and back into my chest.

"I told him that he was wrong, that you'd be here today and he should ask you to come back. Maybe if he had, we would've been better prepared . . ."

There's so much anger and sadness in her face, and her dad's sunglasses sit atop her head.

She continues, sounding almost mad with grief. "What happened today will never be forgotten; it'll be a day the world remembers the strength of the human spirit. That we will not be oppressed and enslaved and *devoured*."

Mouth gaping, I shake my head. "Trinity, what have you done?"

"The thing I should have done from the moment we got free." Her honey-brown eyes reflect the stadium lights, her braids tied back in a thick ponytail, and that pit in my stomach turns into a black hole. "The rebels know what happened, and their fury will be harnessed. Use this opportunity to get that son of a bitch. Hold on, it's about to get bumpy in here."

Trinity chucks her Dezlar onto the concrete floor, stomping on it several times before it's completely cracked and useless.

Horror creeps over me. "What did you do?" I knew Malakyte made a big mistake when he killed Geonni. Now, he's going to pay for it.

"What's she doing?" Deimos's voice is even more panicked as it slices through the air.

"Something I can't take back," Trinity declares, and Deimos and I stare at each other with bated breaths.

"She's going to raise an army and start a war."

Deimos's pause is short. "About damn time."

CHAPTER 60

Trinity does not prepare us for the explosions.

They are dirty bombs, meant to distract rather than maim, but they are effective in completely derailing Malakyte's plans for a showcase performance.

My plans, too, but I have no choice in the matter.

Malakyte and the Titan winner stand frozen on the center podium, looking enraged and confused as the bombs go off all around the circumference of the stadium floor. Away from any spectators, the bombs create seven-foot-high holes in the sidewalls of the arena by the turf, barely visible through the smoke and dust.

Dozens of SSPARROWs flock to the podium defending their dear leader. They immediately fire their weapons into the cloud of gray smoke billowing up onto the arena floor, the stadium onlookers having gone eerily quiet, their shocked screams turning to hushed whispers.

This is my chance.

I bolt.

It's stupid, and I feel entirely small and exposed out on the arena floor as my legs take me across the rubble-covered ground. This is my one shot to get to Malakyte and find the Ringers and stop him from pressing that trigger. I remind myself I can't let my hate seep in again and take root. All I can do is push forward.

Like an anthill exploding, tons of Terran rebels pour out of the holes in the arena, their leader now becoming a martyr, rallying them in fury to their cause. Each one holds up weapons of all types: guns and swords and axes and bats and pipes and makeshift spears. Dressed in plain clothes, they barrel down into the arena as another explosion from the south practically knocks me to my knees. The rebel's faces are twisted in fury about Geonni's death. Raging, infuriating madness bears down, and I'm caught right in the middle of it.

SSPARROWs begin to usher Malakyte and his right-hand lady off the floor, and I can't let that happen.

There's too much chaos and smoke for any of them to see me coming, and I body slam myself right into the Prince of Arianyte.

The two of us tumble right off the platform as I'm enveloped in his dark cape and ice-cold body.

We scuffle for several tense moments, but then the two of us freeze when the lights illuminating the stadium abruptly go out and we're all plunged into pitch darkness.

CHAPTER 61

We fumble around in the darkness for several moments, not knowing which way is up. Red suddenly covers my vision, and, at first, I think it's blood, but then I realize it's the stadium's emergency lights taking over.

Pacey must've cut the power to the stadium for whatever reason.

Malakyte pushes me off him forcefully, his cold hands shoving my chest as I land hard on the turf.

Patrons from the stands begin rushing over the railings and onto the arena floor, some going toe to toe with rebels, others fighting SSPARROWs, but the result is insanity. The only light that illuminates the entire stadium is from the cloudy sky above, and the eerie red lights bathe everyone in a deep, blood-red afterglow.

The ensuing chaos intensifies when Malakyte attacks, rushing me so fast I barely have a second to react.

This is it.

It all comes down to this.

Me versus Arianyte.

After all these years, I'm going to end this—for Gavrielle.

For all those like him.

It's not about revenge. It's about saving others by stopping this monster.

I'm shoved backwards by an icy wind that wafts from him like a snowstorm, my balance tripping me back as my feet cannot catch me. A cold palm connects to my chest and slams me to the ground. I'm more embarrassed than anything as he grins down at me like the Cheshire Cat high on his branch, laughing at me with those evil, incredulous eyes.

Using my legs for momentum, I hop up to my feet quickly, remaining crouched.

From this angle, I see he's sporting a sword at his waist, semihidden beneath his billowing cape. I'll have to watch out for that.

"How'd you get out of my collar?" he asks coolly.

Malakyte jumps for me again, coming at me straight on. I wait, luring him closer and closer, balancing on the balls of my feet.

I swallow before I say, "They must not have been as resilient as you thought."

As he pounces, pointed fangs glint at me. Angling my body in the opposite direction of my intended attack, he falls for my fake. This is my time to strike, and I take it.

Whipping out my sword, the blade slashes him all the way across the chest, and he tumbles sideways, a painful gasp escaping his dark lips. I don't allow him a moment of reprieve as I jump into the air, sword in hand, and a battle cry rives from my throat.

He rolls, missing my sword by such a close margin that it slices his hair, leaving locks of it on the turf of the stadium floor.

"Let me take a little more off the top," I say, smiling a cocky grin of my own at the cheesy line.

Malakyte looks very displeased at his hair, of which I sliced a large cut out of the sleek, glossy surface. I smile at myself for also knocking that stupid crown from his head. He presses a finger to the wound on his chest, looking at the dark blood curiously. It looks so black that I can't distinguish it from his black jacket. I don't know how deep the wound goes, but I hope it burns.

"We found your little stash beneath the stadium, Malakyte. Why are you doing this?" I doubt I'll get a genuine answer.

The question must've made him angry because he comes towards me again, teeth bared. I dodge, but he latches onto my wrist and cranks it behind my back with incredible speed and efficiency. Pain rushes up my arm and into my back like a strike of lightning. Arianyte's dark prince kicks the back of my knees out and I fall, his other hand on the back of my head, slamming my face into the turf. I cry out in rage as his boot swivels on my hand holding the sword, forcing me to let go of it. With one knee on my back pinning me, I realize with horror that I can't get out of his hold.

An instant panic envelops me, a claustrophobic choke hold threatening my very breath—

"You smell a little too divine to be such a pain in my ass today, you know that?" Malakyte purrs from above me, but I curse in response. "I can sense how I make you feel too. From the moment we met, you felt that connection between us. I can smell the attraction on you, hear your heart race when I walk into the room. I may be your villain, but you can't deny the way your darkness dances with mine. Nevertheless, as much as I'd like to continue this song and dance, you're not going to ruin what I've intended for this day. It's going to be for the betterment of Earth and of all Terrans. You'll see it that way, like those so-called Terran leaders likely having aneurysms up in their little VIP box in the stands. They'll come to see how the rebels bombed this stadium and how only Arianyte can make things right. Only Arianyte can protect them. Well, only if we're given the authority to protect them, that is. You and I could've run this world together like I planned, but you had to go and spoil decades of preparation. I am not happy with you, Miss Ruzz."

"It's Kara," I growl through clenched teeth as the pressure he's exuding on my head gets more and more unbearable.

"Kara . . ." It's as if he is tasting my name on his tongue like a fine wine. "Well, *Kara*, you've made enough of a mess here today. It's time you and I have a private chat about how I expect you to behave from this point on."

As if I weigh nothing, he takes a handful of my hair and wrenches me up to my feet by it, causing me to cry out as I stumble around to get my footing. I'm able to snatch my sword up as I go, thank the stars.

"Malakyte," I breathe, panting heavily as my chest rises and falls in succession with my beating heart. I have to try and reason with him, find that sensible man who did make me feel butterflies. "Don't do this. You'll kill everyone here, and the city will be blown to bits. The nuclear fallout alone will—"

"Give the Terrans the pretext to hand over control of Earth to me? Only I will be able to fix the environmental disaster that's surely awaiting this planet if those bombs go off, correct. I'll finally be able to rule this planet the way it was supposed to be done initially. No more Devouring Accords, no more Terrans asserting their authority over me inside their precious little Zones. It'll only be me. My family needs to see how I'm able to liquidate assets efficiently."

I shake my head in disgust. "Why not just take the power if you want it so badly? You don't have to do *this*."

Pushing me forward as he releases his grip on my hair, he laughs—taunting me. Malakyte fishes for the trigger inside his pants pocket, tosses it up into the air, and catches it. It falls back into his hand with a soft plop. "Arianyte has laws that must be followed. Because of Zariya's stunt some forty years ago, I'm on what you Terrans would call a short leash. The more bodies I lose, the worse I appear because bodies are our source of income. It's business, baby, and if I assert my power over this world, there's sure to be immense bloodshed. Another war, one I can't afford to fight. Not because of numbers or cost, but because of optics and loss of bodies. The sacrifice of this city is a reasonable hit. Whatever remains of the Terran government's irrational fears of terroristic rebels bombing their Zones and creating environmental annihilation globally will have them begging the only person who can stop these horrible events. The only person who can save them. That's me."

"No shit."

He smiles widely, white teeth glinting in the blood-red haze of the stadium's chaos. Surrounding us is full-blown madness. Nearly half the people from the stands have come down onto the arena floor and are in a full-fledged battle with rebels and SSPARROWs alike. Where are the others? Are they still below? And the Ringers?

"A classic bait and switch then?" I say, working out his plan in my mind. He wants to stage an attack and frame it on the rebels or Deimos, to then use that as a pretext to have the frightened Terran government relinquish the rest of their control and power over to Arianyte? Meaning he wouldn't need to secretly kidnap children. The Hijacked would be taken right out in the open.

Shit.

And the Terrans will go along with all this too. All his bribing, all the money he's funneled to them and all his promises of stars-know-what had been to butter them up for this very moment. If Malakyte can't take this planet by force, bound to the Devouring Accords and those laws, he'll just change the laws. It's a clever workaround, and a devastating one.

He waves the trigger around. "This is my path forward. Karalevine, you can't stop it. But you can join me on this path." A cold hand reaches out to me, the Prince of Arianyte offering me a deal I don't automatically reject.

"I would have joined you," I say, wondering if it's not a complete fabrication. "I liked you, Malakyte. I thought that I was wrong about Arianyte this entire time. You almost gaslighted me into believing you weren't the monster I had grown up believing you were."

Vulnerability flashes on his face for the briefest of moments, and the pain I see there makes me sad. He claims, "I never expected you to accept such a broken thing, anyway."

That sounds like something I would say.

"I've lived a long, long time, and what I've realized from all of those long years is that time heals all wounds. I'm sure you hate me right now, even cursing my name, but one day you'll come to see that this was all done for you. Perhaps you'll even begin to understand why I had to do it this way. You and I can rule the galaxy together, have power that you couldn't even dream of. Luxury beyond your wildest dreams. No one would ever dare hurt you again, not because I am there to protect you, but because you are the force that makes men's bones tremble to dust. You won't be contained or told to dim yourself so that your brightness does not blind others. I say, blind them all. Burn their eyes out. Let me be that conduit for you, let me take you to the greatness you were born to wield. We can forgive each other and start over. I'm sorry for the pain I've caused you; I've acted irrationally and vindictively out of revenge and anger, but so have you. Neither of us are innocent here, but I'm willing to stop this fighting between us and become the power couple that'll rule the world. I can give you whatever you need more than anyone else can. What you *truly* need."

More than Ardelle, he doesn't say.

His icy hands gently cup my cheeks, eyes alight and alive like he's almost human. Like he actually means what he's saying. Despite all the things he's done, all of his darkness and maliciousness—he *wants me.*

He wants me.

Maybe those broken pieces of me want him too? Because they're too broken to know what's good for them—and what's not.

The black cape attached to his back flaps in the wind; the fallen bodies and those fighting vigorously behind him are nothing but shadowy figures against this bloody hellscape. What's wrong with me? This should repulse me and make me want to stab my sword through his heart, but it doesn't. It sounds like everything I've always wanted to hear, but as I imagine myself in this insane position with all this power and influence, my family's faces flash in my mind as if to remind me that *they* are the ones I've always wanted. They chose me too. They are good for me. I think . . . Yet, the looks on their faces when they realized what I've done and the lies I've told them were looks of real disgust. Would they forgive me for all this? If they do, would it be the same? Could I forgive them for being willing to cast me aside? Forgive Ardelle for his lies and betrayal? I fought so hard to keep them, and I failed. Just like I failed Gav, and Geonni, and the Hijacked—what's left for me to fight for now? How can I stop the person responsible for all that pain and anger when he is offering me the world? How could I forgive myself for all my mistakes if I take his hand and leave here with him? What would that make me?

When I don't answer, he presses even further. "Come with me, and these bombs don't have to go off. I will let your Ringers go, order my SSPARROWs to cease, and you and I will leave here together. If not"— he waves the trigger in front of his face—"these bombs blow."

My stomach drops.

"I'll drop my plans for you, Kara. I'll do it for you."

Does he feel my heart soaring at the words? Can he sense me questioning *everything*?

"*Lies*," a voice from deep within claims. "*He lies, lies, lies.*"

On repeat it continues to bring me back to reality, back to the truth.

I'm being delusional. There are no good outcomes in choosing to go with him. He's a liar, a manipulator, and Zariya knew that—the crystal knew that and was trying to tell me this entire time. As Deimos said, I am the ultimate weapon for Arianyte to wield. I'd be a slave, twisted and warped into a monster exactly like him. Being queen means nothing if you're cruel and a killer and a monster—an identity I've been trying to run from ever since the night I became one at the orphanage. Maybe that's why I feel a connection to Malakyte? You have to be one to know one, I suppose. We're both the biggest monsters on this battlefield, and even if we play on the same side, I lose. Because he's everything I'd become if I allow this dark and sick desire to overcome my morals and my heart.

Watching me carefully, Malakyte interrupts my thought process. "I should mention one thing before you decide." The two of us stand amidst battle cries and the sound of gunfire. I really don't like that mischievous look in his eye. "I've been meaning to inform you of this for some time, and I want to give you this information so that you fully understand what's at stake and the full weight of your choices. Your Ringer, Jance Gallivan, happens to be your biological father."

What. The. Hell?

I stumble away from Malakyte, his words practically knocking me to the ground. I jumble a bunch of nonsensical words that not even I can decipher, and I'm unable to keep looking at that triumphant grin on his face.

"He's unaware of his paternity," he clarifies as my world spins, as if that makes this any better.

"What? H-How do you know this?" I managed to stutter out, disbelief and utter hope rushing through my veins. Could this really be true? Could I believe Malakyte? Why would he tell me this now?

So you'll go with him and save your supposed father, a voice in my head says, the rational part of me that sees this ploy for what it is.

I can't dare to hope it's one based on truth.

That would change so much . . .

Malakyte shrugs, as if this bit of information means nothing. "I know many things about you, Karalevine. If you come with me, I'll tell you everything. Save your friends and your father, save all the people. You'll be a hero, I'll make sure the world knows it. And that you're my future queen, future empress—the way Zariya was. It's what your father would want for you."

He could never know that. This person who has no connection to his own parents could never understand what Jance would want for me— if what he claims is even true.

Could it be true? Could Jance be my actual father? My mind spins. There's too much going on here and so many questions firing, my mind can't keep track of any of them. What am I supposed to do? How am I supposed to choose this? If Jance really is my dad, then I could save him right now, but that also means I lose him the moment I found him.

The prickling behind my eyes infuriates me. I will not allow this monster to see me cry— to see where my weakest point is.

I know what I have to do, what must be done in order to keep everyone safe.

Perhaps this is what I deserve then, for all the bad things I've done. It's not the atonement I thought I would find or the revenge I dreamt of, but it's something. It's what Gavrielle would have done—would want me to do. I have no doubt about that.

And at least my soul would be free. And I can forgive myself after all this time.

This is my atonement, the redemption arc I never realized I was barreling towards.

Saving everyone I love and care for means sacrificing myself.

I'll leave with the Prince of Arianyte, if only because it's the right thing to do. It's the choice the old me would never have made because the old me would fight and claw to stay with the father I always wished I had. To stay with the family I used to wish for on every single birthday. And I still do want to fight, but if it means Jance and Saris and Ahren get set free, and the others don't get blown to smithereens and dust, then I'll lay down my sword.

I can only hope this version of me continues to fight against what Malakyte wants because she's the one that does all the right things.

"Okay," I say, slow and defeated. "If you let the Ringers go, and give me the trigger now, I'll go with you willingly, but not as your prisoner nor your lover. You don't get my heart, Malakyte, you don't get it at all."

The ice returns to his eyes with that last bit, no doubt hoping all his fancy words would've changed things between us. No, I didn't choose the wrong guy—I chose right. Malakyte will find another way to get what he wants in regard to the Terran government, but if I can stop this atrocity today, I'll find a way to stop the one for tomorrow. Destroy him and Arianyte from within, continue the mission Geonni set up for me.

Be the dark horse I was born to become.

Malakyte closes the distance between us, leaving only about two inches between our bodies. It is too close because I can feel the waves of frost pouring off him. I shiver as his hand comes forward and cups my chin, feeling like an ice statue is touching me. Some guy near us screams a death howl, a cry for mercy that nobody answers. There are a lot of cries like his going on around us, and what I'm doing is going to stop it all.

I'm going to stop this, now.

Swatting his hand away, I hold out my own, beckoning my fingers for the trigger. He smirks, flicking his wrist to hold the trigger out before me.

I reach for it, a small amount of relief washing over me now that I'm saving the people I care about most, but at the last minute, right before I grasp it, Malakyte presses the trigger.

CHAPTER 62

My mouth falls to the floor.

"What the hell?" I shout, slapping the trigger from his hands, but it's too late. Fury builds up in my bones.

Malakyte laughs, his pointed canines on full display.

"I'm sorry, I truly am," he says, picking the trigger back up. Glee fills his voice as if this is the funniest joke he's ever told. "You don't actually believe I'm letting these people walk out of this arena alive, do you? There's no reason to leave them alive now. They'll only distract you. I'll fish out their bodies later and get my crystals back. I'll free your Ringers only to appease you, but this is happening. It's done. Let's go."

He snatches my arm and begins dragging me away, just like that.

In this moment, I'm frozen, and my body simply goes with him like I'm his puppet doll already. The bombs are going to go off . . . Ardelle and the others don't know—they'll never get out in time. Maybe they've left? I need to hold onto some hope that they have.

Did he do this because I'm not in love with him? Is this payback . . . all his words, they're lies.

Then my eyes are blinded by the four megascreens powering on.

At first, the screen is black, but then what looks to be some type of amateur film footage begins to play.

My heart soars.

The scene is nothing but a blur of darkness and muffled sounds until the camera finally focuses . . . and the camera is pointed at Malakyte. He's seated in a chair, looking rather stiff, as Deimos is standing to the right of him. Taunting him from the sounds of it, then in an instant his blade is out and barreling down towards the prince's chest.

"Wait!" a female voice yells, panic infused in every octave. *My* voice.

My recording of the encounter between Deimos, Malakyte, and me plays before the entire stadium. Pacey must have been able to hook it up to the trigger mechanism somehow, making it so if Malakyte pushed the button, it would trigger this video instead of the bombs. Pacey Dawson is a certified genius.

Malakyte whirls on me, his victorious face now transformed into one of rage and fury.

He can't stop this. He has no control, and he knows what information is about to become public. I zone back to the recording, the entire stadium stopping in its tracks to watch, weapons frozen midattack.

"What is the Silent Breath?" I ask Malakyte in the video.

"Yes, Malakyte, tell the sweet girl what the Silent Breath is. Speak!" Deimos orders the prince.

In the video, Malakyte's eyes are furious fireballs and his words are laced with frigid ice. "It's a necessary iniquitous."

"Nobody even knows what that word means. Answer the girl's question," Deimos demands, putting the knife to Malakyte's white throat.

Malakyte reluctantly continues. "We must do it for a galaxy-wide government to exist. Otherwise, with the gaps between viable planets and star systems being so vastly apart from one another, one lifetime is not enough."

"Enough for what?" Deimos presses.

Those onyx eyes look up at Deimos, and I know him well enough to know he's picturing a thousand ways to kill that green-eyed devil. "You cannot leave a thing like Arianyte to subsequent generations, one after the other. There's too much risk involved, too much change. If one planet gets a visit from us every half a century, they make necessary changes per their agreements with Arianyte, then a new ruler comes back to say, 'Never mind, things have changed.' It causes instability."

Deimos shoots the alien leader in the leg, and screams ring out across the arena as shocked onlookers watch with wide eyes. Malakyte's lips curl in a snarl, sharp canines bared, clearly hating this dramatic power shift.

Deimos shakes the pistol, making it clear he'll shoot him again and again until he speaks.

"The Silent Breath is an ongoing, systematic harvesting process of carbon-based lifeforms. The extracting process of fresh stem cells from these lifeforms will only confuse you. You wouldn't understand the science: it's too complex. But we turn those viable cells into a serum. That serum is then ingested and it rejuvenates the bodies' cells and makes them . . . young. It keeps them young. Forever. Notwithstanding continual access to the serum, of course.

"There, are you happy now? That's the Silent Breath, and every single planet agrees to it. It's this pretentious planet Earth that refuses to agree. It's why the war was sparked upon our arrival. I'm not doing anything wrong per our agreement with Earth's leaders. We've agreed Earth is exempt from this process."

"Where do these stem cells come from?" I demand, my own voice sounding strange to my ears. The camera looks like it's trembling—because I was.

Malakyte's condescending laugh echoes out wickedly across the silent stadium. His current grip on me as we stand watching the video is getting tighter and tighter. My upper arm feeling as if he's going to snap the bone in two.

"I think you already know the answer to that," the prince answers in the video.

"Say it," I demand, the words booming across the chaotic arena that's now frozen and glued to my voice—my confession tape. To finally turn the public's position against Arianyte once and for all.

My ace.

Didn't see this coming, did you, asshole?

Malakyte's eyes roll in the video and my heart races from what I know is coming. "The children. The younger the source, the fresher and superior the cells. But again, Earth doesn't belong to this process."

"Then what about all those missing kids?" Deimos reminds him. "The Hijacked? We all know you're lying about taking the kids, so admit it. I have the digital fingerprints of you identifying the right children to take, ones nobody would miss or question their whereabouts. You've been kidnapping children under the radar for years, making this serum in secret, violating the Accords to do it. I was getting them to safety, away from you and your experiments and revolting addiction. But you always have a scapegoat, don't you, Prince? I was that scapegoat. And don't be fooled, kiddo. This serum takes hundreds of dead children to create one single dose. They're farmed until they're bled dry. This biological material is almost as rare as what's beating inside your chest. It's why the kids are kidnapped so frequently, why this old man looks no older than you."

Hearing that Deimos has been saving children from Malakyte still throws me for a loop. Despite his insane methods, Deimos has been an unsung hero to the Hijacked, and according to him, Ardelle knew he was taking the kids to safety.

Malakyte doesn't deny it. In fact, he looks almost proud of what he's accomplished, his smirk saying everything for him. Proud he can cheat death itself. Yet standing beside me now, he looks downright furious.

There's no way the people of Earth are going to be cool with this, and he knows it. No matter what happens now, the Terran government will never give him more power, no matter how much destruction he causes. Not after this, they won't. They're up in the stands somewhere, watching this go down live. Terrans from Zones all over the continent and planet have come here today. He wanted them to witness the destruction firsthand, to die with the city, and to send the other officials a chilling message.

I've screwed him, and he knows it.

"Say goodnight, you piece of shit," Deimos sings as his blade comes up yet a second time. I hear myself cry in an attempt to stop him, but those cries go unanswered. The camera jerks around violently with my screams, along with a muffled microphone. It then flashes to dark-blue blood splattering on pristine floors and walls. More cries from me follow, then I'm seen bolting from the room in a panicked run, the camera bouncing around in all directions.

After several curses from me, the video goes black, and we're all encompassed once again in a bloody darkness.

CHAPTER 63

My cackle is the only sound howling out into the stadium stunned in silence. The people are all suspended in shock, likely questioning their very loyalty to a man who's openly admitted to killing Earth's children so he could avoid wrinkles. I swear I also hear the ripple of Deimos's laugh out there somewhere too—amongst the dead bodies and weary souls.

"What have you done?" Malakyte roars at me, latching both hands onto my shoulders and shaking me aggressively. Teeth bared back in a snarl, eyes darker than Coal Black with rage, I now see the true Prince of Arianyte—the main villain in my story.

He's always been the villain, I just couldn't see it.

"Looks like we're both double-crossing liars, huh?"

His howl rumbles my bones.

Snatching me again, he begins dragging me towards the side of the stadium, and I'm like a dog on a leash, not wanting to follow. This changes things. His vehemence towards me puts me in an even worse position than I was in initially when I made this agreement. He could punish the others because of this.

"What about the Ringers?" I ask as he walks over the body of a rebel whose mouth is frozen open in a dying battle cry.

"Where are they? How will I know you'll let them go?"

Malakyte's snicker is as bitter as an orange peel. He doesn't answer.

I pull against him harder, hard enough to stop our advance. Whirling on me, he uses his body to tower over mine. He raises his brows at me, wordlessly asking what I want.

"I want to know they'll be freed. That's the deal, and you've proven you're not trustworthy enough to keep your end of it," I say defiantly. "You lie, Malakyte."

Sometimes I feel stupid with the way I talk to him, that I should be way more concerned with what I say.

"They're outside the stadium in a transport-hover. I'll order their release once I get you and me out of here. Now, *let's go*," he says condescendingly, his voice icier than his grasp as he pulls me violently.

And before I know it, I'm being carted once again towards my terrible future, a small convoy of SSPARROWs and rebel fighters coming alongside us, threatening to drag us into their fray. The smell of death pungent in the air and the iron twinge of blood mixing together are enough to make me gag.

I look around, hoping to see one of my fellow Starseeds out there—they're nowhere to be found. Pacey turned the tide here. She saved all these lives with her creative hacking skills. I hope she knows what a great job she did, that she made a difference in the end, and she's brave and capable and stronger than anyone gives her credit for. I hope Ardelle can forgive himself for what he's done, that he's able to grieve losing his childhood and all hopes of a future he and his family may have. And I hope Jance can . . . I hope Jance can see that he was mine, too. I hope a part of him knows this, knows that I'm his daughter. I wish I had more time to tell him. I wish he could hold me one more time in those arms that have always made me feel safe. I understand why I always felt that way now.

As Malakyte drags me by more bodies of the fallen, both rebels, SSPARROWs, and civilians alike, I try to tell myself this is what's best.

This hit to Arianyte, this video will make waves that go beyond what I could have expected when I began this journey. I'll prevent the full takeover of Earth by this madman, and I did that without losing myself in the process. At least, at the very end, anyway. Maybe I've finally learned something?

Going with Malakyte is my ultimate atonement for all the mistakes I've made, for what happened with Gav. I forgive myself for that. I do. I was a child with an enormous power that got out of control, and when I left him there, I was too scared and young to realize the weight a choice like that would have on me later. Had I gone back and fought for Gav, we'd have both been taken away. Had Arianyte gotten me then, who knows what type of weapon they would've created out of me at that tender age.

Regardless of how I'll suffer in the upcoming future, I can live freely inside my heart knowing I've protected those I care about.

Where Zariya failed, I'll succeed, and that keeps my feet walking along Malakyte's side. Without the drastic measures she had to take, without the death of the ones I love most. I realize in this moment that we're different people, she and I. We may share a soul and this cosmic crystal, perhaps even a similar destiny—but I'm making the choice to go down a different path than her. My own path.

Even if that cost is my freedom, my autonomy. I'll gladly pay it if it means I don't have to make the terrible choice she did.

I may be a prisoner now, but my soul flies free for the first time in my life.

A beeping noise snaps me out of my thoughts and I look around. Malakyte doesn't seem to hear it, but I surely do. It's close, like it's right next to us.

"What is that?" I ask, head whipping in all directions.

Stopping so abruptly I run into him, Malakyte freezes like a predator in the wild. Reaching into his pocket, he pulls out the trigger, and we see that it's the source of the beeping, its red lights flashing alongside it.

They weren't doing that before.

My brows knit in panic, and when I see the gleeful expression on Malakyte's face, my stomach drops ten feet deep.

"Looks like your little hacker only managed to stop the preignition trigger. The actual bomb will go off in the next ten minutes. Regrettably, we won't have time to free your Ringers. My apologies."

He attempts to drag me on farther, but I dig my heels in, horror blinding me.

"Let go of me," I demand, pulling back on his grip. No. No, I won't let this happen. Not after everything.

Malakyte pulls harder, a grip of iron and ice.

"Let go of me!" I shout, raising my sword with my other hand and swinging it down. The dark crystalline blade misses slicing his arm off by a hair. "I'm not going anywhere with you."

Not if they're all going to die anyway. I'd be sacrificing myself for nothing. I'd rather die with them than live a life as a slave knowing what their fate was—that I couldn't save them.

Why is history repeating itself? What Zariya intended so many years ago on that moon was for Malakyte to die with her and the rest of the Starseeds and Ringers. That's why she blew it up—to stop *him*. My heart aches, as only moments ago I felt myself relish in the fact I was going to save those I love and care about. Now, I've doomed them all. But if we've got no choice but to die here today, I'm going to make damn sure this prick is coming with us this time.

Pointing the sharp tip of my sword at his throat, Malakyte freezes, smirk fading.

Before I can stop him, Malakyte swings the sword at his hip out in a long, dramatic arc—knocking into my sword with a loud twang.

I have no time. I must strike now—keep Malakyte here for as long as I possibly can.

I'm unprepared for the strength of his attack, and it knocks me back on my feet several paces. He's not holding back this time.

Don't think, just strike.

Instincts taking over, my Elendril sword swoops and flies through the air, the ornate handle rubbing against my palms. Each hit that connects rattles my very bones. The strength of Malakyte's attacks against me quickly overpowers my slight frame. Jance warned me about this, Ardelle too. My body is my biggest weakness: I'm physically not strong enough to win a fight toe to toe.

I have to be smarter.

Quicker.

Maybe if I get the trigger, I can stop the bombs? That's the ultimate goal, but if I can't, then I'll die keeping this monster here.

Where did he put the damn thing?

The clanging of our swords is all I can hear over my pummeling heart.

Hunching low to the ground, I pop up, letting the top of my skull pound him under the chin. The snapping of his jaw causes my lips to part in a grin as I slink behind and knock both his knees out from under him. My dark sword is at his throat seconds later, and I hold the Prince of Arianyte on his knees.

Not able to lie to myself, it feels good having this bit of power over such an impressive monster.

"Try anything and you're dead," I say, watching as he spits up dark blood from our scuffle. "You're not going anywhere, Malakyte. It's over."

"It's only over for you and the rest of you Starseed trash."

Pressing the blade closer, I draw blue blood. "Don't you dare talk about us that way. Because you're in a really nasty spot, especially since I'm guessing the only way to truly kill you is to rip that crystal out of you or cut off your head?"

His silence is my sweet answer, yet I worry—does he feel my blade trembling? Can I even do that? Can I actually cut off a person's head, even one as evil as Malakyte's?

My hesitation costs me my one and only shot at doing so. At getting the trigger off him too.

Malakyte's elbow swiftly nails me in my bottom ribs, and out of pure pain I stumble backwards, sword out in front.

Stupidly, I allow my eyes a few fleeting seconds to search for the trigger on the ground to see if it has fallen or been dropped, knowing it's around here somewhere.

Malakyte takes his chance and comes for me again, drawing me right back into our conflict.

My sword isn't quick enough and his own slices my thigh a good four inches before I'm able to pull away.

Crystal searing, I refuse to cry out as the blood trickles down to the ruined turf around my boot.

"Looks like that hurts." His words taunt. "Don't worry, my sweet Zariya. All the pain will be over with soon. I promise it'll be quick, and I'll make sure to hold you until it's over."

Zariya? He's lost it.

Coming at him, I dig in my heels and fly, ignoring the sharp pain in my thigh. My hair whips behind me, and a battle cry roars from my throat. We strike several blows but continue missing each other. Fire builds inside as we play cat and mouse. Punches and kicks fly. Demon blades glint red in this light as we both swing our swords in skilled, graceful arches. The urge to use my crystal to blow him to bits is even more tempting when I realize he's landing twice as many blows as I am. Yet, something's stopping me from using it.

"*Wait . . .*" it says.

Wait.

I'm fast, but he's matching my pace. I'm punching and kicking and swinging mostly on instinct, my dodges pure luck and any blows I make even luckier. But I'm wounded from blasting out of that collar, my own crystal damaging my body enough that I'm paying for it now with every single breath. Every movement I make feels like my insides are about to pop.

His age and experience are truly showing in this fight.

I see an opening to kick his ribs, but when I do, he locks his arm around my shin. Hopping on one foot, his pointed teeth are all I can see as he licks his lips with anticipation. Like a ragdoll, he throws me, taking me completely off balance as I hit the ground hard. The fall brutally forces air from my lungs and I cough out what feels like five broken ribs, but I have no time to think about the pain or lack of air coming into my lungs. Driving the pointy end of my sword into the turf, I force myself back up to my feet, using my sword for support. I snarl as I spit blood at him.

Giving me no time to recover, he swings his sword wide and the blade's parallel to my neck, coming in hot. Ducking with wide eyes and a gasp on my lips, I find his gut wide open. It's a stupid move but I have no time to think about it. Like a bull, I head-butt Malakyte right in his stomach. He gasps from the air exiting his lungs by force. The sound is simply delightful, and we both fall to the ground.

It's my only opportunity to grab the trigger.

Diving my hands into his pockets, he doesn't realize what I'm after until it's too late.

Sitting atop him and wasting no time, I press the trigger. It's such a tiny thing, barely bigger than my palm and shaped like a black egg. The lights continue to flash despite my aggressive pushing of the solitary button. I search it gingerly, hoping there's another button, but there's nothing.

How much time has already passed? Certainly enough to prevent Malakyte's escape, but . . .

"Smart thinking, however, those bombs are going off. There's nothing you can do to stop this. You're going to fail, exactly like Zariya did."

Icy arms grab me around the waist as he bucks his hips and bounces me off his lap and onto the turf.

Malakyte bends over me, long hair tickling my cheeks. "And you may have prevented me from exiting this stadium and avoiding the blast, but my crystal will revive me. You, on the other hand, you will die along with your fellow Starseeds and Ringers, and that ludicrous pain-in-my-ass Deimos will get the blast this time too."

His voice is gleeful, almost fueled by madness as he speaks.

"Except I have nothing but time. Time to wait for your soul to reincarnate once again. Once again blinded to the truth of the past—of this day. You'll forget all of it. And I'll ensure that the next time I find you, I won't make the same mistakes as I did this time. You'll be mine the way Zariya was mine before that gutter rat took her from me. I won't fail again. You'll never know, you'll never remember. None of you will remember."

Utter terror shoots through me at his monstrous words.

At a horrendous fate that awaits me, awaits us all . . . on the other side of another life not yet come to pass. All the memories of this life, of the life before it . . . washed away and wiped clean.

And the fact I'll be none the wiser, just as I was blind to Zariya's fate during this current incarnation.

The thought of it rushes in, cascaded not only by unadulterated fear but also rage. Knowing there's no way out, no way to win this fight. It mirrors Zariya's final moments. The parallel is crippling my body in heavy sludge as I retreat further and further into myself, preparing for the brutal end.

For my brutal failure.

Useless isn't enough of an adjective to describe what I am. Pathetic. Coward. Selfish.

Chin trembling, I look around for someone from our group—anyone—to help me. To fix this terrible mess that I've made. I'd even take Deimos right now to help get my ass up off this floor and do something to save us.

But nobody's here. They're all off fighting their own battles in a fight I had a hand in starting.

I'm alone.

Like I was that night at the orphanage when all this began . . . like I've been my entire life.

Get up! I scold myself again, forcing myself to at least grab my sword and go down swinging. My arm is lead as I reach for it, the hilt cold against my hand.

My fingers curl around my sword, the pain in my chest swapping to something else. All I have to do is get up and fight one last time in an attempt to make some sort of difference in the bigger picture of things.

With the promise of his threat fueling me, that power within finally declares that it's time to rage against this psychopath.

With everything I have.

To stop being afraid of its power, to stop hating it for blasting Gav, to finally come face-to-face with the demon within and say proudly—this is me.

Perhaps I found the door to danger and walked through it, pursuing a fallacy of vengeful fever dreams, but I did so with the best of intentions. If perhaps she's sometimes a bit selfish, I can no longer hate that girl— even if her shoes fit.

This is who I am.

Self-destructive monster and all.

It's enough—*I'm* enough.

It gives me the precious strength I need to stagger to my feet.

With gritted teeth and sweat dripping down my back, I haul myself up. Each movement feels like I'm unlocking my skeleton, but as I slide one foot below me, it gets a little easier, then a little easier as the fear of Malakyte's eerie threat falls from me like icy chains being melted right off my body. Huffing with exertion, I rise on trepidatious legs.

Standing, my crystal's energy is flowing through my veins much faster than I've ever known it to. Like a dam has burst against a massive weight, and every part of my body is filling up with the Elendril's power.

Pushing through my psychological and physical barriers must have blasted past the invisible ones I had with my crystal too. It no longer flows impeded by my fear and hatred of it. The antimatter energy is pouring out of my hands and into the sword itself, causing it to glow alight in the purple color of my crystal. Symbols appear on the black blade, glowing wildly as the energy pours into it, lighting it up like it is made of lightning fire. The pearl within the hilt also begins to glow, shining my star symbol along with it. We are one. The Elendril crystal, the sword, and me.

And we are going to kick this guy's ass.

I'm faster, stronger, and filled with power now. Standing only feet away, Malakyte's eyes widen with fear, sensing my crystal's power surging like a rocket's.

He glides in an arch around me, his sword veering through the air like a bullet.

Only by the grace of my speed do I block it with my sword, and we face each other, sword to sword. Eye to eye. Monster to monster.

With a shout of rage, I push the crystal harder into my sword with a flash of brilliant light so dense and saturated it bursts through the red emergency lights like a beacon of hope.

I can feel the power scorching through me. Wild. Deadly. Vicious.

It happens fast and in slow motion all at once. I knee him in the balls, feeling good about my hunch he has similar anatomy as Terrans. He does. He staggers backwards, bent over himself in agony. My new invigorated boost of energy propels me in the air. The glow of the sword is an explosion of light within the darkness of Malakyte's shocked eyes. The reflection of my sword's light bounces off their wide, glassy, horrified surface. For once, he's frozen in a prison that has nothing to do with his cold blood. There's not enough time for him to block me. I'm too fast. The only option left for him is to use his sword as a shield, but the second our blades collide, my crystal's antimatter energy slices right through his and straight down into Malakyte Ardeen's face.

CHAPTER 64

THE ARIANYTE EMPIRE DECREE #3

AS OF MARCH 4ᵀᴴ, IN THE YEAR 2099, THE ARIANYTE EMPIRE RETAINS FULL JURISDICTION OVER EARTH AND ITS NATIVE SPECIES—THIS DAY WILL FOREVER BE KNOWN AS "THE DEVOURING."

It's the first time I hear him in genuine pain. Malakyte's screams are as substantial as the bombs due to erupt under our feet within minutes.

Malakyte is holding his face in his hands, wailing like a banshee on the arena floor. This is my chance to stop him, to end his terroristic reign forever. Not only in this life, but in the next—and for the very last time.

His screams incite zero pity from me.

I swing my blade up, fully intending to cut his head off on the downward strike, when a pinch in my gut stops me midswing. This moment is what I've been fighting so hard for since the very beginning of all this—for so many years.

"This isn't who you are," my conscience or inner-whatever whispers to me.

But this asshole groveling at my feet is going to kill everyone in this city if I don't, I argue back to myself.

And if I don't kill him here and now, his crystal will keep him alive, and we'll all die. Leaving Malakyte to hunt us all down once again.

Repeating this madness.

The sword trembles with my indecision—with my rage. Why am I going so back and forth on this? I made a choice, hadn't I? To be better, but he's . . . he's going to cause so much pain if I leave him alive.

The others would do it. Ardelle would do it. He'd kill this guy and do whatever it took to get what he wanted—he's already proven that. Why do I have to be the good person? Nobody else around here is. Why must I have this stupid moral fiber when all I want is the pain inside me to stop?

Will killing Malakyte make it stop?

Would it make the pain of Gavrielle and Geonni stop?

Will it keep the guilt from destroying me from within like a brain-eating amoeba?

Or is it simply up to *me* to make it all stop? Is this all on me?

I scream, the sword barreling down.

My choice made.

Instead of slicing through the alien's neck, the sword plunges into the arena floor. My knees collapse under me as I use the sword to hold me upright. Tears finally escape, pouring out in rivers of pain and anger and rage and fear.

Dammit, damn being a good person when all I want to do is give in to the worst corners of myself. But really, it isn't what I truly want, or truly need.

What I need right now is my own forgiveness.

Because killing Malakyte as my last act on this Earth won't make the pain stop. Doing what I've done—all these terrible things—it has changed nothing regarding the pain I feel.

Only I can solve that.

And it sucks, it's real shit, but I'm a better person than the one I was before. That doesn't make me feel guilty, it makes me feel proud.

I can only hope whatever higher power that sends us down to places like Earth sees this moment and grants me mercy in my next life. Perhaps keep this sick son of a bitch far, far away from me.

Stars, I don't want to die alone. If only I could find some way to shield myself from the blast, I could—

My neck snaps up, eyes going wide with an incredibly reckless idea that maybe—just maybe—could work.

Remembering Ardelle's training at the bookstore, an insane idea flashes through my mind.

A shield.

Hope—stupid, reckless hope—fills my chest.

"I hope you think about your actions the next time you look in a mirror," I say to Malakyte cruelly. "And remember me for the rest of your miserable existence, asshole."

"Zariya!" he cries, crawling towards my feet pathetically. "Don't leave me here."

"My fucking name is Karalevine!"

Turning, I run towards the bombs as fast as I possibly can.

CHAPTER 65

How many minutes I have, I don't know. What I know for sure is that I don't have many as I hop over Malakyte, sliding my sword down its sheath at my back, and make my way back towards the planted bombs.

I don't make it more than ten feet when a sweet, familiar voice stops me in my tracks.

Not Malakyte's, he's still writhing on the ground and calling Zariya's name, but by a very ruffled and disheveled Naresteé.

"You're not going anywhere, you little bitch," she snarls, her expression crazed. "What did you do to him?" Bloodied and filthy, her makeup and hair are a wild mess. She must have really gotten into it with someone.

She points a pistol in my face, the exact model that killed Geonni.

"I should have killed you all those years ago," she seethes, her inscrutable exterior finally broken. Like a boulder thrown onto a frozen pond, she's cracked. Her words, however, cause me to pause, despite looking into a barrel of a gun.

When would she have had the opportunity to kill me? What is Naresteé talking about? It wasn't the night at the orphanage because she never came into contact with me.

I have a slim chance of stopping this bomb; I can't deal with this.

Without warning, another disruptor pistol comes into play, but this time it's pointed at the back of Naresteé's head, right between her horns.

It's Deimos.

"You'll never get the chance, because if anyone is killing this little brat, it'll be me. Throw the gun, or I'll blast your brains out."

I risk a glance over at him, relieved to see him there despite that absurd comment.

"Now!" Deimos's voice bellows, pressing the gun harder into her skull. He, too, looks like hell, even more beaten up than when we fought at the carnival.

Seething, she hisses right back. "You think you can pull the trigger before I can?"

"Either way, you'll still be dead. Spare your own life and drop the damn disruptor."

Despite the fact that this could get me killed, I have to say it. "She's the one who took Gavrielle, she's the reason your Ringer is dead."

Silence rings out as Deimos contemplates my words. What is he going to do to her? She suddenly looks nervous, and after she takes a moment, she removes the pistol from my face and throws it.

If Deimos is going to exact his revenge, I won't be here to see it.

"Malakyte's bombs are going to go off. Pacey didn't stop them. I think I can, but I have to get to them—*now*!" I say, my voice a panicked plea.

Deimos nods, giving me the signal to go.

"Don't let them out of your sight," I say before I run off, then dash towards what's likely certain death.

Let Deimos take care of Malakyte, stars know he wants to. He can live with that burden because I'm not going to.

So many bodies lie dead around me, and I'm forced to hop and jump and dodge each one of them as I swiftly weave my way towards the exit of the arena floor. Their bodies, those on the ground and those fighting, are a blur as I fly across all the damage I've incurred.

Hope floods me as I see a familiar boy fighting straight ahead. Stars, luck is on my side for once.

"Sylo!" I cry out, making my way towards him. It's dark even in the red light, but he squints and sees me coming. Once I meet him, I explain quickly what's going on with the bombs. "The Ringers are in the parking lot in one of the SSPARROW transport vans." His eyes go wide as saucers at my words. "Get them out and go. I've got a last-ditch effort to stop the bombs, but I can't stay. I've got to go. Get them out of here!"

I'm gone before he can reply.

I swiftly make it to the alcove I hope will lead me down to the catacombs, nearly slipping as I round the corner. My feet follow the dips in the dark concrete tunnels, hoping to the stars that I'm in the correct spot and not on the opposite side of the stadium. With the lights out and my sense of direction turned upside down, I have no idea. Each alcove looks identical to the other, and I easily could be far from the bombs.

Zariya, if you're out there somewhere, help me now, I beg as I continue scampering towards what I hope are the bombs. *Gavrielle, if you can hear me, get me there in time. Help me save them.*

I must get there in time.

I must.

My footsteps echoing are the only sounds aside from my ragged breaths; the cries and sounds of the battle above are completely silenced down here. Whipping around another corner, my chest fills with hope as I see the blue glow of the bombs straight ahead.

"Jupiter's rings," I gasp aloud as I sprint down the steep hundred feet towards the bombs.

Seconds after discovery, I can hear what sounds like a timer ticking down, synced up with each individual bomb. The beeps get closer together with each passing second.

Beep, beep, beep, beep.

The sound is a haunting anthem, promising the death of tens of thousands of souls. Mine one of them.

Beep, beep beep—beep.

My father's, my friend's, my family's—their lives hanging in the balance.

Desperately, I push my legs as hard as I've ever pushed them. I have to make it. I *have to!*

By some miracle, I reach the bombs before they detonate, but the beeping is almost like a racing heartbeat now, barely a millisecond apart.

Wasting no time, I stop and take a deep, shaking breath. Silencing all my panic and fears, I call upon the beast, the monster within me.

My demon, my curse to bear. It's a part of me and I'm a part of it. We're one, and we're going to save this city.

Even if it means I die in the process.

As my crystal's burn grows into an unbearable sear, it lights up like a literal sun in the night's sky.

A star about to go supernova.

Exactly like Ardelle showed me that night at the bookstore, I use my crystal to create a ball of energy, except this time I attempt to wrap it around the bombs. I'm not sure if I even can as my arms outstretch and I watch the antimatter expand out before me. My heart is racing, thundering in my ears as I create a dome around the bombs.

Then the bombs explode before my eyes, with only a heartbeat to spare.

A hot wind hits me first, and I wonder if I'm going to be incinerated right here and now. The explosion hits my antimatter barrier immediately, blowing my hair back in a sizzling whoosh. The heat burns my skin and lashes, causing my eyes to water, but somehow—it holds.

The sight is extraordinary, and I can do nothing but watch in wonder and awe, feeling minuscule in comparison to the radical images before me.

My barrier is the purple color my crystal has always been, except pushed to this level it's burning white hot in many places, shades of Tangerine Orange and Lemon Yellow swirling within it, specs of white lightning bouncing off the interior. The bombs are a witch's brew of Lime Green and Midnight Purple ink as they push against my shield with vigorous power. Small round circles flatten out alongside the barrier, smashing themselves out with white-hot green at the center and purple around the edges. It's an unreal sight, one not too terrible to go out watching, I suppose.

Because even if I survive this without being annihilated or turned into walking cancer, the building will surely collapse on top of me. My antimatter is causing the concrete to rain down. Each layer that falls evaporates to dust the moment it hits the shield, causing more to fall in an endless cycle. Eventually, it's going to collapse on top of me, and this will be my permanent gravesite.

However, I can know for sure this time that I did what was right. That my team—my family—will know what I did, and that I did it for them. They'll know that I sacrificed myself for them because it's what was right. They'll know I've changed.

I've changed in multiple ways.

And that I'm sorry.

I laugh then, feeling the freedom that only certain death permits.

I laugh until tears follow, and I let them fall without inhibition or shame or guilt. I can let all that go now. I can rest, after all these years of pain and rage and hatred.

I can rest.

I am ready.

Closing my eyes, I can feel the bombs subsiding from within my shield, if only a little. Once they've ceased and their energy is spent and neutralized, the stadium will collapse, sealing me inside. I hope my death is quick, stars, I hope it's quick.

My energy is expended, and I can barely hold on, my barrier becoming smaller and smaller as the bombs slowly subside and fade down. The more my shield shrinks, the more concrete falls on top of me. This room is vast, and this will probably take down a third of the stadium.

The dust falls into my eyes, bigger bits hitting my body from above. Chunks that fall are getting larger and larger until the entire area is coming down on top of me.

It's time.

I'm ready.

"Thumbelina!"

My neck cranes towards the voice coming from behind me. Through the rainfall of rock and debris, I see him there, eyes alight in a ruby-red glow that sends my heart blasting skywards towards hope.

Towards him.

"Ardelle!" I shout back. The nuclear bombs aren't completely dispersed. I can't lose the shield now.

As if a powerful wind is keeping the falling debris away from me, the concrete falls everywhere around except on top of me. Ardelle stands twenty feet back, taking cover as he holds off the assault of the collapsing building long enough for me to keep the bombs covered.

Until neither of us can anymore.

He shouldn't be here. Despite my heart thudding wildly that he ran into certain death for me, he has a family. He has Pacey.

My knees give way underneath me as my energy wanes, my eyes as heavy as tanks. Blood drips from my nose and I taste it cresting over my lips. I've pushed my crystal and body so far past their limits today, and I'm barely holding on.

Almost there . . . the bombs are almost dissipated.

I can do this.

We can do this.

"Let it go!" Ardelle shouts from down the wide hallway. "Let it go and run towards me."

I shake my head, craning it towards him. "It's not ready yet," I yell.

"I'm holding up a massive piece. I can't keep it up much longer. Most of the bombs have been unleashed, and there are dozens of feet of concrete above us. It'll be snuffed out. I can't hold it."

"No, just go!" I shout back, not willing to risk it after all this. He'll die with me if this doesn't work.

Silence is my response and I wonder if he actually left, but when I turn to look back, I see him struggling to keep the stadium above me still above me. His arms tremble from the exertion of holding a portion of a stadium over me, and I can see the struggle on his face.

When I look back under my dome barrier, I can barely see the green and purple colors of the bombs.

Maybe I can make it out of here.

"Thumbelina!" he cries, and I hear the desperation in his voice. He will not be able to hold on.

And neither am I.

"I'm coming!" I shout, angling my feet and leaning towards him, knowing I'll have no amount of seconds to spare.

I let my shield dissolve.

With the last of my remaining strength, I push my legs hard, muscles ripping and screaming as I shoot up the hallway incline, cement and concrete collapsing mere feet behind me.

Ardelle's protective cover over me slips as I dart towards him, zigzagging through chunks as big as hovers as they pummel down around me.

I can barely see, eyes burning from dust and debris, my vision a waterfall of concrete.

"Keep going, don't stop," he says as I reach him, the ground at our feet wobbly at best.

I fly by him, placing my hand on his shoulder as I go by.

Ardelle begins to slowly walk backwards, his own protective shield of gravity causing rocks and debris to slide off him. I make it to the first turn, away from the falling debris, Ardelle at least thirty feet behind me inside the rain of rubble.

"Hurry up!" I cry, my voice echoing against the walls, all cracked and buckling under the weight of the moment.

"Go!" he yells from down there, so enmeshed within the debris and dust I can no longer see him. This dumbass is going to sacrifice himself, I just know it. It's something heroic and stupid that he would do, if not to make up for what he's done. I know because it's what I would do too.

"I'm not leaving you!"

No response.

Every heartbeat is a moment too long, as dread begins to seep into my bones.

"Ardelle!" I shout, smoke shooting up from within the area farther down the steep hallway, the spot that was safe for me mere moments ago now collapsing as well.

Dammit, you idiot. I seethe, torn between what to do.

My heart drops as the entire hallway collapses before my eyes, sealing Ardelle in what's most certainly his tomb.

CHAPTER 66

Ghosts linger on Earth because they're not ready to move on. They have unfinished business with those they love, or perhaps despise—maybe it's both. Conceivably, I am that ghost, a white-faced wraith whose feet hold her up amongst the stadium's insides, now half-collapsed and on fire. She's not quite sure what she's doing, the shock disrupting her senses—*my* senses.

What just happened, what I'd seen down that hallway . . . Nobody could have survived that.

Nobody.

Covered in dirt and blood and stars-know-what else, I stare aimlessly down at the wall of rubble where Ardelle used to be. I don't know what else to do.

In desperation, I run back down into the tunnel. The pieces of fallen concrete shake under my feet, many pieces still falling amongst the thick dust filling the air to the point I can barely breathe. My fingernails bleed as I try to move the chunks, but they don't budge. I try to summon my crystal to blast them away, but the tank is completely empty. I can't even muster up sparks.

I yell his name, but I get no answer.

The horror creeps in . . . and I feel so numb, not allowing this to be reality.

Not yet.

Not yet!

Not after everything . . .

My sobs escape me, knowing I don't have the strength to survive this.

"Geez, Thumbelina, I didn't think you cared so much."

I gasp, hearing him but not seeing him. Then, out of the billowing dust, I can make out the outline of his broad shoulders.

Large pieces of concrete fall, the last bits of his gravity magic spent by the look of utter exhaustion plastered on his face. I run to him, slamming into his body as he envelops me, holding me tightly in his trembling arms.

This is when the cracks in my armor finally full-on shatter, and my dam of tears cannot be contained.

"I thought you were dead," I say between sobs. "You reckless idiot, I can't believe you."

Snuggling me tighter, he rests his chin on the top of my head. "I'm glad you're okay, too, Thumbelina."

We stay there for longer than is safe, unable to let the other go.

Holding each other upright, we stagger out of the underbelly of the arena, making our way back out to the stadium floor. The destruction caused a fire on the opposite end of where Ardelle and I are standing. If it wasn't for all the concrete he was holding up and dropping between us, it would've engulfed us in flames.

Once we reach the outside, we see most of the people have fled. Those remaining helping the injured escape before more catastrophic damage happens and additional SSPARROWs show up to contain anybody who lingers.

"Where's Malakyte?" Ardelle asks as we search for him or any familiar face.

"I left him with Deimos." My voice is hoarse. "I found Sylo before heading down to the bombs, told him where the Ringers were. Let's hope he was able to find them and get them out. I left Malakyte over this way."

Helping people on our way across the arena floor, Ardelle and I finally make it to the general spot I left the prince.

But he's not there.

Neither is Naresteé.

I look around, swearing this was the spot.

Then I see Deimos sitting there, cross-legged and pissed off.

"Deimos," I yell, staggering my way towards him, blood gushing from my thigh, my body so weak I can barely walk. "What the hell? Where did they go?"

Deimos looks up at me with slits for eyes, which I notice are massively swollen and red. "That bitch with the horns got me with some kind of powder, shot it right into my eyes. They took off."

I grunt in annoyance, shaking my head in disbelief.

A loud thunder-like cracking comes from within the stadium, the entire thing threatening to crumble in on itself.

"Let him go. He's not an immediate threat anymore," Ardelle says, and begrudgingly, I agree.

"I cut half his face with my sword," I admit, and Ardelle smiles down at me, impressed.

"That's my girl."

Well, we'll talk about that fact later.

Deimos stands up, eyes barely open. "He was still wailing like a little bitch when they took off, if it makes you feel better."

It does. It really does.

The three of us make our way out, and Deimos eventually takes off the second we get outside, no surprise there.

Ardelle and I wander for several minutes as emergency vehicles arrive on scene. The SSPARROWs don't know what to do. To arrest, to detain, or to let everyone go. There are too many people to do either former options, and they're probably questioning their loyalty right about now. Those who were here, anyway. The loyalists will come, and people will be taken in and a narrative will begin to emerge. We can't stay. We can't be anywhere near Arianyte.

My body sags into Ardelle's when I finally glimpse them—our Ringers.

"Jance!" I yell, waving an arm their way.

All our Ringers plus Sylo make a mad dash towards us, and with the new information Malakyte told me, I stumble my way towards Jance, leaving Ardelle's warm body for his.

He doesn't hesitate for a second as he scoops me up into his arms, and the emotion that overwhelms me leaves me with no doubt that I know this person . . . I know this soul. Yet, doubt creeps in as fast as a summer storm, and I can't be sure right now. Even though I want it to be true more than anything.

"Thumbelina saved this entire city," Ardelle says. As he hugs Sylo and Ahren, he explains what happened below the stadium.

Jance looks me in the eyes as he holds my face in his hands, his own misty and soft as he brushes the tears from my cheeks. "You're an incredible kid, you know that? I'm so glad you're safe, that we're all safe."

I worry the others will be upset with me, but to my surprise, I don't see any condemnation on their faces. Maybe it was all worth it, after all?

But something is off. Looking around I ask, "Where's Pacey?"

"She's probably helping some people somewhere. We'll find her," Sylo says, looking around, but I look at Ardelle and I can tell something is immediately wrong.

He shakes his head, his entire demeanor changing on a dime. "She's not coming back with us," he says, his voice barely a whisper, and it's because he's enraged. "My parents took her. I couldn't stop them. They have Pacey. They found her."

"What?" I demand, not understanding. "What do you mean they took her? Why didn't you stop them?"

His exhausted eyes look at me, so much pain there, and I know his heart is breaking. "I couldn't get to her in time. I watched them taking her out. She wasn't struggling; it looked like she was going willingly. I was too far away to stop them. I got my old man with an arrow, but as soon as that happened, they knew I was onto them. They disappeared in the chaos. I failed her, I—"

Our stunned silence is the only response any of us know how to give. The light of our family, taken away. I truly didn't expect to lose one more person tonight, and not ever Pacey. And with the Dawsons' strong connection to Arianyte, I fear this is only the beginning of something very unpleasant for my friend. Something we can't let happen.

"We need to leave," Jance says, and he's right. With Malakyte still out there, we've got to get out of here.

Fast as hell, we run.

CHAPTER 67

We learn a lot in the following days. Yet, the numb feeling within me grows more and more intense with each passing hour of Pacey's absence. At least Pacey is alive, that one fact I cling to with dear life.

Someone I wish wasn't alive is Scarface himself—Malakyte.

I find it ironic that Malakyte now has a similar scar to the one he gave Geonni many years ago.

Payback for what he did to Geonni is gratifying, and I hope he remembers it.

Snow falls silently in the woods beyond the small cabin's windows, which wrap around the entire living room. The television is the only sound as the six of us watch the coverage of the events that unfolded after the Titan Games' finale. None of us makes a noise in the safe house we retreated to after the games, after Pacey's kidnapping. We couldn't go back home, and we risked enough to go back for Sadie, the dog, and to snatch up anything we could quickly carry. Arianyte will surely go there as soon as they can.

This cabin is deep in the woods outside the city, a good hour from Jance's house. It wasn't a terrible place. The one-bedroom cabin with a loft upstairs is cozy and covered with ridiculous portraits of wolves, along with statues and random knickknacks depicting forest animals and mountain tops where eagles fly freely. I envy those eagles. Yet, this place is cold. Not only from the snow and frigid temperature but also because of what made Jance's house feel so wonderful to me—that true feeling of home.

My home.

The beating heart of that home is now a prevalent ghost, her absence haunting each of us.

But I try to take the victory where it was earned, at least that's what I'm supposed to do.

I feel incredibly regretful for letting Malakyte go as I sit in the white recliner adjacent to the couch where Sylo and Ahren sit. Jance, Saris, and Ardelle stand in the kitchen behind us doing chores while we each stay glued to the screen. The reporter continues her coverage of the events.

"The Arianyte leader claims an unprovoked terrorist attack hit the Titan Games' finale event on Saturday night," the news anchor claims, her sleek purple hair reminding me of Pacey. "Bloodshed ensued when known members of the Terran Resistance ignited bombs previously planted before the event began. Sources close to the Arianyte leader say it was an attempted coup on the part of the Resistance. The rebel leader, Geonni Monterey, has been confirmed dead amongst the violence, a full uprising taking place amongst his supporters. Some say his daughter, Trinity Monterey, made it out of the stadium alive and is assembling more followers by the day due to her father's death, which she claims was committed by the Arianyte leader himself. Those reports are unsubstantiated at this time.

"However, other sources are claiming the alleged rebel leader's daughter has leaked credible data from within the occupation itself. Said documents are currently being combed through, but preliminary findings suggest they are authentic and do show Arianyte violating the Accords on multiple occasions."

"Are they ever going to get to him?" I complain to no one in particular, needing to see his disfigured face.

The anchor continues, "Multiple Dezlar recordings of the attack shows a massive brawl between SSPARROW enforcement and Terran rebels, but as you can see in the footage, everyday citizens also took up arms against the occupation as well. Especially after an amateur video was blasted over the massive video screens placed all alongside the area. ZTV has obtained a copy of that recording." The view suddenly switches to a recording of my recording, taken by someone in the stands.

The screen returns to the Terran news anchor after the video plays. "The leader of Arianyte claims the video to be a deep fake."

Malakyte's scarred face appears on the screen. He stands at a podium outside his tower. I lean forward; this is what I've been eager to see. His first appearance since the games. He wears sunglasses, the scar several shades of midnight blue looking like a canyon against his pale skin, likely as angry and seething as Malakyte himself. Loads of reporters stand before him and Naresteé as they shout out questions about his elite team betraying him. My name along with all the others is shouted from the mouths of the reporters. They knew we went up against our dear leader, and nobody goes up against the Prince of Arianyte.

"Nice one," Ardelle comments before Malakyte talks. My lips curl up, just slightly.

Malakyte speaks on the screen.

"I want to assure the people of Earth that the events of the other night are no longer a threat to the city of Zarmenia, to Arianyte, or any civilians of any origin. The terrorists who brutally attacked our esteemed Titan Games did so with an agenda that was meant to disrupt peace between us and incite another war amongst Arianyte and Terrans. Something Arianyte is not interested in pursuing. Several of these terrorists have been captured, many killed. The losses on the side of this pathetic Resistance strongly outweighs that of Arianyte's, and I assure the peoples of Earth, terrestrial or extraterrestrial, that all is well. In terms of the video in question that claims to prove my personal involvement in the kidnapping and murdering of the children on this planet, I assure you it is a deeply convincing fake created to specifically cause doubt amongst the people of Earth."

I roll my eyes at his pretentious claim.

Monsters are nothing but bullies who hide in the dark . . .

The coverage goes back to the Terran broadcaster. "However, since the finale, protesters have been flooding the streets in all major cities, including here, within the streets of Zarmenia. There has been violence on the streets, many attacks on extraterrestrial businesses and persons have caused many extraterrestrials to leave the planet in mass, fearing another war is imminent. Demands for the release of any Hijacked children have been pouring in, and Terran government officials have been systematically deploying raids on Arianyte facilities within their respective Zones. So far, several buildings have been seized, and an investigation into the children found in these buildings is underway to determine if Arianyte indeed violated the Devouring Accords. If so, this could mean war is swiftly upon us."

Aerial footage then begins to play, the screen split into four even squares. Each one is different, yet the same. It shows children leaving four separate buildings, two here in Zarmenia and two others in different major Zones. The kids, some as young as two years old, walk in single-file lines with their hands over their heads as armed Terrans escort them off the property; SSPARROW soldiers on their knees, for once.

If I did anything right, it was this.

Well, and stopping the bombs from killing the entire city and inciting an environmental disaster that would lead to Malakyte gaining complete control of Earth. That, too.

"You did a brave thing, kid. Going back to stop those bombs. I couldn't be prouder of you," Jance says. He must've noticed that I'm doing it again. Zoning off, becoming so numb to everything—shutting down. Too much has happened, and I'm overwhelmed. Even when we had a clear victory in many aspects.

It all has caught up to me, I guess. The emotional weight of everything from that day. I genuinely don't know how to feel besides exhausted.

Physically, emotionally, spiritually . . .

"As opposed to all the wrong things I've done," I counter, not willing to take any amount of credit.

Jance clears his throat. "We've all made mistakes."

He forgives me. I'm not sure about the others.

"And we'll get Pacey back," Sylo says again, the one thing we're all in agreement with.

I look back at Jance; he's already watching me. I can tell he's hesitant, but he knows none of us are going to let this go—let Pacey go.

"Where do we start?" I ask as I look at Jance, debating if I should blurt it out that—*by the way, I'm the long-lost daughter you thought was murdered. Surprise.* Not sure that would go over well. There is still the question mark of who killed my mother, who tried to kill me, but that is a battle for another day.

Soon. I'll tell Jance soon. I need to know if it's one hundred percent accurate before that happens.

First, Pacey Dawson needs to come home.

And we're not going to stop until she does.

"We start by tracking down my parents," Ardelle answers. "Pacey is likely going to be with them. We'll start there."

We all nod in agreement.

I smile for the first time in days, hope igniting slightly.

They better be prepared, because if they think Pacey belongs to them, they're in for a rude awakening.

Gavrielle would be proud, I think as I close my eyes, trying to imagine his face for the millionth time.

I imagine him sitting beside me now, what he'd look like at our age and how he'd be playfully punching me on the shoulder for an ass well kicked. I hope he knows I tried my hardest to bring him justice, to make right the wrong choice that I made by leaving him to Arianyte all those years ago.

I hope he forgives me.

Because as I've found, forgiving myself has unburdened me from the heavy chains that pain and guilt have shackled me with for years. I'll have to work on the other shit, that darkness that fits so eloquently within my soul like it belongs there. But at least for this one thing, I'm free of guilt.

I'm setting Gav free.

While glancing down at my dandelion tattoo, I remember the boy who saved me in so many ways, but who taught me a more valuable lesson later on in life—that saving myself was up to me all along.

EPILOGUE

Malakyte Ardeen sits in front of a sharp-edged mirror, anger simmering at the inflamed scar across the left side of his face. The Silent Breath serum is gradually restoring his eyesight and facial wound extremely slowly. Something about the magic within the sword is highly resistant to the healing properties of the serum. Had he not had a reservoir of stock on-hand to inject directly into his eye, he would have lost his vision in that eye entirely. Both his eye and scar are still healing, and Malakyte wonders if the scar on his face will ever heal completely. Karalevine had done that. His Zariya had done that.

He remembers her words to him vividly, that, whenever he looks in the mirror, he'll think of her.

She is right about one thing: he is thinking of her.

Of all the problems she's been causing him, this entire fiasco is by far the worst.

And why it makes him desire her even more is harder to examine than the scar on his face.

Ludicrous, he realizes. She makes him reckless, and yet, she draws him in like a moth to a flame. His pride and heart hurt more than his face at times. How could she choose that other male over him for the second time in two lifespans? After he gave so much of himself to her, she still rejected *him*. Karalevine wanted Malakyte to see all her broken pieces, yet she shunned his own.

Most do. He had accepted that. However, when it comes to her . . . He couldn't help but feel its sting within his cold beating heart.

"You should be happy at least," Naresteé says, walking up behind him. The black sheets on his bed are ruffled behind her as she stands in the reflection of the mirror. "The Dawsons have the daughter, and they want to collaborate with us to keep her from her brother. They'll be on board with your plans, at least. We'll need all the allies we can get right now."

He makes eye contact with her in the mirror, and her doll-like face remains emotionless. "I want to study her, see what all the parents did treatment-wise to try and remove the crystal. There could be some valuable information there we missed. And yes, allies are imperative for the plan to fall into place."

She huffs softly, resting her soft hands on his shoulders. They slowly make their way down his chest, moving sensually. He tries not to show that his skin itches from her touch. It's not the touch he desires. "You know how they thrive on hypocrisy; it's why their planet almost choked to death before you restored it." Her sweet voice calms him, like it always has these past decades. She is his right hand, she'd do anything for him, but she isn't Zariya. "Soon they'll be begging you for the Silent Breath again. The possibility of eternal life is too much of a temptation for them to stay away for long. They'll do anything to avoid death by aging. So cynical, these humans. This will pass. You'll be able to turn this around; it's only a matter of time. They'll be eating out of your palm once again in no time at all. That brat Karalevine won't be able to stop our plans."

Malakyte brushes her hands away and stands, unable to stand the sight of his reflection a moment longer. "If my family hears about this incident—"

"They'll hear only what we want them to hear. They won't come here. They have too much to deal with to come all the way out here over this one hiccup."

If they come, Zariya—Karalevine—would be in genuine danger. More than she'd ever be with him. He would never hurt her, never let her be hurt—even if that means going against his own family. He must keep her safe, keep an eye on her. Because he lost her once, he almost lost her twice, there's no losing her again. He'll make this right.

Make her his.

Make this entire planet his.

Prove to them all he's meant to be the leader of Arianyte, and not just a prince, or a page—but a king.

An emperor.

"You really need to get a handle on Karalevine; she's the cause of this entire mess. Look what she did to your face, Mal." Naresteé tries to touch him again, but he brushes her off a second time, and her face falls.

"I have plans to take care of the Star. She's simply more tenacious than I had anticipated." And he hates that his heart ticks up at that little fact about her.

"By the way," Naresteé tries again, standing before him and brushing a strand of hair behind his pointed ear. "Why does Karalevine believe Gavrielle Abraxas is dead?"

FROM AWARD-WINNING AUTHOR
ARABELLA K. FEDERICO
THE MARK OF DREAMS AND DARKNESS

More by Arabella

Gavrielle is still alive? What? Find out what's become of Gav in the epic sequel, The Mark of Dreams and Darkness, available now in all formats. The audiobook now has a triple cast featuring Graphic Audio's, A Court of Thorns and Roses, Jon Vertullo as Gavrielle. Along with Connor Brannigan as Malakyte, and our leading lady Nikki Grey returning as Karalevine. Stay tuned for the epic finale, The Mark of Shadows and Starlight.

By scanning the QR code below and signing up for the Arabella's Army newsletter you can get access to exclusive scenes from Malakyte's POV. Does his obsession with Kara sound romantic, or straight up stalkerish? Well, just wait till you see this special scene, revealing a huge secret to Kara's past that you can't get anywhere else.

Want to show Arabella some love? Please consider leaving a review on your favorite bookish platform like Amazon, Goodreads, Barnes and Noble, and wherever you like to leave your reviews. Reviews help Arabella tune to her reader's needs and desires, and reviews are always greatly appreciated. Don't forget to tag Arabella on social media if you loved this book.

ACKNOWLEDGMENTS

When I was young, I always dreamt of magical worlds where epic tales of people fighting over good VS evil, where magic reigns supreme and all those childish things were not set aside. Instead, they thrived. In these worlds, no Prince Charming was there to save the princess. The girl is the hero for once, she was the warrior. It took me many, many years to finally write this story, but after all the trials, delays, and discoveries, I was finally able to bring it to the world. To say this book is anything short of a dream come true is an understatement. It's truly everything to me, and I hope after reading it you feel all the love, time, and emotional effort I put into this project. If it made you feel something—anything—then I did my job as an author. However, this amazing novel couldn't have come to life without all the help and support I've gotten over the years. To begin, I need to thank my mom and dad, who've always pushed for me to pursue my dreams, no matter how big or unlikely they may be. You guys have always seen my truest potential, even when I doubted myself. The support from you both is unmatchable, and I hope to see you at the premiere when one of my books becomes a movie or TV show, because that day will come. Next, I have to thank my sister Sabrina, to whom I'm more than grateful that you're always there when I don't know what to do, or which path to take, and for all the times you've walked me off the ledge. Every writer needs a rational voice to bring them back to reality when it all becomes too overwhelming, and you've always been that rock for me. We both know the magic that can happen when we believe in something, and your good energy fills this book up with magic all on its own. Your enthusiasm for this project is unparalleled and I couldn't imagine a better cheerleader to have in my corner. I'm so grateful for you and your support.

Second, I must give my upmost gratitude to the industry professionals who have truly made this book a reality. First, to Chersti Nieveen and the entire team at Writer Therapy, including Andraea Jones and Ben

Stapley, whose outstanding knowledge of storytelling craft took this diamond in the rough to a sparkling, beautiful gem. Chersti, your passion, commitment, vision, and talent have made the absolute difference in this book. Not only that, you have taught me so much about the craft I love so much, expanding my knowledge and skills far beyond what I thought I'd be capable of. All the extra time, effort, and attention for me and this book is beyond appreciated, and I truly wouldn't be as proud of this story if it wasn't for you and all the hard work you and your team put in to make this story as beautiful as it is today. You saw what I knew was there all along—potential. Yet, I needed that last bit of guidance to bring it to that professional level. And together, we took this story to a place I always believed it could get to. I genuinely hope it has made you proud.

In addition, thank you to my amazing line editor Sarah Hawkins. Thank you for all your hard work and detailed analysis.

To Stefanie Saw from Seventhstar Art, who took me on last minute and created an amazing cover that no doubt is genre specific and beyond gorgeous. It's genuinely one of the most beautiful covers I've ever seen, and I'm totally not saying that because I'm biased. Your art skills are amazing and you definitely understand what makes an amazing cover.

To Samantha Pico from Miss Eloquent Edits for graciously taking me on as a client and doing a stunning job on my formatting. You have been so generous with your time and work; I am so grateful to have you as a part of this project. The inside of my book looks as stunning as the outside, and what a beautiful cherry on top.

Third, I want to thank all the beta readers, ARC readers, my street team, and every member of Arabella's Army for absolutely killing it and bringing my vision to light. Every like, comment, share, post and repost, for sharing my book and helping boost its visibility-thank you. Some of you guys are the ones who saw the book at its worst, and through your critiques, made the book better. I learned so much from all of you and couldn't be more grateful to you. A special thanks to Nereida, Alexandra, Lara, and everyone else who beta read for me time and time again.

Last, I want to thank my amazing Booktok community. As I write this, I have no assurance that this novel will see much of the magic on Booktok. However, I do know that I've got a place there; a home. You all have been such a light in my life as I walk through this journey, and

I couldn't have done it without you. We love books, all of us, and the power of Booktok is undeniable. It's touched me in my career long before this book was ever released, and I can only wait in anticipation to see what other magic Booktok has waiting for me in the future. To all my supporters and followers, I adore you and truly hope you enjoyed the book. I've met so many wonderful authors and readers on Booktok, and can feel safe being my goofy, authentic self there, which is worth more than gold.

I think back to the young girl who came into school early just to be able to write her Lord of the Rings and Spiderman fanfiction, dreaming of the day she could write an amazing story of her own. That girl would be so proud of what she accomplished, of how hard she worked and all that she's done to make this dream a reality. Being a published author takes courage, no matter who you are. It's brave to put your heart out into the world for people to analyze and criticize. However, just like it takes courage and bravery for the princess to save herself, it so too takes all the same amount of vigor to do something as crazy as this. But I've always said, writing is my destiny-my purpose. It always has been. I hope, if you've made it this far, that you go for your dreams, too. That you make your dreams come true, just as I have. No matter how big or unlikely they may seem to the outside world, no matter how scary that battle may seem, you become that warrior; and you don't ever stop fighting for your dreams. Because dreams are worth every battle, any fight, and all the sleepless nights of hard work that go into them. They're all worth it.

About The Author

Arabella is a loving dog mom who enjoys art, roller skating, good TV shows and movies, and all things fantasy and supernatural. When she isn't writing she's often drawing character portraits, making content on her social media accounts, and helping other aspiring writers realize the dream of becoming a published author. Arabella loves to inspire and teach the craft of writing to others and finds fulfillment in sharing her knowledge to the world in hopes she can give back to those who taught her along the way.

You can find Arabella on social media by searching Arabella K. Federico or visiting www.ArabellaKFederico.com